Sex and Shopping
A Wicked Words erotic short-story collection

Sex and Shopping

A Wicked Words short-story collection

Edited by Lindsay Gordon

BLACK LACE

Wicked Words stories contain sexual fantasies.
In real life, always practise safe sex.

This edition published in 2006 by
Black Lace
Thames Wharf Studios
Rainville Road
London W6 9HA

Toys	© Stella Black
Nothing But This	© Kristina Lloyd
Beautiful Things	© Cal Jago
Customer Satisfaction	© Maya Hess
Priceless	© Mathilde Madden
O	© Nuala Deuel
Gone Shopping	© A. D. R. Forte
Seams and Ladders	© Fiona Locke
Sweet Charity	© Monica Belle
Shopping Derby	© Heather Towne
Shop till you Drop	© Carmel Lockyer
Changing Rooms	© Kate Pearce
Grandmother's Teapot	© Madelynne Ellis
Living Doll	© Primula Bond
Sex and Shoplifting	© Mae Nixon
Getting Good Designer Outlet	© Saskia Walker
This Very Boutique	© Portia Da Costa
Rummage	© Elizabeth Coldwell

Typeset by SetSystems Limited, Saffron Walden, Essex
Printed and bound by Mackays of Chatham PLC

ISBN 0 352 34076 2
ISBN 978 0 352 34076 4

Contents

Introduction and Newsletter

Strange how desires for different things merge and spark like crossed wires. How it all gets tangled up and we're driven by our wants and needs. If the Buddhists are right, then we're driven purely by cravings and anxieties – cravings for things, and anxieties when we don't get them. And if nothing else, shopping is proof enough. Because being a consumer is all about the craving and the need for things in shops and stores and malls ... but it's also about the anxiety of looking at what we don't own and will never be able to buy, and the battle with the temptation of buying what we really can't afford. And it's all about being seduced by the gloss and presentation of items, and the promise that our lives will be better and happier if we just own that handbag, or that pair of shoes, that dress, the earrings and accessories that go with it ... Kind of like sex. This is what I like and want and need and I want to get it from him, or her, or both of them at the same time. And it's frustrating if I don't get what I want when I want it. I want to be desired and I want to desire; to be seduced and seduce. I want to shop around for the right deal, try out things, consider, weigh up, consult, go back for a second look, or just throw caution to the wind and splurge. We have expectations and we want to do business.

It makes our hearts beat faster – we become different creatures with different motivations when we shop for things, for sex, for satisfaction. We may not even recognise ourselves afterwards. And this roller coaster of anticipation, excitement, desire, irresponsibility and satisfaction is something our wicked authors have capitalised on with these naughty stories. But shopping isn't a substitute for sex here. Oh no, not at all. Shopping is sex. The wires get all crossed . . .

And short-listing this anthology was harder than an average woman finding a pair of black trousers or jeans that fit. The choice was bewildering – shoplifters, changing rooms, human mannequins, teapots, toys, lingerie, internet bargains, male auctions and even selling yourself online for cash. I wanted them all. Every damn one. You see, I needed them all. They're so good. You wouldn't understand. No one would. I need help. There should be someone I can call . . .

Lindsay Gordon – Summer 2006

Want to write short stories for Black Lace?

Please read the following. And keep checking our website for information on future editions.

- Your short story should be 4,000–6,000 words long and not published anywhere in the world – websites excepted.
- Thematically, it should be written with the Black Lace guidelines in mind.
- Ideally there should be a 'sting in the tale' and an element of dramatic tension, with oodles of erotic build-up.
- The story should be about more than 'some people having sex' – we want great characterisation too.
- Keep the explicit anatomical stuff to an absolute minimum.

We are obliged to select stories that are technically fault-less and vibrant and original – as well as fitting in with the tone of the series: upbeat, dynamic, accent on pleasure etc. Our anthologies are a flagship for the series. We pride ourselves on selecting only the best-written erotica from the UK and USA. The key words are: diversity, surprises and faultless writing.

Competition rules will apply to short stories: you will hear back from us about your story *only* if it has been successful. We cannot give individual feedback on short stories as we receive far too many for this to be possible.

For future collections check the Black Lace website.

If you want to find out more about Black Lace, check our website, where you will find our author guidelines and more information about short stories. It's at www.blacklace-books.co.uk

Alternatively, send a large SAE with a first-class British stamp to:

Black Lace Guidelines
Virgin Books Ltd
Thames Wharf Studios
Rainville Road
London W6 9HA

I liked defying him but I knew it was risky I knew

Toys Stella Black

'Stella. I told you. One toy only.'

'But I want the Ami Yumi doll and the Ami Yumi cat, what's the point of having one and not the other?'

'I told you. One toy only and if you argue with me I will take you into the car park, I will take your pants down and I will spank you. Do you understand me?'

I considered lying down in the middle of the corridor marked 'Action Toys' and remaining supine until he bought me exactly what I wanted. I am five foot three, after all, and eight stone. Petite in one sense, but difficult to move in the other. Still, even I, immersed in lovely fantasy as I was, recognised that a 23-year-old woman having a tantrum in the middle of the Toy Palace might cause more problems with the security department than was necessary. He was a kind Daddy, a good Daddy, a cruel Daddy, a perfect lover and role-player, but he would not be able to explain himself to the outside world. The outside world would not understand. But the outside world, at this moment, was of no importance. We had our world. We were playing. He was hard and I was wet and it was bliss.

'But!'

I liked defying him but I knew it was risky. I knew that he meant it. I knew that if he became annoyed, if I overstepped the mark, he would tan my arse for me and it wouldn't be easy. He had a hard hand, and if he didn't feel like using that he used a Mason and Pearson hairbrush, or sometimes a paddle. It wasn't easy. I had the bruises to prove it.

But somehow, I never actually believed he would do it,

he could do it, until he actually did it. And here in the Toy Palace, one of my favourite places by the way, here in the Toy Palace, amongst the Wheebles and Whoozits, he just looked like any other good-looking 32-year-old man in a dark coat.

The discerning eye would know that the coat was Gaultier. He did have money, a lot of it as it happened, he had inherited a fortune when he was 28, and he was prone to indulge himself as a result. He was a hedonist, but without the self-destruction that that sometimes implies. And now, he was my big Daddy. He loved it. I loved it. I was his naughty girl. We were free.

I gazed, lost in the biggest toy shop in the world. Well. That's what the sign said. It was what the Toy Palace believed. THE BIGGEST TOY SHOP IN THE WORLD. This meant a fantastic kingdom of plastic and wood and primary colours. It meant that Barbie had a private jet and the Star Wars 'Republic Senator' had a snake-like tongue with which to threaten his enemies. There were Froggies and Doggies and Pony Rescue and Playmobil sniffer dogs all of which could be explored for hours on end.

I never became tired of it, though the Daddy sometimes became a little impatient and would take me hard by the hand and march me to the till where I was allowed just the one thing. Only one. Though no price limit! Well, even with that restriction. You try it. One toy in the biggest store in the world?

'I've spoiled you, Stella,' he would say. 'I've spoiled you, and I've created a bad girl.'

Rules were made to be broken. He made them, I broke them.

The rules said I was to be polite in the shop, not ask for things, not whine or sulk.

He took me by the hand and led me over to a large aisle entitled, 'Dressing Up!' Masks stared down at us. Fanged freaks, dragons, one-eyed zombies and scarred

Nazis – a hideous gallery of imaginative prosthetics and sinister teeth. And on to the outfits. There was nothing you couldn't get. Your baby could be a monkey, a duckie or a pumpkin. Your son could be a fireman, a Bob the Builder, or a Dementor. The teenager could be a cool ghoul, a night slasher or a high seas rogue.

He dragged me past all this to the teenage girls section. If he makes me be a Tinkerbell I'll never speak to him again, I thought, though Skeleton Bride was good, as was Dragon Geisha and Zombie Cheerleader. My spirits rose.

'There are nuns,' I informed him.

'You're not being a nun,' he said. 'It's not Monty Python. Just stand there.'

A young man appeared. His face was not his advantage. Indeed, his face could easily have taken its place amongst the Halloween masks. He was wearing a green nylon uniform with 'Toy Palace' and a castle logo embroidered in red on his chest.

'I'm looking for a witch.'

The assistant didn't say, 'Aren't we all?' as I would have done, but displayed an expression as wide and dry as the Gobi desert.

'Over here, sir,' he said in the voice of Shaggy from *Scooby Doo*.

Daddy stroked the back of my neck and, overpowered by fatherliness and his smell and my compulsion to take him into me, I nearly cried.

'I don't want a bloody witch outfit,' I said. 'I want . . .'

The shop assistant, walking ahead, did not hear.

'Don't be rude,' he said calmly. 'We've got to get something for Suzanne's Halloween ball. I'm putting you in a black net skirt, thigh-high boots, seamed stockings and PVC pants. We're getting the skirt here – the boots and knickers you'll have to wait for and, I might add, I will be caning and buggering you when you are wearing them.'

I stared at him innocently. I knew this costume would

look good with purple lipstick, dark eyes ... I knew I would flip myself over for him, let him push the net over my head and cane me, slashing onto the PVC until my flesh started to sweat inside it and I would grow wet into that pervy plastic fabric.

'I don't want the witch. I want the cat!'

I put some gum in my mouth, chewed it, stared defiantly at him for a couple of seconds and then walked off in the opposite direction, past shelves piled high with farm animals, past plush badgers, past mighty Action Men with inmate muscles and criminal leers.

I knew he would like the sight of my disappearing rear, little white Chanel shorts with a gold chain around the waist, Punky Fish jacket, Japanese teenager socks, Betty Page pumps, open toe, black velvet, high, with tiny polka dots and dear little bow on the back of the heel. They were the most adorable things you have ever seen, a mixture of pure pervert and adorable innocence that is very difficult to achieve in a shoe.

He loved them. Well. He should do. He had bought them.

The shoes were new. We had gone round the shops in his chauffeur-driven sedan, smoothing our way through Bond Street and Mayfair.

The peculiar boutique, hidden away in a mews, seemed to be designed for people like us. I expect he found it in a 'specialist' magazine. I hadn't realised there were so many of us around. I saw another Daddy with a naughty girl sitting on his lap, a beautiful Eurasian, mid-thirties, extending her foot to a kneeling assistant while her lover nuzzled her neck.

She walked up and down, showing him the little white boots. They were laced up to the knee of her bare brown legs and teamed with a pair of white culottes and a striped Paul Smith blazer. I thought they were marvellous but her daddy shook his head and said, 'No.' I swear she cried. I thought he was going to slap her but he kissed her on the mouth and pointed to a lovely pair of dark-green faux crocodile stilettos with four-inch heels.

We are around, naughty girls. We can do anything. And will.

My Daddy – not my real Daddy of course, he died years ago – my pretend Daddy indulged me and fucked me and spanked the arse off me when I was rude to him, or didn't present my cunt when he asked me to, and we had fun with our minds and mutual attraction. And his dick.

So off I went, away from him and his witches outfits, disappearing around the Mermadia Sea Butterflies, past Simpsons Monopoly and something that the Furbys had bred. Past a 'Winged Puffball', past a knight fighting a dragon with *jo lan* ninja martial moves, until I was lost in every sense, subsumed by thoughts, surrounded by animatronics. Then. Oh my God, Daleks. There they were, in every shape, size and form. Dalek pens, Dalek lunch boxes, remote-controlled Daleks, Dalek T-shirts, Dalek tins. Annihilate. Exterminate. Destroy. I felt a rush of genuine pleasure. Daleks have always made me feel very very happy.

You might ask, and it would be fair to do so, how the terrifying metal maniacs of Who lore infiltrated the psycho-sexuality of Ms Stella Black, unfettered tart of the perve parish? But there is a link between terror and safety and sex, my friends.

Deep in the memory cells of the parasympathetic nerve system there lurked old stories of omnipotent robots whose mission it was to destroy all; and some-where out there there was a male person destined to protect me from them. At an age when Dr Who was God, and God was the Father I had no real Father, only a distant grave and a strange disappearing act and no explanations. There was a deep longing for a protector; a man who was easy to admire and before whom all enemies fell. A man whose style reflected self-confidence and insouciance and a mighty intelligence gathered from many planets over centuries of time travel.

My childhood, if it could be called that, was an odd one. The early years were full of Cybermen and Ice-Warriors and Yeti, all scaly and furry and whispering and scary. Somebody whom I could not remember put me to bed during those years. He was nice and he loved me and then he went. I searched and looked and prayed to the God the Father invented by somebody at school but he never came back and I faced the world alone. Now he was here in a different form. A form that understood me. And loved me. And played and played.

Of course I wondered whether I would marry my role Daddy, whether we would *end up together*, though I didn't fancy having to talk to his boring friends or explain myself. I didn't fancy silent breakfasts and the mundane detail of morbid domesticity. I mean I would have liked to have been engaged in a camp 1950s way. But, in the end, the sex was spectacular and absorbing and enough. We were distant but close. Our world was safe and sexual and imbued with complete trust and perfect understanding.

The best moments were lying slumped against each other in the back of a limo, smelling of the night's scents, some bar cigarettes, me Paloma Picasso, him Givenchy, warm, his hand playing me, making me wait for it, winding me up.

Men had bought me jewellery in the past; they didn't understand the toy fetish. I didn't really want jewellery, I always lost it anyway, I wanted love, as we all do, and I am cursed with wisdom. I know that love is more than a bling thing from Tiffany. I know it is about time and trust.

Daddy arrived in November, at a dance in an earl's mansion in Belgravia. I think I had fucked the earl once or twice in the past, in the Cap d'Antibes or somewhere. I was Roxy Music in vintage Anthony Price. Most of the men had dismissed me because I was cleverer than them. I got incredibly bored and went to explore the magnificent residence which was one of those places with an indoor pool, Ionic pillars and several original Chagals. Around the third floor I found a bathroom the size of an apartment with two marble sinks, gold mirrors and a free-standing bath adorned with a parade of Floris and Jo Malone.

Nobody would have been able to resist that and I did not. Off came the moire dress.

I was relaxing in delicious hot waves of geranium scent when he walked in. I was, of course, completely naked, though my modesty, such as it is, was protected, to an extent, by the high white walls of the Victorian bath.

He didn't say sorry. He hardly looked at me. He simply padded across the soft white carpet, pulled out his dick and went to the loo. I did not provide him with the gratification of staring at his organ, curious though I was, as one always is. Instinct told me that he was fine in that department. It's a talent I have. Assessing dick size by the reading of the personality. I am rarely wrong. I'll tell you how to do it sometime. It's quite useful.

He sat on the edge of the bath, lit up a cigarette and smiled at me through the smoke.

I soaped myself, particularly my breasts, which weren't particularly dirty, in the usual sense of the word. I looked at him straight in the eye and lathered between my legs. Then I stood up and rinsed myself with the shower, ensuring that he was allowed the full advantage of a rear view that, with thoughtful presentation, could cause a bus to crash into the back of a police car.

Finally, I lay back into the water, legs spread, toes on the edges, little crimson nails winking at him, little crimson lips slightly parted to reveal my clit.

He took his time but we both knew it was up to him to lead. The water nearly went cold. I'm not a patient person and neither do I sit in cold water for any man, even if he is one of the darkest and best looking I have ever seen. At last he stood up and gathered a vast white towel from the silver rails.

'Come to Daddy,' he said. 'It's time for bed.'

I was home.

We fucked for a fortnight before we found our mutual core. It was after a night of anal sex. It's a strange thing, anal sex. It always makes me feel violated and small and submissive. I have to be taken to it very slowly, and with some dominance. He quickly discovered that.

I was lying on my stomach on his bed, wearing a pair of pink cotton pants and matching socks and very little else. I was reading the *Beano* and eating sweets and being very Nabokov. I got some chocolate on his counterpane and he was furious.

'For God's sake, Stella,' he said. 'It's eighteenth-century silk. You can't dry clean it, it will destroy it.'

'Well, it's very stupid to have it on the bed then,' I responded, popping another candy into my mouth. 'Give it to the V and A or something.'

I turned the page to Dennis the Menace and Gnasher.

He didn't say anything. He simply took the *Beano* and the packet of sweets and placed them on the bedside table. Then he ambled over to the dressing table where, amongst a line of antique clothes brushes, there was a silver-backed hairbrush that had once belonged to an aged aunt.

He grabbed me, spread me over his knee, ripped down the Lolita knickers and beat me with that silver-backed brush.

The sound rang out as a slap into the room. God knows men have spanked me before. I seem to bring it out in them for some reason. But this took me by surprise as we had not discussed it. The stings became harder and my flesh hotter. I yelped. Then the erotic flush turned into red pain. He slapped my thighs and then returned to my arse, again and again, for about twenty minutes, until the arousal and discomfort melded and I eased smoothly into the true transcendence of total submission.

He went all the way, spanking me, fingering me, spanking me again until I wept and said, 'I'm sorry. I'm sorry. I won't do it again.'

My pants were then removed completely and his fingers, lubed with Vaseline, eased into my back passage.

'Play with yourself, Stella. I want you to relax.'

So I brought myself to orgasm as he fingered me slowly and did as I was told. For once.

He kissed me on the lips, and pushed me face down over the edge of the bed. I was kneeling on the floor, but my forehead was pressed into the aforementioned eighteenth-century silk.

He left me there for a minute or two, knowing that I love to wait for it. My smacked bottom was presented red and animal-like to him. My cunt was wet. And slowly, his dick wrapped in rubber, he eased himself into me. Very gently. In and further in. I was naked now, except for the knee socks, snivelling and moaning but turned on, allowing him through.

There was only me and him and his dick and my anus. Somewhere there were our smells and the smell of chocolate. I went somewhere, returned, went away again. He started to thrust harder, letting himself go and surrendering to his ejaculation.

Later, after smoked salmon sandwiches eaten naked, he tucked me underneath the white duvet. We were naked and together and close.

After that he took charge.

Once he made me stand outside the gates of a school yard wearing a St Mary's public school uniform. My dark hair was in bunches tied with pink plastic baubles. God. I even had a tight white shirt and a green and yellow striped tie. Very St Trinian's. Very me. I looked as if I had a whisky still in the science lab and a racehorse in the dormitory.

I was chewing gum and swaggering about with my satchel when he pulled up in the BMW.

Seeing him, I dropped the lipstick which I had been applying into a Hello Kitty compact mirror, bent down, and gave him the full vision of a round butt framed by a grey pleated skirt and barely covered with white cotton panties.

He wound down the window.

'Get in, Stella, and stop showing off.'

He drove to his flat in Knightsbridge. There was a grand drawing room with huge portraits of relations and a lot of tassels and upholstery. There was a statue of a horse and a bust of John Donne and several seriously valuable eighteenth-century banquettes. There was a woman painted by Reynolds and a grand piano made in 1820. It was like the John Soane Museum without the entrance fee.

Homework was a dry Martini and a blow job delivered with genuine affection. I liked to torture him with my mouth – I liked it when he nearly burst and just had to fuck me or he would die.

'Ladies and gentlemen, please note that the Toy Palace will close in ten minutes. Please make your way to the checkout area.'

I don't know how long I had been lost in aisles of Twinkleberries and plastic princesses.

Somehow my trolley had filled up with Daleks. I simply don't know how they got there, by themselves, probably, knowing them.

If he doesn't let me have these, I thought, I am going to pay for them myself. I'm not leaving this shop without a Dalek and that is all there is to it.

He was waiting at the till. The witch outfit was in a carrier bag.

I knew he was about to blow. It was my pleasure to press the button of that detonator. I love being annoying to men, I just do. I can't help it. But only with the men with whom I am in love – the others? I'm not interested in playing with them.

'Where have you been? I've told you about wandering off.'

'So get me a mobile. Or tether me or something . . .'

'Don't you dare speak to me like that!' He was furious. 'The more I give you the more you take.'

The last time he had been so cross we had been in Harrods and I had made him wait for more than ten minutes by a handbag counter. He hated waiting. Who doesn't? But he was rich enough not to have to queue for anything, and didn't. Everything was delivered. Tailors came to him. His assistant arranged things.

Anyway the time in Harrods he dragged me into the ladies' loo without taking any notice of the uniformed attendant, a plump woman in her mid-fifties. As she stared in silence at us, he bent me over the marble basin, lifted up my miniskirt, pulled down my pants and spanked me until I couldn't sit down for a week. I remember seeing my face in the mirror, over the gold taps, a picture of flushed cheeks and pain and then wishing he would stop because it was too much, but he went on and on, a real good smacking so that you knew you had been punished and you would feel the heat throughout your lower body for hours. And then wetness . . .

The attendant didn't bat an eyelid and calmly accepted a £50 tip.

Daddy had a huge erection and propelled me down the escalator and into the waiting car so quickly my feet hardly touched the ground. And bliss, over I went, over the back of the drawing-room sofa, knicks down, arse up, wet pussy, buttocks still red. Then his fingers in, him kissing me, dick in, filling me up. We came together in one of those rare moments of pure mutual understanding and physical release.

He pulled my hands away from the bars of the trolley where they were gripping so hard my knuckles had turned white. He didn't even look down at the Daleks, of which there were about twenty, and one of whose voice-activated mechanism was chanting in the familiar (and well-loved) tone of threat.

'Exterminate.'

'Exterminate.'

'Destroy.'

I smiled.

He glowered and his eyes flashed dangerously. 'I've had enough of you.'

'But...'

'No.'

'But I want...'

'No.'

'If you don't let me have a Dalek I am going to scream and it is very likely that you will be arrested.'

'If you utter another word, young lady, I will take down your pants and I will spank you here, on your bare bottom, with your shaved puss showing, and I will not stop until you beg me for mercy and perhaps not then...'

We faced each other in a sexual stand off, bluffing, seeing who had the nerve to go the furthest. It was usually me. He had a job, after all, with responsibilities and position. I am an ex-porn star. I could always go for it. My reputation and sales could only be enhanced by bad behaviour. Blimey. The biography alone had sold a million in America. *I Stella*. Hardback. Paperback. Lots of colour photographs. I'm very marketable, you see, being rampant and the holder of a 1.1 degree in philosophy. I can talk post-fem and Foucault and even the *TLS* likes me. Particularly after I slept with one of the (female) editors.

Anyway, if I had been arrested my publisher would have been most gratified and would have assumed that I had hired a private publicist.

Daddy won. Well. I allowed him to win.

People stared as we exited and I was being told off.

Jim the chauffeur (navy uniform, gold buttons, peaked hat) was standing by the car in the car park smoking one of the Benson and Hedges cigarettes that his friend smuggled in from Belgium.

'Successful trip, sir?'

Daddy didn't say anything, but merely pulled me around to the bonnet of the sedan, pushed my head over it so that my face was down and my arse was raised towards him.

Jim ground his fag out with the sole of his immaculate black brogue and got in the driving seat where he watched through the window.

Daddy pulled my white shorts down. No knicks, bare arse, long socks, heels. He slapped my right buttock with the full force of his hard hand. There were no preliminaries, no more threats, no easing into it with erotic slaps – he just smacked hard. And then another on the left. I yelped.

'Ow!'

I didn't have time to assess the situation, to think about Jim watching us, or the risk of being seen. The pain seared into my arse and took all thoughts away.

Smack. Smack. Smack.

He hit me with the flat of his hand with all his strength for ten minutes. It was a hard spanking and I knew I had asked for it. He went on and on until he smelled and felt and heard my genuine supplication. I was wet and weeping and desperate for him. Ah me. There's nothing like romance.

'I'm sorry.'

He reached down and picked up the shorts, which were now on the ground. Then he hugged me and helped me gently into the back of the sedan where I lay with my head on his lap and my arse naked, hot and wet and tearful. He stroked my hair and kissed me.

Then he handed me the biggest Dalek of the range. Radio controlled, twelve inches, flashing lights, automated head movement, poseable gun and arm, blast sound effects, authentic voice mechanisms and illuminated eye.

'You make your Daddy very very happy.'

Stella Black is the author of the Black Lace novels, *Shameless* and *Stella Does Hollywood*.

Nothing But This Kristina Lloyd

I call him the Boy although he isn't. He's skinny enough, it's true – as skinny as the kids who do backflips in the square – and there's not a single hair on his flat brown chest. But his age is in his eyes, eyes as green as a cat's, and when I look right at him, though we're meant to be ignoring him, I see eyes that might be a thousand years old.

He's been following us for half an hour, weaving among the crowds, his flip-flops slap-slapping in the dust of the souk. 'Hey, mister! Hey, lady!' he keeps calling. 'You wanna buy carpet? Teapot? Saffron? You wanna buy incense? Come, come! Come to meet my uncle.'

His urge to 'come, come' sounds grubby and erotic and the refrain pulses in my head like some dark drumbeat, weird enough for me to wonder if it's going to bring on one of my migraines.

'Lady, you wanna buy handbag? Real leather! The best! Hey, mister, nice wallet for you! Look this way! You are my guest. Come!' The Boy averts his eyes, head down and spinning, and the whole song and dance routine seems a pastiche of the real hustlers, an empty act he can turn off at will. No wonder he can't look at us: we'd see right through him.

'I feel like David bloody Niven,' mutters Tom.

Tom's posh as fuck, so self-assured and confident you don't even notice it. He's relaxed and ironic. A bit on the prim side, it has to be said, but I adore every hot salty inch of him. I like to draw him, standing, sitting, lying, sprawling, my futile bid to capture him in charcoal and pencils. In evening class, I learnt to draw not just the object but the space around it. I learnt to see absence. 'What's not there is as important as what is,' said our tutor, although personally I'd contest that with Tom. I'm quite a fan of what's there. Naked, he's pale and softly muscled with strong swimmer's shoulders and thighs like hams. Sometimes I sketch his cock, big and randy or just lolling on his thigh, framed in dark curls, and when I show him the end result he'll invariably wince. 'Oh God,' he drawls, looking away and sounding slightly camp. 'You're so *vulgar*.' But he can't help smiling and I know deep down he likes it.

'*Pssst!*'

It's the Boy. I can't see him, only hear him. The medina is crammed with noise, its maze of tiny streets choked with the scents of paraffin, leather, spit-roast meats, sour sweat, baked earth and strong rough tobacco. Here and there, the souk opens out, exposing its squinting stall-holders to a livid blue sky. But for now we're in the thick of it, two clueless pink-skins in an ancient labyrinth, lost among beggars, hawkers, shoppers, mopeds, donkey carts and big wire cages squawking with heaps of angry hens. The Boy's hiss slices through the chaos, clean as a whistle, but I can't spot him anywhere.

I'm disappointed. I'm supposed to be relieved because the official line is he's been annoying us from the off, prancing around like some mad imp of consumerism, urging us to buy this, buy that, buy the other. The thing is, we do want to buy a carpet, a nice Berber runner for the hallway, but he's probably on commission and, besides, we'd rather do it in peace.

My disappointment tempers the arousal I'm half-ashamed to acknowledge. At first, I couldn't be sure it was sexual although I suspected it was. Heck, it usually is with me. And then I knew damn well it was when my groin flickered its need and I grew aware of my inner thighs, filmy with sweat, sliding wetly as I walked, my sarong flapping around my ankles. But it's a weird kind of sexual. It's not as if I fancy him, this slip of a lad with the calm, creepy eyes, but I'm drawn to him in a way I can't identify. He keeps dropping back from us to sidle among the crowd or prowl at a distance, elegant and stealthy, stalking us like prey. My money's in a belt. I must have checked it a dozen times. I don't think he's a thief though.

I don't know what he is. All I know is he's sparked off in me some intrigue, some furtive hunger that makes me not quite trust myself. We keep walking, Tom and I, and within the humid fabric of my knickers, I'm as sticky and swollen as a Barbary fig.

'Pssst!'

His call sounds so close I actually look over my shoulder, expecting him right there, but no sign. It's as if he's invisible, some mythical djinni up to no good or a golem from the old Jewish quarter, laughing to himself as I pat my money belt once again.

'Seem to have shaken him off, the little shit,' Tom says mildly as he unscrews his water bottle.

I realise Tom's not hearing what I hear, making me question my senses. The heat in this place stupefies me and I haven't been sleeping well either. At night, after an evening of jugglers, magicians, fire-eaters and snake-charmers, the bedsheets tangle themselves around my legs, cobras for the pipe-player, and my mind whirls with madness and enchantments. To soothe me, I think of the stillness beyond the town: snow-capped mountains, end-less deserts and a black velvet night sprayed with silver stars. But I sleep fitfully, slipping in and out of dream-scapes, grotesque and lewd, and I wake each morning sloppy with desire. When I sink onto Tom's cock, drowsy and heavy, I feel fucked already, post-coitally limp, as if I've been possessed by an incubus, a gleeful demon who screwed me senseless as I slept. My limbs seem to liquefy as I ride Tom, awash with vagueness, remembering feral creatures, how they pawed at my flesh, and priapic monsters with gas-mask faces, rutting in steamy swamps.

I don't imagine we'll buy a carpet today. I'm not really in the mood. Feeling a tad psychotic, to tell the truth. But I hide it well. I'm probably just premenstrual.

A few minutes later and the Boy's with us again. I don't see him but I smell him, a pungent sexual whiff as we pass stalls selling metalware, shards of sunlight glancing off pewter, copper and brass. Then, in the shadows behind, I see two green beads peering out from the gloom, points of luminescence, freakishly bright. My heart pumps faster. Among so many brown-eyed folk, those eyes are hauntingly strange, non-human almost. He doesn't belong to these people, I think. An outsider, perhaps; a man who leaps across gullies high in the Atlas mountains, surviving on thin air.

'Oh, God, there's that smell again,' complains Tom.

A few yards ahead, the Boy darts beneath a tatty awning. He's wearing filthy, calf-length shorts and his legs, I notice, are dark with hair. He's a youth, I think, and then some. Old enough, I'm quite sure, to go snuffling under my sarong.

'It's foul,' says Tom. 'Really fucking rank.'

I think he's talking about the Boy. I think he's smelled his appetite and is repulsed. Then it dawns on me he's talking about the tannery. When we were last here, I was about ready to retch with the stink of it but now the tannery's just a backnote and it's the Boy's odour I'm getting. It's as if my senses are tuning in to him, to the sound, smell and sight of him, and everything else recedes. The whole thing's starting to make me nervous.

Tom offers me the water before taking a swig himself. He has beautiful manners, partly because he's from Surrey but stemming too from a naturally submissive streak he doesn't fully acknowledge. He's no pushover, believe me, but his gentle manner, combined with a curious intellect, makes him tend to the deferential or at least a fascinated passivity. Give him a good book and he's lost for hours. Give him a good woman – or better still a bad one – and he's lost for months. I took him away from someone else. Well, he left her for me at any rate. Two years down the line and we're still in love, half-daft and quite besotted.

But I'm no fool. I know damn well if some other woman caught his heart he'd be gone in a flash, leaving me spitting with rage. I like Tom a lot. I want to hang on to him. I want to keep him mine. But all I can do is hope for the best. And meanwhile, I try to catch him as I can, all those impossible charcoals and pencils, all that seductive permanent ink.

My favourite sketches are the ones I do in bed at night, Tom lying there with his mouth agape, dreaming eyeballs quivering beneath his lids. I love him so much when he's fast asleep, when he doesn't even know he exists. Tom doesn't realise I do this. I keep the sketches well hidden, my treasured possessions, proof of all the hours I stole from him while I watched him sleep. I have bouts of insomnia, you see. It's not only out here.

'Half a mo'. Batteries,' says Tom. He edges past slow, swathed people, and I wait for him by a spice stall. Black strips of tamarind and threaded figs hang like jungle vegetation over sacks heaped with nuts, dried fruit, tea leaves and herbs. SNORING CURE – NEVER FAIL! says a sign and APHRODISIAC FOR THE KING! proclaims another. The air is powder-dry and colours catch in my throat, scarlet, copper, ochre and rust, an earthy rainbow of seasonings that makes me cough like a hag. 'I have medicine! Never fail!' cries a djellaba-hooded man, and I protest my health, realising there's some seriously dodgy shit for sale here: a turtle strapped to the canopy's scaffold, bunches of goats' feet, dried hedgehogs, chameleons, snake skins and live lizards flicking around in giant-sized jars.

'*Pssst! Lady!*'

His voice goes straight to my cunt. The sensation's so strong he might have tongued me there. My senses reel and I turn, catching a glimpse of sharp brown shoulder blades before he's swallowed up by the crowd. Across the way, Tom's holding a pack of batteries, appealing to a stallholder who looks out with a half-blind gaze, his eyes veiled with cataracts. A woman with a wispy beard jostles me. Instinctively, I check my money-belt and I see the Boy just feet away, throwing a backwards glance, an invitation to follow. I cannot refuse him. I don't even question my options. I just go.

As I move, Tom turns. He catches my eye, nodding acknowledgment of my direction. It's fine, he's cool. He rarely makes a fuss. And, should we lose each other, we've both got our phones. An image comes to me of my mobile trilling away, whiskery rats nosing the screen where the words 'Tom calling . . .' glow for no one. I push the image away. It's not important. But the Boy is.

Anxious not to lose him, I squirm through the crowds, keeping his shorn head in my sights. A man with a monkey distracts me briefly and for a terrible moment I think I've lost him. Frantic, I whirl around, a vortex of faces blurring past me, colours racing. He's gone, he's gone. But seconds later, I have him again. I watch as he vanishes into an archway so narrow that at first I think he's ghost-walked through a wall. Panicking, I hurry, elbowing people aside. Somebody curses me but I don't care. I'm high with fear. I don't know why I'm following him. I only know I can't stop. Dark eyes flash around me, and my cunt's pumping nearly as hard as my heart. I'm in the grip of something scary, my juices are hot, and I try to remember if I've eaten something funny. Maybe I stood too close to those desiccated hedgehogs. God knows what they were for. God knows what I'm doing.

In the alley, I pause to catch my breath. I've got the Boy in view again. The alley's cool and whitewashed, not much wider than a person, and a few feet in, the racket of the souk goes dead. There's no one around but us. Suddenly, it is so still. So silent. My own breath surrounds me, a whispering rush like a seashell to my ear. I walk on and yet I don't think I move. I just pant. The sun doesn't fall here, but the alley seems to shine with its own light, the white walls reflecting each other in a numinous glow, and I wonder if this is it. I wonder if I'm dying on an operating table, my soul sailing up to enter the kingdom of heaven, or to at least try tapping on its door. I want to look back to see where I've come from but my head's far too heavy. I can't turn.

There is nothing but this: me, my breath and the Boy. It's as if I've slipped into a chink in the world.

Several yards ahead, half-crouched, he creeps along with cautious grace. His slender torso is sweet and supple, the rack of his ribs visible beneath grimy fudge-brown skin. The scent of him drifts in his wake, pheromonal and ripe. Civet, perhaps, or musk. How pliant his body must be, I think. How smooth his skin, how eager his hands, how tireless those beautiful, plum-coloured lips.

I follow, both of us keeping a steady pace, then the Boy stops, poised low. His arched spine protrudes in a knobbly ridge and the stubble of his hair prickles with light. I freeze, feeling I ought to, and realise I'm barely breathing. Then, slowly, the Boy swivels his head around to face me. And that's when I nearly keel over. Because the eyes that look into mine belong to no man on earth. For several stunned seconds, I stare back. They are cat's eyes: green as gooseberries with black slit pupils.

Fear thumps me in the gut but I cannot scream. I cannot move either. I can't do anything. I just gawp, rooted to the spot.

He smirks and turns away. I think I must be in one of my dreams. Soon, I tell myself, I'll wake at the hotel and I'll straddle Tom's cock in a trance of remembering. I'll rock back and forth, head swimming with a post-human dystopia, a stinking medieval market peopled with DNA freaks or inter-species offspring. Look around and they all seem perfectly normal till you spot their webbed feet, forked tongues, folded wings or dog-fang teeth. And I'll climax and so will Tom. Then we'll get up, have breakfast, take a bus to a town with tiled palaces, koi carp and orange trees, and we'll buy something lovely in Spanish leather or cedar wood and everything will be all right.

The Boy creeps forwards. I'm so scared and I'm so wet. But wet is winning. I follow, turning a corner then another until he ducks into a small archway in the wall. Moments later, I'm there too, head down and heart hammering as I descend three worn white steps.

In front of me, a cool cavernous chamber opens out. Hung with tapestries and oil lamps, its edges are banked with stacks of carpets, and in a far corner stands a cluster of earthenware jugs alongside sacks of grain. Sunbeams, soft and fuzzed with dust, slant down from high plasterwork arches, a tranquil light for prayer. It smells of straw and mice.

I catch a glimpse of the Boy as he flits from one stone pillar to another then stays there, hiding. Sitting crosslegged on a tall pile of carpets is a bald, muscular man with dark skin and heavy brows, his jawline shadowed with bristles. He's bare-chested, whorls of black hair clouding his pecs and making a seam over his neatly rounded paunch. He looks like a cross between the Buddha and a thug. It's not a look I'm familiar with but I do like it. He has a small, neat smile, and he's observing me steadily, chin propped on his fist. I get the feeling he's been expecting me.

'Hi,' I say, trying to sound brave.

I walk deeper into the chamber, across the flagstone floor, shoulders back. I know this man is going to fuck me and, frankly, I'm ready for it.

No one replies. The man keeps watching me, smiling. Though I'm still scared, I have an inkling of a new confidence. I'm starting to feel powerful and ageless, like some whore of the Old Testament. The Boy emerges from behind his pillar to lean against it, arms folded and smirking. His attitude's changed. He has the jaded, haughty air of a rent boy, hard faced and sleazy. It's attractive in a sick kind of way. His eyes are normal too. Well, relatively speaking. They are the most astonishing sea-green – *National Geographic* eyes – but they are normal in that they are human. I must have been seeing things earlier, a trick of the light, nothing more.

They both watch me as I sashay forwards. I feel deliciously easy. I'm a harlot, houri, concubine, slave. I could dance like Salome, seduce them with a strip show, except I don't have seven veils, just sarong, vest and Birkenstocks.

Besides, my guess is, these guys really don't need seducing.

'You chose well,' says the man, addressing the Boy.

Now hang on, I think. Didn't I just walk here myself of my own free will? Then I correct myself. Who am I trying to kid? I've been picked up, haven't I?

'My uncle,' says the Boy, grinning and nodding at the man.

Uncle tips up his chin in a curt greeting. 'Show her to me,' he says to the Boy.

Barefoot, the Boy saunters forwards. He parts my sarong, exposing my legs, and presses his hand between my thigh. All the weight of my body is suddenly in my cunt, resting in that skinny hand. My gusset is damp and he paddles his fingers there, grinning at me before latching on to my clit. He rubs through the fabric, judging my expression. I want to appear impassive but the smell and touch of him makes me dizzy with longing. Truly, I can't remember ever feeling so horny. I guess I don't manage to pull off the cool, composed look because the Boy chuckles softly. In a whisper, he says, 'Ah, you like that, don't you? Hot little bitch.'

Well, you got me there, I think.

'She's OK, Uncle,' announces the Boy. 'Nice and wet.' He tucks the gusset aside then pushes two fingers up inside me. My knees nearly buckle. 'Really wet,' he adds, stirring his two fingers around. In the silence, I hear my juices clicking.

'Excellent,' says Uncle in a thick, languid voice. 'We have a willing woman.'

'A willing slut,' says the Boy, 'who wants to get fucked.' He seems to be relishing the words, testing their strangeness like an adolescent keen to rid himself of innocence.

I'm relishing them too. I like being objectified. It takes the heat off having to be yourself.

The Boy, still working me with his fingers, slips his other hand up my top. He strokes me through my bra before pushing up the cups to squeeze and massage. My nipples are crinkled tight and he flicks and rocks them, bringing my nerve endings to seething life. Then, just as I start to feel I'm losing myself, falling open to ecstasy, the Boy pulls away and crosses the floor to Uncle.

It's a cruel, desolate moment. I'm about to protest but before I can utter a word, the Boy has sprung up onto the carpets, leaping from a standstill like a mighty ballet dancer. On his haunches, he straddles Uncle who reclines, mouth parted, to suck on the Boy's fingers, offered like dangling grapes. The Boy cups the man's shiny head, supporting it, and Uncle goes slack with surrender, eyes closed in bliss, as he slurps and snuffles on a sample of my snatch.

Now, I'm not averse to a spot of guy-on-guy action but I've only just arrived and I'm feeling a touch neglected. So I walk towards them because, dammit, I want to play too. As I near, they stop their weird feeding and, holding the pose, look down at me with benign curiosity, blinking heavily. It's as if they've never seen me before. Jesus, it's creepy. Without smiling, they continue to stare and blink for what seems like an age. A pair of green eyes and a pair of bright brown ones.

Then Uncle perks up, his expression changing to a villainous leer. He looks seriously gorgeous, like he ought to be behind bars. Sneering, he sits straight, swinging his legs over the edge of the carpet-pile, and delves into the crotch of his baggy pants. His pants are slate-blue silk, and a materialistic impulse asserts itself because that's just the shade I want in the hallway. I consider asking for a thread so I can choose a carpet with a matching weave but the moment passes. I have a different object of desire, other needs to gratify.

'Suck my dick for me,' says the man, grinning. He releases a big fat erection, wanking it gently, the muscles of his beefy arm flexing under dark skin. It's a beautiful brute of a cock, arrogant and obscenely large.

'Dirty bitch,' adds the Boy. He still sounds like a kid trying out rude words. 'Suck the man's dick.'

I'm happy to oblige. The stack of carpets are almost shoulder height and all I need do is lower my head to engulf him. His pubes tickle my nose and, butting deep within my mouth, he's superbly stout and powerful. My head bobs between his thighs and I'm getting weaker and wetter as I dream how it'll be when this beast slides into me. The Boy drops to the floor and I feel him at my feet, nuzzling my ankles then crawling under my sarong. I spread my legs for him and feel him rising, the heat of him on my skin, his shorn, silky head, his tongue trailing a path up my inner thighs. He pulls down my knickers and I feel him between my legs, his hot breath on my cunt before his tongue, so delicate and perfect, dances over my clit and squirms into my folds.

Oh, my. That tongue has truly been places. Like his eyes, it could be a thousand years old, a tongue that's pleasured geisha girls, ladyboys and Babylonian whores. Fingers fill my cunt, a thumb rubs my arsehole and moments later I'm coming hard, gasping around Uncle's cock, Uncle clutching my head, keeping me steady for fear I neglect his pleasure in favour of my own.

'She's a slippery little bitch, isn't she, huh?'

Uncle's voice is loud enough to carry across the chamber. He's talking to someone else; not to the Boy, and certainly not to me. I pull back and turn, wiping saliva from my mouth.

Tom, of course. Hell's teeth, I'd forgotten him. He's standing within the white stone archway, looking somewhat dazed. Really, I'd completely forgotten him, forgotten the man I love. Well, I guess fresh meat can do that to a girl.

Tom stares, mouth sagging dumbly. I worry for a moment, fearing my blue-eyed boy is going to be appalled, but I can see he's interested, absorbing the scene. It's that fascinated passivity again. 'My God,' I can almost hear him say. 'You're so *vulgar*.'

'Come, come,' cries Uncle, jumping down from the carpets. 'Welcome, my brother!' He pumps Tom's hand and claps him on the shoulder as if they're the best of mates. 'You want her to suck your dick too, huh?' Pleased with himself, Uncle laughs over-loudly.

I think Tom's had a hit of whatever I've had, the scent of dried hedgehog or something. He smiles. I know exactly what he's going to say. He's going to say, '*I* don't mind' in that sing-song way he does when I say, 'Shall we have coffee here or there? Rice for dinner or pasta?' It can get a bit annoying, to tell the truth. He looks at me; his smile's ironic. '*I* don't mind,' he says, and I realise he knew that I knew he was going to say that, and his tongue's in his cheek because he knows all that knowing will amuse me. Long-term relationships can be so nice.

The Boy, on his hands and knees, peeps out from under my sarong to edge a cautious pace forwards. Then he's motionless, watching as Uncle leads Tom to a low bank of carpets, stacked at three levels like a shallow flight of steps. A hazy shaft of sunlight falls across them, revealing tiny squalls of dust as the men clamber and sprawl across this wool-woven stage. Uncle sits on the higher level, legs akimbo, and Tom lolls within his silk-clad thighs, head resting there as he yields to an off-centre shoulder massage. Uncle bows forwards, murmurs in Tom's ear, and Tom smiles gently, stretching his spine in a discreet arch, his pleasure private and contained, as the man kneads with big oafish hands.

I stand there, entranced, hardly able to believe what I'm seeing. The Boy edges closer, moving gingerly as if wary of disturbing them. Sitting back on his heels, he watches intently as Tom relaxes deeper in to the massage, occasionally grunting.

When Tom and I fuck, a glazed expression sometimes settles on his face. His eyes close, his mouth drops open, and he looks completely gone, blanked out with bliss as I move on top. He's got that slightly dead quality about him now, and when Uncle reaches forward to remove his T-shirt, Tom acquiesces, raising his arms, as docile and obliging as a sleepy child. He doesn't even protest when the Boy pads forwards to nuzzle his pale chest. All he does is smile fondly and, like a basking chimp, he stretches his arms back, exposing their white undersides, tendons taut, his dark patches of armpit hair attracting the Boy who tentatively sniffs, a hand sweeping broad caresses over Tom's flexing body. Tom is clearly loving it.

Well, you sly old tart, I think.

I can't take my eyes off him. I wonder if they've drugged him. And then I'm clearly not thinking straight myself because soon I'm wondering whether it actually *is* Tom. Perhaps someone – or something – has got inside his body because I've never seen him like this before. Tom likes to size up situations, to tread carefully, to fret unnecessarily; and he's never shown even the slightest interest in men. And now look at him, pushing the boundaries of his experience as if it were a walk in the park. I start to fear I may never get him back.

But then I notice his smile fading and he moistens his lips, a small moment of nervous desire. It's exquisite, so tender and Tom-like, and I feel I know who he is again. I see his Adam's apple bob in his throat and, in his neck, a hint of tension, as he tests the air for a kiss. The Boy bends over him, their lips meet, and lust flares in my groin. I watch a knot of muscle shifting in the Boy's jaw, movement in Tom's neck, and I'm all eyes as, without breaking the kiss, the Boy reaches down to unzip Tom's fly. Tom's erection springs out, weighty and lascivious.

I don't know what I want to do most: watch or join in.

Then Uncle grins at me, rummaging around in his silky blue crotch. He exposes his cock and moves it against Tom's face, tipping it back and forth like a windscreen wiper. 'Come here,' Uncle says to me. 'Bring us titties.'

He's dead right: I want to join in. So I cross to them, whipping off my top half as I do so. Greedy and urgent, I scramble up onto the carpets and Uncle welcomes me by holding out a brawny arm. He opens his mouth and I fill it immediately with soft pink breast, pressing a hand to his crisp chest hair, my body pushing against the bulk of his belly. His tongue lashes my nipple and he delves under my sarong, searching eagerly for my hole. With a force that makes me gasp, he plugs my wetness with thick, crude fingers. Grinning up at me, he holds my nipple between his teeth and gently pulls on it, stretching my flesh. I hold his gaze, daring him to keep right on going.

For the first time, I notice how stunning his eyes are. They're a hard amber brown, sparkling like topaz. But this is no time to be romanticising, because the guy's moving us into position, my sarong and belt are off, and I'm utterly naked, poised above that prodigious cock, buttocks split in his big rough hands, cunt wide open. With heavy luxury, I sink down on him, groaning all the way until I'm stretched and stuffed to capacity.

Truly, it's a beautiful moment, made more beautiful by the fact that beside me is Tom, being sucked off by the

Boy. They're both naked too, Tom with his knees apart, the Boy's shorn head bobbing in his crotch, his pert little butt stuck up in the air. Sprawled against the carpets, Tom has an arm flung wide, eyes closed, mouth open. I've never seen him looking quite so dead. I wonder if his expression's the same when I go down on him. My guess is not. All the same, I try and commit that face to memory, thinking maybe I can reproduce it some time in charcoal and pencil.

Tom must sense me looking because as I start to slide on Uncle's cock, he reaches out with a blind hand to stroke my arse. In that tiny affectionate gesture, I feel such a connection with him, such warmth. And I feel free to fuck like there's no tomorrow, knowing Tom and I are united, mutual support in mutual depravity; for richer, for poorer; for better, for worse.

Uncle clasps my hips, bouncing me up and down, and I'm as light as a doll in his hands. This man can do what he wants with me, I think. And I don't mind if he does. It's a while since I've been overpowered. The two of us mash and grind, silk hissing beneath me, sweat forming on my back where sunlight heats my skin.

'Hey, brother,' calls Uncle, addressing Tom, 'does she like it in her ass? Huh? A big prick in her tiny little asshole?'

Tom's too zonked to reply immediately. He just sprawls there, half-dead, before his head rolls sideways, eyes still closed. When he finally speaks, it sounds as if it's costing him an enormous effort. 'Probably,' he croaks.

The Boy pulls away from him. Tom groans in despair.

'Dirty little slut,' says the Boy excitedly. His cock is ramrod stiff, its ruddy tip gleaming, and against his scrawny frame it looks grotesquely large. He springs off the carpets, takes a small copper can from near an Aladdin's lamp, and pours thick clear liquid into the palm of his hand. 'Uncle,' he says, 'you in her pussy, me in her ass. Bam, bam, bam. We fuck her hard, yes?'

Uncle laughs lightly.

'No,' I whisper. Then louder: 'Yes. God, yes.'

The Boy leaps back onto the carpets, lubricating his cock with lamp oil. Tom groans again. I reach out, feeling sorry for him, and Uncle, gent that he is, shuffles us closer. I lean over to kiss Tom and he responds eagerly, our tongues lashing awkwardly as Uncle pounds into me. Sweat dribbles down my back into the crack of my buttocks and I feel the Boy's greasy fingers press against my arsehole. He wriggles a finger past my entrance and I'm groaning into Tom's mouth as the Boy opens me out, forcing the ring of my muscles wider, making me slick and ready.

'Keep her still,' urges the Boy, and Uncle obliges, his cock lodged high.

'Lean over,' orders the Boy and I obey. His knob nudges my arsehole and pushes into my resistance. I think I'm going to be too small for him, my other hole too full, and that it's all going to hurt like hell. I make a feeble cry of protest.

'Don't pretend,' snaps the Boy. He grasps my hips then there's a flash of pain and, with a sudden slippery rush, he's fully inside me, and I'm swamped by dark, fierce pleasure. Uncle calls out triumphantly. I feel I'm on the brink of collapse, the intensity of having both holes packed so solidly taking me to a place I didn't know existed. I gasp into Tom's mouth, quite beyond kisses now, as the two men start to drive into me. Bam, bam, bam, as the Boy said. I have to pull away from Tom. I need air. I need to groan and wail.

Beneath me, Uncle's face is flushed with exertion. He spots me looking at him and he grins, meeting my eye with a deliberate gaze. There's the weirdest kind of friction going on inside me, the two men jostling my body as they fuck. And then I know I've lost it. I know pleasure has reduced me to lunacy because I see something wild in Uncle's eyes. His pupils contract and, for a moment, they are like the Boy's: bright with black, slit pupils.

It's the light, I tell myself, the light, the light. And I can't bear to look. I flop forward onto Tom, seeking a kiss, wanting the reassurance of his mouth, his nose, his face. I'm close to coming and so is Tom because the Boy, gorgeous greedy creature, is sucking him off again. As the two cocks shove fast and hard inside me, I nudge my clit and then gasp into Tom's mouth, our lips so hot, so wet and loose: 'I'm coming, I'm coming.' That sets him off and he groans and pants, his body twitching as he peaks. My orgasm rolls on and on, and Tom is still gasping into my mouth, still coming. It feels sublime, orgasm-without-end. Our lips slide and smear, and nothing else can touch us. It's as if we're melting into each other at every breath. And I am him and he is me, and we are all ecstasy, all delirium, all gone.

Sex, I think, will never be the same again.

We didn't buy a carpet for the hallway that holiday. But sometimes it's like that. You go out hoping to buy one thing and come home with something totally different. I've stopped drawing Tom in the middle of the night as well. I don't feel the need any more. I don't have that yearning to capture him. Because I have my Tom, I have him entirely, from now until the end of time. And if I ever start to doubt it, I just need to picture his face, glazed with rapture at the point of climax. He doesn't know what he looks like. I don't know what I look like either. People don't, generally speaking, do they?

All I know is that he'll never look at another woman like that; he'll never be able to. Because when he comes, something shifts in his eyes. He rides the wave, annihilated with bliss, the two of us breathing so hard and so deep. And when he looks at me, his beautiful blue eyes have black, slit pupils. And I am him and he is me. And I know we are possessed.

Kristina Lloyd is the author of the Black Lace novels *Darker than Love* and *Asking for Trouble*.

Beautiful Things Cal Jago

I have always loved beautiful things: exquisitely crafted pieces of jewellery; elegantly cut cloth forming tailoring perfection; the awe-inspiring works of fine art that hang in galleries and the homes of the wealthy. Yes, beautiful things are an important part of my life. Just as important though, is the process by which they come to be mine.

My life is divided fairly equally between my small but successful PR firm in Oxford, my bright and spacious modern loft apartment just outside the city centre and, my favourite environment of all, shops. Fashion boutiques, shoe shops, jewellers, book stores – all of these, amongst others, have the ability to send my pulse rocketing. Because, as much as I try to control these urges that I have, the emotional and physical responses provoked by a shopping trip are simply unparalleled. Retailers are my salvation. It is a simple fact: for me, few things beat the thrill of acquiring new things.

I know that, for some, the credit card is the Holy Grail but I'm a cash kind of girl. Crude, some may say. But somehow, for me, cash lacks the quiet desperation of 'slapping it on the plastic'. And besides, beautiful things deserve crisp notes being counted into a perfectly manicured hand.

And so it was that one afternoon, after a particularly fraught time with one of my more demanding clients, I found myself standing on a pavement looking through the window of Serendipity, a jeweller's that had caused quite a stir when it had opened six months before. In fact, 'jeweller's' doesn't seem the right word; that somehow implies fusty, traditional and endless rows of diamonds and yellow gold. Serendipity wasn't like that at all. The owner was a thirty-something designer who, with a flourish of metals and stones, had brought a quirky coolness to accessorising the discerning women in the town. The pieces on sale were largely one-offs made by the owner herself although some of them were bought in from an array of exotic locations. They were unique, striking, beautiful. Expensive, of course, but isn't it worth it to have something so exceptional? I had perused a few times before and had even bought a couple of items – an unusual turquoise pendant and an armful of silver bangles, which chimed as I moved. But this time, before I'd even entered the shop, I knew that things were different. This time I was after something very special.

The owner looked up and smiled as I entered. She didn't look so much arty as businesslike. Like me, she wore an impeccably cut suit; classic black, the jacket tailored tightly around her narrow waist, its hem flared over the curve of her hips which, in turn, were hugged by flattering bootcut trousers. Her blonde hair, however, was piled up on her head, held in place with a mass of pins. It was a laissez-faire look, totally befitting an artist, the technique for which I had never quite mastered with my own long dark hair.

A young woman stood towards the back of the shop trying on a selection of silver rings. They were pretty much the only items openly on display which could easily be handled as most of the merchandise was locked in cases. She sighed heavily as she tried on the rings and then rejected them, looking around to see whether anything else caught her eye.

I wandered through the shop inspecting the jewellery, taking in countless exquisite items. I imagined how the pieces would feel displayed on my body: fine, delicate chains grazing my collarbone, heavy pendants nudging insistently at my cleavage, chunky metallic bracelets and chokers gripping my flesh, their coldness pressed against my fevered skin.

I stopped abruptly as my gaze settled on a strand of perfectly formed golden moonstones. At certain angles the spheres appeared almost translucent yet the next moment, from a slightly different position, a spectacular amber sheen was visible as an inner glow that seemed almost to float across the convex surface.

Breathtaking.

I forced myself to look away and caught the owner's eye, gesturing towards the cabinet.

'You'd like a closer look?' she asked, stepping towards the glass.

I nodded. 'Please.' I felt my voice waiver as I spoke and cleared my throat.

She removed the object of my desire from its glass prison and draped it across her hand, suspending the necklace in front of my face.

'So beautiful,' I whispered, reaching out to touch one of the perfect stones. It felt cool against the heat of my fingertips. 'May I?'

She smiled, seemingly pleased that I had the good taste to recognise its flawlessness. 'Of course. They're stunning, aren't they? I brought them back from Burma and then set them in the silver. It's so difficult to find good, pure examples of even the blue moonstones over here, let alone these golden ones. They're so rare. And so lovely.'

I smiled and nodded and felt a little light-headed as I took the necklace from her and marvelled at the weight of it. Holding it in one hand, I moved the fingers of my other hand across the stones, gently gliding my skin over each sphere one by one. I closed my eyes as I caressed them, my fingertips lingering on their cold smoothness. I felt my skin prickle and had to stop myself from actually gasping. All the signs were there; this was the one. This was perfect.

The girl trying on the rings sighed dramatically. 'Do you have any smaller ones?' she asked.

The owner frowned slightly. 'There are all sorts of sizes there,' she said. 'You might just have to try a few, I'm afraid, until you find one that fits.'

The girl sighed again and pouted. 'I've been trying them,' she said, sulkily. 'Have you got any more out the back?'

The owner forced a smile, turning away from me slightly so that she could keep an eye on her. 'What sort of thing were you after?'

'Not sure.' She smiled sweetly. 'But I'm sure I'll know it when I see it so if you could bring anything else out . . .'

The owner edged towards the young woman, suspicion furrowing her brow. She looked from me to her; me, a professional thirty year-old in a smart suit carrying a briefcase, her, the sullen, slightly scruffy teenager who just seemed out of place in such a shop. Her gaze settled again on me. Placing the necklace gently on top of a display cabinet beside me, I smiled sympathetically and rolled my eyes. 'It's fine, I'm not in any hurry,' I assured her.

The owner returned my smile, relieved. 'I'm sure we can find you something,' she said firmly and immediately moved to the teenager's side, mentally trying to account for every bit of stock she had so much as looked at. Which was perfect actually because, as soon as she left me, I silently scooped the necklace into my palm and nudged it with my fingertips, forcing it a little way up the sleeve of my jacket. Then I placed my hand in my trouser pocket.

OK, yes, I know what I said before about the thrill of counting crisp banknotes into a manicured hand and so on and that still stands true. I really do enjoy spending. But, for me, shopping trips don't always entail expenditure. Sometimes, my desire to simply take is just too overwhelming and the thrill I get from that is deeper and more potent than watching a cash register eat my money as a sales assistant asks me whether I want to keep the hangers.

My heart thumped. I stood still for a moment and tried to regain my poise. If you truly wish to go undetected, even after you have left the shop, you obviously cannot show any physical sign of guilt. This includes bolting from the premises at the first possible opportunity. I glanced at the owner, checking that I hadn't been spotted. What would happen, I wondered, if she had seen what I'd done?

I imagined the grip of her hand on my wrist as she stopped me from walking away with my precious pickings. When she had spoken to me about the necklace, her voice had been low, throaty, authoritative. Would she still sound so in control when, digging her fingers harder into my flesh, she would accuse me of theft?

'I saw you,' she would insist, her face just inches from mine.

I would simply smile as her hand dived, determined, into my pocket. She would frown, perplexed, as she rummaged around and then come up empty-handed. Then she'd plunge it in again, forcing it down, down into the depths of my silk-lined pockets, her fingers slipping on the smooth, shiny material and sliding down a new route, surprising her with their sudden misdirection. The beauty of customised clothing; concealed pockets. Her smooth palm would roam across my bare thigh tops and I would hold my breath until her fingers located what she wanted.

'It's one of my little idiosyncrasies,' she would say quietly, her fingers moving ever higher up my legs, the stones of the necklace trailing cold across my skin. 'As a businesswoman, I'm quite keen for people to pay for what they take.'

I would hesitate, trying to ignore the exact location of

her hand whilst determining the best course of action. Her cool measured stare would confirm that remorse was probably a wise option.

'OK,' I'd say, doing my best to look genuinely devastated by my bad behaviour, 'I'm sorry. Of course I'll pay.'

She'd smile. 'Yes, you most certainly will.'

And then she'd spin me around, flip me over the display cabinet, raise my skirt unceremoniously, and mete out a just punishment until I truly repented and orgasmically vowed to mend my klepto ways.

I shook my head, forcing myself to return to reality. Whilst the very real danger of getting caught is always there and adds an irresistible frisson to proceedings, I can think of nothing more humiliating than the fall-out of being found out. The reality would not, after all, be a sensual spanking from a sexy blonde but bad coffee in a police interview room, a trip to the magistrates court followed by a couple of column inches in the local paper, and a fine, imprisonment or both. But actually, if I'm being honest, the thing which makes me baulk most at being captured isn't the humiliation, the punishment, the inevitable criminal record. It's the fact that, if I end up in the shit, it would mean that I wasn't any good. It would signal absolute failure on my part as a thief. And that simply isn't true.

I forced myself to focus. The owner looked bored with the girl now. She had tried her best to find her something but the young woman appeared to have lost interest. I anticipated their exchange would shortly come to an end so decided it was time to make my move.

Suddenly, the shop door flew open and a man entered looking flushed and out of breath. All three of us immediately turned to look at him, so forceful was his entrance.

'If anyone owns that silver Audi outside, you'd better go and move it,' he panted. 'You're about to get a parking ticket.'

'Shit.' I looked at the owner, startled. 'Two seconds,' I

said, waving a random two fingers in the air. I dashed out of the shop before she had time to speak, slowed down only by bumping into the man who, by now, was having a full-on rant about traffic wardens.

Almost before I knew it I was out on the pavement. Perfect. I marched quickly as the blood rushed in my head and white noise roared in my ears. As every inch of my skin buzzed and a familiar tingle crept the length of my body, a wide smile stretched across my face.

My first act of retail deviance was when, aged seven, I slipped a miniature bottle of perfume into my new grown-up handbag in the local chemist's. It was a pretty, shapely bottle, you see, and I wanted to look at it again at home. So I took it. It made sense to me to do that but, of course, I knew it was wrong. I'd held my breath to the point of giddiness as I left the shop, convinced that I was going to be caught. I was terrified but exhilarated as I galloped along the high street and then home feeling ready to burst. And it was a thrill which lasted for the hours I sat in my bedroom with the door firmly closed, touching the glass and admiring the way the light caught its contours. Actually, it was a thrill that never really went away.

I have stolen ever since. I love the sheer excitement of it; the rush I get from palming the item, feigning nonchalance and then racing home with my newly acquired treasure. It is something which, once experienced, I was never going to stop. Some steals are more exciting than others, depending on the item or the circumstances or my mood, but there's always some sort of thrill to be had.

I've stolen lots of things over the years, obviously: silk scarves, cashmere gloves, lingerie, jewellery, leather goods, books, hosiery ... And perfume, because old habits die hard. Expensive things. Beautiful things. Never the usual bars of chocolate and lipsticks, even when I was a teenager. The items always have to be worth it. It's not about me being a snob or having to steal what I can't afford. Things simply have to be expensive because it adds to the excitement – and the beauty. And because I take what is expensive and beautiful I do not steal for the sake of it. I haven't got cupboards full of unwanted rubbish at home; stuff I don't like or want but couldn't, nevertheless, resist taking. Consequently, I have a real fondness for all the items I have taken. One of my favourites, without a doubt, is the shoe.

The shoe was magnificent, the ultimate, classic black stiletto. A simple, unadorned, iconic shape; the mere sight of it made me swoon. I took it to the sullen sales assistant who duly lumbered out the back to hunt it down. When she finally returned, it was to tell me, in a flat voice, that it was one half of the only pair left in the shop. A size five, it was too small for my long slender feet. I was distraught but decided not to be defeated. In spite of it being the wrong size it was, in all respects, the perfect shoe. It was beautiful. So I wordlessly took it from where it hung off the tips of two of her fingers, held my head high and carried it out of the shop. No one tried to stop me. Who, after all, would be expecting a customer to walk out holding one lone, ill-fitting stolen shoe? Often, it's all about confidence. Confidence, attitude and, sometimes, the element of surprise. For the past three years it has enjoyed pride of place on top of the bookcase beside my bed and, at the risk of sounding dramatic, I shall actually be a very happy woman if it's the last thing I see before I go to sleep every night for the rest of my life.

No matter what I've stolen and in what circumstances the after-effect is always the same. It is excitement, but not just the excitement of getting away with a crime. This excitement is far beyond that and it is the driving force that keeps me going back to steal time and time again. The moment of theft is potent and heady. But what comes afterwards absolutely blows my mind.

I have lost count of the number of times my journey

home from a steal has been interrupted simply because I could not wait. In my car, in public loos, in a rickety lift in a multi-storey car park, even in the stairwell at the bottom of my apartment building because my front door a few flights up just seemed like a million miles away; time and time again, hot and wet, I have hurriedly, impatiently triggered the release I so desperately sought. And when I can wait, I can't wait for long. Once through the front door, my beautiful steals clasped in my hand, clothes are shed and my fingers create all that I have thought about from the moment I had walked into the shop and spotted my object of desire. Not that the action that succeeds the steal is always solo. On the contrary, there is sometimes a whole new dimension to proceedings.

My heart wasn't all that thumped on my journey from the jeweller's to home. I had passed countless department stores, cafés and pubs, all of which I could have used for instant relief. But I was determined to wait. My hands shook as I rammed the key into my front door. Images from the scenes in the shop flashed through my mind at speed as I quickly stepped out of my shoes and began to unbutton my jacket: the young woman looking every inch the common shoplifter as she surreptitiously toyed with the rings; the knowing glances the owner and I shared as she fell for my act, convinced that I was the one she should trust; the man's flustered intrusion making my escape so flawless; my initial glimpse of the perfect strand of moonstones and the first time my fingertips touched their coolness. My breathing quickened at my recollections as I entered my bedroom. It was no good. I couldn't wait.

Without wasting another second, I made my way to the bed, kneeling one knee on the edge of the mattress whilst keeping the other foot firmly planted on the floor for balance's sake. I briefly looked up at the huge ornate mirror that rose from behind the wrought-iron head-board. The mirror had been a steal too although, obviously, it wasn't easily slipped into a pocket or dropped into a handbag. It had taken a lot of careful planning, that mirror. But it had been worth it to own something so decadently beautiful. The reflection that stared back at me now was flushed; from collarbones up across throat to cheeks, my skin glowed. One hand slid down the front of my trousers as I half-stood and half-crouched while the other reached forwards to steady myself on the bed. My legs were splayed slightly, completing an image that was positively whorish. I smiled and closed my eyes as my fingers skimmed over my underwear for the briefest moment.

'Caught you red-handed.'

I froze.

A soft, teasing laugh then from someone who knew me too well; someone who knew how impatient I could be at such times.

'It was all your talk of traffic wardens back there.' I straightened up and turned to smile over one shoulder at him. 'It just turned me on,' I continued lightly.

He laughed again. 'It worked though, didn't it?'

I giggled as he came to stand behind me, his hands gently circling my waist. 'Mmm, absolutely.'

One of his hands travelled downwards, stroking the swell of my hip and over my thigh. 'Another job well done, wouldn't you say?' He lifted up the back of my hair and softly kissed my neck. My skin prickled. I was so ready.

'Don't make me wait any longer,' I whispered.

He tutted. 'So impatient.'

'Mmm ... So ...'

'So ...?'

I sighed but couldn't help smiling. 'So ... don't make me wait any longer.'

'What is it you want?' he asked maddeningly.

I rolled my eyes. 'You know what.'

'Tell me.'

I sighed again and he must have felt sorry for me. Well, either that or he was as eager as I was. I felt movement behind me.

'Turn around,' he said and I did as I was told.

We stood facing each other. I held my breath as, grinning, he produced the moonstone necklace from his pocket.

He held his hand aloft, the necklace dangling from his fingers. Fingers which, less than an hour before, had deftly entered my pocket and lifted the stones in the split second before I had strode from the shop. To anyone else his intrusion would have been imperceptible. But not to me.

'An excellent choice,' he said.

I laughed. 'Would you expect anything less of me?'

I reached out to touch the stones but he quickly jerked his wrist, flicking the necklace out of my reach. I frowned.

'Take off your clothes.'

After six years together, that phrase still had such power. Alex, my soulmate, playmate and sometime-partner-in-crime, never tired of watching me strip. He didn't want anything showy. He just wanted me to slowly and deliberately remove each item of clothing until I stood naked before him. He could, he said quite charmingly, see something new and feel some element of surprise every time he saw me undress. I did as instructed, maintaining eye contact with him as each garment was shed.

He nudged one of his knees into mine, pushing me backwards onto the bed. Straddling my thighs, he bent his head as though to kiss me but his mouth hovered no more than an inch above mine. Then, with most of the necklace scooped into the palm of his hand, he held one of the stones between his thumb and forefinger and gently moved it across my lower lip. Its coolness felt almost wet as it glided across my sensitive skin. I exhaled softly as he moved it more insistently and then pressed gently but firmly, forcing my lips apart and allowing the stone, and the fingers that held it, to enter my mouth.

'It really was an excellent choice,' he said again. 'So beautiful, isn't it?'

I nodded in silence.

He released some more of the strand and it cascaded over my chin and throat. I felt the stone inside my mouth touch my tongue, Alex's finger and thumb sliding further between my lips after it. I closed my teeth around the golden sphere, gently grazing Alex's flesh. He quickly removed his hand and the moonstone and shimmied his body further down the bed, his jean-clad lower half making room for itself between my legs.

He reached forwards and trailed the necklace lower. I felt its weight slither down my neck as the stones bumped along my collarbones. He steered them lower, lower, and I closed my eyes feeling them nestle into my cleavage. I felt his fingertips on me then, brushing lightly against my skin as he carefully arranged the necklace over my body. I marvelled at how restrained he could be, how patient, when I knew he was as desperate as I was. I squirmed a little as I felt him shifting the stones around one of my breasts. He rolled one of the stones across the nipple and I bit gently on my lower lip as I felt myself stiffen under his touch.

Suddenly, he drew both ends of the necklace together, pulling them tight and ensnaring my nipple between the hardness of two neighbouring stones. I gasped, surprised by the unexpected movement and the brief burn of pain which accompanied it. The intensity of the heat began to disperse as Alex's tongue began to lap at the buzzing flesh.

I held my breath as his tongue skimmed down my ribcage, lingering over my stomach and then continuing its travels down towards my navel. With my eyes tightly shut, I focused on the incredible feeling and tried to resist the temptation to thrust my hips off the bed towards him. Knowing Alex, if I looked too impatient, he would make me wait even longer before giving me what I wanted. I tensed as I felt a sharp blast of breath between my legs and sunk my fingers into Alex's hair as it brushed inside my thigh. Finally, he had stopped toying with me.

Alex didn't quite make the contact I was expecting, however. Instead, one by one, he began to press the stones inside me. His fingers forced them deeper while, every so often, he tugged gently on the strand provoking exquisite sensations inside me. Full of the stones and his fingers, my heart pounded between my thighs. Each stone and finger moved deliciously, probing, twisting and pushing against my insides. The pressure was so immensely pleasurable it became almost unbearable. I reached for his wrist and grabbed it tightly, not knowing whether to force his hand deeper or push it away. Highly skilled at prolonging agonising ecstasy, Alex was perfectly capable of keeping me there on the brink all night. But, fortunately for me and my impatient ways, he was not so cruel that afternoon. A low moan escaped from deep in my throat as he began to remove the necklace from me. The dragging friction created inside as he pulled each one free caught my breath as my muscles involuntarily contracted around them, trying to keep them from leaving.

Kneeling, he grabbed my slender ankles and eased my legs above his shoulders. The muscles in my calves and thighs stretched taut as he found the angle he wanted. It was the position I wanted too; suddenly and unhappily empty, I ached for the fullness I had just experienced. He grappled with his belt. Once free he was inside me, deep, within seconds. He remained perfectly still for a moment and then, with remarkable self-restraint, he began to move oh so slowly. He drove into me with long smooth strokes and I wriggled beneath him wishing that I could have half the self-control he had.

'Harder,' I said. 'Please.'

He bent down and kissed me, his tongue pushing deep into my mouth and sliding across my teeth while he nipped and tugged at my lips. I grabbed the back of his head, pressing his mouth harder to mine but he reached for my hand and pulled it away from him. In a moment he had coiled the necklace around one wrist and now jerked it downwards, pinning my left arm above my head on the mattress. I gasped in surprise as his free hand secured my other wrist just as securely under his weight. A burst of air broke from my lungs as he stretched forwards and began to tongue my wrist – an erogenous zone I have never fully understood and can often forget about but one which, when remembered, gets me every time. I writhed beneath him, his tongue circling the sensitive spot and sliding across the moonstones which had, just a few minutes before, been buried deep within my core.

'I can taste you,' he murmured and his thrusts quickened.

I dug my heels into his shoulders and pushed my hips towards him to meet his force. As I heard his teeth clatter against the stones and, just an instant later, felt them close around the sensitive flesh of my wrist, my whole being seemed to spasm as ripple upon ripple of pleasure rushed over me. Seconds later, Alex's body went rigid and he shouted out close to my ear as he flooded me with heat.

It took a few minutes to come down from my orgasmic high and bring reality back into focus. We lay curled on our sides, Alex behind me, his chest pressed against my back, his knees nestled behind mine. He absently trailed a finger along my shoulder making my nipples tighten once more. I sighed, utterly sated. My body hummed; my mind felt totally serene.

'What are you thinking about?' Alex asked.

I smiled into my pillow and trailed my fingertips over

the necklace which lay on the bed beside me. 'Nothing much,' I said.

But, as always, he knew me too well. His toes nudged at mine beneath the duvet.

'Well...' I wriggled onto my other side and smiled sweetly. 'As it happens, I did see a rather lovely print in that little art shop on my way home. A female nude actually,' I said watching Alex's eyes light up. 'I think it would look perfect in here,' I continued, already trying to picture the layout of the shop and a potential escape route. 'So I think –' I paused to kiss him lightly on the lips '– I might just have to treat myself.'

Cal Jago's short stories have been featured in numerous Wicked Words collections.

Customer Satisfaction
Maya Hess

It wasn't that Adele Riley enjoyed shopping as such. It wasn't that she wore or understood or even drove her most frivolous purchases. Her wardrobes bulged, her house was filled with the latest technology and her driveway boasted several classic cars as well as a jet ski, a motor home and a small yacht that she'd recently just had to have.

No, it was the handing over of the cash that drove Adele wild – and she always shopped with cash – the easy deal between herself and a hungry salesman; the flicker beneath his glinting eyes as they were briefly connected by a wad of notes; the hardening of his jaw, his forearms, his expression, as he counted out the money several times. It was the potential and the power contained within those little bits of printed paper that thrilled Adele most. The impending burst of authority it gave her. Plus, it also showed that she was loaded.

But once the deal was done and the goods were delivered, once the packaging had been ripped off and the items were no longer pristine, when the thrill of the hunt was over and the open sign switched to closed, Adele pined for yet another frivolous purchase. It was the rush of guilt combined with adrenalin combined with sheer decadence that she was doing something reckless considering that, even though she pretended to be rich, she wasn't really at all.

The phone call came just as the Mercedes salesman came deep inside her. Adele fumbled with her Nokia as she was shunted against the wall, her skirt hitched up over her thighs and one stocking wilting at her ankle.

'Yes?' she snapped. The gathering pulses in her sex joined together in what she knew would be an unstoppable orgasm. She really didn't want to be talking on the phone. But as she listened to what the caller had to say, Adele slowly slid down the wall, pulling her newest lover down to the floor with her as her mouth dropped open and her eyes grew wide and as black as beach pebbles.

Mercedes Man, puzzled, withdrew from his prospective client and took the opportunity to lever his long wet erection between her plump although shocked lips. If this didn't work, he thought, he would sink his face between Adele's tanned thighs. He adored beautiful women; all women. Especially ones who were ripe for a forty thousand pound deal.

'That's disgusting!' she exclaimed, as the stretched wet tip of the erection bumped her lips. 'I just won't allow it!' Adele snapped her phone shut and clamped her mouth around the super-sized treat, relieving the salesman of his concern that she had been referring to his cock. 'Mmm,' she mumbled, gripping the base and taking him deep, getting right back to what she did best: sex and shopping.

The ten per cent deposit was handed over on a less than usual high. The fuck had been good. Not the best ever but enough to get her wet all over again as she gave up, note by note, four thousand delicious pounds. Adele noticed that Mercedes Man – Mr Coombes, Senior Sales Executive – had grown hard again beneath the cut of his fine wool suit. At least there was the balance still to pay. Adele's eyes narrowed to slits as she imagined handing over thirty-six grand but then she grew angry at the thought of the phone call.

'If you could kindly pay the balance by next Thursday, I'll make sure that your new vehicle is sparkling and ready for you, Miss Riley.' Mr Coombes allowed himself an unprofessional visual slurp of his client's breasts. He couldn't help it. Her blouse was sheer, she was braless, her nipples were freshly sucked and, by the look of them, eager for more. He couldn't wait for Miss Riley to pick up her car.

'Next Thursday?' Adele asked. 'That's not much over a week. I'll be paying cash you know.' Her voice was clipped and betrayed nothing of their recent liaison in the photocopying room.

'Is there a problem?' Mr Coombes ran a finger around his collar. He didn't want to lose his commission and certainly didn't want to jeopardise another chance to fuck the divine woman sitting in front of him. He'd meant to have her from behind but had come too soon. Next time, he promised himself, wishing that Mrs Coombes would occasionally oblige.

'Of course there isn't a problem,' Adele snapped. She gathered up the paperwork and stuffed it in her Prada bag. 'Thursday next it is then,' she promised, forcing a smile. She knew, as things now stood with her bank manager, it would be impossible.

The cash machine devoured five of her eight debit and credit cards and the bank cashier refused Adele to even withdraw ten pounds for a ride home.

'Does madam not have a car to go home in? I see that you have five car loans in your name.' The young woman offered a safe leer behind the security glass.

'Of course I have a car. Several, in fact.' Adele swallowed the knot gathering in her throat. She hesitated and retrieved her cheque book and remaining cards from the chute. 'They are all being serviced and polished today.' This was the hardest thing she had ever had to do. 'Could I possibly withdraw five pounds then?' Truth was, Adele couldn't stand paying the extortionate city centre parking fees while on her shopping sprees and preferred to save cash by taking the bus. There was no thrill in feeding a car-park machine when all you got in return was a ticket. A girl had to be careful with her money.

'No, sorry. Like I said, your account is frozen. I suggest you contact your branch manager.'

'Oh I will!' Adele snapped, realising that she was truly penniless. 'How about a pound then?' she asked, offering her most alluring expression.

Dinner was crackers and jam because she had no food in the house and had exactly 27 pence in her purse. Normally on a Friday night, Adele would treat herself and several friends to dinner at an expensive restaurant. She'd promised everyone a feast at the new Thai place but had to feign sickness instead of suffering the embarrassment of having her credit card declined even though it was her finances that were ill, not Adele.

'Shame,' Nick commiserated. 'We'll miss you, Addie, but you get yourself better real soon now.'

'I will,' Adele mumbled down the phone through several tissues to make herself sound unwell. She knew what he really meant was that they would miss her paying the bill although any one of her high-earning friends – Nick the IT consultant included – could afford to pay. It was just that Adele *liked* to pay. She insisted. Always. It was a power thing: unlocking the potential of the cash, however much it was costing her in interest.

To pass the time and until a plan formed (crazy things occurred to her such as seducing her bank manager or, ridiculously, selling off her assets) Adele spent the evening on the internet browsing the most exclusive online boutiques, piling her virtual shopping cart high with goods before making a speedy exit at the last possible moment when her credit card details were required. The pretend cyber-shopping spree didn't even come close to the thrill of buying in the flesh.

'Buying in the flesh,' she whispered to herself, thinking, wondering, plotting. She poured herself another glass of water, pretending it was Rioja. 'Buying flesh, more like,' she said with a giggle while simultaneously Googling the words. Nothing much came up, sadly, because she fancied a bit of sexy diversion from her money worries. There were plenty of dating sites and chat rooms, she knew, but what she really needed was something that combined the buzz of shopping with the naughtiness of seducing the salesman, which she invariably did.

By late evening, Adele had grown desperate and miserable. She'd been unable to find solace on the internet and she was still as broke as ever. 'God, send me a sign,' she said with a sigh, laying her head down on the desk. 'What am I going to do?'

For the first time since her bank manager had called earlier that morning, Adele realised the seriousness of her financial problems. She'd always thought of herself as well off, rich even. Her job as PA paid enough to secure a multitude of loans and credit cards but evidently not well enough to actually repay them. Really, securing cash whenever the whim took her hadn't ever been a problem. And she'd never once considered the prospect of paying it back.

Adele raised her head off the desk just as the email pinged her inbox. She was ready for bed, ready for a little self-comforting with her vibrator but the email, marked as spam, intrigued her.

Debt, Mortgage, Loans getting you down?
UNDERpaid and OVERspending?
Turn your unwanted items into cash – FAST!
Sell those frivolous purchases on our new
STRAPPED FOR CASH auction.
Special introductory offer . . .

'I'd have to sell *myself* to pay off my huge debts,' Adele said with a laugh, about to delete the email. But instead, she stopped and thought. 'Now there's an idea,' she mused, allowing her fingers to brush over the thin fabric of her blouse. Her nipples didn't need any encouraging; they were willing. 'I guess that's illegal,' she said with a sigh, wishing there was a way that she could advertise herself for a date, charge a fortune for the privilege and then, well, who knows.

The computer wheezed as she shut it down, her mind buzzing with possibilities. Just the thought of promoting her assets online drove Adele to strip in front of the mirror and size up what she had to offer. As an afterthought, she snapped the curtains shut. She had been known to play around with them wide open and the light on but now that she was considering selling herself for cash, then anyone who wanted a look would have to pay for it.

'Nothing's for free,' she told her reflection as she drew a line from her full breasts down to the neat V at the top of her exotic holiday-tanned legs. 'And that includes me,' she said with a giggle before dipping a finger between the delicate folds that fastened her most saleable product into a highly desirable package, as the man at the car showroom had found out earlier. For free.

'Just imagine how rich I'd be if they'd all paid for the pleasure of my body.' Then Adele folded herself onto the expensive bedding of her king-size bed and tried to place a value on her assets by climaxing over and over and doing despicable things with the vibrator that surely any man would pay to at least watch, if not join in. 'Forget shopping,' she said, exhausted. 'I'm going into sales and I –' she told herself naughtily, '– am the merchandise.'

It was an ingenious idea – one that would satisfy her craving for a deal and her appetite for men. Adele wondered why she hadn't thought of it before. Just how she would set about her new business venture and market herself, she wasn't entirely sure. She decided to sleep on the problem and dreamed of all her debts dissolving and as many men as she could possibly handle exchanging wads of cash for her insatiable body.

Monday morning and the office was teeming with impatient managers, sales executives guzzling coffee while pinning the phone to their ears, and the hum of business as usual as the staff settled into another week.

Adele, dressed in a designer suit that she had purchased before her financial ice age, slipped quietly into her office, shut the door and booted up her terminal. By the end of the morning, she wanted her new online shopping experience to be available to every man in the country. Her business mantra was simple: make love, make money.

The first time her mobile rang, she ignored it. She was deep in thought about getting herself exposed, literally, and didn't want distractions. But when it rang and rang insistently, Adele finally answered and was once again greeted by a less than patient bank manager.

'Plans are in hand, Mr Wetherby,' she purred down the phone, 'to clear my debts within a matter of months.'

'Oh?' The manager sounded incredulous. And dull, thought Adele, imagining him in an unremarkable grey suit with matching hair and skin that had never seen a tropical beach or been adored by a passionate woman.

'Yes. Fear not, Adele Riley is going into business.' And, failing to impress Mr Wetherby one bit, he demanded that Adele liquidate her assets immediately.

'That's the plan exactly, Mr Wetherby. I can assure you that very very soon my best assets will be melting and earning me oodles of money.' Adele giggled and hung up. 'Right, back to work,' she said with a sigh and began trawling the internet for the type of website that she needed.

By lunch time, she was desperate. It seemed that no such site existed. Instead of her usual visit to the trendy wine bar for lunch, Adele walked several blocks through the city to Nick's glass and chrome office building. She found him eating a sandwich, bent over his laptop.

'Better now?' he asked without looking up.

'Fine,' Adele said, forgetting she'd been ill. 'Nick, I need you to build me a website. An auction website. By the end of today.' Adele offered her sweetest smile and widened her dark eyes. 'Pretty please?'

Nick pushed back in his chair and laughed. 'Addie, if you knew my schedule then you'd realise –'

'Even if I show you this?' Adele lifted her skirt to reveal long slim legs gift wrapped in the sheerest stockings ever and topped off with a tiny strappy triangle of silk.

Nick swallowed, his chest rising from an involuntary breath in. 'No, not even if you show me that.' He returned to his work but was unable to even touch a key because Adele had thrust her hips towards his face.

'You can lick it,' she pleaded. 'And, if you get the work done today, you can have a three-hour fuck in lieu of payment.' She made sure that Nick caught a waft of her natural perfume by running her finger around the lace edge of her panties.

'Just how do you expect me to put that on my tax return?' His eyes narrowed and his lips parted a little at Adele's proximity. He'd always had a thing for her, like all the men in their circle of friends – she was gorgeous, stunning – but really, could he accept her body as payment?

'It's a deadline thing, Addie. A big banking client's expecting a presentation later and –'

Adele didn't want to hear excuses. She was a businesswoman now and had her own deadlines to meet. She lowered her thong and pulled Nick by his unruly blond hair, pressing his mouth into the cleft of her shaven pussy. He soon got the hang of it and purred resignedly as his tongue searched the neat little folds of his friend's most secret place.

'Oh, Nick,' Adele moaned. 'If your web design skills are

half as brilliant as your tongue, then I'm going to make a fortune.'

'I can have it done by six,' Nick murmured, prising apart the sweet lips with his thumbs and driving his tongue deep inside. Then he stopped, looked up along Adele's flat tanned stomach and stared directly into her eyes. 'What, exactly, will you be selling?'

'Take a wild guess,' she said, giggling, and levered his mouth between her legs once again.

Back at her office, Adele cadged a sandwich off the receptionist but it didn't go halfway to satisfying her appetite. How she had finally pulled Nick from between her legs she didn't know, but leaving him without a string of orgasms had set her up for a difficult afternoon. What she had left his office with though was the promise that her new website would be up and running by early evening and all she had to do was list herself for sale by uploading some naughty photos and dirty promises.

After his initial shock at his friend's new venture, Nick had explained how they had an 'off-the-shelf' software product that would suit her needs completely and he would simply customise it to her desired look.

'Classy and expensive,' Adele had instructed. 'I'm going to be charging a fortune so keep it all upmarket.'

'No problemo,' Nick assured and set to work with an uncomfortable bulge in his trousers and three hours with Adele to look forward to later.

Back home from work, Adele couldn't eat even if she'd had food in the fridge. She kept visiting her new online home – a domain that Nick had kindly donated from their corporate stock with a suitably kinky name – but it wasn't until just before seven that Nick called round with the news that the site was finally live. He looked exhausted.

'It's fantastic!' Adele squealed as the page resolved. 'Just what I wanted.'

'I've got a couple of my guys to work overtime to promote it everywhere. They've done hundreds of adult sites so they know exactly where to get you noticed.' Adele lunged at him gratefully. 'That was an extra favour,' he said with a yawn. 'But one that should get your business up and running in no time.'

'Now for your payment.' Adele giggled, took Nick by the hand and guided him to her bedroom. But Nick glanced at his watch. 'Somewhere you'd rather be?' she asked.

'Of course not, except that I still have to see the banking client I mentioned earlier.'

'Poor Nicky,' Adele crooned, her voice enveloping his tired body like a bubble bath. She unbuttoned his shirt. 'Will you take some naughty photos of me for my website before you go? I need something to tease the punters with.'

Adele had already set up her professional quality, extremely expensive, bought-on-credit camera. The huge lens glared at the perfectly made bed and Nick stood behind it, studying the various settings.

'It suits you,' Adele said as she came into view on the camera's display. She had stripped naked and her smooth flesh and perfect breasts and flared hips and glossy long dark hair looked a million dollars on screen.

'What does?' Nick swallowed, pretending to adjust the camera. He zoomed in on her breasts, focusing on a nipple. He took a shot.

'Being behind the camera.' Adele climbed onto the bed, making sure that her legs were slightly apart as her buttocks passed in front of the lens. She heard a frenzy of clicking as Nick got to work.

Within an hour, Adele had a fine gallery of pictures to add to her website. Nick had left reluctantly but not before giving her a tutorial on how to get the best from her new auction site. Soon, a dozen tantalising auctions were on air, each advertising various dates, experiences and thrills and all accompanied by an array of sexy, alluring pictures to encourage opening bids.

The lowest starting price for an evening with Adele, including talking dirty, a sexy outfit and half an hour watching her play with a vibrator, was fifteen hundred pounds. She hoped to net double that. At the other end of the scale, Adele had implied total mind and body possession for twenty-four hours – a do-with-me-what-you-will auction – and the first offer over ten thousand pounds would secure the deal.

'Well, I only want rich people buying me,' Adele said with a grin as she viewed her lovely website. 'Mr Wetherby would be proud of me. I shall have my debts paid off in no time and all the fun a girl could want.'

There was no way Adele could sleep, especially as her body was aroused to the max because Nick had left before his promised payment. So she whiled away the hours by visiting chat rooms and discussion forums, especially the ones where she reckoned rich guys would hang out, and promoted her new website blatantly. Within several hours, she could see that hundreds had already visited her site.

And then it came. At ten thirty, Adele received a system email stating that someone had bid. The thrill! A stranger wanted to pay cash, so far a minimum of four thousand pounds, for the pleasure of her company and as much sex that could be crammed into three hours in a hotel. Adele's exclusive boutique was in business and, best of all, she was the merchandise. She could barely believe it was working. Mr Wetherby would eat his own financial words. *'Hopeless with money ... A shopaholic ... A liability to the bank ...'* His insults had rained thick and fast.

As quickly as her fingers would allow, Adele took a look at the bidder's details but it was pointless because in another few minutes he had been outbid by two hundred pounds and within an hour, nearly a hundred men had registered along with several women, and a dozen bids had been placed.

'This is amazing,' she mouthed as she watched her shopping debts melt away in front of her eyes. By morning, she would be able to call her bank manager and declare herself on the way to solvency again.

'I'm sorry but Mr Wetherby's phoned in sick today, Miss Riley. Can I take a message?' The woman was impatient, her tone clipped.

'Sure. Tell the miserable man that Miss Shopaholic called and she'll be depositing a large sum into her account very soon.' That should keep the weasel off my back, Adele thought, hanging up before the secretary could defend her boss.

Then she went to prepare herself for the biggest date of her life because – and it made her skin dance at the thought – a moment after midnight, someone had bid on The Big One. A stranger had agreed to pay ten thousand pounds to own Adele for twenty-four hours and really, at that price, she wanted to ensure he got the fuck of his life.

'This guy must like shopping, too,' she pondered as she stepped into a gossamer Versace dress, the fabric of which wrapped flimsily around the curves of her body. 'I do hope he pays in cash.' She felt the thin strand of satin between her legs dampen at the thought.

Adele strode confidently into the hotel lobby and was immediately faced with a hundred possibilities. Some kind of conference had attracted virtually every good-looking man in the country and picking out the mystery bidder from among the gathering of suited males would be tricky. Especially as she had no idea what he looked like. Suddenly, the worst occurred to Adele. What if he was ugly, dirty, a madman...

'I'd recognise you better without your clothes.' A hand was on her shoulder and a voice as reassuring as warm honey drizzled in her ear. She smelled expensive cologne, too. Adele turned.

'Oh,' she garbled. 'Are you ... I mean, did you ...'

'David,' he said, extending a hand. 'You are even more stunning in real life.'

'Oh,' Adele said again and found herself being led towards the lift. 'Are you, you know, the one who ...' He could be anyone, after all.

'Cash OK with you?' He winked, raising a brown leather briefcase. Adele relaxed a little, knowing she was well on the way to getting the dreadful Mr Wetherby off her back.

'Fine,' she replied, feeling as if she'd downed three gin and tonics at once. The lift carried them to the fifth floor, by which time her vision was blurred and every nerve in her body stripped to the core. 'Absolutely fine.' And she nearly melted into the plush carpet as she watched David unlock the door to a magnificent suite.

The man was a god. If she'd hand-picked him herself, she couldn't have done better. He was tall, dressed perfectly in jeans that showed off the power of his legs and buttocks, and a pale shirt and linen jacket with his hair, ever so slightly greying in a way that told of experience not age, brushing the collar. He turned, his face essentially clean shaven but with a day's growth adding a rough edge to his impeccably smooth appearance, and said, 'After you.'

'Do you often buy your women on the internet?' Adele asked, quickly checking her appearance in the mirror. She had to think of repeat business.

'Impulse purchase.' He smiled, removing his jacket and laying it over a chair. He placed the briefcase on the king-size bed and clicked it open. Adele begged her mouth not to drop open as a diamond-like radiance burst from within the case. 'Would you like to count it?'

'Oh, yes please.' Adele's fingers twitched at the chance to touch the cash just as much as they longed to explore her client's divine body. She sat on the bed and pulled out the neat wads of notes before peeling them apart one by one and dealing them out in a patchwork on the bed. Then she pulled her long hair from its clip, lay back in the sea of cash and spiked one pencil-thin heel through a crisp fifty. 'It seems to all be there,' she said, not having counted a single note. 'Which means that I'm all yours.' Adele dragged her arms through the money and rolled onto her front, giggling as she heard a champagne cork pop just like she thought she might if the mystery buyer didn't get deep inside her soon.

'Here,' he said, trailing the cold glass along the back of Adele's long legs. 'Have some of this while we talk.' He sat on the bed, his weight making Adele roll towards his thighs. She liked that.

'Talk?' She sat up and took the champagne.

'I've bought you so you have to do as I say, remember?' David rolled up the sleeves of his shirt. Adele liked the colour of his skin, the dark hairs, the length of his fingers. 'Now, tell me why you are doing this. An intelligent, beautiful young woman selling herself on the internet.'

Adele pulled a face, wondering if it was the Versace or her perfume that he didn't like. 'For the money, of course.' She took a long sip of champagne. 'And for the thrill too. Nothing excites me more than exchanging cash and if sex with a –' she drew in breath and glanced up and down his body, '– if sex with a striking man is involved too then . . .'

'You're broke, aren't you?' David poured more champagne and it seemed that he meant for a dose to spill on Adele's leg. 'I do apologise,' he said and bent down to lick it off before it dribbled onto the cash.

'How did you guess?' Her voice was barely there, shattered by his warm tongue against her skin.

'Just a hunch.' David peeled the fine fabric of Adele's dress from her legs, exposing her smooth skin right up to the edge of her tiny knickers. Then he tipped the flute just enough to spill a taste of chilled champagne onto the triangle of silk. 'At least you can afford some new ones now,' he offered before cleaning up the mess. 'Or are you so deep in debt that I'm going to have to buy you over and over again?' David eased the fabric aside and kissed her freshly marinated sex like he was kissing her mouth.

'Oh, I'm very, very deep in debt,' Adele whimpered, lying back again. One moment his tongue was buried inside her then the next it was barely there.

'And why would that be exactly?' David had already pulled off her panties and was now working on the complicated wrap-style dress but opted for ripping the fabric when he couldn't find an easy way to the rest of Adele's body.

'No!' she wailed. 'Do you know how much this dress cost?' She fingered the shredded bodice but soon gave up protesting as David unhooked her bra and doused her breasts in the remainder of his champagne.

'One thousand eight hundred and fifty pounds.' Then he removed his shirt, spread his body over her wet breasts and kissed the indignant retort from her lips.

That he knew the exact price, Adele thought, would normally be quite remarkable but as long as his broad chest was pressed against her body and she could feel the thick hard line of his erection gathering rhythm against her thigh then she didn't care about money or debt or shopping or anything other than climaxing with the weight of this man on top of her.

'I like a woman with expensive taste.' The array of fifty pound notes beneath them crackled as David grinned and worked his way out of the remainder of his clothing. 'Let me guess,' he teased. 'Eighty to ninety thousand pounds in the red although mentally you're well on your way to the half-million mark with every-thing you'd like to own?'

The man's skills of deduction would have impressed Adele immensely if she hadn't been greeted by his naked erection offered conveniently to her lips. She simply nodded and sucked gratefully on the most handsome thing she had ever seen.

'I bet your bank manager loves you, with all the juicy interest you're paying.' Even through the long strokes gliding up and down his shaft, the man maintained his self-control and stayed focused on discovering just how deep Adele's financial troubles ran. He pulled out of her mouth so she could speak.

'Don't talk to me about my bank manager. Not if you want to have sex with me, anyway.' The thought of Mr Wetherby briefly curdled the thrill building between her legs.

'Oh?'

Adele thought for a moment. 'Just think the complete opposite of you. He's a miserable old man who probably hasn't had a fuck in years and he gets his kicks from hassling hard-working people like me.' She licked the silver bead forming on the end of David's cock. She really didn't want to be reminded of her bank manager at a time like this.

'I guess he's just doing his job. You know, protecting the world from shopaholics like yourself.' David gripped his purchase by the shoulders and turned her roughly onto her front. In a moment, his strong hands had lifted her hips and teased open the clear-cut line of her smooth sex. 'Have you ever actually met him?'

Adele's face melted into the cash as she felt the tip of David's erection touch her sex for the first time. 'No,' she managed, crunching a fistful of notes as he ever so slowly worked himself inside her. She moaned, really not wanting to discuss the man further.

'You're not entirely qualified to pass judgement then, are you?' Self-control slipped away with every inch that was lost inside Adele. David reached round her slim waist and ground himself so deep that it was hard to tell where his body ended and hers began.

'Guess not,' Adele capitulated breathlessly as her temporary owner moved skilfully behind her.

'Then don't you think it would be wise to wait until you see him for yourself?'

David was pounding now, sparing no thought for her reply. Her sex pulsed, gripping him, squeezing him as the first stirrings of climax spiralled within. She wanted to come a thousand times and at that moment didn't care a jot about her stupid bank manager. She had a client to please and, aside from her own delight, that was her primary consideration.

'Well?' David insisted, slowing his rhythm, leaving Adele hovering on the brink of her first orgasm. 'Don't you?' The man seemed obsessed.

'Yes, yes, OK. You're right. I should wait until I meet Mr Wetherby before I call him an uptight, nagging old git.'

David seemed to approve and cast Adele onto her back in one deft move. A shower of money rained onto the floor as he plunged inside her again, rapidly working her back to the edge of orgasm, his own climax also imminent.

Adele stared up at the man above her, hardly able to believe that her first buyer should be so perfect. She prayed that he had endless cash so that he would visit her website time and time again. Keen to ensure he did, she pulled him down by his lean, muscle-bound shoulders and wrapped her long legs around his back with her heels digging into his buttocks. She kissed him hard and afterwards he buried his lips in her long hair, working his way to her ear.

'I'm ... not ... uptight ... or miserable,' he said and then his back arced in a series of whole body spasms as the new, deep position finally tipped him over the edge.

Adele felt the hot spurts inside her as her own perfectly timed climax milked David with wave after wave of delicious orgasm. God, she should be paying *him* for the pleasure. They lay, their bodies skimmed with sweat, while Adele stroked and kissed every inch of his body. Then she stopped.

'Why say that?' she asked, sitting up and leaning over him. 'Why would I think you're in the least bit uptight or miserable?' Adele felt her cheeks colour. She didn't think she wanted him to answer.

Instead, David reached for his jeans, took out his wallet and extracted a business card. 'Always a pleasure to meet clients,' he added after handing it to Adele.

'Oh hell,' she said as she read. 'David J. Wetherby. General Manager'. Printed underneath his name and title was her bank's name and address. 'I'm even further in debt now, aren't I?' Thinking quickly, Adele plunged her mouth onto his semi-hard cock, working him back again before he could be angry.

'Deeply, deeply in debt,' he managed between involuntary gasps. 'And it's going to take an absolute age for you to pay back.'

Nick answered his telephone groggily. 'Yeah?'

'It was you, wasn't it?' Adele whispered. David was in the bathroom. Only four hours remained of the date and they'd not yet left the hotel room.

'Me what?'

'That told Mr Wetherby about my website. Go on, admit it.'

'You know Dave Wetherby?' Nick was suddenly alert.

'Well, I do now,' Adele whispered. 'Rather well, in fact. What were you doing showing him my website? He's my bank manager!'

But Adele hardly heard Nick explaining how her shopping website had accidentally become part of the presentation intended for his banking client – the same bank that Adele happened to use – because the not at all uptight or miserable Mr Wetherby had returned from the bathroom and was threatening a refund if she didn't instantly oblige his needs.

Adele smiled and snapped her phone shut while pulling him back onto the bed. 'Customer satisfaction is my main concern,' she said and got right back to work pleasing her client.

Maya Hess has written numerous short stories for Wicked Words and is the author of the Black Lace novels, *The Angels' Share* and *Bright Fire* (published 2007).

Priceless Mathilde Madden

I love the idea of men for sale. Always have. Always will. And although its hard to pinpoint *exactly* why, I think in a nutshell, it's just, when I think about men selling themselves – in any context really, in any sexual context – something deep in my soul seems to sing. Just the thought of it. Men selling themselves. Selling their bodies. Selling their faces, their chests, their arses, their cocks. Offering themselves up to the highest bidder. Displaying their bodies for evaluation. Offering anyone who has the cash the chance to own them for a night. It's such delicious objectification. It's so very hot.

But an ordinary woman like me, with a very ordinary life, doesn't get the chance to experience such things very often. If ever. And even if I did run into some kind of sexy-men market stall on my way home from work, well, I kind of have this boyfriend anyway, so it isn't really on the cards.

So it's nothing but a hot idea really. I never even dreamt I'd put my money where my mouth is. But then my friend Kate starts talking about organising a Charity Slave Auction for the organisation she is working for. And, boyfriend or no boyfriend, I can't help entertaining very unhealthy thoughts about what that might entail.

Talk about divided loyalties. Especially for someone like me. Someone, that is, with no willpower whatsoever. So, actually, divided loyalties, not so divided. Because, you know, I can just go and watch, I don't have to actually bid, or anything.

And so poor Kate – who is completely ignorant of my crazy dirty fetish for men-for-sale – is pretty bamboozled when suddenly I all but beg her to smuggle faithless-me into her auction.

She has many – eminently sensible – objections. Like the fact that it's just boring work. Like the fact I really should be able to find something better to do on my birthday. On my twenty-ninth birthday. Oh yes, because that's when the auction is scheduled to happen. Not exactly perfect timing. (Although, then again . . .)

'Look, babe,' Kate says when I've dodged about half a dozen very good reasons why not. 'Why don't you just go to the pub with everyone – Rex and Pete etcetera – and then go on to a club or something and I'll come and join you when I'm wrapped up. I'll be there by midnight.'

'It's not that, Kate,' I say, in the voice of a three-year-old child who isn't getting any more sweeties. 'It's not that I want to be with you, personally. Well, I do, obviously. But that's not the thing. The thing is I really, really want to come, really –'

'Don't be stupid,' Kate interrupts before I can actually explain. Not that I can actually explain. Not to Kate. 'I can get you into much better events than this. What do you fancy? Fashion shows? Pop concerts? How about an awards show? I could do that, really I could. I know some people at one of the banks that sponsor the Brits and –'

But I manage to stop her there with nothing but a frown and I'm-so-not-that-kind-of-person eyebrows. 'Kate, please, I just want to go. Call it my birthday present. I –'

Kate interrupts again, 'But I don't get it. Why do you even want to come and bid? I mean, you have a boyfriend, Rex, remember? Why not leave the lovely auction lots for us single girls?'

I grin, sheepishly, but then try to give Kate a don't-be-daft expression. 'I'm not going to bid, Kate, I just want to watch. Bit of eye-candy fun. On my birthday.' And I do actually mean that. I do just plan to watch. Really.

'Well, OK, if you really want to,' she says with a sigh and a sort of shrug.

So I never actually do tell her why I want to go so much. I never have to let my kinks out of the bag.

OK, I know it's only for fun. No one is really paying for the men themselves; no one is really paying, well, for sex, but just the idea of it – the men showing themselves off, the women bidding.

Have I made it clear that I find this so fucking hot?

Then, I have to have this conversation. One evening, about a week before my birthday, I'm in bed with my boyfriend, Rex, and we've just had an excellent shag with loin liquefying kinky bits and everything, so he's in a pretty good mood, and I say, 'Rex, you know my birthday?'

My beautiful Rex is sitting up in bed looking somewhere between iconic and gorgeous. He's smoking a cigarette and he's still wearing the scuffed-up pair of black cuffs that I used to tie his wrists to the headboard earlier. His orangey-red hair is sticking out all over the place like some kooky kind of sculpture. He blows out an endless blueish-white plume of smoke before saying, kind of fast, 'It's next week and I've not forgotten.'

'I want to go to Kate's charity slave auction,' I say.

'Yeah,' says Rex, nodding sagely, 'I kind of reckoned that you might. How many are you planning on buying?'

I pick up my pillow and whap him with it. 'None! God, I do have some self-control you know.'

'Yeah, now you say that, but what's actually going to happen when you're there and there are all those gorgeous men parading about for you, up for grabs, and you've got your birthday money burning a hole in your handbag, are you even going to give a thought to poor old me? Stuck at home? After the years of sterling service I've given?' And he shakes his outstretched wrists in my face, so the manacles jingle.

Because, although there are some things that you might not really want to tell one of your closest friends – like that fact that you are super kinky for men selling themselves – it's different with your boyfriend. (Really it is. If you don't agree, you're wrong. I say, tell your boyfriend about your kinks. All of them. Asap. It is so worth it.)

So Rex knows. Actually, Rex likes. Actually, Rex even takes part in pay-for-play role play on occasion. And so, it's not really surprising that Rex saw this one coming.

'You don't trust me?' I say, enjoying the jingling cuffs and put-upon expression in spite of myself.

Rex laughs. He does find my dirty little secrets amusing sometimes. 'It's fine,' he says, still enjoying himself, 'we'll do something just the two of us afterwards.'

And I notice a naughty light in his eyes then. 'What are you thinking?' I say, intrigued but rather worried.

Rex smiles. 'Ooh no,' he says, 'can't ruin your birthday surprise.'

So, on the evening of my twenty-ninth birthday, I'm sitting here, surrounded by smoky clatter and chatter, in a very cramped room above a not particularly nice pub. I'm all on my own, and just starting to get an odd little tingling feeling in my stomach. It's partly excitement and partly a bit of oh-my-God-I-might-not-have-done-the-right-thing doubting. I could be with Rex right now, having a romantic dinner, or in the pub with a huge crowd of my closest friends and hangers-on. And although I have been having lurid fantasies about this evening for (what feels like) my entire life, I can't help worrying. What if it isn't any good? Oh, God, what if it doesn't turn me on?

After I've finished two nervous G and Ts Kate finally appears, looking elegantly harassed – as only Kate can.

I smile, woozily. I'm just a little bit zoned out because I've come straight from work with nothing proper to eat (and, of course, because I am stupidly over-excited about this event), but I tell Kate it's all going fabulously from my front-of-house perspective. And that's when Kate drops a small but perfectly formed bombshell. All her protests about my presence here – and particularly her concerns that I oughtn't to be bidding seem to have gone out the window. And birthday or no birthday, I can't just wallow on Fantasy Island – I have a job to do. Apparently.

Kate slides onto a stool opposite me, sets down her drink and then quietly confesses. 'Charity Slave Auctions aren't really in vogue any more,' she tells me, over the rim of her slightly greasy glass. 'You know, it kind of has sordid associations. But there are so many hot guys who work for Fur Fighters – I just couldn't resist. And it's not like they're actually prostituting themselves, is it? Not really. I got eight lovely meals donated, you're actually bidding on the meal out. See?'

'I see.'

'Anyway, the thing is, I kind of sold the idea to the board of trustees on the grounds that it would bring in shed loads of cash. So it bloody better. Actually that's more or less what they said – only in rather more hoity-toity voices. So the money will talk. I hope. Well, it'd better do if I want them to keep employing me to organise events.'

'Well, it's pretty full,' I say, giving the room a quick once-over head sweep. And it is. In fact the room is heaving. Most of the occupants are women, but I can see the odd male face dotted around too and I wonder if they are here to bid themselves or have been reluctantly dragged along.

'Yeah, well, I know I was a bit obstructive – but

actually, I'm really glad you're here,' Kate says, looking rather sheepish. 'I know it's your birthday and everything; I know I should be doing things for you, but, well, I was wondering if you could do me a little favour?'

Kate bends down and roots around in her handbag for a second, before straightening up to present me with a sizeable brown envelope. She slides it across the table.

I open my mouth to speak, but think better of it and instead take the envelope and peek carefully inside. It's full of cash. I open my mouth again, but Kate beats me to it.

'Two hundred and fifty quid,' she says. 'I don't actually want you to spend it, just, you know, keep the bidding going. And if you end up buying then, well, you're covered.'

I frown at her. Thinking of a hundred and one reasons why this is a bad idea. Not to mention an unethical one. Deliberately driving up the bidding – isn't that the number-one auction crime? And what kind of birthday present is a stack of cash I'm not actually meant to spend? But really my main concern is: 'Kate. I can't bid in this auction. What if I win the bloke? I mean, Rex. You remember, my boyfriend.'

Kate looks annoyed and doesn't notice my mimicking of what she said to me a few weeks ago. 'I've explained all that though. You're just bidding on the meal. If you win the bloke you've got the money to pay, and then you can just go and have a nice meal. But really, if at all possible, try not to win the bloke. There's no profit in it if you win.'

So, well, talk about Kate changing her tune. And really, where does this leave me? Stuck in a room where an auction of apparently gorgeous men is about to take place, where I am duty bound to bid on any specimen that might not be generating enough cash – but if I win one of them I have to quietly go and have dinner with him and his gorgeousness (and the fact I own him) without any untoward behaviour. On my birthday!

But before I can say anything Kate stands up – apologising again, and muttering about not wanting anyone to see us talking – and walks out.

I sit dumbly at the tiny table, clutching my envelope like it contains Weapons of Mass Destruction. And then the room goes dark.

When she takes to the stage a few moments later, I have to say, Kate does her job really well. She prowls around the stage in her tight hot-pink dress, whipping up the crowd into what can only be described as a hormonal frenzy. Behind her, on a line of wooden chairs, the eight men she has on offer look really quite alarmed.

She introduces the charity, giving a sparky spiel about animals and fur – the former being good and the latter being bad. But before we tire of her contractually obliged waffle about the worthy cause, Kate switches gear. 'So now, ladies and ... can I see a few gentlemen here too?' She holds up a hand to shade her eyes from the spotlights and peers into the audience. From the back of the room several masculine cheers greet her.

Kate laughs in response and then gets back to her patter. 'Excellent. Now, I want to see some high bids this evening. We've got a meal for two for each winning bidder and their prize. So bid early, bid high and don't go home empty handed.' Kate plants her tongue firmly in her cheek as an excited cheer hits her.

The first specimen she has for us – and that is the way she puts it, specimen – is Jonathan, from finance. Jonathan is lovely looking, wearing a navy-blue suit/navy-blue shirt combo that makes his dark skin look like molten Green and Blacks. I try not to lick my lips.

I don't need to assist with the bidding on Jonathan. He fetches £160, without even blinking. And in a far corner of the room a table full of girls scream with excitement as their prize weaves his smiling way over to them.

And the ever professional Kate (anyone would think she auctioned off men every single night), rattles on to the next guy – Simon, from IT.

Simon, likewise, is gorgeous. He's a master class in blond spiky hair and a sun-breaking-from-behind-the-clouds grin. Kate wasn't joking when she said she had some hot men in her office. They're delicious. It seems like she's pulled a master stroke with this risqué auction – she's going to make bundles.

When Simon, along with a rather nice meal for two, is sold for another hundred quid or so, I settle back in my chair. I don't have to even think about the furtive envelope on my table, Kate doesn't need little old plan-B me.

But that's where I'm wrong.

The next chap, Keith, isn't quite as drool worthy as Simon and Jonathan. He's not bad looking, but he's not an oh-my-God, head-turning, is-that-guy-a-model-or-what type. And he goes for just thirty-eight quid, before I even have a chance to step in and unethically force up the bidding. Kate flashes me a glare.

So I'm sitting up straight and paying extra attention to the next guy, and when I see him, I forget to breathe for a second. He's kind of gawky. Rangy and red haired. He looks cute, but a little shy. He's actually blushing. And I think it's the blushing that does it, far more than Kate's evil glare – I bid.

And that's where the trouble starts, because my cheeky funny guy might not be America's Next Top Model, but there's something about him, and at least one other person in the audience has noticed it too, and that's all it takes. And then it's just like every eBay auction I've ever participated in – once I've put in a bid on something, I'm committed, it's mine. I've got to have it. And I have to have this guy. It's war! The bidding gets fierce between us. And Kate does nothing to cool things down.

I suppose I might have stayed in control, might have maintained my dignity and bowed out at two hundred quid, say, if it hadn't been for the fact that my guy was wearing very tight shorts that left nothing to the imagination and was quite definitely erect as soon as his price went past fifty pounds. Yum.

And I'm not sure quite what it is yet, but something about that tell-tale bulge tells me this guy could be very interesting. Even more interesting than his bashful stage performance would suggest.

And I guess that's why I'm still bidding even though my brown envelope limit has been long passed. That's why I'm bidding £380. That's why I'm getting out my cheque book and writing a cheque to make up the shortfall from Kate's cash.

And that's why I'm heading out of the door with my purchase and jumping into a taxi on the rainy street.

We don't bother to go and eat – whatever Kate might have drilled into us about the fact I was bidding for the meal. Sod that. We go straight to my place.

In my little flat with low, low lights and soft, soft furniture my purchase looks even better then he did on the stage. And the idea that he seemed to actually be turned on by being auctioned off just won't let go of me. In a way that's even sexier than the fact he actually was auctioned off, than the fact I bought him. I just keep thinking about how hard he got and how hard he blushed.

I love . . .

I don't know if I can even explain it. I love it when men have dirty little secrets. I love it when they are turned on by something nasty, something wrong, something that twists against what society expects a man to be. I love it when men want things like that. When they burn and throb to be brought down, owned, used. And, although I know there are plenty of men that get off on that kind of stuff and are happy to shout it from the rooftops, I love it when the guy in question is all conflicted by his deviant desires. Just like the blushing guy in front of me right now.

It's so delicious. He's so different from Rex, who practically vaults the furniture to get to the ropes in the bedroom and, although I love Rex, I love this new spin on naughty little sub-boy too. It's just adorable. And, actually, I'll probably enjoy this so much more if I make an effort not to think about Rex too much.

I offer my purchase wine rather than coffee, because it's actually still quite early in the evening, and he accepts in a slightly shaky voice that makes me feel all twinkly with excitement. He's even more bashful now – he's biting his lip and not meeting my eye, and I haven't even begun to press the point. Well, not yet.

'You like that I bought you?' I ask darkly, looking at him over the rim of my glass.

'Yeah. Kind of.'

Oh, God, and his face is just priceless. Perfect. He hates that I know it turns him on, that I have that little chink where I can dig and twist.

'And you like that I own you? Right now?'

'Well . . .' But his words die in the air. I wait for him to speak again, but, nothing. Everything goes quiet.

Time seems to stand still for a bit and then I get up from my chair and walk over to him, getting right in his personal space, reaching into his lap, trailing my fingers over a desperate hot erection. 'I think the word you are looking for,' I say, softly, 'is "yes".'

He doesn't reply, so I squeeze the bulge in his tenting shorts harder. He makes a gratifying little mewling sound then. And I smile. And he gets even harder.

So I take a handful of his T-shirt, gripping it in the middle of his chest and twisting the fabric into a bunch, and then – acting like a caveman or something – I use this makeshift handle to drag him into my bedroom, and throw him down onto my bed.

I climb on top of him, straddling his tight skinny body easily. He sprawls beneath me, prone, his arms stretched above his head. He could just be being casual, just lying the way he fell, just lying the way that is comfortable right now, but he looks exactly like he's positioning himself to be tied down. Naturally, I choose to imagine that he is hinting at me about what he would like next. Letting me know what he wants, but can't bring himself to say. And I choose to take that hint.

From a bag tucked under my bedside table I produce a familiar pair of well-used leather wrist cuffs.

My recent purchase looks at them with widening eyes.

'Have you ever been tied up?' I ask, surprisingly breezily.

'Um, nope.'

'Have you ever thought about it?'

'Um.' His face twists into a strange expression. I almost feel like he is trying to hide from me. To climb inside himself. Out of the firing line. 'Um, yes, I suppose,' he says, eventually. So reluctantly.

I hold his gaze. I don't have to say anything to let him know that that vague admittance is nowhere near enough.

'I've always thought it would be hot, OK. But it's also twisted and weird. It's fucked up!' He almost looks angry as he says this, but his voice is catching a little with arousal. He did put himself on sale after all.

There's no debate though. In fact I start to tie him down while he's still talking. I move slowly, buckling his wrists snuggly into the cuffs and then fixing them to the eye bolts that have been part of my bed frame since forever. 'You like it though,' I say. 'You like it even though you know it's "fucked up".'

'Yeah-uh,' he says, his affirmative becoming a soft

moan as he pulls a little against his restraints. 'Oh, God. Yeah. I really fucking do.'

And then he's tied, but not over-restricted. He can still squirm, which feels right. I push his T-shirt up until it is bunched around his armpits, and play about with his elegant chest. I tug a little at the sandy hairs there, just enough to make him squirm and roll, and give himself away.

Not just a submissive, but a pain slut. A pretty, pretty little pain slut. All rose-flushed cheekbones and hard, hard cock. Eager and confused and just far too precious. Priceless.

And once I realise that, I need to make him more uncomfortable. Need to. And I need to do it now. I want to see him hurting, twisting in pain. From the bag, I pull out a pair of silver nipple clamps and dangle them in front of his face. He shakes his head.

'Oh, no.'

'Oh, yes.'

'No. I can't. I don't want this. It's too much.'

'I don't think it's too much. I think it's just right. Perfect. And the thing is,' I say, gently stroking his chest as I speak, 'I get to decide, because I own you. You are bought and paid for and I get to do whatever I want to you.'

'No,' he says. But there's that crack in his voice again, giving away that delicious arousal that I know means he likes the fact I own him, really. He likes the fact I get to decide just how uncomfortable he is. 'I don't think it's really meant to work like that,' he continues. But any further protests die away as his breathing gets heavier.

'Yes it does. For us it does.' And I dip my head and kiss his left nipple, before securing it quickly in nasty jagged teeth. He moans as the jaws close, but he doesn't protest.

And he's harder than ever.

* * *

He is tied down and clamped now. Rolling around on my bed. Not really coherent. Ecstatic. And I'm feeling pretty good myself.

I know where I need to go next. I don't have any option. I'm so wet and I'm rubbing myself gently against his leg. His helplessness, his pain, his liking his pain and helplessness, his conflicted emotions about liking his pain and helplessness, all these things are working together to enhance my spiralling arousal.

I move back. I can't remember when his clothes disappeared but he's naked now, and his hard cock is still as obvious and needy as ever. I lift myself up and move over it. Repositioning and moving him inside.

And, oh, oh, wow! Too good.

I move as he moves. We both slide and glide. It's easy and good. Familiar. He's very hard and the pressure is right where it needs to be, nudging me, pushing me on. We don't have far to go. Either of us. But at the same time, I'm not quite there yet.

I release his wrists so we can both roll over – locked together – and I can watch him moving above me, his long thin body, elegant, powerful, my property. I feel like I'm falling as his thrusts push me down into the bedclothes. And as I fall, I start to soar. Right there. Good pressure. It isn't always this easy, but the build-up – weeks of it – have brought me to just the right place.

He thrusts again and it almost pushes me over the edge. I'm so close to coming now. I just need . . .

I reach up and grab the sparkling metal chain that connects his two nipple clamps. I hold it for just a moment – a delicious anticipatory moment – and then I tug. Not so hard, but hard enough. He cries out.

Oh, God.

I tug again, timing it right this time so his cry coincides with his thrusting.

Oh, yes. Oh, nearly.

I do it again. And then, the next time I do it, and he cries out in pain, I come so hard I barely notice him any more.

When I open my eyes – barely seconds later – I'm holding the nipple clamps in my hand. They're not connected to him any more. And he's slumped on top of me, panting.

I hold the clamps up, not realising for a moment how I could have come to be holding them. And then it occurs to me that I must have pulled the chain so hard as I came that I pulled the clamps clean off. Oops. I bite my lip. 'Sorry,' I say.

And then he lifts his head to look at me. His face is flushed, damp with sweat. But the smirk on his face says it all. He pulls himself up into a half-sitting position, resting back on one elbow and rubs his bright-red nipples, wincing at me. But it's so big and exaggerated a wince, it's almost comical.

'Sorry,' I say again, but I'm finding it sort of funny now.

Rex grins at me. 'It's not funny,' he says, looking kind of like it is.

'Yeah, OK.' And I reach out and rub my boyfriend's poor tender chest myself. My poor wounded soldier. My hero. The things he does for me.

'So?' Rex says, reading my mind. 'Good birthday present?'

I laugh – almost relieved that he has come out of character. 'You should get an Oscar,' I reply, a little laugh lighting my voice.

'That good?'

I shake my head, because I can't believe he doesn't realise that it was. Actually, he probably does. He's probably just fishing for adulation. Well he's fishing in the right place, because I feel very, very adulatory right now. 'It was wonderful. It was ... Oh! The way you play acted

Mr Conflicted for me. That was the best ever! I really, really loved that.'

Rex laughs. 'Yeah, well, I got sick of you going on about how hot that got you.'

'I never thought you could pull it off, though, or I would have pestered you to do it ages ago.'

'Well, now you know I can, I'm just going to play that part all the time for you. No more of your usual Mr Kinky Slut Boy, no more draping myself over the back of the sofa for you and begging you to "please, hurt me", because, of course, you don't like *that*, do you?'

I swallow. Because I'm so fickle and much as I love Rex's new conflicted shy boy, his trademark Mr Kinky Slut Boy is so hot too. Mmm, that bad boy schtick. So good too. 'Well,' I say, hopefully, 'maybe I could, I don't know, mix it up a bit, mix and match?'

Rex shrugs. 'Well, there might be limits. I might have to restrict you to just one persona per playtime, you greedy girl, otherwise it could get confusing.'

Oh! He is beautiful. 'God, no wonder I nearly bankrupted myself for you.'

'What?' Rex looks a bit confused. 'I gave Kate a whole stack of cash for you to buy me with. Didn't she give it to you?'

'Um, yeah, but I kind of went a bit over the limit.'

'How much did you pay?' Rex asks, shocked, and he kind of swallows when he says it. Shocked and aroused. He likes. He likes talking about the fact I paid for him.

'Three hundred and eighty.'

'Shit! Sophie! I told Kate to stop the auction at two hundred and fifty.'

I laugh. I have to. 'And you actually thought she would? You poor naive little whore-boy. Kate saw the glint of my cold hard cash. Why do you think she even agreed to your plans?'

And, God, even though things are pretty light and I

am pretty spent, I still get a tiny tingle when I call him a whore. Because, well, just because. I sigh and run my hands over his body, gently, but still with a kind of possessiveness that even the breaking of the fourth wall hasn't quite dissolved.

Rex moans gently. He's clearly still as buzzy as me.

'Tell me how much you paid again?' he breathes.

'Three hundred and eighty pounds.'

'God, so you wanted me that much? I hope I was worth it.'

'Oh, baby, you were priceless.'

Note: Sophie, Rex and Kate all appear in Mathilde Madden's Black Lace novel *Mad About the Boy*. She is also the author of the Black Lace novels, *Equal Opportunities* and *Peep Show*.

O Nuala Deuel

Inga Loeb was single because she wanted to be that way. She had no shortage of potential suitors, but her independence meant more to her than any number of proposals, any number of velvet boxes from Alexandrov; vows of love and fidelity tumbled over and away from her, as ephemeral as the windstream across an aeroplane's wings.

Inga was an air stewardess; she worked exclusively for a Saudi Arabian businessman with his own Lear jet. It was just one more reason she could offer to the pack of randy dogs that were chasing her tail. *I can't have a boyfriend*, she'd say. *I'm on call twenty-four hours a day. At any moment I might be expected to drop everything and fly out to Europe, to South Africa, to the States.* Her boss, known to everybody as Ali – to recite his entire name would take a good fifteen seconds – was a hard taskmaster, but extremely fair. He smiled at Inga often, and chatted to her when he wasn't working on his laptop, or calling clients from 40,000 feet in the air. It was important to her to know that she was more to him than some kind of drink-fetching robot. He asked her opinion on various matters. He confided in her. Sometimes her duties extended to errands that took place on the ground: purchasing gifts for special clients, checking out hotel facilities for all-day conventions, arranging dinners at short notice at elite restaurants. She had a certain amount of persuasive power, and knew that these gifts were more likely to work if she could utilise them in person. She was an attractive young woman, with glittering green eyes and an hourglass figure that she liked to squeeze into sheer black dresses and high heels, or, when she was relaxing, expensive scuffed leather trousers and thin clingy tops. She turned heads, and she often made them nod too, whenever she asked for something to be done. She was not used to rejection.

For such an inconvenience, she was paid handsomely. She enjoyed a top-end five-figure salary with regular, generous bonuses, and owned a large studio flat in Bayswater and a modest terraced house in Devon, which she decamped to at every opportunity. She had a good circle of friends and an interest in photography, world cinema and jazz.

She was also addicted to online shopping for sex toys.

Inga loved the anonymity of such shopping. She loved too the little routines she had developed on the nights she decided to settle down for some retail therapy with the mouse and the Mastercard. There was always a hot bath first, and a large glass of Rioja. The sash window she slid open as wide as it would go. Miles or Bird or Dizzy on the stereo. Candles. She immersed herself in the hot scented water and closed her eyes to this blanket sensual infill. When the glass of wine was finished, she would feel a little thick, a little woolly in the head, a sensation echoed in the pit of her stomach. Her mind would be turning to silicone and steel, to leather and lubricants. Her long hair fanning out in the water, washing up on the floating bounty of her breasts.

Tonight, on the eve of her thirtieth birthday, she reached for a bar of lavender soap and ran it along the gulleys at the side of her body, where the flesh swept down to the pout of her pudenda; the many nerves bunched beneath her flesh here singing as they awoke to her intent. She pulled out the bath plug and felt the water lowering. Her weight drew her down as the bath emptied. Her pubis broke free of the surface, like an exotic sea creature caught out by the tide. She ran the soap over the hair there, enjoying the lather as it thickened, feeling the cream slither into the frills of her labia. She squeezed her thighs together, and the sight of her long limber muscles becoming defined under her skin, enhanced by the oily light, turned her on more than she expected. She was sleek. She was a thoroughbred. More of her body became exposed as the water gurgled away. The deep curve of her waist. The nub of her belly button. Her breasts settled back against her ribcage proud and perfect, like something cast by a sculptor eager to capture her in her moment of glory. She watched her breasts shudder as she worked the soap against her cleft, creating so many suds now that it was difficult to keep a grip on the bar. The sound of the soap as it sucked and squelched into her quim was deliciously rude. The last of the water gathered in an eddy at the black O of the plug hole and she watched it spin wildly away. She reached down to the low table by the bath and swept up a brightly coloured configuration of moulded jelly and plastic. She flicked a switch and the head of its seven-inch shaft rotated. A separate, bifurcated offshoot vibrated alarmingly. She thrust the vibrator into her pussy, as deep as she could get it, and positioned the buzzing clitoral arouser against her hot little flood button.

Fifteen pounds from *www.honeypot.com*. A bargain.

She came before she could find a rhythm to move against, ploughing the firm silcone into her with fervid abandon, imagining a man crushing her against the enamel surface of the bath, his own senses lost to the pooling of heat that gathered at the tip of his monumental cock. The vibrations were deep and intense. They always produced a different kind of orgasm to the one she experienced with her fingers. It was as if every single nerve ending was being attended to at once by the little machine. It was mind-blowing. Quite often she had a headache after playing with one of her toys; they were that thorough with her. Yet, as had happened now in the empty bath, her skin puckering as she cooled, she had not been able to reach her climax without thinking of real meat pinning her down. Her toys were all about preparation; they couldn't deliver the coup de grâce. Ultimately, despite their sophistication and their lifelike appearance, it was the lack of humanity that failed her. The sound was too mechanised; the smell too synthetic. She loved the rhythm of sex, the measured slap of flesh. It was like the beat of the drums in jazz, it created the spaces within which the music happened. But she could never find the toy she needed to replicate that. And no matter how hard she worked them, there was never the reciprocal sound of a lover losing control: all of these things were what drew an orgasm from her. It wasn't all about direct clitoral stimulation.

Still, she loved the naughtiness of her machines. There was a thrill in using something that was custom-made for the vagina, and for pleasure. Hanging around a businessman for as long as she had, she couldn't help thinking that there was a gap in the market, but she couldn't imagine how it might be filled. All she could do was keep trawling the websites until that border between the actual and the pretend was smudged to the point where it no longer became something worth considering. Tonight she would find herself a toy worthy of a woman entering her fourth decade. She wanted the best there was, and she would not call a halt until she had found it.

Inga rose shakily to her feet and pressed her fingers lightly against her mons. A residual tremor existed there. She was still excited and by the time she had reached her bedroom and jiggled the mouse to chase away the screensaver, knew that she was going to have to trawl the web one-handed. But not to some grinding background of white noise. She dumped the vibrator in her underwear drawer and reached for the beautiful, thick twelve-inch glass dildo she had bought in Amsterdam the previous summer. It didn't gyrate, it didn't throb, and it had a tendency to feel a little chilly, but that was what she craved right now. She sat naked on the office chair in front of the Apple Mac, her legs spread, cunt tilted towards the screen, sliding the end of the dildo all over her fizzing, swollen pussy lips.

She clicked through her bookmarked favourites, enjoying the gentle slip and slide of the tool as she slithered it tenderly across her opening, not yet wanting to fuck herself into oblivion. The filed list of sites that she had previously patronised seemed suddenly too pedestrian; she wondered if she had taken her proclivity too far and become jaded: nothing on the pages aroused her as it once had.

She desultorily ordered some strap-ons because she liked the colours and the quality harnesses. She bought some large steel cock rings of various diameters and a few of the lifelike vaginas, just for fun. But none of it was connecting with that little zone in the pit of her stomach, the place that was like some secret internal mouth forever locked in an O of surprise and arousal.

She grew bored of her usual haunts and typed a few key words into the search bar. *Lifelike, sex toys, ultimate, realistic*. She realised that what she was actually looking for was a man as soon as she hit the return key, but by then she was too engrossed by the jags of pleasure ramping through her clit to consider what this meant. She spread her legs even wider and eased the bulbous head of the glass into her. The shaft of the dildo was a beautifully shaped series of concentric circles, like thick ribs, and she felt each one as she swallowed the fat glass, inch by inch. Her pussy lips rippled around the girth of the dildo. She felt filled up, stretched. The tip nudged up against her cervix and a low moan shifted wetly around the base of her throat. She began to slowly pump the glass cock in and out of her drooling quim as the search results came back. In a daze, feeling her control dwindle, she glanced down the familiar list of names, most of the links coloured red to indicate she had visited them before.

There was one website that had escaped her attention, which surprised her:

www.o.com.

It must be new. She clicked on it, imagining the dark eyes of her imperious ghost lover peering intently into her own as she bore down on the orgasm waiting to be hatched inside her.

David.

She felt herself tip over that invisible edge and had to put out her hand to steady herself as the legs of the chair she was sitting on skidded back away from the table. Her release was a like series of circles that rippled away from that tight little nub of pleasure at the top of her cunt. Whenever she felt her orgasm, she thought of the old RKO sting that appeared before movies, of radio signals buzzing from a mast on top of the world. She imagined the peristaltic spasm of a ring of muscles desperate to squeeze the ecstasy from her body because it couldn't hope to stay intact if they remained behind.

She came back, as she always did, despite the conviction that each climax sent her further away from herself. Reality poured into the gaps of her in the shape of her credit card, the mouse, the chirrup of her computer as it processed any number of little unseen tasks.

'Hi, Dave,' she said, thickly. Her heartbeat felt visible in the skin of her chest. She was exhausted and energised at the same time. The homepage of *www.o.com* contained nothing more than a picture of a male sex doll that was so lifelike she thought it might turn to her and tip her a wink at any moment. Short hair, a cute mouth, chocolate-brown eyes. His body was a pale caramel colour, his prick tumbling halfway down his thigh, soft, but with a heavy weight to it. It had real presence: it drew the eye. Next to the picture, in acid pink lettering, were the words:

Meet Dave. A six-foot tall hunk of hard muscle and good loving. Made with the highest quality materials.

Watch his erection grow as you caress him. Realistic thrusting action. Realistic ejaculations. Awesome sucking and tonguing programmes. Listen to him tell you how great you were afterwards. A stunning piece of equipment, the ultimate sex toy for the discerning woman. Buy now.

How could she not? Despite its four-figure price tag, it was a piece of kit that she must not ignore.

She quickly entered her details and punched the transaction processing key. A few seconds later, a screen appeared thanking her for her order and informing her that her purchase would be with her in three working days. She drained her glass of Rioja and swept back to the bathroom feeling suddenly revitalised, somehow like a teenager again. As she showered away the sticky residue of her climax, she imagined it was because, in a way, she had set up a date. It was like being sixteen again, at college, waiting impatiently for the Friday night and a movie with the class Adonis. Three days was an impossible time to wait. She felt herself shiver in anticipation. Plenty of time to pamper herself. To make the treat something more than it was.

She went out for a walk.

The streets around her home were glossy with long-departed rain. The sodium lights were caught in the sheen-like holes punched in the skin of the Earth, allowing glimpses of wondrous lands beneath. These merged with the smeared windows of countless flats rising to her right. She had been walking for so long she was unsure of where she had arrived at. The windows shivered with pulses of TV colour. Some of the glass was shrouded by net curtains. Others allowed an unhindered view of the rooms inside. She wondered about the people sitting in them. How many of them were about to have sex, or had just finished? How many were in the middle of the act right now? She remembered teenage boyfriends honey fucking her on parents' sofas in front of the television, for hours sometimes, once the frenzy of the first few occasions had burnt itself out. Lovemaking changed, she suddenly realised, as you grew older. You knew how to fine-tune. You knew exactly what you wanted, and how to extract the sensation you craved. There was no longer any hit and miss, any wild abandon. Control was what gave adult sex its frisson, but it was also what stripped it of its magic too.

As if summoning some evidence to the contrary, she turned her head to catch sight of a couple in a kitchen, fucking in the buttery light from an open refrigerator. He had her against the worktop, thrusting into her as her hands slid against the MDF, her eyes closed, her breasts juddering, the nipples proscribing crazed parabolas over their soft heavy background. The couple's domestic setting, the easy knowledge they had of each other's naked body, the way he peppered her chest, throat and face with kisses instructed her that her beliefs were flawed. There was surprise on the woman's face. And the thrill of it was there too; she had been ambushed by him. A smile surfaced, turning into the frown of sweet excruciation, breaking into a smile again as she reached the limit of feeling. She opened her eyes and fixed Inga to the spot. She hugged her man close to her and Inga felt the acres of cold night sky pile in on her. She had never felt so separate, so isolated. At home she had hundreds of pounds of diversion.

By the time she arrived back at her flat, she was so despondent that she could not bring herself to get undressed. She dropped to her bed as the clock on her computer softly chimed the hour. Midnight. Now she was thirty.

Inga awoke to a sound like a flock of birds. She experienced a moment of depression when she saw that she was still dressed in the previous night's clothes. A couple of jelly dongs stood to attention on her bookcase next to a tube of self-heating lube and a pair of padded nipple clamps. A day of glorified wanking lay ahead. She could have anything she wanted, from the slimmest, stubbiest four-incher to the mammoth eighteen-inch pole vault that she needed to take muscle relaxants for. The thought of all that impersonal, meatless meat exhausted her before she'd even flicked a switch.

I need a holiday, she thought, at the same time understanding that she didn't know what she wanted; yet more, that she did, but she couldn't put a face to it.

She traipsed downstairs to the source of that avian sound: a stack of birthday cards on the welcome mat. The sight of so many tributes from friends cheered her and she spent the next quarter of an hour tearing into them. A cup of raspberry leaf tea and a bagel later and she felt more sanguine about her position. Everyone went through a phase of self-doubt. Everyone who masturbated had to swallow a little guilt, a little self-loathing, however misplaced.

She cheered herself up further by remembered friends from college who had been brazen in their enjoyment of themselves: Anna who would always play Madonna's 'Justify My Love' to indicate to others that they must not enter her bedroom for any reason; Kim, who loved to come on all fours, using all of her fingers, rilling them across her vulva like an anemone sifting the sea for titbits; Madeleine, the French exchange student who greased her mons up with groundnut oil and climaxed by squeezing her thigh muscles together with such skill and precision she could manipulate her clitoris while her hands dealt with the hypersensitive flesh of her nipples.

Those times had been good for her not only because she had a steady stream of friends on tap, but they helped to open and close certain doors in her life. She could remember kissing Madeleine on the doorstep at midnight, summer clinging to the blue-black sky, their faces so damp with perspiration they had grown bored of wiping it clear and had let it come. She had tasted of salt and apples. The kiss had been exciting because it was unexpected. It was the first time she had drunk chilled Beaujolais, or eaten fruitcake with Wensleydale cheese. It shouldn't work, but it did. Was that brief flirtation with lesbianism – a kiss, a breast's tip in her fingers, a nervous, trembling thigh pressed between her own – the reason she had not linked up with anyone now? Despite her confidence, the hunger to be a success in her work, was she essentially someone who didn't know anything?

She thought she might cry, or smash a glass, or get roaring drunk. In the end she did none of these things, and merely sat in the centre of a circle of greeting cards, watching for the shadow at the window of something that might take her away from herself, even for a little while.

The knock at the door was almost too tired to rouse her from her sleep. She lurched for it, her desperation shaming her. She signed quickly for the package, so much larger than she was expecting, unable to meet the postman's gaze, in case he was aware of what it was she was receiving. Once she had closed the door, she left the monolith of brown paper and parcel tape and hurried to the kitchen, where she poured herself a large brandy, downed it in a few swift gulps.

She couldn't believe he was actually here. She imagined him uncomfortable and stifled in his packaging. She quelled an irrational stab of panic. He was a toy. *It* was a toy. His penis curled against his thigh, perhaps taped to it, to prevent it from becoming prematurely gorged. His balls. She imagined cupping them, lifting them, measuring their soft weight. She might take one of them, or both of them, into her mouth, feel the underside of his cock twitch and throb against her nose . . .

She approached the package, which was leaning,

almost nonchalantly, against the sofa. She imagined his voice: *Here, perhaps? Or upstairs? You decide.*

She feverishly unwrapped him, yanking him clear of his bubble wrap and shrink wrap, tossing away the yards of cardboard, twisting open the plastic ties, freeing him from his unedifying bonds. She stepped back. He was hunched over, as if in thought. His hair, when she haltingly reached out to touch it, was soft, real. Suddenly she was gushing, setting free words that she had never spoken, never imagined she would ever say: *I love you. Will you marry me? I love you. I love you.*

She started to cry, both in gratitude that she had been able to purge the entreaties from her system, and in disgust of her need, at the weirdness that was rushing into her life. She wiped her eyes and pushed him back onto the sofa. She was mildly shocked at the feel of his shoulder muscles; there was yield but there was also – *God how could there be?* – resistance too, as if he had thought for a second about denying her the satisfaction of bullying him. He lay, not like something synthetically rigid, but with relaxed presence, his body observing gravity's laws. His arm flopped naturally over the edge of the sofa. His head was tilted back, revealing the cartilaginous ridges of his throat. She watched, rapt, as his left leg, hooked over the armrest, moved to the rhythm of a heartbeat. It must be hers, fooling her, surely they wouldn't go to so much trouble?

He said, 'You're beautiful.'

There was the slightest suggestion of digitisation to the voice, a minuscule click at the start and end of the sentence, but it was a relief to hear it. She had begun to believe that a real body had been dumped on her doorstep and she wasn't sure how she might deal with that. The spookiness of the situation receded; this was a doll. A very good toy, but a toy nonetheless. She let her dress fall to the floor.

'David,' she said, her voice thick with anticipation.

'Yes, darling?'

She reached behind her and unhooked her bra. 'It's time to get my money's worth.'

The phone rang towards early evening, as she was slowly putting together the ingredients for a dinner she didn't want.

'Inga, hi. It's Cass. Ali has been called out to Milan. An emergency meeting concerning the hostile bid for Judd Janeway. He's expecting a series of negotiations. Could go on for two, three days. The jet is prepped and on standby. Sorry it's such short notice. There will be a car with you inside twenty. OK?'

The names of these companies were like phrases of foreign languages heard in passing. They meant nothing to her. She knew Ali was into as many companies as there were fingers on his hands, perhaps as many as there were rings on his fingers, but none of them rang any bells. It was part of a world she didn't understand, or hoped to fathom. Venture capitalism, in the main. Which sounded to her like a fancy term for opportunism. Get rich quick. Good luck to him. It was obviously working. Was it a coincidence that he was single too? Like her he claimed it was what he wanted to be. But maybe like her it was a question of protesting too much. Sometimes people never asked the question, and she told them anyway. Too often, recently, when she said it it seemed more like she was trying to persuade herself.

For the first time in Ali's employ, she wondered about him, about her and him. Was there some alchemy between them, on a level she had yet to unveil? Such a scenario seemed too convenient, and too Hollywood, in a way. The driven businessman and his help, at different ends of the food chain, yet inhabiting the same space, sharing the same life, give or take a million or two.

She had never seen Ali with a woman, had never even spotted him appraising female clients, or the girls that moved sinuously within his striking range on the streets of Manhattan, Prague or Barcelona. There were ample opportunities for him to sate any pang, yet she had never paused in her knocking on the door of his hotel suite at the sounds of passion from within. It never happened. She had never had to divert the queries of an inquisitive husband, nor, for that matter, any inquisitive wife. Ali seemed to be asexual. It was as if any dalliance with another person was somehow wasteful in terms of time; he was more interested in spreadsheets than bed sheets.

Inga had never really considered him in these terms before, either. Perhaps because she had been unknowingly put off by his neutrality, but possibly because he did not spark anything visceral within her. He was an attractive man in many ways; he was lean and wolfish, with hooded eyes and a full mouth. His hair was slightly longer than the conventions of his career permitted, and its blue-black gloss was shot through with seams of silver. He was unusual looking, and therefore sexy. But his lust for profit had turned his features into something that was beyond what could be construed as predatory in sexual terms. He had the killer in him. She had heard him laughing over a competitor's liquidation. For him, fucking was something to be done metaphorically, and only ever in the ass.

The car, with its tinted glass windows and inscrutable driver, whisked her through the rain-soaked streets of West London. On the Westway, as the great glass edifices of the Paddington Basin streaked by, she felt a prickle of anger towards Ali, the way he summoned her whenever he wanted, as if she were something cryogenically suspended at those times when she wasn't fetching and carrying for him. Her life was not on hold when she wasn't working, despite the handsome payments that bolstered her bank account. For the first time since taking the job, she felt resentment.

She closed her eyes, breathing deeply. Things were

coming to a head. And that was good, she reasoned. Questioning her position meant that something wasn't right somewhere. The money was good but the karma wasn't. Perhaps this was an indication that she was about to make choices based on who she was and what she wanted, rather than what everyone else demanded from her. That was the key to making the break from childhood. Being yourself. It was just that, for over twelve years, that was all she had done.

Her cunt ached. Whenever she moved, his smell rose from the apertures in her clothing. Slices of action from the day flashed into her thoughts, like stills from some forbidden portfolio. She reached down and massaged her pussy through her uniform.

'You have beautiful breasts . . . I'd like to suck them.'

His mouth opening, his eyes swooning shut: her nipple disappearing between his ice-white teeth, the leading edge of his tongue settling against her tit. His lips pursing, drawing her nipple to a taut exclamation, rolling it around his mouth.

My God. It was so real. It was real. She had laughed out loud.

Rising to his feet as she knelt on the sofa, his hair falling over his eyes. Holding his penis as it thickened, peeling back his foreskin to reveal the swollen shape of his desire. Her vagina suddenly slick with juice as she realised such a beautiful, huge, sculpted prick was seconds away from filling her up. The feel of the tip squirming against her folds, almost sliding off her. The inches. The light tap of his balls against the top of her thighs at the end of that delicious first strike. His breath on her spine. The thrust, the sensation of being unravelled as he partially withdrew, as if the organ were no more part of her, than him. The cushioned spring of pubic hair. Her name in his throat as he quickened. His hand encasing her breast, palpating her, squeezing pleasure from her pores.

My God, my God.

Her orgasm burst out of her as she reached around to feel his hard quivering buttocks clenching with the force of his own. She felt three, four, five hot silky spasms deep within her. He withdrew and liquid pearls frothed from her crease. She dabbled her fingertips in it and brought them to her nose. Fresh seed. How did they manage that? She glanced down at him; he was sweating, his skin flushed. His erection was subsiding, but she had knelt and sucked and licked at him, marvelling at the taste of his semen, enjoying the way that her ministrations were reviving the corpse of his penis. He was hard again within a minute. She slurped at him, giving him her entire repertoire of kisses, flicks and nips, enjoying the way he filled up her mouth, the way he groaned and ground his hips against her face. She sucked him hard and fast, than let him fuck her mouth slowly, barely touching him with her tongue and lips, providing the merest amount of friction. Then back on with the full throttle, then easing off. He was writhing. He came in the middle of another bout of frenzied sucking and she was impressed that the quantity was less this time. The manufacturers had omitted no detail.

She had left him on the sofa as the car drew up outside. 'Sleep well, David,' she said. 'My David. We'll be together again soon.'

Now she came again as her fingers writhed in the slick created by her memory, her legs rising, feet knocking the chauffeur's headrest. She could barely stifle her cry, and decided not to. She didn't care if the driver saw her. As she froze in the instance of her climax, she saw his eyes in the rear-view mirror, her own face behind it, her mouth a red-rimmed O of surprise and elation. The tide receded; she blew him a kiss.

'Tell Ali,' she said. 'Tell him what you like. If he fires me I'll thank him for it.'

A twinge of shock, of fear, of disbelief, as she stepped from the car at Heathrow and headed for the departure lounge. Don't look back. Do not look back.

Two hours later, she was exhausted. She had been busy with pre-flight checks and had served Ali aperitifs and dinner shortly after take-off. Now Cass was briefing her on the itinerary once they landed in Milan. She couldn't concentrate. All she could think of was David. She realised she had made a decision. She was going to leave her job. She had never felt tired at work before, and it wasn't solely due to David's athletic lovemaking. Her tasks were tedious. The thought of carrying on like this for even another week, let alone another year, made her feel sick to the stomach. As Cass talked of hotel lunches, guest lists and corporate goody bags, Inga was reminded of the chauffeur. A spike of panic ripped through her. His voice, as she stepped clear of the car, had been bracketed with a little digital click, as had the captain's just now. At least he had an excuse, speaking through the intercom. Or was she just imposing little bits of David on to the humdrum, trying to spice up that which could no longer be enlivened?

Cass materialised by her side. 'Ali would like a word,' she said.

Was it the change in pressure as the jet sank towards Milan that caused her voice to sound metallic? Inga suppressed a giggle. She needed a holiday. First chance she got, she was off to the beach. With a *very* large suitcase.

Ali was ensconced towards the rear of the jet, behind a series of heavy curtains. His desk was piled high with papers requiring his initials. He processed another dozen of these before lifting his head and indicating she should sit down.

'I understand you've had a change of heart regarding your career path?' he asked her. His hooded eyes never looked so raptor like. She felt like a morsel being proffered by a bird handler.

'How did you . . .?' she began, but he held up his hand, his eyes closing slowly, as if to say *You don't know me by now*? 'Yes,' she said, firmly. 'I've worked for you for a long time. I think it's time for a change.'

He nodded. 'And which job is it that you're tired of?'

Inga blinked. 'I don't understand.' She spread her hands. 'This one. I'm tired of this one.' The first needle of doubt. Fear was in this cabin. It was trying to place a suffocating mask over her face.

'Not the other job then?'

'I don't have another job.' Her heart was beating too hard. As if part of her knew what he was talking about.

Ali stood up and walked around the desk until he was closer to her than at anytime during her employ. He unbuckled his trousers and let them fall to the floor. He was naked underneath. She felt the cabin sway, the lights fade. For a second she thought the cabin had succumbed to some mechanised fault and was pitching out of the sky, but then everything righted itself and she saw that it was only the sight of Ali's cock, of David's cock, that had taken her to the brink of fainting.

'I don't . . .'

'No. Clearly you don't,' Ali said, pulling up his trousers and leaning back against the desk. 'There's a reason why I keep the details of my businesses secret from my employees. But now that you're handing in your notice, I'll share it with you. I own a number of companies, but my main interests are in the synthesis of the best elements of the human and the machine. That and sex. Sex is the most ancient of businesses, flesh and metal hybrids the most modern. I like that. I like the balance. The poetry. All of my sex toys are modelled on me. Even David. Your boyfriend. How does it feel to know you've been fucking your boss?' He smiled. 'You've tested lots of models for me over the years, and I'm extremely grateful.

I doubt we'd be where we are now if it wasn't for your exhaustive research into dildos and dongs.'

'That wasn't my job.' She could barely speak now. Alarm signals were blaring all over her mind.

'It *was* your job,' he said, moving towards her. He placed a hand on her shoulder. 'But now your contract has been terminated.'

She felt his fingers at the back of her neck. She made to speak but her throat could produce only a click. She felt something snap.

Her vision shrank to a small white O. Nothing.

Nuala Deuel is the co-author of *Princess Spider: True experiences of a Dominatrix*, and has had short fiction published in numerous Wicked Words collections.

Gone Shopping A. D. R. Forte

Usually, I make a point of disliking the distracted cell-phone users. The drivers going ten miles under the speed limit, the idiots arguing in the middle of the grocery store aisle with their spouse or kid or pool contractor, blissfully blocking the tomato sauce from those of us who actually want to get our shopping done. Yeah, I could wax poetic about the stupidity of people on cellphones. And then, of course, I turn out to be just as bad.

Although perhaps with much better consequences ...

I blame it all on Aunt Michelle, of course. She called just as I was sitting at the stoplight waiting to turn into the mall parking lot. And that woman can talk. With her the gift of the gab isn't a gift; it's a holy calling. But she makes it interesting, and I was still only halfway through an update on Uncle Joe's latest boating disaster by the time I'd parked.

At least I had an earpiece, but still I walked into the department store and paused just inside the entryway, forgetting why I was there.

'... and *then* the bucket of fish fell over. Slopped all over the ever-lovin' deck and just soaked my pants.'

I grinned silently at Aunty Mish's plight.

Jeans. I was here for jeans because Stan had accidentally washed two of the last three functional pairs I owned in hot water. With a red shirt. Sometimes I wondered if it was too much to ask for a lover with at least some modicum of common sense.

Stan's ability to quote John Donne in bed and expound on the Realists at length was charming. But when faced with the condition of my poor, unwillingly tie-dyed jeans, the Realists paled. Not to mention the fact that I loathe clothes shopping. Offhand, I could have thought of probably ten other things I would rather have spent my hard-won Friday morning off from work doing. But here I was.

'... Anyway. At least he'd had the life jacket on. Honestly, I think your uncle is the dumbest man alive sometimes.'

'I feel your pain, Aunty Mish. Believe me, I feel your pain.'

The door behind me opened and I stepped out of the way to let a woman with two teenagers and a noisy family of various and sundry ages pass. I really needed to just hurry up and get this over with; I could always call Aunty Mish back later. Or not. I was more than capable of multitasking, but either way I couldn't stand in the store entrance all day. And the last, littlest various and sundry was holding the inner door open by sheer will-power, and looking over his shoulder at me with a 'hurry up, lady!' expression.

Stifling a sigh so Aunty Mish wouldn't hear, I followed the other shoppers into the store and over to the rows of garish orange plastic carts. I probably didn't need one, but what the hell. OK, shopping cart: check. Women's clothing: to the left.

I've never bothered with the sections in clothing stores. They mean exactly squat to me. What the heck is a 'Misses' anyway? If I can find a pair of pants that fit, I simply consider it a miracle and thank the great deities of retail. So with my sights set on the distant racks of denim, I wheeled the cart around and started off.

Ah ha! There was a sale tag. Perfect. I stopped and continued to make agreeing murmurs to Aunty Mish as I dug patiently through the tangle of hangers and size tags. I swear, why the clothing industry thinks all women come in the same five or six sizes is beyond me.

'So how's that boyfriend of yours?'

'What?'

I wriggled a hanger free and considered the jeans on it. Beaded spangles on the pocket, but I supposed I could live with a few sparkles. Every piece of female apparel I looked at seemed to have been made for the teenage pop-star crowd, regardless of the section.

'Your boyfriend,' repeated Aunty Mish patiently. 'I never remember his name. But then, you never talk about him.'

'Oh. I . . .' I didn't know what to say. What could I say about Stan?

I racked my brains, trying to think of something suitably positive and affectionate. But standing there, faced with the choice of silver grommets or turquoise beads to adorn my backside, I wasn't feeling particularly generous towards Stanley. Deciding on the grommets as the lesser humiliation, I flung the pair into the cart and confessed to my aunt.

'It's Stan. And honestly, he's a pain in the ass more often than not. But he's decent in bed and he's smart. I guess that's about all there is to it.'

'That's all there is to it?'

I rifled through another row of hangers. 'Yes. What else should there be?'

'What do you think?'

She had me there. What else should there be?

We did all the right things. Books. Art. Candlelight on water. Long conversations. But I knew it was just going through the motions, and if I tried to argue the case to Aunty Mish she would see through it in a heartbeat.

I sighed, loud and audible this time. 'OK, OK, you win, but no lectures, darling. I'm happy enough.'

There was a pause while she thought it over. 'OK. No lecture. But . . . you should be more than happy, Frannie. You should be ecstatic. Life's too short. Got it?'

Yeah, tell me something I didn't already know. 'Got it, Aunty M. Now talk about something else, please.'

She obliged, rambling off about my brother's baby's

newest two teeth while I turned to search for a dressing room. And found it blocked for repairs. My luck I would come shopping in the middle of renovations.

'... but I can't figure out how to open this picture attachment.'

It was a plea for help. Great.

Luckily Aunty Mish isn't a total computer illiterate, but I still didn't want to do tech support in the middle of the lingerie section. I started walking while I tried to talk her through the download of Charles Jr's pictures, still looking for a dressing room. And found it, tucked behind rows of khakis. At least I think they were khakis, because Aunty Mish had lost herself in the complexities of .abm files versus JPEGs and I was having a hell of a time trying to extricate her.

But once I felt sure she wasn't going to delete half her registry trying to save five baby pictures, I took my spangly selections from the cart and headed into the dressing room. I had no trouble finding a vacant stall without too many failed try-ons piled on the floor; I was the only one in the place.

I bolted the door and kicked off my sneakers. Then I stripped off my sweatpants, hung them over the stall partition as I bid goodbye to Aunty Mish, promised to call her later and turned off the earpiece. I reached for the first pair of jeans. And that's when the stall door next to me banged shut and I looked down to see a pair of decidedly male feet in sandals next door.

My first thought was to yell in a loud and unfriendly voice that he was in the wrong room. Until my gaze fell on the discarded clothes lying in my own stall. Dockers khakis, 32W, 34L. Ralph Lauren polo shirts. John Ashford sweater, XL.

Crap.

He had to have overheard me talking to Aunty Mish and if I could see his feet, he damn well could see mine, French manicured toes and all. His own feet were worth a second look. Smooth, well-kept nails, nicely defined ankles and just hairy enough to be sexy male without being caveman. I found myself imagining what the rest of those legs looked like. Amazing what not being on the phone can do for one's powers of observation.

I knew I should just play this off and act casual. Or put my pants on and get the hell out. But I did neither, simply stood there with my face burning, ogling the feet of a complete stranger as he undressed. Which he did without the least compunction. His shorts pooled around his ankles before he whisked them up, and then I jumped as they flopped halfway over the top of the partition.

'Sorry. Didn't mean to startle you. You can go ahead you know. I don't mind really.'

I could hear the laughter in his voice. And he was pulling on jeans, one leg at a time. Rustle. Zipper. I took a deep, deep breath and tried not to squeak when I spoke.

'Uh, thanks. I guess I should be the one apologising.'

A laugh. A deep, masculine laugh. 'Not at all. Mistakes happen.'

I fumbled with the clasps on the hanger and managed to get the jeans off after three tries. My fingers had apparently turned into blocks of wood at some point, or at least that's what they felt like. I got both legs in and pulled the pants up. Only at that point did I realise he now knew for a fact I'd been in my underwear. And would be again when I took these off. Never in my life have I been more tempted to shoplift. Just walk out of there and worry about paying for the jeans at the counter. Or not. Because he might walk out and see me. This would have been hysterical really . . . had it been anyone but me.

'So do they fit?'

'I . . . er . . . what?'

'Do they fit? My sisters spend hours obsessing about finding pants that fit right. I think I've clocked them at three hours just on buying jeans before. But then . . .'

Zipper. One leg off, then another.

Boxers or briefs? I wondered.

'. . . they're fifteen and seventeen. So it figures.'

'Yeah, well, trust me, it gets harder with age,' I replied drily. I looked at my reflection. Surprisingly enough, these fitted, and the silver grommets didn't look half bad. I hadn't noticed it before, but a tiny silver horseshoe dangled from the belt loop over one hip. I jingled it and tried to decide if I had the metaphorical balls to take them off with him still there.

He was trying another pair on now, and in no great hurry apparently.

'But once you find a nicely fitting pair, it's worth it. From my perspective anyway.' He laughed again, teasing, and I found myself smiling in response. Never mind that he couldn't see.

'Oh really?' I jingled my horseshoe again, not really believing that I was striking up a flirtation in this situation. Yeah, I'd lost my mind for sure.

'Absolutely. I'll admit it; I'm a guy. I have the utmost appreciation for the loveliness of the female form. In denim, in khaki, in silk. You name it.'

Now I laughed out loud. 'Lovely, huh? Well, I certainly hope I can live up to that description.'

He paused. 'I'd offer to come around and give you an opinion, but I wouldn't want you to think I'm a total asshole.'

I leaned on the mirror and crossed one ankle over the other. Might as well be comfortable if I was going to have a full-blown conversation, right? 'I haven't gotten that impression so far. But I don't think I have the nerve to ask you for an opinion either.'

Another pause. I could tell he was still facing the mirror. I imagined him standing there, hands on hips, wondering what to say next.

'Can I offer one anyway? And you not throw something at me?'

'Offer away.' Why was my heart beating so fast? I waited.

'Well, I don't have a foot fetish or anything, but if your toes match the rest of you, I think lovely more than describes it.'

I covered my mouth with my hand and stared at the ceiling, laughing silently in disbelief. I felt like I'd been drinking champagne. Suddenly I didn't care about proper any more. 'I think that's the sexiest thing anyone's ever said to me.'

When he laughed, I heard the edge of nervous relief and I almost walked out of the stall then and there and knocked on his door. He'd been worried about *my* reaction. Simply insane! 'Well, you're most welcome.'

Zipper. Rustle. He was taking the second pair off. And then I decided, what the hell. What had Aunt Mish just said? Life's too short. Might as well make it interesting.

I waited until he had pulled them completely off before I asked, 'So, boxers or briefs?'

Silence. And then he laughed. 'Gentlemen don't tell.'

'There. Now I'm disappointed.'

I pushed away from the mirror and started to take the jeans off. My own underwear was starting to get decidedly damp. God, I couldn't believe I was getting worked up flirting with an unseen guy in a bloody dressing room. I didn't even have the excuse of being desperate. I had Stan. And hard on the heels of that thought was the realisation that I didn't want to think about Stan. Not right now.

'Oh, don't be disappointed. Give me a chance to critique the fit of those jeans over dinner and maybe I'll tell.'

Oh, he was smooth.

'Promise?' I asked.

'I said "maybe".'

'You don't make it easy do you?'

He started laughing. 'At the risk of sounding lame, no. I try to make it as hard as possible.'

I sat down on the narrow shelf under the mirror, and laughed until the tears ran down my face and my stomach hurt. Finally, when our laughter had subsided to chuckles, I looked down and saw that he had come to stand in the corner closest to where I sat.

'OK,' I said between gasps for breath. 'Dinner.'

'Great! Where would you like to meet?'

We haggled over a few places and finally agreed on a sushi restaurant across from the mall.

'At six?'

'Six is perfect.' I shook out the jeans I'd been holding, and waved them under the partition so he could see the horseshoe. 'I'll be wearing these and a pink sweater.'

I knew he was taking in every detail. I could almost see him nodding. 'Duly noted. I'll be waiting next to the aquarium and wearing sandals.' A pause and a little laugh. 'Wow! The only woman in the world who knows instantly what she's wearing to a date.'

I stood up and turned to the partition, my toes facing his. 'I don't like to waste time making up my mind.'

'I can tell.' It was a compliment. 'You're definitely unique.'

'No, actually I'm Francesca, a.k.a. Frannie, a.k.a. various other less flattering things.'

A laugh. 'I'll stick with Francesca. I'm Cal.'

'Nice to, umm, meet you, Cal. Although I'm not sure meet is the word.'

'Me neither, but it works as well as anything.' He sighed. 'Right. Now I have to go figure out what *I'm* wearing tonight.'

I giggled. He was teasing again. Stan never teased.

He stepped away and I saw him pulling on his shorts, buckling his sandals. His arms and hands were like his feet. Dark hair. Definition even though there was no real muscle. Long fingers. No-nonsense hands.

Damn. If just those parts of him had this effect on my panties, what would seeing the rest of him do?

I pulled my sweats down from the partition as he opened the stall door and stepped out. He paused for just a moment outside my stall and through the wooden slats I could just make out a tall lean body. A runner's build. Holy Hot Mystery Men Batman.

'See you at six,' he said.

'I'll be there. Jeans and all and fully dressed, I promise.'

'Bye, Francesca.'

And with a laugh, he was gone. I stood there, clutching my sweats and grinning and wondering just what the hell I'd gotten myself into.

'I have a date.' I stuck my head around the downstairs bathroom door and peered into the living room. He was reading with the TV on. 'With a guy I met in the dressing room.'

'Uh-huh.'

I waited but nothing more was forthcoming. With a sigh, I double-checked my get-up for the last time, turned off the bathroom light and walked into the living room.

'You don't believe me.'

Stan looked up from the book for all of the five seconds it took to roll his eyes at me.

I shrugged. 'Don't say I didn't tell you.'

He waved at me, never looking up. 'Have a good time. You look pretty.'

And that was all.

I'd been honest, I told my conscience. Yes, the truth was so outlandish it seemed nonsense. But something in my voice, in my face, in my posture would have given it away. If he had bothered to look.

But he hadn't and, thinking about it, I don't know that Stan had ever bothered to look that closely. I don't think he ever figured it necessary. And that was why I left the house and headed once again for the mall complex without a trace of regret.

As promised, he was waiting. Leaning against the wall beside the aquarium and watching a self-important goldfish make its way through the pillars of the plastic sunken castle. I stopped and I watched him, drinking in that scene and committing it to memory forever. Watching him just as the hostess was watching. And the two women to my right. And the teenage girl holding her boyfriend's hand and trying to appear not interested.

But when he looked up, his gaze found only me. I knew then what the favourites of the Bourbon kings must have felt like, being singled out by the one look that told me I was desired and chosen above all others. And I felt the envy of every other woman in that restaurant lobby as I walked, like one bewitched, to his side and smiled up at him.

He smiled back, and those eyes. Those eyes the colour of bottle-green glass polished smooth by the sea. I was bewitched, helpless to do anything but gaze at him as he bent down to brush his lips ever so modestly against my cheek and rest his hands, only for a burning, delicious moment, against my hips.

'I'm so glad you decided to come.'

'You thought I wouldn't?'

He nodded, full lips curving in a self-conscious smile. 'I thought you might decide it was just too crazy after all.'

'Crazy has never been a deterrent for me I'm afraid.'

I couldn't help it, I had to touch him. I reached up and brushed my fingers along the stubble of his jaw. One of those five-o'clock-shadow boys, no matter how often he shaved. I wanted to feel those rough cheeks brushing the insides of my thighs. I wanted those lips moving in slow kisses all over my body. I wanted that dark spiky hair dripping sweat as he lay over me, his hands braced above my head so he wouldn't brain me against the wall with every rough, hungry thrust.

So this was lust. And this was passion. And crazy *had* never stopped me before. He blushed like a boy, something I'd never expected from my confident, dressing-room suitor. But his voice was as powerful and beguiling as ever.

'Don't look at me that way. I'm being tempted to suggest we just skip dinner totally.'

'Fine with me. I want an answer to my question, remember?'

He threw his head back and laughed, and slid an arm around my waist. 'Just for that, we'll have dinner and go to a movie *and* go for a walk. And *then . . .*' He pressed one finger to the tip of my nose. 'I'll take you home and kiss you goodnight right there. And that's all you'll get, missy.'

I stuck my tongue out at him and we walked to the hostess's podium giggling like schoolgirls, his arm still curled comfortably around my waist. Holy Mother of heaven. If I didn't know better, I'd have thought I was falling in love.

I knocked the phone off the dresser in my hurry to answer it, dived after it and then sat on the floor to talk. Grinning as I answered.

'Meet me?'

Damn, I loved the sound of his voice. 'Where?' I asked.

'I don't know. For coffee? I don't care; I just want to see you. And I picked last time.'

I tried to remember if he *had* picked last time, but I'd lost track. Was this the fifth date or the sixth? I was still racking my brains when he gave an impatient sigh fifteen seconds later.

'You know what? Screw that. Meet me at the mall and come back to my place and I'll make you breakfast.'

'Breakfast? It's three o'clock.'

'Right. You come over this afternoon; I'll make you breakfast in the morning.'

I was speechless. Here it was. I'd longed for it, thought about it constantly, fantasised about it and dreamed of him asking me. And now I had no idea what to say. 'And what do I tell Stan?' I wondered aloud.

'Tell him you're coming over to fuck me silly. It's not like he'll listen anyway.'

I sighed. Cal was probably right. After the first night, I'd simply told Stan I was going out, going shopping. Never mind that every time I came home empty-handed. He barely looked up.

I think Stan knew; I think he cared even less.

'Meet you in an hour,' I said.

We met at the ice-cream counter and then walked from store to store for an hour, sharing a cone. Tangling our tongues with each lick. Hands in each other's back pockets like a couple of starry-eyed youngsters dropped off at the mall to buy hassled parents a few peaceful hours. We didn't care. Halfway through life isn't too late to fall.

When we finally got sick of the ice cream and dumped it in a convenient trash can, we found ourselves before the mall entrance of The Store. Our store. Other people had special songs, special restaurants and cities. We had the men's dressing room at a department store. I wouldn't have traded it for the most romantic boulevard in Paris.

'Want to visit old haunts?' he asked with a mischievous smile.

'I'm game if you are.'

And so we wandered in without apparent hurry. Through rows of polyester cotton, denim and lace, and soft wool blends, until at last we found ourselves in the dressing room once again. Most of the stalls were partitioned off with yellow tape and construction notices, and a makeshift wall obscured the front entrance, forcing us to go around it. We did, and found ourselves alone except for a crowd of dust flakes whirling in the air, which smelled of plaster and raw wood.

Cal turned and slid his hands under my sweater. Hands warm and slightly damp on my bare waist, he pulled me close. His mouth was mint-chocolate-chip sweet from the ice cream; his tongue hot and impatient. He licked the corners of my mouth and purred in appreciation.

'You taste good.'

I giggled nervously. Wasn't this what I'd been hoping for?

But it's a really, really bad idea chimed the voice of reason. Bad, stupid, utterly humiliating, criminal-record kind of bad.

'We can't do this here.'

'Can't we?' His hands slid further up my torso; his fingertips pressed against the underwire of my bra. 'Tell me, Frannie, if you'd seen me before the dressing room, wouldn't you have fucked me that day?'

'No,' I whispered. But his fingers were under the wire and the satin and I wasn't so sure any more.

Suddenly he pulled away and looked over my head. He frowned a moment and then smiled. 'Come on.'

'What? Wh...?' But he was already heading for the first aisle of stalls and down to the very last one on the row.

'Here.'

He pushed open the door and pulled me in, then bolted it behind. The room was big enough for both of us but he blocked me from taking so much as a single step away from the closed door. Hands on the wall to either side of the slats, he kissed me again, hips rubbing mine. And I felt the warm heavy bulge pressing through his jeans into my stomach. His need; like mine. Hot. Urgent.

'I want you to undress for me. In front of the mirror.' His teeth tugged at my lower lip. 'Tease me.'

Tease. That I could do. I hooked my hands into the

waist of his pants, pulling him closer, grinding that lovely hardness into me.

'Then will I get an answer to my question?' I asked, laughing.

He frowned for a minute, and then smiled as he remembered, but he was short of breath already and growing more so. 'You'll get anything you want.'

'Fair enough.'

I squeezed past and spun around, looking at him from the other side of the room. Christ on a bike, the man was hot. He leant half on the door, half on the frame and lifted a finger, twirled it like he was stirring a drink.

'Face the mirror.'

I made a face, but obeyed. And then hesitated. This was so not the thing to do, and two months ago would have been all but unthinkable. But now I had Cal, standing behind me with his gorgeous, naughty smile and his hard-on, and so now ... now I didn't care.

I reached for the zipper of my sweatshirt and tugged it down half an inch. Black satin bra and the shadow of cleavage. I looked up and found his gaze in the mirror; he smiled approval. Another half-inch; another pause. And then I dragged it all the way down until the zipper pulled apart entirely and I could shake the sweatshirt off. I saw him move, saw his hand stray to his groin. Still smiling.

One bra strap; another. Then the hooks, and the bra joined the sweater. I reached for the buttons on my pants and only then remembered I was wearing The Jeans, silver horseshoe and all. He, of course, had noticed from the start. He always noticed. Well, I'd leave them on. For now.

Instead I turned my attention to my naked breasts, the nipples already tight with excitement. I pinched them hard and felt the pleasure swell between my legs. Harder. I bit my lip and looked up at Cal. The lazy casual smile was gone. I said his name once, not loud, barely more than a whisper.

But he came to me.

He crossed the dressing room in a single long-legged stride to stand behind me and curve his hands over my upper arms. His lips touched my neck, soft, while the rough promise of beard on his chin and cheeks grazed my bare skin. It sent chills through me – that kiss, raising the hair on my neck and my arms, making the muscles of my stomach clench. His hands took mine away from my chest, brought them behind me.

'Touch me.' It was a low growl and still a plea. But he didn't even have to ask. I wanted to touch him, kiss him, do everything I could think of with my mouth and my hands and my body to him.

Easier said than done. I fumbled with buttons, trying to think past his cashmere-sandpaper kisses on my neck and his pinching, kneading, stroking hands on my naked tits. For a frustrated moment I wondered how women in historical romance novels ever managed their forbidden jollies dealing with cravats and waistcoats when I couldn't even get a fucking pair of jeans off a man. But at last my efforts were rewarded.

And it figures, it was boxer briefs after all. Smiling, I wriggled my fingers through denim and one hundred per cent cotton and found his cock. Though heaven knows it wasn't hard to find at all. I could just barely get my thumb and middle finger wrapped around it. Sweet Jesus, I'd never even known they came in this size. I pulled it out and began to stroke him up and down, rubbing the tip against the skin of my back, and he moaned. His hands closed hard on my breast and my stomach and he went still.

'God, Frannie.'

As I stroked down, I let my touch keep going, let my fingers run light and tickling over his balls still tucked safely into his briefs, and I won a short involuntary thrust against my back.

'Like that?' I asked.

Only a sigh for an answer. His eyes were closed.

I ran one hand back up his cock, reaching around to squeeze his ass closer with the other. At the tip I could get my fingers closed around him, and I jacked him off until I felt a tiny spurt of pre-come, wet and warm on my back. And answering wet delicious warmth in my own jeans.

His hands were sliding down my front now, opening my jeans, tugging them down. I let go of him to help, pushing the material down to my knees, but when he reached for my panties I stopped him. I found his reflected gaze, his eyebrows lifted in a silent question.

'No need for that.'

I bent forwards so that my ass and my pussy were raised to his view, and braced one palm on the mirror. I'd bought these panties just for him. For today. I hadn't lied *every* time I told Stan I was going shopping; every now and then I'd come home with a few special purchases.

Now I pulled the folds of lace apart over the seamless crotch and teased my bare slit with one finger, half-breaking my neck in the process just to see his reaction in the mirror. His expression was all I'd hoped for. And then we heard the rustle of fabric, footsteps, movement. We stopped breathing. A stall door banged somewhere towards the front of the dressing room.

Grinning, I began rubbing my finger against my clit harder, rubbing it in circles and figures of eight as I got wetter and wetter, and Cal's face blushed redder and redder. He shook his head at me, mouthing at me to stop. But I ignored him. Hadn't he asked to be teased?

From the distant stall, came the sound of clothing being removed. Poor guy had no idea what he was missing just a few walls away. I slid a finger into my pussy, then another. I bent my head and arched my back down. I'd lose the pleasure of seeing Cal's tormented desire, but I knew the effect I was having. I wriggled my fingers deeper, then began sliding my hips back and forth, moving my hand in counter thrust; shivering as the air of the dressing room touched my flushed, perspiring skin.

And then I almost jumped. Hot hard flesh pressed against my ass; a strong male hand gripped it. He slid his cock across my soaked lace panties, pushing it into the yielding softness beneath. My fingers got out of the way. And then ... then I thought I must scream or burst as the head of his cock squeezed into my super-aroused pussy. And that was just the tip. Oh God.

I flung my other hand out for support against the wall beside the mirror and winced at the slap it made. But I couldn't judge if the noise was loud enough to be heard. The blood was rushing to my head and Cal was thrusting into me with slow strokes, going deeper every time. And I couldn't think at all. I bit my lip and ground myself against him, loving the bursts of pleasure every time I pressed an extra-sensitive spot. Not caring about anything but Cal inside of me.

A stall door banged far, far away. It meant nothing to me, lost in pleasureland, until Cal's hands on my waist pulled me upwards. He slid out and I squeaked in disappointment, but his fingers covered my lips as he spun me around. He knelt and dragged my boots off, my jeans. And then as he rose, he lifted my thighs.

I tried to help, bracing my feet on the shelf under the mirror, and almost fell, clumsy with desire and distraction. But he laughed softly and held me, worked himself back into me. And then, with the cold mirror on my back and my arms around his neck. With him kissing me hard to stifle my moans of pleasure because his magnificent cock was sending my pussy and my clit wild with satisfaction. And because all the rest of him was sending everything else in me wild with happiness.

There, in that dressing room as I came and came and came all over his cock. As I heard him grunt and sigh, and felt come running hot down my legs. Then I knew what it was like to really and truly make love.

'You still owe me breakfast,' I said, once we'd safely made it out unnoticed and were casually strolling among rows of socks as if nothing at all unusual had happened in the last hour. As if we hadn't just committed a Class-A misdemeanor.

'Are you coming home with me?' he asked, arm about my waist, fingers tucked intimately under the hem of my sweatshirt. I sniffed him. Sweet musky smell of cologne and sex and faint laundry detergent on his clothes. I cuddled closer. Why was I even still haggling over the decision?

He leant down and whispered in my ear. 'Hurry up and decide. My underwear's all soggy.' He paused, then added in an aggrieved tone, 'Which is *your* fault by the way.'

I laughed. 'Quit being such a fusspot.' I turned down an aisle and grabbed a packet of cotton boxer-briefs from the shelf. Large. 'Here.'

He looked down and smiled. 'I see you were paying attention after all.'

He looked up and I couldn't find anything to say. Not with those eyes looking at me like that.

Life's too short.

'On second thought, put them back,' I said. 'You won't need any once I get you home.'

He grinned. The package fell to the floor and I was being kissed. Really kissed. And I was ecstatic.

Aunty Mish would be glad. And Stan? Well, he'd complain for appearance's sake at first. And, of course, he'd complain to everyone else about me too, but then it would be over and he'd go back to his books and his pontificating. And God help his next girlfriend and her laundry.

* * *

On the way to the parking lot I dug that troublemaking cellphone out of my pocket with the hand not holding Cal's and called Aunty Mish to tell her I'd gone shopping and found a perfect fit.

A. D. R. Forte has had several short stories published in themed Wicked Words anthologies.

Seams and Ladders Fiona Locke

When he doesn't get off at Tottenham Court Road I know he is following me. And when he meets my eyes with that unnerving frankness, I realise he wants me to know.

Several seats become available as the train disgorges its passengers, but he remains standing. Right in front of me. He's tall, with silver-flecked hair and dark compelling eyes. Elegantly dressed in a sombre, old-fashioned suit. And about twice my age. Against my will my eyes flick upwards and I avert them quickly when I see he's still looking at me.

He had been there on the platform almost every day, watching me. Not ogling. No, his scrutiny was more like a military inspection than a prurient leer. I had the sense that I was on parade and I felt myself standing just a little straighter, a little taller.

He always got off with me a few stops later, at Tottenham Court Road. Then we would go our separate ways once we were above ground. And while his brooding gaze excited me, it was always a relief to escape its intensity.

But today I remained in my seat as we reached our station. And he didn't get off either.

The train rockets through the subterranean labyrinth, carrying me away from the bookshop where I work. My boss will not be pleased.

Its brakes shrieking, the train shudders to a halt at Oxford Circus and this time he does make a move. But it's only to sit down – directly opposite me. The carriage is nearly empty. I glance at the doors and debate whether I should get off and double back. I wonder if my companion will do the same. But something makes me stay.

The doors close like a promise withdrawn and I feel exposed by his bold stare. My decision to stay suddenly seems reckless – an offer I'm not sure I'm prepared to make. I shift in my seat, fidgeting. My nylons whisper nervously as I cross my legs and I see him smile to himself, as though they've imparted a secret to him.

I tug feebly at the hem of my too-short skirt, flushed with warmth at the sense of exposure. He makes no secret of staring at my legs. Normally I welcome the attention. Even at work. *Especially* at work. After all, it's the reason I dress the way I do: a cross between air hostess and librarian. I wear my long blonde hair pulled back, a few wisps framing my face appealingly. Just a whiff of suppressed sexuality.

I've always been an incorrigible flirt and I know how to display myself to be admired. This man is no different from any other I taunt and tease. I could see he liked my legs, so my hemlines got higher. So did my heels.

But that was when *I* was in control. Now he's raised the stakes. Now *he* is the hunter.

Bond Street. When I see he still has no intention of getting up I make as if to rise myself. He tilts his head with an expression of amused curiosity, his sensual mouth curling in a knowing smile. I feel toyed with. I don't like having the tables turned. It's like forgetting all the steps to a dance I choreographed myself.

I stand up hurriedly, stumbling in my heels, and reach the doors a second too late. They hiss shut in front of me, trapping me. Chagrined, I turn my back on him. Unease coils around me as I sense his eyes, exploring me like a stranger's hand. I pretend to rummage in my bag for something, a pathetically transparent ruse.

'You've got a ladder in your stocking.'

His presumption shocks me and I stand immobile, not knowing how to respond.

'How very careless,' he tuts.

I round on him. 'It's your fault. If you hadn't . . .'

Hadn't what? Looked at what I was flaunting? I turn away again in a huff.

The plastic seat creaks as he stands up. I've provoked him. The hairs on the back of my neck rise, tingling. His trousers brush my calf and I stand like a statue, my stillness inviting more. I can hardly breathe. When I feel his hand in the small of my back I gasp, but don't move.

'You should be more careful,' he continues, his posh accent low and silky in my ear. I close my eyes, shivering at the feel of his warm breath on my neck. The hand slides lower, until it rests on my bottom. My cheeks clench involuntarily and the hand creeps another inch lower.

I grip the hanging strap above me tightly to steady myself against the rocking motion of the train as the hand slides down the back of my left thigh.

'It's just here,' he says, pressing his finger gently against the little hollow behind my knee. 'I expect you snagged it getting up in such a rush.'

The reproachful tone weakens me. I don't really care about the stockings. They're only an inexpensive Lycra blend, after all – some cheap multipack buy. I have others. But the rebuke insists I acknowledge the damage. Shifting my weight to my right leg, I turn the left one in, twisting it to look down at the desecrated black material. Anticipating a huge tear, I'm surprised when I see it's only a tiny run.

'Is that all?' I laugh. 'It's nothing hairspray or nail varnish can't patch.'

His face looks like a priest's in response to blasphemy. A perfectionist, then. A connoisseur who knows exactly what he likes and expects it to be immaculately presented. My stomach flutters.

I don't even notice when the train stops again. The doors whoosh open and a few people push past us into the carriage. I look at the platform, debating. Neither of us moves. The doors close on Marble Arch and the train lurches into motion again, heading steadily westwards.

'I'll send you a new pair,' he says coolly. 'If you'll wear them to dinner with me.'

He speaks with the effortless confidence of one accustomed to getting what he wants. Determined not to feel humbled, I search my mind for some cheeky rejoinder. Nothing comes. My hesitation only secures his advantage.

He leans in to whisper, 'And when I say wear them, I mean wear them *properly*.'

He says it with a gravity that implies more than just keeping the seams straight, but I don't have the breath to question it. I press my legs together at the tacit threat. The thought of being subjected to his exacting scrutiny fills me with both dread and desire.

'OK,' I say at last, my voice a meek little squeak.

I'm expecting something black, but he surprises me. The stockings are flesh-toned, a colour I've never owned. What's the point of leg-coloured stockings when you can just go bare?

The stockings shimmer as I shake them out of the packaging and admire them. I have never seen anything so sheer in my life. They're pure nylon and utterly weightless – like cobweb. I finger the material with fascination, drawing it across the back of my arm.

A seam runs down the back of each stocking to meet the pointed tip of the French heel. The maker's lavish white signature decorates the top welt, which is doubled over and sewn in the back with a small finishing hole – something I've only ever seen in old pictures.

At first I'm certain that the stockings are too big. However, when I hook my thumbs into the welt and begin gathering the material into a roll I realise that they don't stretch at all; they're exactly the length of my legs. He has a sharp eye.

I point my right foot and slide it into the stocking, gently unrolling it and drawing it up my leg. The silky sensation is an unexpected delight. So these are 'proper' nylons. I suddenly understand what all the fuss is about.

I clip the garters into place, twisting round in the mirror to straighten the seam. A perfect fit. My leg is encased in glass. It shines and gleams in the light. The reinforced heel and toe resemble a ballet slipper and I point my toes, showing off my high-arched insteps in the mirror.

Eager to see the whole effect, I gather up the other stocking and dip my toes into it. But as I tug the nylon up and over my knee it catches on a ragged fingernail. I gasp in dismay and disentangle the filaments that have pulled loose.

I don't want to look, but I have to. And sure enough, where the nylon has snagged is a puckered little line like a cat scratch. Right across the top of the thigh. I smooth the threads down, but the imperfection stands out like a spill of ink on a wedding dress.

Bugger.

I close my eyes in a moment of childish desperation, praying that when I open them the line will be gone. It doesn't work.

Maybe it's not as bad as I fear. I look up at my reflection, pulling the stocking tight and examining it. No, it's every bit as bad as I fear. And while such a rip wouldn't bother *me*, there is no way it will pass muster with *him*.

Dejectedly I look at the clock. I still have an hour. There might be time to sort it out.

I peel myself out of the stockings and dress for dinner. A short slinky little black velvet number with a pearl choker. Black strappy Roman sandals with stiletto heels. A bit goth, a bit glam. But it showcases my legs, which is what he wants to see. In proper nylons.

Ruined proper nylons in hand, I deliver myself into the

mercy of the nearest upmarket lingerie shop. I feel like a desperate parent furtively trying to replace a child's dead pet, but it has to be done.

With a sympathetic wince, the matronly woman behind the counter tells me sadly that they don't stock vintage nylons.

'Vintage?' I repeat, feeling ill.

'Oh yes, these are the real thing,' she says, holding them admiringly in her manicured hands. 'Authentic. Nineteen-forties. Marlene Dietrich might have worn these. They're lovely, aren't they?'

I feel as though I've eaten a raw egg. I put my head down on the counter.

'We do have reproductions,' she assures me. 'I'm not sure we can find you an exact match, but we might have something that looks close enough.'

I raise my head, my eyes wide with hope.

She takes my hand in both of hers and pats it as though consoling a grieving friend. 'Come on, love, let's have a look.'

It's nearly an hour later that I leave the shop wearing the nearest thing she could find. I wouldn't know the difference. I can only hope he won't either.

His approving smile as I walk towards the table calms my jangling nerves.

'You look lovely,' he says.

I release the breath I've been holding and sink into the chair. 'Thank you.'

He offers me a glass of wine and looks down at my lap. I cross my legs obligingly and the nylon gives a soft rustle. I sit with my legs out to the side to give him a better view.

'How do they feel?' he asks.

'Silky,' I say at once, remembering the first pair. These ones aren't nearly as fine. 'They're barely there.'

He smiles.

Encouraged, I cross them again to tease him, pointing my toe and raising my leg, showing off like a sex kitten. He edges his chair closer to me and I place one foot on his knee. His hand slides over my instep and up the length of my sleek glossy leg. The transparent barrier enhances the caress and my sex grows warmer in response. His eyes darken as he traces a finger along my calf and I wonder nervously if the seams are straight. Blushing, I withdraw my leg.

'They're very nice,' he says at last.

Relieved, I take a sip of wine.

'But how did the ones *I* sent you feel?'

The wine becomes a solid lump and I force it down with a loud swallow. My cheeks burn as I drag my gaze back up to meet his. What can I possibly say?

Slowly he rises from the table, just as the waitress arrives to take our order. He takes my hand and addresses the surprised girl. 'I'm terribly sorry, but I'm afraid it's just the wine. Something's come up and we'll have to leave.'

I'm speechless as she takes his money and abandons us. Finally I find my voice. 'You're not serious!'

But the cool gleam in his eyes assures me that he is. 'I did say you were to wear them properly,' he reminds me. 'And you're not wearing them at all.'

His frown makes me tremble with more than fear. I know there will be a reckoning before the night is over.

'Look, I...' My feeble protest peters out under his piercing stare. I bite my lip, blushing. He can see exactly what his censorious tone is doing to me.

'Juliet.'

I squirm at the way he makes my name sound like a reprimand.

'What?'

'Tell me why you aren't wearing what I sent you.'

I blush. 'I snagged them.'

He gathers my hands and looks pointedly at my chewed fingernails. 'I'm not surprised.'

Abashed, I pull them away, shoving them out of sight behind my back.

'Where *are* the ones I sent you?'

'In my bag.' I hadn't dared to throw them away, even though they were ruined.

At his expectant look I fumble the clasp open and hand over the wispy nylon, cringing as though relinquishing contraband to a customs officer.

He shakes his head over them before tucking them into his pocket. 'Right. You have a choice. You can come with me and rectify the situation. Or you can go home.'

He makes me feel like a naughty child. I can be sent to bed without supper or I can stay up and play grown-up games. My knees are weak.

As my stomach gives a plaintive grumble I whisper, 'OK. I'll go with you.'

The shop is a shrine to vintage glamour. Mannequins with hourglass figures model the fashions of bygone eras while a warbling voice sings an old wartime tune on a scratchy turntable. Pictures of screen goddesses adorn the walls: Rita Hayworth, Louise Brooks, Audrey Hepburn.

'Sorry, we're just closing!' comes a perky American voice from the back of the shop.

A door opens and a young Bettie Page lookalike scampers out, high heels clicking on the floor. A leopard-print party frock flares out below her knees and her heels are so high I marvel that she can walk at all. She stops short, grinning flirtatiously at my companion. 'Mr Allardyce!' she exclaims. 'Such a pleasure to see you again so soon!'

I realise that I have never even asked his name, though I'd given him mine, along with my address. He's made me reckless.

'Elaine,' he says, smiling. 'Look what I've brought you to play with.'

As I blink in confusion, he gestures ostentatiously, presenting me like an offering.

Elaine looks me up and down. 'Oh yes,' she says, nodding her head with the enthusiasm of an artist asked to perform. 'This the one you bought the stockings for?'

I chew my lip.

'Yes,' he says heavily. 'Only I think I'd like to see the full effect.'

'Always my pleasure, Mr Allardyce.' She gives me a last appraising look while I try to puzzle out the 'always'. 'What a delightful surprise.'

I'm just a piece in a museum collection. A piece in need of restoration. Nervously I turn to him, a worried question in my eyes.

'Don't worry,' he says in a voice that does nothing to reassure me. 'When Elaine is finished with you you'll hardly recognise yourself.'

She grins and releases my hair from its clasp. 'The gentleman knows what he likes,' she says, addressing the comment to him in a tone that tells me it's an inside joke. She hasn't spoken to me once.

My eyes widen. I came here thinking this was about replacing a pair of stockings. But he has far more in mind. At the same time the fear of the unknown is exhilarating. And the way they're discussing me ... It objectifies me. It pushes the same buttons as being stalked on the Underground. I can feel my knickers growing damp as I surrender. My silence is consent.

Elaine takes my hand and leads me towards the back of the shop. I cast a glance over my shoulder in time to see Mr Allardyce lock the door and turn the CLOSED sign around.

He's right. Two hours later I hardly recognise myself. My hair cascades over my shoulders in glorious 1940s waves. Deep-red lips and smouldering bedroom eyes transform my face into a vision from the silver screen. The impeccable cut of the charcoal-grey suit gives me an enviable wasp waist. And the tight pencil skirt makes my long legs seem even longer.

'Perfection,' he declares, admiring Elaine's handiwork. 'Absolute perfection.'

She beams proudly. 'Thank you, Mr Allardyce.'

He turns to me at last. 'Now we can go to dinner.'

Captivated by the glamorous stranger in the mirror, I can't resist pulling 'come hither' faces while he and Elaine agree on a price behind me. The figure makes me gulp, but I don't let it show. The gentleman knows what he likes.

'Oh, I almost forgot,' he says. 'She'll need a new pair of stockings too.'

I feel like Eliza Doolittle at the embassy ball. Will my accent be his next project?

I draw stares back at the restaurant, but I enjoy the attention. I'm also grateful he's finally decided to let me eat. I'm starving.

He has me sit with my legs on display. Sheathed in vintage nylons. Seams straight. No ladders.

Afterwards the black cab takes us to a cobbled mews near the V&A. As he leads me into his immaculate terraced house it suddenly occurs to me to wonder what he's doing on the westbound Central line every morning.

He offers me wine and directs me to an elaborately carved Victorian sofa in front of the fireplace. My eyes scan the room, taking in its elegant but tasteful furnishings. He sits to my left, positioning me to afford himself the best leg show, indulging his predilection as well as my vanity. His eyes roam from my toes to my hair, drinking in every detail.

'You're the quintessential vamp,' he says. 'You were born in the wrong decade.'

It's a peculiar compliment, but undeniably true. I stretch my legs out across his lap and he strokes them. He pinches the nylon between his thumb and forefinger, pulling it out away from my skin and letting it fall back. I'm surprised at the way the stockings crease at my knees and ankles, where the nylon isn't taut.

Lifting my right ankle, he unlaces the shoe and slips it off, cradling my warm satiny foot in his hands before releasing it.

'You do have lovely feet.'

No one's ever told me that before. I'm flattered. And now I want to play.

Intent on gaining the upper hand, I press the ball of my foot into his crotch. He begins to stiffen immediately. I had hoped to outmanoeuvre him by making the first move, but he isn't taken aback by my forwardness. Redoubling my efforts, I grind my foot against him, caressing him through his trousers.

When I offer him the other foot he strips it of its shoe as well. The sandal falls to the floor with a soft thud. I place both feet on the growing bulge in his trousers and he sighs contentedly as I curl my toes against his hardness. I tease him, rubbing my legs against one another and enjoying the sibilant hiss of nylon. My sex responds to his arousal as well, moistening in anticipation.

But the stimulation doesn't ruffle his composure. With impossible nonchalance he says, 'I've been watching you, you know.'

Something in his smile belies the innocence of the comment. My legs cease their manipulations as the penny drops. He isn't referring to the Tube journeys; he's been to the bookshop where I work. He's seen the smut I sell, flashing the customers a coy grin and a glimpse of cleavage. He knows what a prickteaser I am. He's probably even followed me home, tracing my commute back from the shop. It would be creepy if it wasn't so erotic.

'Now then,' he says, interrupting my epiphany. 'We have some unfinished business to take care of.'

'We have?'

'Your carelessness.'

Oh. That.

He raises my legs like a gate and gets to his feet. I can't guess what he has in mind as he retrieves one of my shoes and slips the leather lacing free of the grommets.

I giggle nervously. 'Is that so I can't run away?'

Ignoring my question, he runs his hands up the fronts of my shiny thighs and I moan softly at his touch. The tailored skirt clings to my legs and he snakes his fingers under the hem. When he reaches the garter clips he flicks them open with surprising skill, releasing the stockings. He's done this before. Many times.

'Lift up.'

I obey and his fingers slide underneath my legs to release the clips at the back. The nylon goes slack and he peels the stockings down one by one. My legs and feet tingle at their exposure to the air, sensitised from their silky bondage.

'On your back,' he says. 'Legs up.'

I'm embarrassed for him to see my feet so close up out of the stockings. I haven't had a pedicure in weeks and he doesn't hide his disapproval. I knew he was a perfectionist – how could I have let that slide? I should have painted my toenails at the very least.

Flustered, I lean back, raising my legs. I'm mesmerised by his control, the effortless way he has of putting me completely under a spell.

I look away as he draws the ruined stockings from his pocket. Without a word he takes my hands and crosses my wrists. Then he winds the stocking around them.

Blood pounds in my head. The position draws my knickers tight against my pulsing sex and I squeeze my legs together. I flush deeply as he pulls my arms over my head and secures them to the scrolled arm of the sofa. The position humbles me intensely and my legs begin to tremble with the effort of holding them up.

'Bend your knees.'

I do as he says and he strokes his thumbs over the balls of my feet, making me shiver. He wraps the other stocking around my knees, tying it securely.

'There are ways to punish naughty little feet,' he says, measuring his words. 'Feet that don't present themselves properly when instructed.'

Though his voice is low and seductive, there is something military about him, a natural authority that reduces me to quivering compliance. His demeanour promises punishment for every misstep. With slow deliberation he doubles the lacing from my sandal, then doubles it again, making a small whip of four looped lashes. He snaps it against his palm and I jump, imagining its bite against my vulnerable feet.

Pushing my bound knees against my chest, he holds my ankles in position as he raises the leather. He brings it down smartly across both feet and I gasp at the sharp sting. I strain against the stocking that binds my wrists, but the nylon is surprisingly strong. I'm not going anywhere.

He flicks the lacing across my tender soles again and I yelp and writhe. The helplessness is intoxicating and I abandon myself to the pain as another stroke falls. Then another. My feet are hypersensitive and the delicate skin tingles unbearably. But the feeling is exquisite. The tingling spreads up along my legs, awakening sensations I didn't know were possible. My body is alive with the delirious fusion of agony and bliss.

When at last the whipping stops I plead for more with my body, flexing my feet, presenting them. But he cups them in his hands and presses his lips against the burning, throbbing arches, stimulating me beyond endurance. I shudder as he drags his tongue along each sole, dipping it between my toes.

Panting, desperate, I throw my head back as his skilful tongue explores every inch of my punished feet. I barely even notice the hand untying the stocking at my knees.

My legs fall open and he trails his fingers over my inner thighs, spreading me open even further. My gyrations cause my skirt to ruck up underneath me, revealing my soaked knickers. The throbbing, insistent urge between my legs is so intense it makes me light-headed.

With his tongue, he traces a path from my right thigh to my swollen sex. When I feel his hot breath against me I arch back, thrusting myself forwards in a wanton display. I feel like a wartime whore entertaining the troops, demanding satisfaction of my own. He pulls back to unzip himself and I gaze hungrily at his cock as he stands over me. I want him to take me. I want it rough, cruel, nasty.

But his game isn't over yet. Taking hold of my feet, he positions them on either side of his cock. Eager to please, I squeeze his length between my high arches, rolling and kneading the hard shaft. My soles feel every throb and twitch of his desire.

His breathing quickens and his eyes drift closed for a moment. But he opens them again immediately, returning his gaze to the naughty feet servicing him. I'm amazed he can stand. Balancing his cock on the instep of my left foot, I tease him with the toes of my right, a burlesque trick that comes naturally to me in my new incarnation.

I watch his face intently and see that he won't last long. I press my feet against him, hard, sliding them up and down the length, revelling in my brazen performance. The climax overtakes him and I position my feet to catch every hot jet of sperm as it dribbles across my insteps and between my toes.

My tormentor is pleased. A contented smile spreads across his face, crinkling the corners of his eyes. He parts my knees again and I close my eyes as he peels away my sodden knickers. He leaves them at half mast and I squirm, giving a little whimper. I can't wrap my legs around him; I have to hold them up. I can just imagine the picture I present – dolled up like a vintage screen siren and dishevelled from my lurid exhibition. My hands tied, my hair mussed and my knickers round my knees. Everything on display. Shameless.

I bite my lip when his fingers begin to stroke me, teasing the damp folds and deliberately avoiding the spot that will make me explode. I grind eagerly in response to his touch, begging for release. I'm unable to help myself with my hands restrained and he exploits my weakness fully. He teases me, dipping his fingers inside me and swirling them round. Finally, the torturous fingers converge on the hard little bud of my clit, brushing it lightly. The pleasure mounts astonishingly as he draws his fingers along the crease on either side, coaxing breathless cries from me until I'm ready to scream in frustration.

But then he stops. With a desperate moan I yank at my bonds, pleading with my eyes. His hands drift away from my sex and he slides my knickers to my ankles, taking his time, playing with me. At last he slips them off and I notice with surprise that his cock is already beginning to harden again. I marvel at his stamina, feeling even more defenceless and vulnerable.

When he moves to spread my legs I flex the muscles of my thighs, resisting. He exerts a little more force, prising my knees apart easily. I quiver as he kneels above me, his cock now fully erect. But I don't want to be passive. With a defiant smile I raise my right foot and plant it in the centre of his chest, pushing him back firmly.

But he is stronger than I am. He grasps both ankles deftly, wrenching my legs wide apart.

I gasp at the show of power and a wave of excitement flashes through me. The head of his cock demands entrance and I struggle as much as my position will allow, torturing myself by delaying it.

At last he drives himself inside, filling me up, pounding me with merciless force. I drown in my helplessness, crying out loudly with every hard thrust. It's too much for me. The deluge of sensations bursts throughout my body and I clamp my legs together around him, bucking and twisting as the spasms surge through me, assaulting me, overwhelming me, devastating me.

As I drift back down to earth, his features swim into focus. I manage a drunken lopsided smile, but speech is beyond me. He unties me and I wince at the pins and needles in my arms.

Before sending me home in a cab, he helps me tidy myself. He puts my new stockings in a carrier bag and inspects my fingers again, tutting at the jagged nails. 'You'll need a manicure, of course,' he tells me, arching an eyebrow warningly.

Of course.

I want to tell him I'm sorry I was a bad girl. Except that I'm not.

'Wear your new suit to work tomorrow,' he instructs, his eyes glittering. 'With proper nylons.'

Oh yes, the gentleman knows what he likes, all right.

But so do I.

I sit opposite him on the crowded train, dressed as ordered. I press my thighs together primly, enjoying the soft rustle that makes him smile. Slowly, I slide the hem of the skirt up over my knees, drawing it hissing over my thighs. As it creeps steadily towards the stocking tops I make sure he can see my fingers.

I watch him watching me, his eyes focused on the gleaming nylon. And slowly, deliberately, I place my hands on my knees. I curl my fingers like a hawk's talons, hooking my torn fingernails into the delicate material. His eyes widen slightly and I give him a sweet smile as I dig in and drag my nails up my thighs, tearing the stockings. Ruining them.

The expression on his face is well worth the price I'll pay for it tonight.

Fiona Locke's short stories have appeared in numerous Wicked Words collections. Her first novel, *Over the Knee*, is published by Nexus Enthusiast.

Sweet Charity Monica Belle

'What am I supposed to do, Mrs Townshend?'

'Pick a costume and one of the blue buckets, Lizi, then get out there and get the money in!'

I couldn't help but smile in return for her big cheesy grin, but mainly I felt silly. Charity is charity, but wandering around a shopping centre on a Saturday afternoon dressed in an animal costume? Still, like Neil said, it was for a good cause. I would just have preferred it if Neil had turned up on time.

'Where do we change?'

'In there where the costumes are, dear. Don't be long, most of the team are already out there doing their thing!'

Another cheesy grin and another nervous smile in response. I went into the room she'd showed, which seemed to be some sort of janitor's closet, only there was a pile of bright-blue buckets with the charity logo on the side and a rack of costumes. There were four costumes.

A gorilla. Not really me.

A tortoise. Definitely not me.

A hippo. No way!

A leopard.

That was more like it, slinky with spots, and just about my size. Also furry, and sure to be hot. I hesitated a moment because I had no way of locking the door and anybody might have walked in, before quickly stripping to my knickers. Only then did I discover how difficult it was to get into the leopard suit. There was a zip starting under the tail, so I more or less had to insert myself up the thing's bum, only once I'd got my top half in my legs wouldn't go, leaving me jumping around the room with my knickers on show, which was the exact moment a man I'd never seen before in my life walked into the room.

He smiled, to which I managed to return a sort of leopardy look. I was earnestly wishing I'd kept my bra on, but there was really no choice. I could either stand there looking a complete fool until he'd put his own costume on, and he'd already selected the tortoise, or I could strip off again and hope he was enough of a gentleman not to take a peek at my tits.

'Would you mind turning your back for a second, please?'

'Yeah, sure.'

He turned his back. I removed the leopard suit. He pretended to fiddle with the fittings on the tortoise costume while I climbed back into the leopard suit. I put one leg in, then the second, tugged the material gratefully up over my bum, and discovered that there was no way on Earth I could get the upper part of my body into it too. He continued to fiddle with his costume. I wriggled, I writhed, and every single movement seemed to accentuate my bare breasts.

Finally he spoke up.

'Are you sure you wouldn't like a hand with that?'

'No . . . really, I'm fine.'

'I think you're supposed to take the head off first.'

He'd half turned, catching himself an eyeful and a scowl, but he was right. I did have to take the head off. That way I could undo the zip all the way and get my arms in, then put the head back on. The relief as I closed the zip across my chest was huge, but it was nothing to covering my face, which must have been roughly the colour of blackberry juice.

I was dressed, and did my best to maintain a dignified efficiency as I picked up the bucket and left the little room. It wasn't that easy, not when the leopard suit fitted like a second skin, while it was impossible to walk without the tail bouncing up and down on my bum. Mrs Townshend gave me her big cheesy grin.

'Go get 'em, girl!'

All she got back was my leopardy look, now the full range of my expression. I set off with my tail bouncing behind me, smack into Neil coming the other way. He recognised me straight off, probably because he could see every contour I have through my fur. He kissed my leopardy nose and gave me a smack on my leopardy bum before moving on in with just one word.

'Later.'

I knew what he meant, just what he meant, my favourite little treat for helping him out with his fundraiser, which you can bet put a spring in my step. Soon I'd reached the populated area, and began shaking my bucket, while wishing I'd had the sense to put some money in it so that it jingled. I was going to go for the door out to the car park, but there was this nasty big tiger there who growled at me, and that wasn't the only animal in the centre.

A lion and a rhino had staked their pitch on either side of the main doors, while a pair of elephants were guarding the lift. A zebra and a warthog had the mezzanine floor, and there was a crocodile lurking outside Smith's. I grabbed the upper mezzanine, shaking my bucket and shaking my tail around the café tables, until I'd got enough coins to make a decent jingle.

Time for a drink. Off with my leopard head and I bagged a caramel macchiato to sip while I looked down on the floor below. Now we had the whole menagerie out, and the last three animals had taken the main aisle on the first floor. My peeping tortoise had the lift station, right underneath me. I could have poured coffee right down the back of his shell, only it wouldn't have been fair. He had tried to be a gentleman.

Some goofball had gone for the hippo suit, and he was making a serious fool of himself, dancing about with his monstrous backside wobbling behind, and I say 'his' because it had to be a man. No woman could ever bring herself to behave like such a complete idiot. I had to laugh.

Then there was the gorilla, my gorilla. It had to be Neil, as there was no way he was the hippo. I rather liked him as a gorilla. No, I fancied him as a gorilla. Maybe it was my accidental bit of exposure, maybe it was his naughty promise, maybe I was just in a horny mood, but it was kind of fun and kind of kinky. Maybe when I'd got a bit more money I'd start to stalk him, and pounce on him. Then we'd see what happened.

I went back to work, or rather, hunting, stalking the tables, pouncing on lone individuals who stopped for a drink, picking off the stragglers in the café queue. When a female stopped to get her brood chocolates I was right there behind her, helping them keep their weight down and saving them from the dentist. When a huge old bull paused to count his change I was lingering hopefully beside him. When I spotted a fine young male coming up in the lift I was ready to get him.

Before too long my bucket was getting heavy. I was beginning to feel I'd done my share and maybe it was time to think about my main prey. A glance from the balcony showed he was still about, as big and black and hairy as ever, scratching his armpits in the hope of extracting change from a herd of little old ladies. He hadn't seen me and I moved back from the edge, now stalking in earnest.

The lift was glass, too open. I sneaked down a flight of stairs and on out onto the first floor, keeping to the cover of a stand of umbrellas. He was as before, unsuspecting as he fed a pastrami on ciabatta into his gaping maw. Now was my moment, to take him while he was eating. I crept closer, from stand to stand, stall to stall, answering the cheeky comment of a cockney costermonger with a hiss and a swish of my tail, my attention fully on my prey.

Still eating, the hapless gorilla had begun to walk away from me, towards the tinkling fountain at the centre of the first-floor plaza – a fatal mistake. I crept closer on velvet paws, any sound I might have made muffled by the water, my every sense alert, one leg in front of the other, slowly, softly, and a final rush, to allow my hand to close on one firm masculine buttock within the hairy confines of his gorilla suit.

He nearly left the planet, dropping the piece of sandwich he had in his hand and choking on the piece he hadn't. Two pats on the back, a little purr and a little rub and I'd fled, treating him to an insolent wiggle of my tail as he stood gaping, more like a goldfish than a gorilla. I'd thought he would chase me, and planned a careful line of retreat so that if he did catch me there would be nobody to see what I got for my cheek.

I didn't get anything, not even a little run to get me breathless and wanting it. He just stayed where he was. It was typical Neil, all horny for me in the bedroom but too shy to be a little daring. I knew what to do about that. First things first though, my social responsibilities as a leopard in aid of famine, and then I could deal with my own rather different hunger.

Mrs Townshend oohed and aahed over my contribution and said several things with exclamation marks. I gave her my best leopardy look, emptied my bucket and went back to the fray. She was right. I'd done well, and now it was time for a little fun. I was going gorilla hunting, in earnest.

First, I needed a lair. Mrs Townshend had one, so maybe there was one above it? A brief foray confirmed that there was, and better still, unused. Next, there was that special little something, my naughty secret. A brief attack on a pair of penguins escorting some young and

I'd collected enough in my bucket to fulfil my needs. Now I really was a naughty girl, using charity money for improper purposes, highly improper purposes. I would give it back, of course, but it was still naughty, and I like that.

I knew my territory now, and made Abigail's Accessories without the gorilla spotting me. Abigail, or possibly one of her assistants, supplied me with what I needed, a dinner candle of the short variety, just right for naughty girls, or even a naughty leopard girl. I was glad she couldn't see my face, because you know that when a single girl buys a single candle it's not necessarily going in a stick.

Now for the hunt. I had my tummy fluttering, and felt as naughty as naughty can be. Out on the mezzanine the zebra had stopped to browse and the warthog was snuffling around a likely looking troop of housewives. I slunk past, taking care not to be seen from above, and as I climbed the stairs I saw my prey. He was at the far end of the aisle, holding his bucket out to a pair of suits, his shaggy black back towards me.

I crept forwards in the shelter of the stalls, ignoring a yet cheekier comment from my cockney costermonger and sidling sideways into the shadow of a stand of sunglasses. Still the gorilla talked. I moved forwards, loath to interrupt his foraging but determined I would get him this time. Slowly I crept forwards, from shadow to shadow, from Woolies to Marks to Macs, the last ensuring that he had no chance of picking up my scent on the wind.

At last the suits moved on. I stepped out boldly, walking up beside him to run a hand down his furry back to his furry buttocks. He jumped just like before, but I'd already moved away, this time taunting with a deliberate wiggle of my leopardy tail and an ever so meaningful crook of one leopardy finger. Now he came after me, slow and steady, six foot six of hairy black gorilla with his eyes fixed on my wiggling tail. I sped up. He sped up too, and we were running laughing down the aisle, oblivious to everyone's the stares.

Where I wanted to go there was nobody to stare, just the blank end of the side passage and the door to some offices, unoccupied on a Saturday. My own little nook was open, and I slid inside, my head poked out, one finger to beckon and one long leopardy leg to entice. He came on, now eager, hunched low and scratching under one arm, then stood high to beat his chest and show off what a big strong dominant male he was. I already knew.

I slipped inside. He followed. I jammed the door with a chair and cuddled close, rubbing my body against him to feel the power of him against my breasts and tummy and legs. I nuzzled his face as he returned my embrace, his hands slipping low to cup my bottom, so like a man, impatient, but now I didn't care. I let him feel, his big hairy gorilla hands cupping my furry cheeks, squeezing and feeling with all the ardour of the first ever time, for all that he'd held me a hundred. He only let go when he lifted his hands to his head, but I shook mine.

'Uh-uh, I want you the way you are. Be a gorilla for me, only I want my special treat too.'

He answered with a grunt, just right. I ducked down to my bucket, feeling the heat in my cheeks as I took out the candle. He knew, he'd seen, he'd done it for me a dozen times, but it still made me blush, so hot, and that heat went straight where it belonged, hotter still as I whispered into his ear.

'You know where this goes, don't you?'

This time I got a double grunt. He took the candle. I was purring as I went down, eager to be taken straight away, and as I was. There were lots of chairs, just right for a naughty girl to kneel on while she gets her special treat. I chose one and climbed right on, pushing out my furry bottom and reaching back to lift my tail, surely all the invitation any man could ever need?

It was all he needed. He gave a single throaty grunt and closed in. I gave him a wiggle and closed my eyes, eager to lose myself in my fantasy as he gave me what I so badly needed. I felt his hands on my body, tracing the outline of my hips and thighs, my bottom and my breasts, stroking me through my fur. His front pressed to me and already I could feel the big excited bulge beneath his suit, ready for my body, ready to fill me right up to the top of my head.

I gave him another wiggle, encouraging him, and his hands had found my zip. My mouth came open in a sigh as he drew it down, nice and slow, allowing my costume to open and make me available to his big gorilla hands, his big gorilla mouth, his big gorilla cock. Now I hung my head, leaning on the chair, my back pulled in and my knees set wide, presenting myself to him the way he likes me, the way he knows means he can do as he pleases, especially that one special thing.

He began to touch, the hair on his hands tickling my cheeks and between, to make my muscles tighten in anticipation. I sighed again as he ducked down low, nuzzling his face in between my cheeks to rub my pussy and send shiver after shiver of pure joy all the way up my spine to my head. He had my costume right open, my bottom pushing out of the unzipped hole, bare and wide, everything showing in an open invitation for what I wanted. I heard the rustle of the crinkly plastic of the candle wrapping and I could hold back my words no more.

'Put it in . . . go on, right in . . . nice and slow.'

I spread my knees wider still as I spoke, really flaunting myself, like the naughty rude little show-off I am. He could see the target, I knew, my back pulled in as far as it could go, my cheeks spread wide, open and ready, ready for the candle to be slid in where it belonged, right up my pussy, slid in to give me just a teasing touch of that gorgeous full feeling and drawn slowly in and out, fucking me, tormenting me. I let him do it, knowing he was only getting me ready for the real thing and that the more he teased the better it would be when I got it. In and out went the candle, making me gasp and sigh, wriggle my bum and clutch at the chair, until at last I couldn't bare it any more.

'Go on, you bastard, do it ... do it, will you? Make me ready and just ... just fucking do it!'

I screamed out the last words, but all he did was move the candle in and out, faster still, until I was whimpering with frustration and need. He was doing it on purpose, I knew, because he wanted me to say it, like the dirty little schoolboy he was at heart, like most men are. Not that I could resist, and he knew it, but I was wiggling my toes and thumping my hand on the back of the chair in frustration before I finally cracked and the dirty words began to spill from my lips.

'Up my bum, you bastard! That's what you want to hear, isn't it? Now do it ... stick it up my bum ... stick it ...'

My words broke to a long low sigh as he obliged. I felt the candle touch me in that so naughty place. I felt myself open, accepting the long hard shaft deep inside me. It felt so nice, holding me just a little open and filling me up, but better, far better, it felt so naughty, so gloriously naughty, to have something up my bottom and in front of a man.

I was whimpering with pleasure as he let go of the candle shaft, leaving it deep inside me with just a little bit sticking out, and purring as I positioned myself for entry and gave him one more encouraging wiggle. It's so nice to feel bare and to feel rude in front of a man, a man who appreciates my feelings and responds to me, a man like Neil. He knows what I'm like too, and what I'd be thinking as I knelt for him, open and ready behind, with a candle up my bum, as he quickly adjusted his suit to pull himself free. Now it was gorilla time.

He gave a throaty grunt as he moved up behind me, making me giggle even as I felt the hot hard head of his cock press to my leg. One huge hairy hand moved down between my thighs and he was guiding himself into me, bringing my mouth wide in a gasp of pure bliss as I felt myself open and fill. I adore that full feeling. There is nothing like it in all this world, and now I had it, in my own special way and more, kneeling, with something up my bum and a gorgeous great gorilla to fuck me.

In he went, all the way, until I could feel the thick shaggy fur against my bottom, ticklish and warm. His hands found my hips, holding me tight as he began to move inside me, back and forth, in and out, and with every push jamming the candle in to remind me that it was up my bottom. I was gasping immediately, wriggling myself onto him and drumming my feet on the chair for the sheer overwhelming ecstasy of what he was doing to me.

He felt bigger than ever, although I was accepting him with ease. It was as if he was filling not just my pussy but the whole of my being, right up to the top of my head, which is exactly the way it should be. He was good too, taking his time, slow and deep, then hard and fast, and slow and deep once more, until I was dizzy with pleasure and knew that all I needed was that one tiny crucial touch to take me over the edge.

I tried to hold off, savouring the pleasure he was giving me, but it was just too much. My hand went back, but as I found my sex he grunted. My own hand was gently but firmly removed from between my thighs, only to be replaced with his own, or rather his big hairy gorilla paw. It was something he'd never done before, one more rude, loving detail to our repertoire, and I was babbling thanks even as he began to rub me.

He was fucking me too, short awkward thrusts, as he held onto me around my belly and hip, but hard and satisfying, while his body was pressed tight against my bum to make the candle move with each and every push. I was going to come, my vision hazy with pleasure as I let my hand stray to my chest, stroking my painfully stiff nipples through my fur as my feelings rose, with my entire mind concentrated on what he was doing to me, how well he had handled me.

As my thighs and tummy went tight a moan escaped my lips. I thought of how I'd teased him, wiggling my spotted furry bottom until he decided to have me despite the risk of where we were. I thought of how I'd bent over for him, my bum pushed out first in fur and then bare naked for his attention. I thought of how he'd teased me, easing the candle in and out of my pussy when he knew full well where it was supposed to go, until I'd broken and begged for it. I thought of how he'd fucked me, how he was still fucking me, how we'd look, me with my bare bottom sticking out of my leopard suit while I was humped by a big hairy gorilla. I thought of what he was doing, bringing me off under his fingers as he fucked me, and with that I came.

I screamed and I screamed again, oblivious to the danger of getting caught, and I would have screamed some more if one great hairy hand hadn't closed over my mouth. He held me like that, still fucking me, still rubbing me, tight in his grip as I rode my orgasm, through one blinding peak after another, until at last I could hold on to it no more.

With that he took his own pleasure, gripping me by the hips and driving himself deep so hard he had me gasping again immediately. I was so sensitive I thought my head would burst as I shook it urgently from side to side, but he was done almost immediately, whipping his cock free at the very last instant to speckle my bum with hot wet seed.

I had barely come down from my high when we heard the sound of voices, and there was a frantic scrabble to get ourselves decent. Whoever it was passed by, but with my excitement gone so had my daring, and we left our cubbyhole as quickly as we could, sneaking out one by one to mingle with the shopping crowds once more, only now I was wearing a happy grin under my leopard mask as I worked.

Twice more that afternoon I passed the gorilla as we came and went with our buckets, and each time I gave him a little squeeze where it would do the most good. I was keen to get home too, feeling a little sticky and up for more fun, so I went down to Mrs Townshend as soon as I decently could. She didn't mind, happy with my takings, and I quickly changed back, no longer a leopard girl.

I was just doing up my second shoe when I heard Neil's voice behind me.

'How did it go, Lizi? Did you enjoy it?'

He knew full well I had and I turned to give him a cheeky answer, to find myself looking up at a large hippo.

Monica Belle is the author of the Black Lace novels, *Noble Vices*, *Valentina's Rules*, *Wild in the Country*, *Wild by Nature*, *Office Perks*, *Pagan Heat* and *The Boss*. Her stories have also appeared in several Wicked Words collections.

Shopping Derby
Heather Towne

Eldon revved the engine. The morning girl from JACK 103 dashed out into the middle of the sun-baked parking lot, chequered flag in hand.

'Stanley's Fine Wine and Spirits Shoppe, corner of Rochester and Marion!' I yelled over the din of the engines and the crowd, and the president of the Chamber of Commerce with a bullhorn. 'Do you know where that is?'

'Yeah!' Eldon responded. 'We're going for the bottle of absinthe first?'

We looked at each other. The guy knew his stores, their merchandise. The government-run liquor outlets didn't carry the Green Fairy, but private wine shops, like Stanley's, did.

I held up my copy of the shopping list that I'd just been handed two minutes earlier. 'I thought we'd knock off the tough stuff first, then mop up the rest in a sprint to the finish.'

Sunlight glinted off Eldon's wire-rimmed glasses, his brown eyes shining. 'I like your style.'

The list quivered in my hand, the excitement and anticipation growing.

The morning girl glanced nervously at the ten seventeen-foot U-Haul cube trucks assembled in front of her, motors running, then at the Chamber of Commerce guy safely ensconced in the portable stands packed with shopkeepers and curious onlookers.

'On your marks!' the president bullhorned.

Truck horns blared.

'Get set!'

Engines revved.

'Shop!'

We were off, lumbering across the parking lot, a converging line of rumbling cargo vehicles headed for the industrial park exit roads. The Shopping Derby was on.

Each truck contained a man and a woman – ten teams randomly formed from the twenty people randomly selected out of the hundreds of applicants to compete – a map of the city, a book of Yellow Pages, and the shopping list of one hundred items we were supposed to purchase in twelve hours or less. Cellphones, BlackBerries and any other type of store-communication device were banned. The contest was a test of shopping skills and stamina, knowledge of the city and its stores and their wares; the results judged on price and quality, as well as quantity.

We were at the head of the thundering pack when we hit the first traffic light that led to the city proper, careful to obey all traffic regulations and speed limits as required, of course. An Air-JACK helicopter hovered over our heads, monitoring the race.

'What's after the absinthe?' Eldon asked.

Planning ahead – good. I was way ahead of him, though, prioritising items with my ballpoint based on purchasing difficulty and probable store location, seeking the coveted cluster effect to cut down on travel time. 'A purple leather bustier,' I answered. 'I'm pretty sure the Underwear Drawer on Clarence carries purple ones – at a reasonable price.'

Eldon brushed his brown hair over to the right and glanced at me. 'Don't just be pretty, be sure.'

I got a good feeling he and I were going places.

We watched Trucks 4 and 7 steam off to the right down the four-lane street.

'Wal-Mart,' we said together, shaking our heads. They had a big box two blocks to the west.

Most of the items on the shopping list weren't the usual generic junk you buy at a big department store, however. What skill does that take? But there were some; the easy stuff, worth less points in the grand scheme of things.

The light stayed red, taunting us.

'You know the city pretty well?' I asked, phone book and map bouncing up and down in my lap, in time with my legs.

Eldon drummed the steering wheel and said, 'Drove a cab before I got my CGA.'

The light changed at last, and we chugged off into traffic, eastbound, both of us scanning the horizon for bottlenecks. The clock was ticking.

'What do you do for a living?' Eldon asked, checking the rear-view mirror the recommended every ten seconds.

I was zipping through the shopping list for the fifth time. 'Huh? Oh, I'm a purchaser for Coachways – the bus manufacturer.' Not that that was going to be of any help. All the items on the list were personal products – housewares, clothing, health goods, sporting equipment, kids' stuff – not industrial components.

'Go!' Eldon hollered at me, rocking to a stop in front of Stanley's Fine Wine and Spirits Shoppe. The place had just opened; timing is everything during a shopping binge.

I dashed out of the truck and into the store, telling the man sporting the 'Stanley' nametag exactly what I wanted, loud and clear. Communication is critical in getting the right product, quickly.

He waddled around the pub-style counter and plucked a dusty bottle off a wall shelf, then glanced at the idling truck out front. Eldon was already in the street with the rear doors open, ready to load.

'Shopping derby, eh?' Stanley commented. He casually scratched his salt-and-pepper beard with the bottle top. 'Great idea by the Chamber. I got in as a sponsor on that one right off the bat. I knew it would get loads of publicity. What're you and your partner going to do with the ten thousand if you –'

'Just bag the bottle, Stan,' I gritted.

I flew out of the store, tossed the booze up to Eldon in the back of the truck. He dropped it in a cardboard box, then jumped out, as I slid behind the wheel. We were off.

Traffic was picking up, along with the heat. I hugged the outside lane, keeping things rolling. My heart was pumping a mile a minute, and so, apparently, was Eldon's.

'Buy a lot of stuff at the Underwear Drawer?'

'On occasion,' I said. 'Like any naughty girl.'

We looked at each other.

I made the kerb in front of the lingerie and sex toy emporium in five minutes, then leapt out and scooted inside. I knew just where to go – and not from studying flyers, ad bags, store layouts, websites, or the Yellow Pages, either.

I spotted the rack of leather bustiers near the rear of the store and started flipping. The rich aroma and texture made me a little dizzy. Black, black, black, red, red, white ... no purple!

I made tracks for the green-haired clerk behind the cash register. 'Don't you carry any purple leather bustiers, Nancy? Size medium.'

She fluttered her false eyelashes as I clawed the countertop. 'Well, um ... if you don't, like, see any on display ... we might, um, have some –'

'Get one!'

She dropped the crotchless panties she'd been pricing and scurried off to the storeroom. One of the many things this competition was going to test, was how well you handled the hired help.

She was back in under a minute with my leather bustier, right colour, right size. I fingered the requisite bills off Eldon's and my combined roll and handed them to her. You had to pay your own way in the derby – that was the entrance fee. Only the winners would be reimbursed. Thriftiness was important, therefore, as it always is with any good shopper.

I grabbed the bagged bawdywear and sailed outside. Eldon was in the cargo cube, bent over arranging boxes and padded mats, preparing. His hard buttocks roundly filled the rear of his tan Dockers. Sweat rolled down my back and into my shorts.

He spun around. I threw him the bag. He boxed it and jumped down out of the truck, colliding with me. My breasts bounced off his chest, stunning me, thrilling me. And impulsively (so unlike the way I shopped), I grabbed the guy's head between my hands and kissed him.

The frenzy was getting to me, I guess.

We stared at one another. Then he pushed me back and bolted for the cab of the truck. Still, even as he ran away, I sensed a connection deeper than commerce between the two of us.

World Cup Germany soccer ball – Kick It! on Gertrude, the store adjoining the new indoor soccer facility. It paid to read the newspapers, which Eldon did scrupulously.

This time I flung the cargo doors open while my partner raced into the store. He was out with pace in a matter of seconds, a silver Adidas soccer ball bearing the 2006 World Cup logo in his hands. He kicked it up to me where I stood on the edge of the truckbed, along with the comment, 'Nice legs.'

The pale-pink shorty-shorts I was wearing for action *did* do a good job of showing off my long legs. Two-mile daily jogs had turned them summer lean and brown.

'Thanks,' I said, jumping down.

He caught me, kissed me. His lips were soft and slightly wet. He darted his tongue into my mouth, tussled with my tongue, and a tingle shot through me. I broke away, damp and breathless and even more pumped for the hunt.

I slid behind the wheel and gunned the engine.

'They should have a Fat Boy barbecue at Grillers on Fort Street,' he said, scanning the shopping list from the passenger seat.

'Thought so,' I muttered, strangling the steering wheel, his warm hand riding my bare thigh.

We squeezed into the alley next to the barbecue store; there was no parking on the street. Eldon ran inside while I flopped the rear doors open. Then I thought about the size and weight of that jumbo propane cooking apparatus, and I started after him.

But he was already back at the mouth of the alley, a store clerk guiding one end of the rolling barbecue, hustling to keep up. Good help wasn't hard to find, once you demanded it.

The two men heaved the grill into the back while I fidgeted behind the wheel. The doors finally slammed shut and Eldon slid in next to me. We rolled.

'Does the Constantine Nursery on Shell carry that type of fern?' I asked, pointing at the jumping list in his hand. My finger slipped, poking him in the stomach. He was hard under his conservative green golf shirt, and ribbed.

Eldon shook his head, sweat beading his tall forehead. 'I doubt it. Their inventory is mainly flowers – annuals and perennials and the like. They don't carry many non-flowering plants. Greenthumbs on Cavalier has plenty of plants, though.'

I nodded, grinning. 'I knew there was a reason I brought you along.'

I rode the rear of a Smart car until it jittered off into another lane.

The Greenthumbs on Cavalier was closed. Eldon spotted that two blocks away. I hung a U-turn and headed for their other location on Adelaide. I was shaking again – not with nervousness, with excitement.

The second Greenthumbs was open. We both piled out of the truck. Large greenhouses are notorious for scattering their living wares all over God's half-acre, staff often as difficult to find as marigolds in January. So four legs would be better than two, in this case.

I located the fern section first, the plant we were seeking peeking out from behind a mini-forest of its scruffier cousins. We carefully loaded the greenery into the truck.

Then I pushed Eldon against a side panel, pressing my lips into his, my overheated body against his body. It was a sauna in the back of that truck, but we were already too sweaty to care. We swirled our tongues together, Eldon's hands sliding down my back and onto my bum. He gripped and squeezed my taut little buns, his erection pressing hard and yearningly against my stomach. I moaned into his mouth, fingers riffling his hair.

We broke apart in unison.

'*History of Canada, 1497 to 1750, The Years of Discovery*, Jock Miller?' I gasped.

'University Bookstore, for sure,' he exhaled. 'But that's way over on the edge of town.'

'Used bookstore?' I snapped, clutching his shoulders.

'Yeah,' he agreed, almost cracking a smile as he stared at my rapidly rising and falling breasts. 'The Learned Worm on Florence. They carry used textbooks. At least they did when I –'

'Let's go,' I hissed, shutting him up with a kiss.

By hour six we had fifty-two items crossed off our shopping list, snug in the back of our truck. The JACK guys in the chopper informed us over the radio that three trucks had already been ticketed and one towed. And two other trucks were running fine, but their passengers had broken down – screaming at one another on the sidewalk as they hopelessly floundered. Long-haul shopping can wear on the nerves of the best of companions. Especially when you don't know what you're doing.

We knew what we were doing. Each item purchased, checked off our list, was rewarded with a hug or a kiss or a grope, or all three, depending on the pertinent parking circumstances. We were brimming with adrenalin, the finish line and prize money in sight; turned on rather than tired out.

'Romeo Busante hand-dipped chocolates, dark, twelve pieces in a heart-shaped box!' Eldon called out to me over the roar of the road.

I swiped perspiration off my forehead and smiled. 'A girl's best friend. Better Than Sex, Waterfront Drive.'

He squeezed my leg. I puckered a pretend kiss.

It was almost cool in the little stand of trees in the park behind the Waterfront Shopping Center, what with the shade and the breeze from the lake. But not for Eldon and me.

He was on top of me, cupping my breasts through my damp T-shirt, licking my nipples. I shimmered with delight, staring up at the fluffy clouds drifting by on the brilliantly blue sky, the box of Busante's resting comfortably on the grass next to us.

'Yes,' I urged, when he closed his lips over a rigid clothed bud and sucked on it, flooding me with even more heat.

He bathed my T-shirted breasts with his tongue, sucking and biting my nipples, before finally pushing my top up and baring my boobs. I flung my arms over my head and arched my back, begging the earnest accountant to ravage my chest.

He grasped and squeezed my slippery breasts, flicking a cherry-red nipple still harder and higher with his tongue, the dizzying tingling sensation driving me wild. I twisted my head around in the grass, and he pushed my tits together, slashing his tongue across the stiffened peaks of both of them at once. I closed my eyes, my body vibrating.

He mauled and sucked on my breasts until, finally, I grabbed his head and brought him up to my mouth, my pussy as wet as the lake.

'We should really hit the road,' he said, foggy glasses riding his forehead.

The guy sure knew how to tease a girl. But that could be forgiven, even encouraged, because he sure knew how to shop.

I rolled over on top of him, our lips locked together. Then I levered a hand in between our flaming bodies and covered the hardened outline of his cock with a warm palm. I squeezed and rubbed him, and he moaned into my mouth, throbbing in my hand.

'Yes, I suppose we really should hit the road,' I breathed, rolling off of him.

I brushed grass out of my hair and pulled out my T-shirt in an effort to dry it, as Eldon shifted into gear.

'Dungeons and Dragons Howling Orc miniature, War Drums set?'

'The Sorcerer's Apprentice and Sons, on Euclid,' he replied instantly.

I touched his arm. He goosed the gas.

We weren't the only ones to find the mouldering storefront sepulchre of geekdom, however; the Truck 8 contestants were there ahead of us, though still far behind us in the overall race. The woman was arguing with an H.P. Lovecraft lookalike behind the counter, brandishing a shopping list that showed only about twenty checkmarks.

'You've got to have this stupid troll!' she wailed, shoving the list in H.P.'s face. Her braided brown hair was coming apart at the seams, the back of her neck a blistered red.

Her partner, a pale pudgy guy with a goatee, stood next to her, shoulders hunched, rocking back and forth, lips moving as if in silent prayer. His glassy eyes and demeanour were testimony to a terminal case of shopping stress.

'Madam, it is an Orc, not a troll,' H.P. intoned, folding his parchment fingers together. 'And, as I have already explained to you, I had, unfortunately, but two of that particular miniature, both of which have been purchased from me in the last hour. Perhaps you may obtain one at –'

But the woman wasn't listening, she was screaming, tearing at her hair, her companion rocking faster.

We exited, beelining for Dougie's Black Hole at the Springside Mall. One thing every experienced, time-wary shopper knows: you don't argue with store staff – either they have what you want, or they don't. And if they don't, you move on.

We scooped up the figurine and then wrestled with each other in the cab of the truck, Eldon's busy hands shopping for purchase on my most private of possessions. The vying for buying supremacy had thrown us together, and brought us together, our passion building alongside our cargo, the heat of battle inflaming us to take chances we'd never take outside of an all-out shopping derby.

'TanFan burnt-orange paisley dress, extra large,' I stated, after Eldon had stored the Greek-language Nana Mouskouri CD from Second Sound Sensations in the back. 'There's a vintage clothing store on Marlborough.'

'Why vintage?' he asked.

'TanFan went out of business right after Chip & Pepper.'

He cracked a smile.

Traffic was heavy, but I drafted in behind a bus, and we were hanging a right onto Marlborough in the time it took most people to tear open their credit card bill. Eldon followed me into the funky boutique. I didn't ask why; I knew why. I was going to try on the dress even though it was unnecessary, and too large, and he was going to help.

I stripped off my sticky T-shirt in the crowded cur-tained change booth, Eldon dropping to his knees in front of me. He unbuttoned and unzipped my shorts, yanked them down, leaving me bare, bottom and top. My legs shook and my arms goosebumped as he ran his warm hands up and down my legs. And when he ran them up over the swell of my buttocks, and gripped my cheeks, I squeaked.

His breath steamed hot and humid against my moist naked sex. I wrung the paisley dress in my damp hands. He let slip his tongue and licked me, and I almost tore the threadbare garment to threads.

'Jesus, yes,' I whimpered, leaning back against the wall, the man's tongue caressing my lips.

He held me by the bum and lapped at me, sending me shivering. I discarded the dress and grabbed onto his hair, pulling him into my dewy need. A heavy languid heat consumed me as he wriggled his tongue inside of me, and I gasped to fill my lungs in the suddenly breathless confines. And when he spread me apart and flicked at my button, I just about melted in the man's mouth.

I had to put a stop to it, for the good of the team. I just couldn't take any more. And I wanted physical culmination to come with contest culmination, as I knew he did, too.

So I jerked his head back, bent down and kissed him on his shiny lips. I helped him to his feet, then spun him around and tried *him* on for size.

Taking his spot on the floor, I unzipped his pants and pulled him hard and needful out into the open. The merchandise was just as advertised, and I admired it with my soft swirling hand, testing and teasing its length and strength. I took his swollen head into my warm wet mouth, then half his shaft.

'Fuck,' he groaned, startling me with the curse word.

I gripped his thickened base and bobbed my head, lips sliding back and forth on his pulsing manhood, tongue cushioning the veiny underside. I cupped his pouch as I sucked, squeezing and tugging.

'That's enough! That's enough!' he cried, grabbing at my bangs.

I pulled him out of my mouth with a soggy pop, the both of us very much on edge.

Four hours later, ten hours in, there was only one item left on our shopping list: a fold-out futon. We weren't cocky, but we had a good warm feeling that we were well ahead of the rest of the field. And even if some of our competition managed to somehow buy all one hundred items, we were confident we could beat them on quality and price.

'The Futon Factory on Bishop?' I asked, cradling the Yellow Pages, balancing the map in my lap.

'Sure, if you want to pay full price. But when I was monitoring local TV commercials this past month, I'm sure I saw an Al's Unpainted Furnishings spot advertising a sale on just that product. Wanna give it a try?'

He looked at me just a little smugly, and I could've kissed him. Did, in fact, right on the dimpled chin. 'You haven't been wrong yet,' I said.

He spun the wheel to the left, and ten minutes later we were in the gargantuan parking lot of the Al's Unpainted Furnishings warehouse on Clairemont. 'Shellacless' Al, owner and star of a hundred annoying TV advertisements, was there to greet us on the cavernous showroom floor.

We told him what we were after. He said he had it, but we'd have to get it. Al had rock-bottom prices, and customer service to match.

Eldon and I lugged the futon out of the store and into the glaring sunlight, heaved it aboard the truck. It was hot heavy work, but we were so keyed up we hardly took notice. We stood in the back of the truck, amongst our one hundred prescribed and purchased items, panting with exhilaration. Then Eldon shoved me down onto the futon.

He closed the cargo doors to only a crack, felt for me, found me, ready and willing. I pulled him down on top of me, his hard body fitting neatly against mine, the discount futon creaking, but standing its ground. He kissed my lips, my nose, my neck, licked and bit into my neck. I wrapped my arms and legs around him and nuzzled his hair. His tongue trailed up over my chin, into my waiting mouth.

It was dark in that giant shopping cart, but a sliver of light and a previous familiarity with each other's bodies showed us the way. No words were exchanged. There was nothing to say now, just do. We might be finicky shoppers, but we knew what we liked.

Eldon rolled my T-shirt up over my breasts and fingered my achingly hard nipples. He took them in his mouth, each in turn, sucking on them, as I clawed my shorts and panties down, my head spinning. He released my breasts long enough to strip out of his own pants and underwear. Then he was on top of me again, sliding inside of me at last.

I grasped his bare bum as he pumped me, sweat streaming off his face and onto mine, his searching tongue swarming into my mouth. He clung to my quivering breasts and I clung to his clenching buttocks, his hips moving faster and faster, filling me with sensuous joy.

I started to shake, my body a live wire, a wicked tingling blazing up from the wet-hot friction point where we were joined, where Eldon pistoned away. A scream caught in my throat. He threw back his head and grunted. I shuddered, he jerked, the inferno of our ecstasy engulfing us. I flooded with wave after wave of warm wet delight, as he emptied himself inside of me.

We collected the ten thousand dollar prize money, all right, and were reimbursed for our purchases (which we got to keep). The next closest couple only managed to muster a measly 86 rather overpriced items.

But we didn't go running out shopping for engagement rings, or starter houses, or anything like that. Eldon was married, after all, as was I. We'd come together for a brief encounter during the madness of the derby, sharing our passion for purchasing. But now that the buying spree was over, we returned to our families.

I got custody of the futon.

Heather Towne's short stories have appeared in numerous Wicked Words collections.

Shop till you Drop
Carmel Lockyer

'My name is Elva and I'm a spree shopper.'

I'd never had to say it before, and I wouldn't have said it now, if it hadn't been for my business partner.

Harbir made it a condition of our continuing business relationship that I dealt with my 'problem'. We were making a great living as multicultural marketing consultants until he decided my shopping habit was out of control. It wasn't, but he'd always been a fuss-bucket and the loan underpinning our prestigious Islington offices was a special EU one that supported business specialising in diversity: if he lost me as a partner, or I lost him, we'd have to pay back the capital at once. Not good.

He insisted that spending every lunch hour shopping was excessive. I told him his was a stereotypical masculine response. We argued for the first time since we'd met at college: him the economics whiz kid and me the linguistics queen. The only thing we had in common was the desire to be in charge – 'boss genes' we called our shared obsession.

But now Harbir wanted me to stop shopping for a week – to prove I could. I got as far as Wednesday, but then I cracked and sneaked out at coffee break. When I came back: one decaf skinny latte and a pair of Prada sandals to the good, and several hundred pounds on my credit card to the bad, he was waiting.

'You need Spree Shoppers Confidential, Elva, and you're going to take a month's leave of absence for "personal development" reasons and get this sorted out,' he said.

'Oh come on, Harbir, one little pair of shoes . . .'

He gave me the stern look that Sikh men are so good at and I admitted the truth, because disappointing Harbir was like kicking a puppy.

'And what shall I tell Sadhika about this addiction?' he asked, sadly.

Sadhika was Harbir and Pavitar's daughter, a totally beloved and spoiled child.

'She's only three years old, Harbir, why would you tell her anything?'

'But it's the principle – she looks up to you, Elva, you know that.'

I did. I sighed. 'OK, you win. A month, but I'm going to work from home – you couldn't survive for even a week without me.'

'Whatever you say, Elva.' He smiled his sad smile again and handed me a little laminated card with the Spree Shoppers Confidential Freefone number on it. I hated it when he did that: got me to do exactly what he'd already decided I should do.

The first couple of days I refused to ring the number. I was sure I could quit, cold turkey. On the fourth day, my credit card maxed out in Homebase and I came home in a taxi only to realise although I'd just bought rich-chocolate-coloured paint for my dining room, I would have to stack it in the spare bedroom along with the aubergine-coloured paint I'd bought for the same room six weeks ago. I was sure I was not out of control but maybe, just maybe, I needed to rein myself in a little.

So I rang the number on the card and was connected to an adviser called Sarah who went through a telephone questionnaire with me and then invited me to attend a meeting the following day in West Kensington. So I went.

It was a mistake to go to Harvey Nichols first. I realised this as soon as I pushed open the door to the meeting room, and had to turn sideways to get myself and my four big shopping bags through the doorway. The faces of the four women and one man in the room proved me right: they all looked as if they'd been forced to suck salted lemons.

'You must be Elva,' said a blonde with a clipboard. I thought she looked like a miserable Afghan hound. I nodded.

'Welcome to Spree Shoppers Confidential. I'm Sarah, your sponsor. Well, we can all see your problem.' She pointed to my bags and I tried to hide all four of them under my chair. 'You'll have to start with isolation. Here's the agreement: you commit to staying home for a fortnight, and one of us will call you every day to make sure you've managed to survive an entire day without purchasing anything – I'll give you my card so you can call me when you feel weak – and if you can get through fourteen days we'll start you on some supervised shopping. We'll order groceries and other staples for you and have them delivered. You can make a list of what you need while we continue the meeting.'

I gave her the evil eye – that crack about 'when' rather than 'if' you feel weak was fighting talk – but Sarah simply looked down her long nose at me, handed me a card, a notepad and a pen, and carried on.

'So, Malcolm?' She turned to the only man in the room.

'Hello, my name is Malcolm and I'm a spree shopper.'

'Hello, Malcolm,' they all chorused.

'This week I've been soooo good,' he squealed. 'Adam and I are going on holiday and I've only bought two pairs of Bermudas – normally I'd have a new pair for every day of the week…' He chuntered on about his purchasing history and I tuned out.

The card was laminated. Perhaps Spree Shoppers Confidential owned shares in a laminating firm. I read the details carefully. It was a pledge. I agreed to isolate myself from 'pernicious shopping experiences', including malls and high streets, airport duty free lounges and department stores, for a fortnight, and SSC agreed to visit me during this period, to provision me and to give me a 24-hour telephone support service. This service – excluding the cost of a fortnight's food, for which I would pay them in advance and in cash – would cost me £800. I wondered if I was allowed to bargain. Probably not.

The woman next to me, wearing a pair of Lucite earrings which I was sure were vintage Zandra Rhodes, leant over and whispered, 'Hi, I'm Charlotte. Don't let Sarah get to you – she's a bit of a tartar but everybody else is nice. I did the isolation pledge and it worked for me.'

I nodded gratefully and got on with writing my food list. If I was going to be banged up at home for two weeks, I at least wanted to look forward to my meals.

When everybody had spoken, Sarah ended the meeting and took my notepad from me. 'Dulche de leche ice cream, truffle oil, organic smoked salmon ... are you planning to set up a restaurant?' She wrinkled her long nose.

I merely smiled at her and led the way to the nearest hole in the wall to get the cash she'd need to buy my groceries.

'My name is Elva and I'm a spree shopper.' Behind me and below me, something astonishing was happening. I could feel a tongue, slow and hot, working its way around my right ankle, gently teasing its way up my calf. A hand, equally warm and slow, was massaging my lower spine, making its way downwards in tiny incremental circles and tender pinches. When the two met, which I guessed would happen somewhere around mid-thigh, I was going to lose the ability to speak. I was already squirming a little on my special ergonomic typing chair. I lowered my eyes without moving my head. I could see a pair of tight grey uniform trousers with apple-green piping, well filled out, but the rest of Stephen was out of sight, and I didn't dare glance down.

'Hello, Elva,' chorused the other shopaholics.

'I'm not sure what to say,' I began, and I wasn't, mainly because Stephen was now nibbling his way up my calf, and the sensation was making it impossible for me to concentrate. I felt his other hand reach round the chair and between my thighs, sliding under my skirt.

But I'm getting ahead of myself, aren't I? Let's go back to the pledge.

I wasn't feeling so confident by the next morning. Sarah dropped off my bags of food and I'd spent several hours putting them away and then researching menus to keep me happy for two weeks – I'd fallen asleep with a pile of recipe books piled on the bed. But daylight brought a different story: I needed a mandoline if I was going to do stir-fries, a steamer for rice, a couscousier, a spring-based cake mould ... I needed, in fact, to go shopping.

I rang the office. Harbir sounded rattled. 'Elva, I can't stop to talk, I have to go into a meeting with the Schaerar account people tomorrow.'

'Schaerar? They're not due for a debrief until next month.'

'I know, I know, but they've asked for a progress report and I need to prepare.'

I wished him luck and hung up, but I felt uneasy. Harbir wasn't good with clients; that was my end of the business. He made figures sound dry and boring and never knew how to put a good spin on statistics – he was a genius at gathering data but a complete drongo at presenting it, whereas I could make information shine. I wondered about teleconferencing the meeting but if I couldn't see the Schaerar people I wouldn't be able to interpret their responses to Harbir's results. This was turning out to be one of the worst Monday mornings of my life.

I tried to brainstorm the problem, but nothing occurred to me – there was no obvious solution. If I went to the office I'd break my isolation pledge and forfeit my £800: I knew I'd never get to Islington and back without diving into a boutique somewhere along the way. If I didn't go, Harbir would probably depress the clients so much they'd pull their marketing contract. It was a lose-lose scenario.

What did I always do when I couldn't solve a problem? I went shopping. But that avenue was closed, barricaded, shut off, and fuck-off barriers and big flashing red and blue lights were telling me I could not pass that way. Life was, to be honest, bloody awful, and it still wasn't even 10 a.m. yet.

I wandered into the kitchen and made coffee. I could certainly do with a new cafetière, I thought, or maybe a dinky little espresso maker ... damn, I had to stop thinking like a shopper!

I fished out the SSC card and called the number. Within seconds the receptionist connected me to Sarah's mobile. I did not want to whine to her, but somehow the whole story spilled out and her reply was prompt and practical.

'I'll be there by lunch time – we'll set you up a webcam. That way you can conference with your office and I can keep an eye on you – every time I call you, I can check you're actually at home. We've had people use mobiles before to try to fool us they weren't out shopping.'

I drifted back to the desk and rang Harbir – who sounded mightily relieved I'd be able to take part in the briefing. Then I gave our IT guy Sarah's number so he could co-ordinate with her on whatever was needed to get this multimedia conference up and running. I couldn't help wondering what else was possible with technology and as soon as my fingers hit the computer keyboard I knew the answer: online shopping.

I was good. I was strong. I held off even going near the internet until after Sarah had been and installed the software and hardware that made up the webcam. Then I let my fingers do the walking.

I ordered a batterie de cuisine to be delivered as a priority, and didn't forget the various exotic bits of kitchen equipment I'd been salivating for the night before. I found a place where I could try out hairstyles online, and decided that as soon as my house arrest ended, I was going to have a radical makeover. I tracked down a pair of second-hand Zandra Rhodes earrings on eBay, but they weren't as nice as Charlotte's so I decided to keep looking. In fact, I had a wonderful afternoon and evening, shopping, bargaining, browsing and skipping from one site to another – it was amazing what you could buy over the internet.

The next morning the IT guy rang to say he'd sorted out a system and if I sat in front of my PC, put on the headset Sarah had left and accessed a certain http address I'd find myself talking to him in person. I did, and I was! I was actually looking at my own boardroom table, with the IT guy sitting on one side and Harbir on the other. Suddenly I realised I hadn't checked what they could see of my room, and rushed to push three coffee mugs out of sight behind the monitor, as well as checking swiftly over my shoulder to see whether there was any intimate stuff in view: personal photographs on the walls or stuff like that. I made a mental note to order a folding screen as soon as this call was over – I didn't want the world and his dog being able to look at my décor.

'Hello, Elva,' said Harbir, and his voice came right out of my computer. I damn near jumped out of my skin. I'd expected to have to pick up the phone to talk to him, but there was a tiny microphone on the desk and it routed straight to my speakers.

'Hi, Harbir,' I said into the headset and he grinned broadly – full marks to technology. I got rid of him as soon as I could and was immediately online, browsing for a screen. I visited Habitat, the British Museum, the

V&A, and about a dozen Japanese and Korean sites before finally settling on a 1920s Arabian Nights screen inspired by the work of Aubrey Beardsley. It was beautiful and the second-hand shop selling it guaranteed next day delivery by courier. I was getting to like this! That was when I ordered the ergonomic typing chair – if I was going to spend all day in front of the computer, I needed to be comfortable.

And that's where I was now, in my new chair, with my folding screen behind me, and my webcam switched on so I could take part in a Spree Shoppers Confidential meeting. It wasn't the first SSC group I'd attended remotely, but it was the first in these circumstances. From the corner of my eye I could see a curl of apple-green ribbon spilling from its grey box and resting on my desk – was it in view to those watching me? I leant forwards slightly to push it out of sight. Big mistake. It brought me within reach of Stephen's fingers. Not only was I sitting in a virtual meeting, with a virtual stranger sliding his fingertips and tongue up and down my body, out of sight of the other participants, but I was lying through my teeth.

You see, after I'd done all the practical shopping, I thought I deserved something for me. A little reward. And as I was browsing the web, I found a beautiful site, Orchard Erotics, where I could order a hand-made corset or basque, tailored to my body, without ever leaving the house. I couldn't resist. I registered with the site and a few moments later received back an apple-green email containing my password.

Once I got inside Orchard Erotics I was enthralled. It actually was a virtual shop. I could hear the music playing in the background, a pianist tinkling 'It Had to Be You', my footsteps sounded against parquet flooring or vanished into deep grey carpeting as I navigated the site, and members of staff, drawn like elegant caricatures, welcomed me as I passed them. There were small salons opening off the main corridor, and each displayed one beautiful item: a pair of grey kid elbow-length gloves, an apple-green bustier with French knickers, a wisp of grey tulle, like a tutu, over a pearly suspender belt, a pair of embroidered stilettos in green, which nearly stopped me dead – I was sorely tempted to go in and look at them more closely. But I continued until through one doorway I saw a beautiful green basque modelled on a glass body. It was difficult to remember this was all an illusion. I wanted to put my hand out and touch it.

Suddenly a little cartoon man appeared, white haired and fashionably slim, with the perpetually surprised eyebrows of a facelift addict. 'Madam,' he said, his voice coming from the speakers exactly as Harbir's had. 'I am Mr Theo. Thank you for gracing our emporium. Have you chosen a colour and fabric for your garment?'

I knew I wanted silk, but I hadn't decided on a colour. I was thinking about apricot and I said so, feeling rather silly for talking aloud in an empty room. There was a split-second lag.

'Apricot. I see. Would you consider peach, perhaps?'

That annoyed me. Already somebody was trying to influence my choices, and I knew exactly what I wanted. 'You claim to deliver whatever the purchaser desires – and I desire apricot – can you do it, or can't you?'

The little cartoon figure drew himself up to his full (tiny) height. 'Madam, Orchard Erotics can, and will. It will take two or three minutes for our systems to analyse your computer, printer and so on, and then we can proceed to measurements and swatches. Please feel free to do something else until you hear the bell, at which point I will be delighted to continue our fitting.'

I wandered off for more coffee and a quick interrogation of myself. Was I breaking the pledge? Absolutely: if you thought about the spirit of it, but definitely not if you focused on the letter of it. Was I going mad? Absolutely: if you thought talking to little cartoon men was a sign of poor mental health, but definitely not if you considered it as part of a quality online shopping experience. Did I need an apricot silk basque? No question about it – of course I did!

I heard a gentle chiming and returned to the computer. 'Dear madam, we can begin. First of all, we have sent colour swatches to your inbox, if you would care to print them you can choose a colour to suit you. We cannot guarantee the colour match will be perfect, of course, but we have optimised them to work with your printer. While they are printing, if you would care to transmit your measurements via the screen?'

I looked at the computer to find a ghostly female figure had appeared. It looked like the chalk outline drawn around a corpse in an old detective story, except it glowed neon blue. I entered my proportions in the boxes by the side and watched as the figure's shape morphed to match mine. Finally we got to the colours: I lifted the sheets from the printer and glanced over them.

'Sugared Apricot,' I declared. There was the same tiny lag and then my little cartoon shop-man wrung his hands, looking worried.

'Madam, are you sure? We find many women are happy with Tokay, a lighter, more flattering colour.'

I sighed. 'Look, I know what suits me. Sugared Apricot will be great.'

The imaginary man looked at me pleadingly. 'Please, madam, all we want is for you to be utterly happy with your basque. It would be remiss of me not to mention that the shade you've chosen could make some skins look a little sallow.'

I grinned. 'Not mine.'

He sighed. 'If only I could be sure. Ah. I have a happy thought. Does madam have a webcam?'

And, of course, madam did. I switched it on, held up the swatch to my face and the little cartoon man clapped his hands with pleasure. 'It's perfect, no, it's beautiful.

Madam is utterly right. Thank you for putting my mind at rest. Your garment will arrive by courier before 5 p.m. tomorrow.'

Good service, I thought, as I logged off. Very good service. Mind you, the price was exorbitant. What they delivered had better be superb.

Right then though, with Stephen's fingers gently probing me so I could hardly think straight and my own body betraying me by heading for orgasm at the rate of an express train, the phrase 'good service' was one I wished I hadn't thought. Under my dress, I was wearing the apricot basque Stephen had delivered a little earlier. It had definitely been an error of judgement to bind Stephen's ankles to the chair with some of the apple-green ribbon from around the box – what on earth had I been thinking about?

I'd totally forgotten about this bloody SSC meeting, that was the problem. The whole day I'd been running backwards and forwards to the front door, collecting one item after another from couriers, assembling furniture, trying out new kitchen appliances and, in between, reading back through the Schaerar file and checking our metrics against reports on marketing trends across Europe. I was knackered. So I crawled upstairs for a quick shower, and when the doorbell rang again I ran down, in my bathrobe and my hair wrapped in a towel, to answer it.

And there he was. Stephen – blond and smiling, dressed in his grey and green uniform, holding a large grey box with green overprinting and tied up with a huge green bow.

'Elva Jones?' he said on a rising note, but his eyes went down, past my breasts, somewhat uncertainly constrained by the robe, all the way, slowly, to my wet feet, and he smiled. I've generally preferred dark men, but Stephen's smile changed all that in a second. He looked … naughty. Not smutty or sleazy, simply like somebody who was doing something wicked and thoroughly enjoying it. I'd never seen a man with such a sensual expression, nor one who was fitter, to be honest. Every inch of him, packed into his well-cut uniform, was toned and honed, and I was willing to bet he had a great six-pack.

I realised I hadn't answered him. I nodded, unable to take my eyes from his curling gentle mouth.

'I have a delivery for you, from Orchard Erotics' he said and his voice was insinuating, as though he was propositioning me.

I held out my right hand, wordlessly, checking the security of the knot on my belt with my left. He shook his head, still smiling into my eyes.

'Mr Theo insisted I should check the fit,' he said.

'Mr Theo?' I could hear my voice was shaking.

'Mr Theo said you were a lady who was very certain of her wishes, and it was my job to be absolutely sure you were happy with our work. Mr Theo said he'd never spoken to anybody as demanding as you were.'

'Demanding?' I didn't think of myself as demanding, and I wasn't sure I liked the idea.

'Oh yes.' His voice was caressing now, and so quiet I had to lean forwards to hear his words. 'We like demanding ladies; we cater for their every need. We are –' he paused, gazing down the front of my robe with unconcealed greed '– enthralled by them.'

'Bloody hell,' I muttered.

'And it seems my timing was perfect,' he said with a grin, hoisting the box higher with one hand and freeing the other to reach out and touch my collarbone. 'Although you ought to go and finish drying off – you have water droplets on your neck.' And he put his wet fingertip in his mouth.

Well, I was lost. Here was a blond love god, flirting with me in the most outrageous possible way, in the middle of the afternoon, with me dressed in no more than a robe and the fading fragrance of L'Air du Temps shower gel. A day in the office was never as exciting as this. Who said shopping was bad for you? I beckoned him in and sat him down on my ergonomic chair.

I should have gone upstairs and got changed, of course, but once I'd actually got my fingers around the box he'd delivered, I couldn't drag myself away. The box itself was a work of art – it had a raised surface, a little like crocodile skin, but when I looked closely, each bump was actually a tiny body part. There were pert little breasts in pairs, and women's curving buttocks, alongside tighter, more defined masculine arses, fitted between them were curvy female bellies and taut male ones, the latter with tiny lines of hair travelling from the navel downwards. No matter how hard I peered at the little anatomical details, I couldn't find any genitals. It was all tasteful and erotic – it was as if somebody at Orchard Erotics had sat down and thought about how to make the whole experience into a sensual adventure. The sense that such attention to detail was being paid was exciting, but also weird – as though a complete stranger was paying more attention to my sexual desires than I was myself. It was personal shopping taken to a whole new level.

I put the box down on the table and rubbed my hands over it, feeling the little bumps and nubbins warming my hands in contrast to the slippery green silk ribbon. Stephen followed me. I plunged my fingers into the cascade of ribbon crowning the box, until I found a loose end, and pulled. The whole elaborate display began to unravel, hanks and coils of ribbon spilled down the side of the box and, as I was lifting the lid to find out what was inside, I felt Stephen behind me – so close behind me that if I'd breathed in deeply, we'd have been touching.

I turned swiftly. He was smiling submissively. 'Let me dry your hair first,' he said. 'That way, when you try the basque on, you'll get the full effect.'

'Let you dry my hair? Do you think I'm mad?'

He shook his head slowly. 'No, I think you're very sexy,' he said.

It was my turn to shake my head. He sounded sincere, and he was abso-fucking-lutely gorgeous. What did I have to lose?

I led him to the kitchen, plugged in the hairdryer and handed him my brush before sitting down on a stool. He turned me gently away from the mirror and put down the equipment, before taking the towel from my hair and massaging my hair thoroughly and sensually. I felt as if I were about to melt right through the chair and end up as a puddle on the floor. It was both relaxing and exciting. From the feel of his fingertips against my scalp I could imagine how they would feel against my breasts and thighs and, because I was leaning against him, I could smell his light cologne and each time he moved I could feel the ripple of his abdomen. After a while he picked up the dryer again and began to work on my hair, by which time I was putty in his hands, almost literally. It wasn't until he put down the brush and touched me gently on the shoulder I realised he must have been able to see right down inside my bathrobe all along. I looked up, into his smiling face, and decided I didn't give a damn.

I pointed to the new jazzy coffee machine, which was steadfastly refusing to produce cappuccino for me. 'You make us some coffee,' I said. 'I'll just go and take the towels upstairs.'

I ran for my room, found my best panties (Patricia Fieldwalker champagne lace, as worn by a female character in the as yet un-premiered *Man About Town* movie starring Ben Affleck: I took my shopping seriously, in case you hadn't realised!), grabbed a quick squirt of Nina Ricci to top up the shower gel fragrance and dithered about whether to go back down barefoot or in heels. Eventually I decided on a pair of ballerina pumps in black velvet. I retied my robe and checked in the mirror. Stephen had done a good job on my hair, but it was the aura of lust that was truly making me look so good. He'd given some volume to my black bob so it looked like bed-hair, and I was flushed and dewy from sexual excitement, so my skin bore a rosy underglow. The white robe though, looked too medical, as though I'd escaped from a hospital ward. What did I have that would work? Ah yes, a burgundy Nicole Farhi puffball dress. Its incredibly low and sculpted neckline meant I'd never worn anything under it, because I'd never had anything to support me properly but not show straps – it would be a perfect test for the basque, and it flattered my dark complexion too.

I ran back downstairs and paused in front of Stephen who looked suitably impressed. He was holding two cups of frothy coffee too. I urged him into the dining room, which doubled as my office, and he sipped the coffee as I plunged to my armpits in the shredded tissue paper that filled the grey box, and drew out the basque. It was utterly beautiful. It glowed like ripe fruit and felt as soft as peach fuzz. I sent Stephen back into the kitchen while I put it on, then called him back in.

'You look amazing,' he said. His voice was husky and I could see his hand, holding the coffee, was shaking slightly.

'Elva means olive in Welsh,' I said, for something to fill up the moment in which I wanted to drag him to the floor and shag him senseless. 'My mum's Welsh, you see, and she thought Elva was a good name to go with my olive skin – my father's Italian.' I took a deep breath and got hold of myself, although I'd rather have got hold of him. 'Put that cup down, I don't want you to spill anything. Now, do you think Mr Theo will be pleased?'

'What? Oh. Yes, of course he will, it fits perfectly.'

I looked at him and he blushed.

'Mr Theo did ask you to check the fit of this garment, didn't he?'

He nodded, but he couldn't meet my eye.

'So –' I wandered over to my computer – I could see him in the blank computer screen as he swivelled to watch me. '– if I login now, Mr Theo will be expecting to hear from me, will he?'

Stephen nodded again, and then shook his head. 'Um, not exactly.'

I turned. 'You lied?'

'I wanted to see you in the basque – it wasn't exactly a lie.'

I watched him narrowly. He looked ashamed but also expectant – almost as if he wanted to be caught. 'Hmm, you wanted to see me . . .' I walked back to the Orchard Erotics box, tipped out all the tissue paper and beckoned him forwards. When he stood in front of me, I popped the box over his head – he looked completely stupid.

'Can you see me now?' I asked, almost giggling.

'No,' he said and his voice was full of suppressed excitement. He was getting off on this. I put one hand on his chest and heard him gasp. Then I unbuttoned the first four buttons of his uniform and found he did, as I'd thought, have a nice set of abs. He also had tiny tight nipples, like summer fruit – raspberries – crinkled with arousal. I ran my fingers across them and heard him groan inside his cardboard prison.

I pushed him across the room until the backs of his legs were against the new chair, and then pressed down on his shoulders until he was sitting. I could see that he was aroused by the way his grey uniform tented across his groin, so I unzipped his trousers and let his erection spring free. He started to lift the box from his head, but I pressed down on the top of it with one hand, to let him know that I was in charge, before I straddled him, lowering myself gently onto him, pulling the panties to one side and guiding him inside me with my other hand. First his hands gripped the arms of the chair, then they moved forwards blindly to touch me. I felt his fingers slide across the fabric of the dress, then reach underneath to find my skin and move up until they located the edge of the basque. Then they crept down again until his right hand made a soft fist against my clitoris and I could feel his knuckles moving gently against me, and his left hand teased my pubic hair.

I was glad I'd chosen the pumps, I couldn't have done this in heels.

I braced my feet against the floor and began to rise and fall on him, not able to move too much or the wheeled chair would slide away from me. It was excruciatingly good to have to be so limited, so careful, and each movement brought a mini-explosion of pleasure. Very soon I could feel myself about to orgasm and just as I wondered how the hell I was going to come without sending the chair skidding away from me at the crucial moment, Stephen grabbed my hips and pulled me forwards until I could feel the boned edge of the basque pressing against his lower abdomen and like that, all off balance and tangled together, gazing into the blank surface of a cardboard box, I came.

And just as I was wondering what to do next, I heard the chiming of my computer.

I looked at my watch – 4.30, time for my SSC meeting!

I grabbed the box off Stephen, and dragged him out into the hall. 'Listen,' I whispered, 'I've got a meeting. Now I want you to stay quiet and still and be as good as gold and then maybe I won't tell your boss what a naughty boy you've been. In fact, I might even let you come, next time – OK?'

He pouted. 'I'm not so great at staying still.'

That was when I made him sit on the floor behind the chair. I grabbed a big hank of green ribbon and tied his ankles to the base of the chair. 'Just coming,' I warbled into the microphone, 'I'm having a bit of a problem with my webcam. Be right with you!'

I sat down and twisted round to look at Stephen. 'Remember what I said.'

He smiled devilishly. 'Yeah, you said you were just coming.'

And that was why, when I slapped the button connecting me to the virtual meeting, I had a courier tied to my chair, a brand-new, expensive set of underwear and a Spree Shoppers Confidential meeting to get through.

'My name is Elva and I'm a spree shopper,' I said. Stephen's tongue began its journey and I froze, unable to think of a single word.

'Elva? Talk to us!' Sarah demanded.

'Sorry, I'm ... a bit overwhelmed actually. It's really great how close to you I feel,' I said, as Stephen's fingers slipped under the lace of my panties and began to play in my pubic hair. From behind me I heard a low sound, a little like a groan.

'Is that a cat, Elva? I didn't know you owned a cat,' Sarah said.

'Oh, it's only this tomcat who creeps in from time to time – I don't seem to be able to keep him out,' I said, as Stephen's fingers slipped inside me and his thumb began to circle my clitoris. He growled again.

'Oh, it's purring, isn't that nice,' said Malcolm.

'Look, perhaps you lot could do your bits first and then I'll be ready,' I said.

Below me, Stephen made a noise like a tomcat on heat and then whispered, 'You feel ready now, to me.'

I leant back and wrapped my hand around his mouth to shut him up. Then I braced my feet on the chair supports so he could slide his fingers deeper inside me, and I set the rhythm for his pulsing thumb on my clit by pressing my own thumb against his lips, so when Sarah said, '... and in conclusion, let's all congratulate Elva on her first shopping free week,' my cries of delight could be heard quite clearly, and I hope they thought I was simply excited by my success. And in a way, I was.

A short story by Carmel Lockyer also appears in Wicked Words *Sex and Music*.

Changing Rooms Kate Pearce

Julia Marcham studied her reflection in the three unforgiving mirrors of the changing room. She'd given up trying to be thin in her teens after realising she liked the food she ate to stay in her stomach rather than be flushed down the toilet. The cruel fluorescent light made her skin look pale and highlighted the faint glints of silver in her dark-brown hair.

'I look like crap. Everything I try on me looks like crap.'

'I beg your pardon, miss?'

Julia turned to confront the sales guy who stood in the doorway of the cramped changing room. He wore the store uniform of a white open-necked shirt, which looked good against his tanned skin and tailored black pants.

She spread her arms wide in a gesture of despair. 'It's Ms and look at me.'

He looked, his grey eyes moving over her with a deliberate seriousness. 'You're right. That dress does look like crap.'

She struggled to get at the zipper on the side seam under her arm. 'That's not what I said –' she glanced at his name tag '– Tom, the dress is fine. It's what I'm trying to squeeze into it that's causing the problem.'

He came to help her with the zipper, his long fingers sliding against her bare skin as he carefully eased the teeth apart. She breathed in the scent of his aftershave, Calvin Klein if she wasn't mistaken. At the nape of his neck, his black hair was cut ruthlessly short as if to resist a natural urge to curl.

He straightened before she gave into an urge to lick the spiky strands. She reckoned he was six foot tall, four inches more than her and a good few years younger than her thirty-three.

He hesitated, the dress in his hands. 'If it's OK with you, I can help. It's not busy tonight. Can you tell me exactly what kind of an outfit you're looking for?'

Julia studied his calm face and took a deep cleansing breath. His relaxed manner was beginning to rub off on her. And dammit she was desperate.

'I need a dress that will make me look ten years younger and two dress sizes smaller. I have to attend a party. My ex-husband and his new pencil-thin bimbette are going to be there.'

Tom nodded as if he completely understood. 'And you want to dazzle him with your immense style and beauty.'

Julia smiled. 'Well, I'd like to pretend I have those things for a few hours.'

'You do have them. The first thing you need to do is believe it.' He touched her arm. 'Turn around for me. I want to get a good feel for your body shape.'

OK, so she hadn't expected confidence-building techniques as well as dress suggestions but she was worried enough to listen to anything. She finished revolving, feeling like one of those tiny ballerinas on a music box.

'You have a great figure.'

Her eyes snapped open. 'I do not.'

'You're the perfect hourglass.' He whipped out a tape measure. 'Let's see if I'm right.' He slid the tape around her plain white cotton bra. Her nipples hardened against the cold plastic. 'Thirty-six.' He lowered the tape to encircle her waist. 'Twenty-six.' Somehow he pulled her even closer before he dropped the tape to her hips. 'Thirty-seven.' He held the tape in place and trapped her against him. 'I'd say that was pretty damn close.'

She looked up at him as his body heat warmed her flesh. 'Men don't like this shape any more. They like sticks on endless legs.'

'That's where you're wrong. Some guys pretend to like

that kind of woman because they think they should. Trust me, most men prefer what you've got.'

A slow sense of excitement burned through Julia's stomach as he held her captive with the tape. Her body leant into his until her nipples grazed his white shirt front. She wanted to rub them against his chest until he groaned and offered to suckle them instead.

'So do you have any suggestions?' Her voice sounded husky and full of promise.

'Yeah, I do. But if you're going to go for this, then let's do it right. Let's start from the top.'

He picked up her belongings and ushered her along the narrow corridor to the very end of the squashed cubicles. With a flourish, he produced a key. 'This changing room is for our special clients and, tonight, you're one of them.'

Julia stepped into the thick carpeted space and simply stared. The stark white scarred walls and unforgiving mirrors were replaced with beige and cream walls, subdued lighting and elegant furniture. She dropped her purse on the chaise longue as Tom deposited her possessions on one of the chairs.

'This is nice. I can't say I've ever been in a changing room like it before. You could get a pool table in here and even play.'

Tom smiled at her as she took in the four mirrors, one on each wall. He gestured at a table in the far corner. 'Tea and coffee on the table. Help yourself. I'll be back in a minute.'

Julia helped herself to the excellent coffee and then lay back on the chaise longue. Tom seemed like a nice guy. Would he really be able to find her something outstanding to wear? He was right, of course. Beauty came from within. If she didn't believe she was desirable, how on earth was she going to convince anyone else? For a while, after her husband ditched her, she hadn't felt anything at all. But it was time to get over him. It was time to clean out the last remnants of her old life and get on with the new.

It was warm in the room and she started to relax. She almost jumped when the door opened to reveal Tom, his arms full of boxes. He managed to settle everything on the floor without dropping a thing and, as a bonus, gave Julia a nice view of his tight little butt as he bent over.

He straightened and turned to face her. 'I think I got everything, Ms . . .?'

'After all the help you're giving me, you can call me Julia.' She held out her hand and he shook it, his fingers firm and steady over hers. He extracted a large pink box from the tangle on the floor and placed it on the table.

'First things first. You have to get the foundations right.'

Julia patted her cheek. 'I have foundation.'

His charming smile warmed her. 'That's funny, but I think you know what I mean. The garments you wear under an outfit are just as important as the ones people get to see on the outside.' He held out a flesh-coloured silk and lace bra. 'I reckon you must be at least a C cup. Try this one on.'

Julia took the bra without thinking. It was sheer and underwired and slightly padded. 'Is this one of those bras that makes everything sit up and beg?'

He moved behind her and ran his fingers down her bra straps, stopping when he reached the swell of her breasts. 'We call them sheepdog bras.' He cupped her breasts drawing them higher and pressed them together. 'You know, round 'em up herd 'em together and pen 'em tight.'

She shivered as he weighed her breasts in his palms. Would he scream and run when she unhooked her bra and revealed silicon-free, gravity-prone real woman flesh?

As if he sensed her indecision, he held her gaze in the

mirror. 'You're going to have to trust me here. I can leave you to shop alone if I make you nervous.'

Still staring at him, she undid the front clasp of her bra. He let out his breath, the force of it warm against the nape of her neck. He returned his hands to her breasts; his thumbs covered her nipples.

'Sometimes I pray that I'll come back as a bra in a future life.'

Julia relaxed her shoulders and allowed her breasts to rest more firmly in his hands. 'Not as a pair of panties?'

'Well, maybe a matching set.' After another subtle caress, he released her and took the old bra out of her unresisting grasp. With deft hands he gathered her breasts, adjusted the straps and hooked her into the new one.

'Hey, I have cleavage!' Julia squeaked. OK, maybe Tom had a point. Her breasts definitely looked great trussed up in the fussy little bra. For a change they were nearer her chin than her stomach. 'What do you think?'

He remained behind her. His hands rested at her waist as if they belonged there.

'You don't think it's a little too much?' Julia shivered as he studied her in the mirror.

'I like it. The soft colour makes your skin look great and I love the way the fine gauze at the top hints at your nipples but doesn't actually show them.'

Julia took an experimental breath. Although her breasts threatened to overflow the fragile structure they remained covered. Behind her, Tom went still. She realised why when she felt the press of his erection against the swell of her butt. Not gay then like most of the guys who worked in women's wear, despite his dress sense and fabulous looks. Lust threaded through her and not in a bad way. Getting a rise out of a handsome guy wasn't something she was used to.

She licked her lips and stayed put, allowing him the

intimate contact. 'So is there anything else I need to go with this bra?'

He cleared his throat. 'If you're going to really kick ass, I'd suggest stockings and high-heel shoes. You want your ex to be wondering what the hell is going on under your dress. You want him to catch a glimpse of stocking, a hint of cleavage, a whiff of your perfume. You want him to want you.'

Julia nodded slowly. 'Yes, that's exactly right. I want him to want what he can't have and realise what he's thrown away.'

Tom met her gaze in the mirror. 'By the time we've finished, the guy you take to the dinner party is going to be all over you.'

'And that will make my ex even madder.'

They smiled at each other in perfect accord.

He opened another of the pink boxes and picked out a suspender belt which matched the bra. 'Do you want to try this on?'

Julia stepped out of her panties. Tom knelt in front of her. His unshaven cheek brushed her stomach and she shuddered. He placed the belt around her hips and settled it in place. She could smell her own arousal, wondered if he could to. His mouth was so close to her sex.

'If you sit down, I'll help you put on your stockings.'

Julia stretched like a cat as she sat on the edge of the chaise longue. Having a beautiful man dress you was certainly enough to get her juices flowing. She imagined he was her slave, his naked body oiled and ready for her.

'Do you work out?' The question escaped her before she could stop it. Jeez, now she sounded like a fourteen year old.

'Yeah, I do. Can you tell?'

She deliberately took her time checking him out as he gathered the first stocking on his hand. She wanted to push him a little, see what he would do. 'I'd see better, if you took off your shirt.'

She held her breath. Here it was, the moment of reckoning when he had to decide whether he was willing to go along with her or rapidly retreat.

'How about you unbutton my shirt and take a look while I put this stocking on for you?'

Julia allowed him to place her foot on his knee and then leant forwards to work at the first button of his crisp white shirt. His fingers felt delicious as they glided up her leg stretching the thin silky stocking until it reached the soft skin of her inner thigh. His fingers brushed her mound as he attached the stocking. Three of his buttons undone now. With two more to go before his shirt disappeared into his pants.

He lifted her other leg, set to work on the next stocking, as she undid the remaining buttons. She admired the soft silken sheen of her legs and the sight of his bent head between them as he carefully adjusted the stocking on her thigh.

'You'll have to let me undo your belt.'

He glanced up at her, kept his hands on her thighs. 'OK.'

She moved closer, and struggled to release the clasp. He groaned low in his throat as she tugged at his shirt. The front of his shirt was wet with pre-come, the crown of his cock tried to force its way out of his pants.

Julia touched the wet tip with one finger. He was big, much bigger than her ex. She opened the last button and exposed his chest. Damn the man was fine. Black chest hair, not too much of it, well-defined abs and soft-brown nipples which were already tight.

'Should I stand up and see how everything fits?'

Tom shook his head. 'We're not done yet.' Without turning, he drew a shoe box out of the pile on the floor. Inside were strappy red shoes with four-inch heels.

'I'll be about six foot if I wear those.'

'How tall is your ex?'

'About five ten.' He stared at her, one eyebrow raised.

'Oh my God, I'll tower over him in these. What a great idea.'

He drew a scrap of silk out of his pocket. 'You'll need panties as well.'

Julia frowned at the three strings and triangle of lace. 'They're not really qualified to be real panties. They have no side and no back.'

Tom dangled them in front of her on one finger. 'But they have their advantages for your date and you get no VPL.'

She allowed him to slide the strings up her legs and lifted her hips so that he could arrange them around her butt. 'No visible panty line I understand, but how will my date benefit?'

'I'll show you.' He placed his hands on her knees and pushed them apart until he could fit his shoulders between them. 'Let's imagine I'm your date for this dinner party. And let's suppose I watched you get dressed and know exactly what you're wearing under your beautiful dress.'

He touched the triangle of satin with his finger and thumb. 'I'm going to be hard and ready to fuck the whole evening.' He circled his fingers over her clit and caressed her until she could see it through the cloth. 'Do you think I'm going to wait all night to get a taste of you?'

Julia angled her hips forwards, inviting his touch, needing it. He bent his head, pushed the satin aside, and licked her already swollen clit. A shock of pure lust surged through her. She slid her hand into his hair.

'If I was your guy, I'd find a quiet spot and go down on you until you came in my mouth. Preferably somewhere your ex could catch us.' He circled her sex with the hard tip of his tongue and kept licking her into his mouth. After a while, he added two fingers and slid them deep inside her. She felt herself build towards an orgasm, tried to trap his head between her thighs.

He pulled back, his face in the soft light wet with her

cream, his pupils dilated so that almost no grey colour was left. 'If I was your date, what would I do? Stop now and leave you wanting me or carry on and let you come?'

Julia smiled at him. 'You'd let me come so that when we got back to the other guests they'd all know from the look on my face that I'd been sexually satisfied and didn't need my ex any more.'

He grinned at her and ducked his head back down. 'I hear you.' His quick clever mouth moved over her again and she let go, grinding her sex into his face as her climax thundered through her. He kept lapping at her, brought her back down slowly, gentling his touch until she opened her eyes and sighed.

'OK, you've convinced me to go for the bra, the ridiculous panties, the stockings and the suspender belt. What's next?'

Tom got to his feet and wiped his face on his handkerchief. 'You forgot the shoes.'

Julia stood up. Thanks to the shoes, her eyes were almost level with his. 'Oh yeah, the shoes. They work for me too.'

He swallowed as she cupped his balls and erection through his pants. 'If you're going to help me find a dress, the least I can do is help you get rid of this.' She smiled into his eyes as she slowly unzipped his pants. His cock was hard and ready for her. Bigger than her ex's, bigger than she'd ever had before. 'I've always had this fantasy about going down on a man half-naked in a changing room.'

He smiled as she grasped him around the base of his shaft and sunk to her knees. He was already wet as she delicately licked the crown and penetrated the swollen slit with the tip of her tongue. His hips jerked forwards, pressing him against her closed mouth. When she glanced up, he looked almost desperate.

'I promise, if you let me come in your mouth I'll find you the best dress you'll ever own.'

'And I promise you this will be the best blow job you will ever have. We older women have skills a bimbette can only dream about.' She drew him deep into her mouth and towards the back of her throat. He felt huge and deeply satisfying. She loved the feel of a man's cock in her mouth, the texture, the taste and the hardness. She loved making a man come.

He groaned as she sucked and dug her fingers into his muscled buttocks. She wished her ex could watch her through one of the mirrors on the walls. She'd love him to be hard and unsatisfied. He'd always said she had the mouth of a hooker. Tom shuddered and pushed his hips forwards as his come flooded her throat.

She waited until he stopped thrusting and gently released him. He gave a shaky grin.

'Hey, I think that qualifies you for the staff discount.'

He helped her stand and drew her into his arms. She laid her head on his shoulder and allowed herself the luxury of being held. His heart bumped comfortably beneath her cheek until it resumed its regular rhythm.

'Are you ready for the dress now?'

He tucked in his shirt and zipped his pants before turning to the largest of the stacked boxes.

Julia frowned. 'You only brought one?'

'Yeah, but this is *the* one. Trust me.'

He brought out a dress with an A-line cut skirt and a deep V-neck bodice. It was made of silk in Julia's favourite blue-red, a colour she used to wear a lot.

'It's not black. I need black. I'm too old to wear red.'

He frowned right back at her. 'Now that *is* crap. You look great in red.' He walked towards her, his expression purposeful. And how exactly was she supposed to resist a gorgeous hunk of a man who'd just given her a spectacular orgasm?

With a sigh, she allowed him to lower the dress over her head and settle it around her hips. He turned her to face one of the mirrors and she reluctantly opened her eyes. She almost didn't recognise herself.

'I look ... OK.'

He studied her reflection in the mirror. 'No, you look fucking fantastic.' He brought a chair and set it next to her. 'Humour me. Put your foot up on here.'

She did what he asked and realised that she could see herself reflected in all four mirrors. He kissed her mouth, the scent of his aftershave mingling with the baser smell of sex. Her legs looked impossibly long in the four-inch heels and sheer stockings. He circled her, one hand cupping his groin.

'Let's imagine you are at that dinner party again. It's late in the evening, you think all the other guests have gone and you are alone with your guy in the dining room.'

She closed her eyes as he stopped behind her. 'And I have my foot up on the chair because ...?'

He stroked the back of her calf. 'Because your shoe was loose and you wanted to tighten it before we left.'

'Of course it was, I get it now.' She bent forwards towards her shoe, arching her back and pushing her butt closer to his body. 'And?'

'And you succeed in distracting me. My cock is already hard for you. So I slide my hand up the back of your leg, like this, until I reach the top of your stocking.' She shivered at the cool touch of his fingers as he caressed her skin. Her body was already heating, readying itself for more pleasure.

'You are wet now, because I've already tasted you earlier in the evening.' He touched the string of her panties. 'I know you are ready for sex. I'm thinking I could fuck you real fast before we leave.'

Her nipples tightened into two aching buds as he carefully folded her dress out of the way and bared her buttocks.

'I'm wondering if you will let me.'

She reached back to grab his hand and placed it firmly over her breast.

'No one will come in here, they'll think we'll be in the hall or that we've already left.'

His fingers slid underneath the tiny satin triangle of her panties. He angled her knee slightly to one side so that she could see his fingers working her sex in the mirrors.

'Christ, you are soaking. I need to fuck you so bad. I'll be quick.'

She tensed as she heard his zipper opening and the rip of a condom packet. How would he feel at this angle? He was so big.

He gripped her hips; she saw his face in the mirror, not as calm as before, his focus and determination unmistakable. She bent her head and watched his cock slide inside her. Her sheath clamped around him and he groaned.

'This'll be quick. I'm too turned on. I promise I'll make it up to you later.'

Julia rocked as he withdrew and plunged forwards again, his strokes long and fluid. He continued to hold her hips as he thrust deeper. Her sex tightened around him and she fought off the urge to climax. She pictured the dining room and the door opening to reveal the shocked faces of her hosts and her ex and his girlfriend.

'I think we have company.'

Tom kept his pace even, his right hand dropping to play with her sex. 'Do you want me to stop?' He held still, only his fingers kept moving. Julia imagined the look on her ex-husband's face. She rubbed against his fingers and crushed them into her swollen flesh. 'Oh, God, no. Let them see what I'm really like.'

Her climax crashed over her, making her sheath spasm and clench around his still-thrusting cock. Tom came too, only his hands at her waist stopping her from falling forwards off the chair. He slumped over her before bringing them both down to the floor.

She gave him an embarrassed grin. 'I'll have to buy all this stuff, now. It probably needs dry-cleaning.'

He touched her cheek, his expression tender. 'Don't forget, you get the staff discount.' He helped her up, out of her party clothes and repacked them in their respective boxes. It took her no time to don her street clothes. She went to gather the boxes up but Tom stopped her. With a grin, he backed her up against the wall.

'So now we've played out your fantasy, are we OK to go to this fucking dinner party tonight or not?'

She kissed his cheek. It really was a bonus dating the son of the owner of one of New York's most prestigious stores. Still, Tom must have worked miracles to arrange all this for her. Busy running one of his father's companies, he hadn't actually worked on the shop floor for at least ten years. She studied his face, the hint of passion that lingered in his grey eyes, the hard youthful firmness of his body as he pressed her against the wall.

'I think I'm ready to go now.' She ran her finger down the zipper of his pants. 'That is, if you promise to fulfill the new set of fantasies you've just planted in my brain.'

He smiled down at her. 'Baby, I'm looking forward to it.'

Kate Pearce is the author of the Cheek novel, *Where Have All the Cowboys Gone?*

Grandmother's Teapot
Madelynne Ellis

Birthday time again. That means another round of shopping in the china section of the local department store and, as usual, probably ending up at the factory outlet among the seconds. My grandmother, dear old thing, is not entirely with it most of the time, but she's still batty about teapots: whimsical, stylish, oriental, classical, she's got it, and she expects one from each of us every birthday, without fail. And God help us if she gets a matching pair. Co-ordination is the key, and I don't just mean with each other. We have to make our visits to her domain too, just to memorise all the teapots on display. It's a job that I'm especially lousy at. Teapots, I ask you. I don't even drink tea.

So, it's Saturday afternoon, my last chance to find a present before the birthday gathering tomorrow. I'm browsing Debenhams' china section, phone in hand, to check what's on offer against my photographic cataloguing attempt. Good job Grandma seems to have missed the mobile phone revolution. She never realised that I was snapping pics during my last visit. Not that all these hazy pixels are helping much; the range here is pitiful. And I'd swear I'm looking at the same display as last year.

That's when I walk into Richard. And I mean walk into. Balance recovered, nervous greetings exchanged, we fall into step, side by side, phones before us, flicking through near identical images.

'You know she hides some of them, don't you?' he says.

'Did you get the one in the pantry?' I ask.

'Yep, and the one masquerading as a flowerpot in the bathroom. I spoke to Aunt Val the other day, and she says there are another five in the coal shed hibernating with the tortoise.'

'Grandma has a tortoise?'

Rich nods sagely. 'I think it's concrete.'

'This is hopeless!' I snap my phone shut and glower at the price tag on a cobalt-blue sugar bowl.

'Feeling rebellious?' Rich asks, following my gaze. 'Coffee?'

'Hell, yes.'

Two cappuccinos, a chocolate muffin and an eclair later, and I suppose I ought to explain who Richard is, because, well, we're not actually related. Rich was Gran's first and last attempt at fostering. Nobody else in the family thought it was a good idea. I mean, what single 55 year old wants to take on a troubled teen? Still, Gran had a way about her. Still does as far as teapots are concerned. Anyway, Rich turns up, all straggly black hair and attitude, and, oh, be still my beating heart. I was in lust and, well, he was trouble.

Seven years I've been chasing him. I watched him date four of my best mates before I got so much as a peck on the cheek, and that was Christmas with Gran holding the mistletoe. But I guess I haven't exactly been a prize catch, not until recently when I miraculously scooped a job and a life. I had a set of straight As and a First, but no fashion sense or musical taste worth mentioning. Rich on the other hand has always been the king of grungy cool. Skate/punk/surf/whatever. I've never been entirely sure. All I know is that the floppy fringe that masked his smoky eyes set my pulse alight, and a glimpse of his biceps or chest would inspire hours of daydreaming. I didn't masturbate in those days. I never had the guts, but it's amazing what you can do with imagination and a pillow.

'So, what's your plan?' he asks, as he licks cake crumbs from his thumb. I watch, mesmerised by the motion of his lips. It's only a short step to his bare throat. Some of the piercings have come out these days, and I'm more likely to see him in a business suit than faded combats and a ripped T-shirt. But he still has that magical allure that makes me want to explore the contours of his face, and draw him into a deep hungry kiss. I wonder if he'll get dressed up for Gran's party.

'No idea. Factory shop, maybe.'

His brow creases. 'You'd get Lily –' that's my gran '– a second? Cheapskate!'

I turn away from his gaze, feeling a bit mortified. 'I've got a student loan to pay off.'

'So have I.'

I bite into the remains of my eclair, determined to look aloof despite the blush I can feel spreading across my cheeks. Rich just laughs. 'Hey, I've got an idea,' he says. He swings his chair onto its back legs and points up at the poster on the wall behind me. 'We could make one?'

'Excuse me?' I turn to face the poster, which informs me in a combination of brown and orange swirls that there's a pottery exhibition on at the museum, with workshops where you can throw your own pot. And he calls me a cheapskate! At least I was going to part with some cash. 'So what, we're just going to head over there and throw a teapot? I doubt I could manage an ashtray.'

'It'd be original,' he coaxes, already pulling on his jacket.

'It'll be a bloody mess.'

He holds my coat open for me, and buttons the front. When his fingertips graze my skin a frisson of energy charges down from my throat to my cunt. 'Live a little. She'll love the fact that we've tried.' He takes my hand, and that's it, I'm lost in some rose-tinted haze. Live a little! What I'd like to do is live a lot. I'd like to take him home and exchange Mr Bear for Mr Bare.

By the time we reach the museum, there's a certain anticipatory heat between us. Everyone remembers that scene in *Ghost*, where Patrick and Demi get all smoochy at the wheel. Rich is still holding my hand when we sit down after our two-minute crash course. I reluctantly let go of his fingertips. My palm is sticky and warm. I surreptitiously bring it to my mouth, breath in deep and flick my tongue across the palm, imagining I'm licking his skin. I want to taste him so badly. I want to bite into the muscle of his shoulder, draw loving caresses across his chest and tease open the buttons of his fly one by one until the treasures beneath are revealed.

Neither of us has ever done this before. Rich peddles and I throw. The clay is soft and oozes sensuously over my fingers; with only a hint of pressure it responds to my will. A shape grows up from the flared base. I run both hands up and down the column of clay, my gaze flicking back and forth between the sculpture and Rich's expression. I guess it's pretty obvious what my mind is focused on. I try not to meet his eyes.

'Funny shape for a teapot,' he remarks.

My gaze remains at groin level. 'This is the spout,' I say, as I trace my thumb lovingly back and forth over the tip, while imagining his cock poking rudely from his fly.

Rich's attention is fixed upon the motion of my hands. His foot pumps hard making the wheel spin faster and my up and down rhythm grow frantic. I want to be working him, not clay. I'm seeing his skin darken, and hearing his breathing turn into a pant.

Abruptly, Rich stops peddling, and the clay column crumples.

'Not bad,' the instructor commiserates, hurrying us off so she can install another pair. She doesn't even bother to remove my artistic impression of brewer's droop from the wheel.

'What now?' I ask Rich as I wash off the clay. Maybe he'll slip his hands inside my shirt, tweak a nipple and conjure a teapot like some street magician. Then we can forget this crap, and he can take me home to bed.

'Flea market,' he announces instead.

The second my hands are out of the water, he drags me across the street towards the most decrepit building in town. I'm itching even before we cross the threshold, just anticipating the world's worst jumble sale, patronised entirely by bag ladies and whiskery men in string vests.

Actually, it's not nearly that bad. Inside, the hall is divided into a collection of tiny curio shops. Rich obviously knows his way around. He leads me through the narrow aisles past the goth stall with plastic bats and made-to-measure coffins, past the indie vinyl dealer, the used-book dealer and finally at the back to Pottery Palace. Which I have to say is false advertising. Killer Crockery would be more accurate, considering the alarming angles of the shelves.

'Normally I try this place first.' Rich gets out his phone. 'It's always good for a bargain.'

The stall owner, a matronly woman in a chintzy smock, nods appreciatively.

'Well don't just stand there.' He gives me a playful shove. 'I'll take the shelves, you do the boxes.'

I realise immediately that this involves standing with my butt in the air or scrambling about on the floor beneath the tables, but what the hell, I do as instructed. Grandma's worth it, and so is Rich. I flash him a smile, and wiggle my arse as I bend over, then pretend not to notice his eyebrows twitch in response.

Most of the china collection is composed of incomplete tea sets, chipped milk jugs and the occasional gravy boat. It's ten minutes before I even get a glimpse of a teapot beneath the lurid 70s tablecloths, and then it's one Gran already has.

Rich doesn't seem to be faring any better, and we're

taking so long the stallholder starts shifting impatiently from one foot to the other. Finally, she shoves the money-box into a drawer.

'Pay the bloke next door. I'm going for a bacon butty and a cuppa.'

I'm about ready for another drink, myself. The dust in here is incredible. I lick my lips, ready to suggest to Richard that we quit, when I find it. The most hideous, squat, evil-looking teapot you could ever imagine. It's the unfortunate offspring of the night Salvador Dali met H. R. Giger. The thing is so appalling that I can't stop looking at it. My gasps of incredulity bring Rich to my side.

'What is it?'

'Erm . . .' I hold the misshapen beast out towards him.

'Are you sure that's a teapot?'

'Well, it's got a spout and a handle.' I'm not entirely sure how you get the water inside, but hell, Grandma's not exactly going to make many brews with it. It just gets to sit on a shelf somewhere being a 'collectible'.

'Definitely different. Bravo you.' He lands his palm on my upthrust rear, nearly knocking me into the crockery. If that's not excitement enough, my heart starts to thunder as his fingers feather across the back pocket of my jeans. I've been waiting for this for so long, all I can do is open and close my mouth like a goldfish.

From my back pocket, he slides one finger down the seam between my cheeks. When he nears my cunt, I jerk upright into the tabletop. Ouch!

'Er, you're groping me,' I say, flailing.

'Am I?' He raises an eyebrow, then sinks to his knees as I turn around so we're virtually nose to nose, and all I can think is that I'm a bit slow today. A crack on the head has got to be at least worth a cuddle, and all I'm getting is a staring contest. I try not to strain forwards. I really want to lean in and force a kiss, except I'd really prefer it if he'd lean in and take charge.

'Wow! It can't be.' Rich jerks away before our lips even come close. He crawls along the floor and plucks the treasure from a box of porcelain ladies.

'That's not a teapot.' I press my knuckles into my eyes. We were so close. If only I'd had the nerve. 'It's a figurine.'

'It's a teapot.' His eyes briefly glaze. 'How the hell did it get here? Fuck! It must be a copy.' He tips the thing over and peers intently at the base. Evidently, from his smile, it's the genuine article. 'Amazing! Collectors snapped these up in two thousand and three. They only made thirty. I tried to get her one last year, but they were going for silly prices.'

'But what is it?' I tentatively place a hand upon his arm.

It's obvious, the minute he turns it around – a scene from the *Kama Sutra*.

'Oh, my God! Teapot porn! We can't give Grandma that.'

'Watch me.'

'I'd rather watch you do something else.'

It just slipped out.

Rich cocks an eyebrow at me, still holding the wanton teapot. 'Such as?'

My tongue is swollen. I flick it nervously across my teeth, then swallow slowly.

'Well?' He traces a finger across my cheek. 'What is it you're so desperate to see me do?'

'Masturbate,' I squeak. I've been thinking about it for years. Ever since I caught a glimpse of him one time as I crossed the landing at Gran's. I've never forgotten the way his bare cheeks clenched or the slick sound of his palm sliding up and down his shaft. 'But it's specific, and a bit perverse.' Shit!

'What, like here and now perverse?'

'Kind of.'

My nervous system starts a jig and, as if by magic, my

knickers are sopping. I wasn't actually thinking here and now. The stall owner could come back any moment, but I guess I'm in live dangerously mode today, or else the crack on the head has resulted in temporary insanity. And the right accoutrements are within easy reach.

'Right here, right now?'

I can't decide if he's really nervous or if he's just teasing me to see how wet he can make me. Chances are I already look like a slobbering beast. I wipe a hand across my chin just to make sure I'm not drooling.

'So this is what gets you off at night, is it?' And then I know he's laughing at me, but there's a hint of adulation too. Actually, the way he's eyeing me up me is weirdly wonderful. 'OK, I'll do it, if you show me your tits.'

I go rigid. 'No-o!' Despite the protest, I'm already mentally assessing today's underwear choices to see if they're up to scratch: plum-red twinset with panels of pink roses. Not my ideal choice for an exposé, but definitely acceptable.

Still going with the bump on the head theory, I cast several glances at the adjacent stalls to check there are no other spectators. They wouldn't be able to see me anyway without leaning over the table. Then slowly, I inch up my top.

'Very nice.' He feasts on the swell of my curves. 'Now lose the bra.'

'Rich.'

'Please.' He licks his lips. 'I need something to get me in the mood.'

Pretending to myself that I'm at home bathed in flattering candlelight and not on the grotty floor of some indoor market stall, I tip my breasts out of the underwire, and do my best Jane Austen ballroom flirt. Unfortunately my coyness isn't working because the moment the cool air touches my skin, my nipples crinkle and point towards him like the indiscreet lust indicators they are.

'Oh, yeah! I always knew you had great tits.' He

flutters his fingertips over his fly, where there's now a clearly appreciable swell. 'Now roll the nipples between your fingers.'

Hesitantly, I obey. He's supposed to be the one performing here, not me. Although, confession time, the way his eyes are feasting on the motion of my fingers is turning me on. Heat starts to build in my womb, and my breasts start to feel heavy and ripe. I could do the whole go-go dancer routine and jiggle for him, but instead I settle for, 'Your turn.'

Rich's superstar smile just broadens. 'OK, but you've got to stay like that.'

I freeze in the act of pulling my top down. Wicked, wicked boy. He leans in close, sucks one protruding nipple into his mouth, then releases it with a pop. Now I really am melting and trembling with seven years of unfulfilled desire, and I'm so glad I'm kneeling because my legs are weak.

Rich pulls back and his hand returns to his fly. I lick my lips as he slowly unveils his cock, imagining the taste of his skin, salty and musky and sweet as honey. I get one great glimpse of him as he pushes his hand inside his underwear and cups himself, but then his hand covers all the good bits. Still...

Shit! There's a grin on my face like a kid on Christmas day. I roll my shoulder in nervousness, which drops my jumper back over my breasts. Rich's eyebrows immediately shoot upwards. 'Up,' he demands.

'Let me see, then.'

He gives his hips a sly tight-arsed flamenco-style wiggle, which just inches the waist of his jeans down a fraction. The black denim clings to his snaky hips, but my vision is firmly focused on the V of flesh visible between the open teeth of his zip. This time, when he moves his fist along his shaft again, the head of his cock winks at me, hot and cherry red. Then his thumb comes over the top to gently massage the sensitive eye. He bites his lip to contain his gasp of pleasure. Slick and dewy his helmet shines. I want to lick him, love him, but this is no after-dinner tease. We're in a public place. Time is against us. He's going to be quick and, sure enough, his pulls sharpen into rapid jerks.

This is too quick for me, after all these years of fantasising. If it's going to be over soon I want a closer view.

I don't touch him, just shuffle up close and cup my breasts. The light in his eyes sparks with appreciation. He understands.

Iron dressed in velvet; his erection spears my chest. This close I can see everything. His slitted eye peaks at me from between my breasts. I can smell the rich musky heat of him.

Rich pulls my top tight across my collarbone, as he slides with slippery urgency. 'Wouldn't you like to come too?' he asks. His hands cover mine, and he uncurls my fingers from the flesh.

Taking each nipple between thumb and forefinger, while his palms cup the weight, he takes control.

Immediately my cleavage is raised and more pronounced. But I have my hands free too. Valiantly, I resist the urge to cop a feel of his tight arse. Instead, I push a hand inside my fly. Despite the comfortable ease with which I do this, it's a first. Never, ever have I performed like this for a man, never mind considered doing it in a public place. But I'm so hot my fingers glide over my nub without hesitation, sending divine swirls of steamy lust right through my abdomen and into my chest, to where Rich is thrusting. Within seconds, my clit is hard.

'Cool it,' Rich says.

I don't want to stop. I want to come, but something in his voice pulls me back from the edge and makes me ease off a fraction. His next breath comes out hard. Clearly he's struggling to hold back too. His face is flushed right across his cheekbones and brow, and there's a dry raspiness to his words.

'She's coming,' he hisses.

'Then come faster.' I breathe the words into his navel.

'Oh, Lordy!' He pumps harder and suddenly it's a mad dash to the finishing line before we get caught. On cue, my orgasm swells again, which is just as well because I can sense the stall owner's presence. But I'm there, and so is Rich. I watch his seed ooze in sticky jets from his body, so intimate, and so stickily pretty.

Rich's knees buckle. He braces himself against a table. 'This is not finished yet, no way,' he says as he draws away from the pearl necklace he's left across my breasts. Clumsily, he plants a kiss upon my lips. I can taste coffee and muffin, but time's up. A big wet smooch will have to wait, 'cause we need to get the hell out of here.

Rich plucks a paper napkin from somewhere and goes to wipe away the shiny dew. I slap him away, and rub the seed into my breast. I just manage to scoop my breasts back into my bra and pull down my top before the stall owner actually arrives. Rich turns his back to her to surreptitiously fasten his fly.

'Find anything,' she enquires. 'Must have done. You've been here a bit.'

'Yeah.' Rich hands her the woman and the behemoth. 'These two.'

I manage to control my mirth until we reach the front doors, but then that's it. The laughter bursts from me, full force, and I don't even mind the fact that it's started to rain.

'Where exactly did the perverse bit come in?' Rich asks. He's patting me on the back as if it'll help control the giggles.

'Teapots,' I manage to squeal. I hold up the bag containing our acquisitions, and he squints at them curiously a moment, then at me.

'Oh, I see.' He laughs. 'Guess I didn't quite hit the mark, then.' His face goes suddenly serious. 'You used to spy on me!'

I straighten and, holding his gaze, slowly nod. 'But it was only the once, and by accident.'

Rich sucks his lip, which makes him look ever so deliciously vulnerable. 'Coming over them always felt so much more subversive than smashing them.' Out of nowhere, there's a shadow behind his eyes, and I know he's seeing into his past. 'Lily was far kinder than anyone else I ever stayed with. At least she tried to understand, but she never understood my anger or how to deal with it. After the first few times I freaked out at her, I realised that I couldn't carry on or she wouldn't let me stay, so I found a different way of rebelling.'

'And her prized teapots just happened to be there,' I finish for him.

He nods.

'I definitely still think you should christen this one.' I draw *Kama Sutra* lady out of the bag.

'I can't believe you're such a little pervert.' He peers intently at me. 'Are you really only interested in seeing me wank?'

'I never said that was it.' I shrug. 'Hey, I've got my perversions, and I'm sure you've got yours.'

'So what happens after I come?'

I picture a saucer. My pink tongue lapping like the cat who got the cream. Unconsciously, I lick my lips, but Rich seems to be reading my thoughts. He starts to laugh again.

'It's not that funny.' I prod him maliciously.

'You want to lap up my cold jizz! Eeeuuww! Why don't we just bypass the wank and you can blow me and swallow?'

'Because . . .' My favourite all-occasion get-out clause. 'Just because.'

Because you denied me all those years ago when you kicked the door shut at Grandma's, so I never actually got to see you shoot your load.

'Fine,' he says. 'Tonight, then. At Lily's.'

* * *

Rich turns out in his full black finery: spray-on leather jeans, skintight T-shirt, baggy shirt and chunky kick-ass motorcycle boots. He's too beautifully scrumptious for words. I want to grab him and run upstairs the moment he sets foot through the front door, but I'm forced to wait while he does meet and greet with Gran and all the aunts.

Normally the teapots go on display the moment the guests arrive. My hideous contribution already has pride of place on top of the mantelpiece, but somehow Rich manages to avoid handing his over yet. Still, I have to squirm in my seat for twenty agonising minutes before we manage to sneak away.

We go up to Rich's old room, where coats are piled on the bed. Rich dumps them in a corner, while I jam a chair under the door handle. When I turn back, he's already on the bed, perched among the pillows.

'Now.' He coyly flutters his eyelashes.

'Now.'

He shrugs off the shirt and T-shirt, leaving behind some kind of tribal trinket on a leather thong, which then lies against his naked chest. I expected pewter, but he surprises me with jade. He's hairless, bare, apart from two slender silver hoops through his nipples. Later, I promise myself, I'm going to suck him and roll the rings around my tongue.

'And the rest,' I demand.

He's already hard by the time he takes off his pants. I perch on the end of the bed to look at him lying there, exposed for my pleasure, and the rush of seeing him touch himself while I'm still fully clothed is heady stuff. I'm thinking, I could really get off on this kind of control. Rich is too busy getting a rhythm to notice that I've awakened to a new kink.

There's no subtlety, no slow teasing strokes down his body like I'd make to arouse him. It's all straight to the root.

My breasts tingle with the memory of him thrusting

against me earlier as I watch his hand piston. But when I place the teapot on the bed between his thighs, he shakes his head and laughs. In fact, he's suddenly laughing so hard he seems to have forgotten what he's supposed to be doing.

'Stop it. Rich!' I climb onto the bed properly to give him one of my vicious rib prods, which works a treat, but not in quite the way I'd anticipated. His cock flexes in greeting, and he claps a hand around my wrist.

'You want it, you got it,' he says. 'But for the record. I'd much rather just fuck, because you've denied me that pleasure long enough already.'

Our eyes meet. I gulp. 'Denied you?'

'Yeah.' His voice is all syrupy, fudge sauce, chocolate-and-vanilla sundae scrumptious. Not that there's anything much vanilla about this little scenario. 'For years, every time I looked at you, you turned away. You never said more than two words to me when you came to visit, and I had to get Lily to help catch you with the mistletoe.'

Oh ... My ... God! 'You fancied me.' I glance down, but that just gives me an eyeful of his beautiful cock. 'I thought you hated me. You always went upstairs when I came around.'

'Yeah, and we both know what I was doing up here.'

'But, but ...' I flounder. 'You could have said something.'

'Right. And risk looking like a complete jerk when you told me to piss off. Yeah. I did my best, but I couldn't even get to you through your friends.'

'That's what Dawn, Tina and the rest were about?' I suddenly twig.

'All pushovers next to you. But not this time.'

His cock flexes between us, and somehow I'm on my back with him above me.

'So what do you say we agree that the teapots have seen enough action, and fuck instead?' he says, his smoky-grey eyes looking right into mine from about two inches away.

I'm stunned and confused, still coming to terms with his giant revelation, when he lifts my legs and strips off my knickers, then hooks them over the spout of the porno teapot. My skirt ends up around my arse. Two fingers dip into my heat, tease over my clit and push into my core. With precious urgency, his thumb rolls upwards and, from out of nowhere, the faintest hint of orgasm spikes beneath my skin. I'm so turned on by his lust for me, and by everything that's happened that I don't resist when his weight presses me hard into the duvet, and his cock slides deep into my cunt. I just writhe, loving it.

Rich lifts my top, exposing my breasts, then clamps my wrists above my head and slips me his tongue. His kisses match the driving heated urgency of his rocking hips. And whoah ... Heaven! All I can do is match his urgency as he rubs his totally naked body against my semi-clad one.

Sprays of stars crackle. Springs creak, and the head-board collides with the wall. They must be able to hear us downstairs.

'Are you all right in there?' The door handle rattles, and we both jolt in fright.

'We're fine, Aunt May.' Actually we're more than fine, because Rich is biting the pillow to contain his cries as his cock bucks and I'm on the edge of the precipice ready to fall.

'Well, hurry up. We're about to do the cake.'

'Will do.' Rich wedges a hand between us and finds my clit, which is enough to undo me completely. I come hard around his cock.

'What are you doing in there, anyway?'

'Just coming. We'll be two ticks.'

Madelynne Ellis is the author of the Black lace novels, A *Gentleman's Wager*, *The Passion of Isis* and *Dark Designs*.

Living Doll Primula Bond

'If I increase the payment will you do it all night?'

Robin flicks an imaginary speck off his pristine white shirt, gazing at a point just past Francesca's bare shoulder. His chin twitches, up and sideways, as she knew it would. He's found what he was looking for. His own absurdly handsome face, surely surgically achieved, reflected to infinity in the mirrored walls.

'You know I need the money.' She fingers the spaghetti-thin strap of her borrowed camisole. Robin plucked it from the New Collection rail when she arrived for work this morning and ordered her to wear it. Nothing else was said, but she knew that modelling the stock meant she was finally part of the team.

'You're not wearing it right.' He smoothes one neat eyebrow then moves round behind her. He takes hold of the velvet ribbon running beneath her breasts. He pulls it tight, jerking her about as if dressing a child. The lilac chiffon drifts and tickles her skin so delicately that she feels naked wearing it. Her breasts puff up through the fabric. She needs to take a deeper breath. He's crushing her ribcage. It would be heavenly being paid to prance about in couture fresh from a Parisian fashion house, if she wasn't so bloody cold.

'You have to emphasise the empire line.' As he brings his hands round to the front, his palms brush across her nipples and she jumps. He pauses, measuring the remaining lengths of ribbon. She closes her eyes. Her nipples are stiff as pokers. She holds her breath, hoping to hide her obvious response, wishing he'd hurry up. Her nostrils draw in the tang of his expensive cologne and that makes her nipples tingle. She's never been this close to her boss before. Never noticed how delicious he smells. But it's no good. She has to breathe out again.

'Keep still.' Robin fusses about, hands flying, not noticing that they keep nudging at her breasts. And there it is, the perfect bow, nestling voluptuously between them. 'I knew it. A perfect fit. I'm renowned, you know, for telling a woman's exact size from fifty paces.'

'I'll do it all night,' she says weakly, pulling away from him. 'But only because you don't pay me enough.'

'You're just a trainee sales assistant, Fran. The most junior we have. What do you expect?' Robin clears his throat and swerves round her to peer through the door at the cobbled street outside. 'When and if you reach managerial level you'll get a raise.'

'It's Francesca. And I still don't get the point of doing it all night,' says Francesca, rubbing the goosebumps on her arms. 'Nobody will see.'

'That's where you're wrong.' He opens the door and the little bell tinkles. A blast of cold air rushes in. It's meant to be summer, for heaven's sake. The sales start soon, which is why he wants this lot shifted. 'There's plenty of passing trade along Cute Street. It may be nothing more than a sleepy little alley by day, but it's also a cut-through from all the pubs and clubs. It's like Amsterdam round here after midnight. You'll see.'

'Amsterdam?'

'The stag nights. The whores in the windows.' He flourishes his arm to usher Fiona and Lottie in from their lunch break. They shrug their jackets off as they twitter their apologies for being late. Robin and Francesca both wince to see that the silk camisoles he also made them wear are now creased and smelling of smoke after being bundled in the pub for an hour.

He chews his lip as they bustle into the staffroom. For a rare moment he's lost in thought. The draught from the door is annoying Francesca and she fiddles with some hangers. She finds herself staring at Robin Fosdyke's butt. With his physique, if you knew no better, he could be a sportsman or a male model. She can see the muscles in his back, how broad his shoulders are when he's not constantly twitching and gesticulating. She must still be flustered from the way he accidentally touched her. Lovely hands. Her nipples are singing again. What a waste! Such a cute arse on a man with zero interest in women. She can just imagine those tight buttocks bare, clenching, pulling back, thrusting hard to fuck . . .

Her stomach twists with sharp desire. She bites her lip, tastes salt blood. And Robin presses the door shut.

'Hideous, they are.'

'Who?' Francesca dips into the fitting room to grab at her handbag. Her turn for lunch. 'Fiona and Lottie? Oh, they're just a bit overweight in those camisoles. They'd look better in the sailor jackets –'

'I was talking about the whores! In Amsterdam!' Robin's hands flap up to his ears and down again. 'They straddle these manky three-legged stools like ageing milkmaids, selling their wares to the salivating hordes. All illuminated with ghastly purple neon.'

They both turn to examine their own shopfront. Francesca has nearly finished dressing it. There are no hookers, no three-legged stools. No mannequins, even. Just a chaise longue upholstered in sumptuous red velvet, a riot of crystal-drop chandeliers and a pile of kimonos looking for a home.

'And if the ruse doesn't work?'

Robin flounces towards the antique desk in the corner, presses a key so that the till flies open. 'It's not a ruse, Fran. Or a gimmick. It's a marketing ploy. And it's our last chance.' He pulls out a wad of twenties, ruffles them under his nose. Francesca can smell the money. 'If you do it properly the punters – sorry, the customers – will be flooding in tomorrow morning, just *mad* for our petticoats.'

'But if they don't?'

He slams the till drawer shut and flourishes his arm to embrace the shop. 'Then Cute shuts, Fran, and we're all out of a job.'

She takes a break at a point when no one's passing along Cute Street, and lies down on the velvet chaise longue. It's past midnight now. She's been virtually motionless since the shop closed, standing as instructed in the window, hands resting on jutting hips, one finger hooking her diaphanous skirt right up her bare thigh to show the curve of her buttock. The old rose ball dress droops off one shoulder to seduce the passers-by.

It's a breeze. She spent last summer standing stock-still on an orange crate halfway up the Ramblas in Barcelona with all the other mime artists. She told Robin at her job interview how she decided to wear nothing but a coat of shimmering white paint and some see-through voile, and became the goddess Diana.

The best part of the act is the shock people get when you move. As the goddess Diana she'd aim her bow and arrow at a kid getting too close. Or shake her head very slowly, watching people's mouths gape open as she did so. Or once, when a guy reached out to poke at her, she licked her finger and ran it very slowly up her snatch.

As Cute's dishevelled mannequin she's already had some fun. The women are the obvious and best victims, because they notice more. Even scurrying down Cute Street after work they slow down, drawn like magnets to the intriguing boudoir she's created. If only Robin could see their reaction.

First they see a prim sprigged tea dress tossed across a pile of jade-green cushions as if impatiently discarded, unbuttoned to show an uplift burgundy bra and matching knickers. A row of Cute's signature baby-doll dresses hang from an invisible wire, dancing every so often in warm jets from the heater she's hidden behind the chaise longue. And several pairs of sequinned fuck-me stilettos are kicked about on the creamy fake-fur rug.

They're hooked by the display. She slides her hand down her leg to lower herself oh-so slightly into their eye line as they press their noses up against the glass. They don't see her immediately. They look past her at the two other mannequins positioned centre stage. One glares haughtily sideways, wearing a midnight-blue ruffle shirt and pair of mannish powder-blue capri pants. These are unzipped and the mannequin's hand is inside the trousers, tugging at a filigree lace thong.

The other doll is half turned as if trying to run away. It wears a virginal white flapper dress with strings of pearls dangling between its pointed breasts. It stares demurely downwards, but Francesca has rouged the nipples so they are clearly visible through the muslin. Not only that, but after Robin went home she used her mascara to paint a triangle of curly hair over the pubes and added shocking-pink stockings.

The early evening routine has been easy. A pair or group stops to ogle the flapper's saucy details, then lingers over the other clothes and shoes. One girl glances at Francesca, hovering mournfully in the background in her Cinderella dress. Francesca yawns. Unconsciously, the girl catches the yawn. So Francesca winks. Then the girl jumps, and elbows her friend to look, and Francesca smiles or shrugs her shoulder. Or lets a tear trickle down her cheek. And they giggle and twitter and wait for her to do something else, but she never does.

Just now a tall blonde girl in a tight white minidress and a deep fake tan started preening herself in the window. Francesca waited for a moment. Too much solitude. Time for some action. She was stiff and aching after all that controlled posturing. Keeping her hands on her hips she cocked her knee, very slowly, to step across the hidden fan heater. Then she bent over, Marilyn Monroe style, offering her cleavage to the world, the moons of her backside to the empty shop, and let the air billow the flimsy dress right up round her fanny.

The blonde girl froze, her hands caught up in her Brigitte Bardot hair. Francesca smiled, shivering with pleasure as the warm air blew up her legs. The heat was like fingers moving up her skin. She kept her eyes wide and unblinking like a doll's as she wriggled and parted her legs a little more under the swirling dress. The air ruffled the tight curls on her pussy. Her sex lips puffed open, the heat fondling her there.

The blonde's face was swimming in and out of focus. This reminded Francesca of her dancing days at drama school, the way she preferred to stare away her audience and her nerves so she could concentrate on her private moves.

Francesca allowed herself to blink, just once, and the blonde blinked back, lowering her arms. Francesca ran her hands up her thighs as the dress floated round her, tweaked the tiny scarlet knickers to one side but snapped them back again. The girl's mouth parted. Francesca bent lower, her breasts threatening to tumble out of the hand-sewn bodice. Now she could feel the warm air swooping up her body, too, teasing her nipples. She lifted her hands to fondle her breasts, which were now level with the blonde's face. She swayed, squeezing her breasts, tweaking at the frills over the bodice so that her already hard nipples popped out.

The blonde's fingers were fluttering down her neck. She was biting her lower lip. Francesca ran her tongue across her lower lip, too, to make it pout and glisten. Each one mirrored the other. The blonde pressed the palms of her hand against the window as if trying to push her way in, her breasts in the tight white dress squashed against the glass. Francesca dropped to her hands and knees and crawled nearer. Her breath, and the blonde's, made twin clouds on the glass.

There was a raucous burst of approaching male laughter. The blonde smeared a wet red-lipstick kiss against the window, then tottered away into the night.

The clock on the town hall has just struck midnight, and Francesca's tired and bored. The women were fun to tease, especially that sexy blonde, but none of the passing blokes has noticed the window. Why would they? Men aren't interested in pretty clothes. Well, not unless they're Robin Fosdyke. And now the women are out on the town. They're not in shopping mode at this time of night. She's going to have to tell her boss that his bright idea isn't going to work.

She lies back on the chaise longue and closes her eyes. Cute Street is deserted. Everyone's gone home. She adjusts the heater so that it blasts right up her body. She fingers the gorgeous ball dress. Robin let her choose whatever she felt appropriate for tonight. It's called the Cinderella dress because it's designed to look as if it's been shredded into beautiful rags.

She whisks the fragile chiffon back and forth across her thigh and instantly her pussy pricks and pulsates. The chiffon drifts off her breasts and her nipples prick once more into life. She arches her back with renewed pleasure, tipping them upwards in the soft warm wind. She opens her eyes and looks at herself. Her breasts are swelling out of the bodice and her nipples are standing up like raspberries, the colour of their arousal complementing the dusky pink of her dress. She smiles at the thought – raspberry for arousal – and strokes just her fingertips over the burning nipples. Oh, yes. Did she say that out loud? Electric currents shoot directly to her cunt.

She settles back, flicking her fingers over the red points, teasing herself. She cocks one knee, lets the other fall sideways. Again her pussy lips open. The heater breathes on her. She rubs the palm of one hand across her nipples, just peeking out of her bodice, and slides the other hand under the floating skirt. She can stop all this if she hears footsteps out on the street, become a posing mannequin again. It's all part of the story, didn't you know? Party girl sprawled on sofa, ravished and abandoned, dress falling off her.

Her fingers find the warmth inside her and it's so wet. She gasps as her fingernail scrapes against her clit. Her sex lips close round her fingers, starting to throb. Flurries of lust radiate up her as she strokes the tender skin. She arches her back, her head falling backwards. Somehow that accentuates the pleasure. She also knows it's a good balletic posture. She can hold it if need be. It will look deliberate, artistically composed, the three mannequins like a tableau in oil.

Her fingers are deeper inside now. Her pussy is trying to close round them in little frantic twitches. Her hips start to jerk with the sensation. The velvet is soft against her buttocks. Her fingers are busy, probing and sliding. The heater purrs, and she's moaning, or purring, too. Nobody can hear through that plate glass.

There's a scraping sound on the pavement. She's supposed to be standing up, but no point moving now. She'll slow down the action so you can barely see it, but no need to stop, is there? She's here to shock people. And she can't stop, anyway. So shock it is. Excitement is sparking through her. The scraping footsteps slow, and stop. It's been so long since she touched herself. She can make them think they're imagining it. Nobody will come barging in tomorrow and tell Robin it's a public disgrace, he should sort his window out. They'll think they imagined it. She presses her hand over her nipples, the points pricking into her palm. Her other hand is between her legs, hidden by the dress.

Someone is outside, peering in. She turns her head, snaps her eyes wide open. That'll spook them. But all she can see is a pair of legs. Male legs. Faded jeans cut low and loose to show a strip of flat brown stomach. A student? A builder? Musician? Hands shoved in pockets. Could be any kind of guy. But he's not going to show his face. He's standing halfway across the cobbled walkway, so his torso is in shadow. She can't know if he's seen the doll coming to life.

Well, let's give him a show, then. Let's see if he'll go straight home and buy this Cinderella dress for his girl-friend. The dress modelled by the masturbating man-nequin. A bubble of laughter swells in her throat. She runs her tongue over her lips, keeping the rest of her, her splayed legs, her jerking hips, totally still now. Her eyes will glitter in the spotlights. But a mannequin's eyes are supposed to be dead, aren't they? She parts her mouth, lets him see the glistening greedy saliva on her tongue. Runs her tongue over her teeth. The man's hands shift in his pockets. One pocket rips slightly, but he's still watching.

She waits a beat then starts her hand moving again, up and down between her legs, dropping her knee so that the dress falls away to show her hand fiddling inside the tiny knickers. The man's hands move also, and she can see the outline of his cock growing now, pushing up under his flies – oh, how good that would feel inching up inside her.

He's taking a step to the side, as if to move on. No, no. Francesca lifts her hand off her breasts, tugs the fabric away and there's a delicious whisk of heat over her. Her nipples spring upwards again and she leaves them exposed, lies back and shuts her eyes as they harden into points. Her hand moves faster between her legs and she looks through her eyelashes and sees he's still there so she works herself up until she's nearly there, too late realising her juices will run all over Robin's prize dress, but she's coming quickly. When she opens her eyes again the man in the jeans has gone.

It's 9.30 a.m., and Francesca's brushing her hair in the fitting room. She fell fast asleep on the couch, basking in the heat, her fingers still tucked inside her. She feels pretty good actually. Hopefully Robin won't know she fell asleep on the job. But there's no result yet. No queue of baying customers . . .

'And no fucking Lottie!'

Francesca gapes at Robin, who is prowling round the shop like a cat on coals this morning. He glares back at her. 'If she deigns to come in, she's getting the sack.'

There's something different about him today. It's his hair. Normally it's combed and waxed into a state of polished paralysis. Today it's sticking up all over like a little boy's bed hair. In fact, he could look almost cute if he wasn't done up like a Russian complete with epaulettes, frogging and black breeches.

'Right. If I'm a Cossack today, you can be the empress. Put this on.' He tosses her another garment from the New Collection rail, and goes to open up.

It's a biscuit-and-cream empire-line dress, trimmed with lace. A bit Jane Austen, but she may as well enjoy the clothes while she can. If last night's charade didn't work, she'll be in her combats and flip-flops and back out on the street quick as you can say catwalk.

She stretches and yawns, and drops the dress over her head. It fits perfectly. Her breasts lift sensuously, ready to spill over the low neckline and she twists about, admiring herself. She piles her hair up, like the blonde in the minidress did. She arches her throat, stretches her lips to show her flickering tongue, like a starlet posing for a camera. Last night was weird. She thrusts her tits out. She shivers. Weird, but fun. Her nipples are buzzing.

Then behind her in the mirror she sees Robin. The morning sun shafts straight into his eyes. They're tawny, like a lion's. Ridiculously long lashes. He's watching her through the gap in the curtain.

She flushes. He'd have gone mad if he'd seen her last night, wearing the most expensive dress in the shop and frisking herself in front of a lone male who was patently never going to come in and buy anything. Or maybe

Robin would have liked it. Maybe he'd have got turned on. Before she can stop herself she licks her lips, shimmies round, and whispers in a little Marilyn voice, 'How do I look?'

He doesn't dismiss her, as she expected. He comes closer, looks her up and down, slowly. Not with the habitual jerk of his head like an impatient blackbird. But lingeringly, as if he actually likes what he sees.

He fingers the lace just above one nipple, peels open the intricate folds, then says, in a low voice she's never heard before, 'Totally fuckable, as always.'

'What did you say?' She gasps, turns it into a silly giggle. 'Why, Mr Fosdyke . . .'

He opens his mouth to say something else. She wants him to repeat it, just so she's sure, but behind him the little bell on the shop door tinkles. Robin clicks his teeth. Then he lifts his wrist pointedly to check his watch. 'Lottie?' he barks over his shoulder. 'You're fired.'

But it's not Lottie. No fewer than five customers are piling in to the shop.

'It's the living doll!'

They jostle Robin out of the way, dragging Francesca out of the fitting room and twirling her round. 'We want whatever she's got!'

Francesca's glad Robin persuaded her to do it once more, because she's here again. The blonde.

It's much warmer out there tonight. It's Saturday. Word must have spread since the other night, because she's hardly stopped performing all evening. She's put on a different little act every time. She's smuggled in some wine and once she's grabbed her audience, each performance has become more risqué than the last.

But it's just her and the blonde right now. The blonde is wearing a tight purple vest and splashy printed ra-ra skirt. Robin would have a fit. But Francesca thinks those clothes are dead sexy. She's wearing the Cinderella dress again, and both girls are getting turned on, daring each other silently to see how far they'll go, mirroring each other's actions through the barrier of glass. Hands running up and down their legs, pushing further and further under their skirts. The blonde was the first to lift hers, show her waxed snatch. So it was Francesca's turn to get a shock.

Now she's on all fours. The blonde can't exactly crawl about in the street, but Francesca can crawl in her window. She's licking the pane where the blonde's mouth is pressed, and the blonde has tugged her vest down to rub her pink nipples up against the glass.

As Francesca wriggles with pleasure she feels her dress ruffling up over her bottom. She must be imagining it. Too much wine. Too much play-acting. But the blonde has pulled back. Her hand is clapped over her mouth, staring at something behind Francesca. Then the spotlights go out.

There's only the streetlight now, and the fringed red bordello lamp in the corner that Francesca plugged in earlier. Some sort of fuse must have blown. Robin will be furious. But now Francesca feels something else, a finger, maybe two fingers, running like spiders' legs over her buttocks and, yes, up her butt crack. She tries to fling herself round. But instead she's pushed roughly forwards. She catches sight of herself in the window, breasts half out of the dress, mouth hanging open more in desperation now than arousal.

The blonde is grinning now, her tongue caught in the corner of her mouth. Who the hell is in the shop? They haven't got a weapon, otherwise the blonde would be looking alarmed. Unless she thinks it's all part of the act. Or unless it's the blonde who's the thief, with some kind of accomplice who's broken in, come up behind Francesca and is touching her . . .

Any minute someone will come along the street. Francesca struggles to get up. She could scream for help, but no one will hear her. As she flounders on her knees the intruder slaps her hard. It stings, but then the sharp pain radiates into a shocking warm pleasure. She twists over her shoulder but all she can see is a pair of faded blue jeans as the guy kneels behind her. One pocket is slightly ripped.

'You watched me the other night,' she gasps, widening her eyes at the blonde to beg for help. But the blonde ignores her, curling a lock of her hair round one finger and swaying a little as if to invisible music. 'You like our clothes? Take what you want!'

Keep talking. You won't get hurt if you talk. But something hard, gun-shaped, is pressing up against her arse, moving from side to side to edge her butt cheeks open. Hands rub over her buttocks, sore where he slapped her, then on, up her ribcage. Don't rip the dress. Robin will kill me. The blonde is biting her finger, still grinning.

'Like the clothes?' There's a pause. 'I designed them.'

Francesca tries to focus on the reflection in the window. Her eyes are wide with confusion. Behind her there's just a shadow.

'Who the hell are you?' she demands hoarsely. 'Mr Fosdyke said nothing about any designer. You mean you've come from Paris . . .'

'No, no, no.'

He's unzipping his flies. She's not scared now. This is something to do with Robin, and the shop. He's pissed off with her. Sent someone along to catch her out, and punish her.

It's a cock wedged up between her buttocks. A warm heavy cock. She's trembling hard now. If this is Robin's idea of punishment, well, bring it on.

The man leans over her so that she's trapped inside the frame of his legs and arms. He brushes his hands, his fingers, his wrists, over Francesca's breasts, then cups them. The blonde bends low and scoops her own breasts out of her tight top, starts to fondle them just there in front of Francesca's face.

'Someone had to check on you.' He pinches her nipples hard. 'Your boss doesn't pay the window dresser to lap dance, does he, Fran?'

Her body recognises him before Francesca does. Her nipples shrink into hard points. Outside, the blonde is still swaying with her own private pleasure. Seeing her own naked breasts hanging there in the window, realising who he is, sends a shock of excitement through Francesca. She rocks herself against his caressing hands.

Footsteps approach along the street. The blonde turns her back and puts her mobile phone to her ear, shielding Francesca and her invisible lover. They keep perfectly still. Francesca's nipples are taut, and aching. Robin's cock – because it's Robin, isn't it? – nudges into her crack, growing thicker, hardening between her butt cheeks, pushing them apart. Francesca is breathless, fighting every urge to grind against him. This is her boss, Robin Fosdyke, kneeling behind her in the shop window, shoving his cock up her arse.

'They can see. People will see,' she gasps.

'So earn your keep. Let's give the punters a show they'll never forget!'

Sure enough a group ambles past. They glance at the window. Surely they can see? If he doesn't care, she doesn't care. It's his call. No such thing as bad publicity, after all. Francesca lets out a moan as the people move past, feels her legs slide open. He holds her steady, but starts to bend her forwards. The slight movement catches the eye of one of the men in the group outside.

Francesca is down on her elbows now, her backside up in the air. She wants to be watched. That's her métier: the performer, the artiste. The window is her private podium. She starts to rub her aching pussy against

Robin's stiff cock. Up to him, actually, to stop all this. And he's doing no such thing.

She's wet with excitement now. Her breasts are rubbing against the fake-fur rug, nipples burning with the friction, and she wriggles her hips with ferocious pleasure, bumping against his groin. He accepts the invitation, cupping her bush now and running one finger up the wet crack, pushing it between her pussy lips, circling slowly inside as if searching for something.

Francesca moans again. She can see the blonde's long bare legs and other legs and feet, too, on the pavement. But two more fingers dive up her. Her breath blows clouds on the cold window, blotting out any audience.

His knob is pushing into her now. She's opening up wider to let it in. He lifts her hips to meet him. His fingers thrust in, his stiff cock prodding up behind, and she's more than halfway there. She stretches her throat as another moan fills it, and she sees that sure enough a small crowd has gathered outside. Although their hips are rocking visibly now, she snaps her face into a mask, and the people nudge each other doubtfully.

She's pinned down by his fingers, by his cock, she can feel his thighs taking some of her weight, her soft buttocks squashing on to him. Her thoughts as she stares out at the shuffling crowd are centred on what he's doing to her, the fact that that pert butt she admired just a couple of days ago is doing what she wanted it do to. Flexing and thrusting, banging it in to her.

Something darts like a hare across her intoxicated mind. She's careful not to move her lips, though, as she articulates it. 'But I thought you were gay!'

There's a brief silence. She can hear very distant murmuring from outside. Then Robin just laughs. She wonders if he is keeping his face still enough. He drags his fingers from her cunt with a wet slipping sound. Shit! She's ruined the moment. He's just been playing with her. Of course he doesn't want her. This is just a teasing, a punishment. How embarrassing. She tries to shift away from him.

But then he grabs her hips and drags her backwards, slides her onto his waiting cock. He's right inside her now and she jerks forwards as he slams up her.

Funny how the act of fucking can be robotic if you want it to be. If they're successful, the crowd will think they're just a pair of dirty dummies, at it in the shop window. And the rocking makes her so horny, now they've started in earnest. Her nose bumps against the glass with each thrust. Robin's fingers dig into her with each thrust, his soft balls banging against her at first then retracting with his own desire as he speeds up, getting closer to his own climax. How has she turned him on like this? Why hasn't he answered her?

He doesn't alter his rhythm, just rocks her forwards as he pulls back, thrusts again, up her from behind, letting out his own low groan.

The pricks in their pockets will be shifting and stiffening as the guys watch. They'll shove their hands in there, rubbing the growing, throbbing length in their trousers. They might be muttering obscene comments to each other, but finding it harder to speak as the sight of Cinderella and Robin fucking gets to them. They might want to push the blonde up against the window, she's so sexy – but she's gone. Where? To find an orgy of her own? With no one real to fuck they'll just have to pump their spunk uselessly over their hands instead . . .

Robin suddenly stops. His cock is throbbing, filling her. She blinks slowly. That's what creepy mannequins do. He tugs at her hair, yanking it out of its pins, letting it cascade down her bare back, stroking it for a minute as if she's a wild horse, and then he starts thrusting hard, violently, lifting her off her knees with the force of it.

She has no idea if her face is still composed. She knows she's going limp, and her mouth has dropped open. Her thoughts scatter as he jerks faster and faster inside her tightening pussy. She can just imagine that cute butt flexing and thrusting. The pleasure spreads through her, heat racing through her until she hears his breathing quicken and then she's coming and moaning and he's gripping her to keep her on her knees and to keep himself inside her as she weakens and he judders his own climax into her.

Her mouth is open as she gasps for breath. He's holding her tight. The group outside shuffles away.

Robin pulls his cock out slowly, and juice trickles down her thighs. She lifts the skirt of the dress away from her legs so as not to stain the chiffon.

'What's going on?' she asks, blushing red hot. 'I thought you were gay!'

Robin is looking gorgeous. He's zipping those jeans up over that flat brown stomach, old shirt unbuttoned, hair a mess. Lips wet with excitement. He pulls her over and kisses her, tongue forceful in her mouth.

'You're not the only one who can put on an act, you know.'

They do it again in the fitting room the next day, after counting the takings. He fucks her from behind quickly, staring at her in the mirror as her breasts and hands press against her reflection.

It's all the hornier because he's outrageously camp today. Pink satin shirt. Obscenely tight trousers. Deliberately twitching his butt from side to side, deliberately flapping his hands about, raising his voice ...

But now he's just come inside her and he's stroking her wet pussy, licking his fingers one by one as she smiles at him.

The little bell on the shop door tinkles.

'What the fuck,' he grumbles, zipping his white trousers over his softening erection. 'Lottie's got the sack, Fiona's got the day off ...'

'And I've got a promotion,' Francesca says, pulling her green kaftan casually to cover her damp bush and flinging the curtains aside. 'Robin? Meet Eva. Our new trainee.'

And as Robin shakes the hand of the blonde, she and Francesca smile at each other and wink, very slowly. Just like living dolls.

Primula Bond is the author of the Black Lace novels, *Country Pleasures* and *Club Crème* and her short stories have appeared in numerous Wicked Words collections.

Sex and Shoplifting Mae Nixon

I'd pegged him as a shoplifter almost immediately. When you've been in security as long as I have you develop a sort of sixth sense. No matter how natural they try to act and how skilled they are at pocketing the goods, in the end they always give themselves away. I watched the grainy black-and-white image flickering across the monitor. There was a hard little knot of tension under my ribs and the hairs on the back of my neck were standing to attention.

'We'll get him this time, I'm sure. He's one of the best hoisters I've ever seen, but he can't fool me.' Jeff, my assistant, and I hunched over the tiny monitor. 'I've got Tony and Mike on alert. The minute we spot something they'll pick him up.' Jeff was whispering though we were alone in the small control room and I realised that he was as keyed up as I was.

There's something unbelievably exciting about catching a shoplifter in the act. Adrenalin rushes to my head and every nerve ending in my body becomes alive and tingly. We peered at the row of monitors watching our target amble with deliberate slowness between the racks of cashmere knitwear. Cashmere is popular with shoplifters because it's light, easy to conceal and can readily be turned into hard cash.

The target was a man in his thirties dressed formally in an expensive suit and shirt with no tie. Over the top he wore a long old-fashioned overcoat – the better to conceal his haul – and with his neatly cropped short hair he reminded me of a movie hero from the 1950s. He looked elegant and respectable and somehow solid and reassuring; all useful assets when you're in the hoisting business. Perhaps it was because the monitors were black and white, but as I watched him move across the screen, slipping between the racks of cashmere with the grace and deportment of a dancer, I realised that he reminded me of Cary Grant.

'He's a smart one isn't he, Jeff? You'd never suspect someone dressed like that, would you? I bet he's been at it for weeks.' My voice was a throaty whisper.

The man on the screen casually slipped a cardigan off a hanger and slid it under his coat.

'Got him!' Jeff hissed in triumph. He picked up his walkie-talkie and issued brief orders to our two floorwalkers.

I watched the action on the bank of monitors as he was intercepted by Tony in his security uniform, quickly followed by Mike. Each holding an arm, they led him away and disappeared out of the cameras' range. My heart was drumming. I stared into the screen he had so recently occupied. An empty hanger on the rack was the only evidence that he'd ever been there and I realised that I was holding my breath.

'Do you want me to handle it, Tess?' I could tell from his voice that Jeff longed for the opportunity to interrogate the shoplifter, but I had other plans.

'No thanks. I want to take care of this myself.'

I walked along echoing corridors, my high heels clicking against the tiled floor, towards the interview room. This was the part of my job that I loved the most. I'd worked my way up from security guard to floorwalker, store detective, security chief and last year I'd finally made it to regional security manager; the first woman in the chain to make it that far. My base was our flagship Oxford Street store and the security department was housed in the vast basement.

As I strode around the store in my smart suit I experienced a real thrill of power and competence. There was nothing more satisfying than apprehending a thief. Somehow it made all the hard work and long uneventful hours staring into a television monitor worthwhile.

But more than that, it was a thrill and, dare I say it, a turn-on. It was the most exhilarating moment of achievement and it bordered on the erotic. Since, these days, I seemed to be married to the job, it was more or less the only excitement I got and I intended to make the most of it.

When I arrived at the interview room, the suspect was already seated, his booty spread out on the table in front of him. Much to my surprise there were a couple of cashmere scarves and a leather wallet that I hadn't spotted him taking even though Jeff and I hadn't taken our eyes off the monitor from the moment he'd entered the store.

He was good, but I was better. By the time I called the police to arrest him, he'd be eating out of my lap. He'd be as eager to come clean as a Catholic in the confession box.

I sat down and nodded to Tony and Mike to leave the room. I sat back and looked at him. I crossed one leg over the other slowly so as to allow him a good glimpse of thigh. I rested one hand on top of the other on my knee, knowing that my scarlet-painted fingernails added to the effect. I sat there silently, allowing the quietness in the room to grow threatening. Suspects always expected a barrage of questions but I liked to put them on the wrong foot by remaining quiet. Silence was one of the most effective weapons in my arsenal. It demonstrated my control and their helplessness and usually got me the results I desired.

I took the opportunity to take a good look at him. He'd seemed handsome on the screen but, in the flesh, he was breathtaking. His hair was raven black and fashionably tousled and his features were chiselled and masculine. His suit was made from the softest, purest wool. His overcoat, folded over the back of a chair, was Italian, lined in purple silk.

Though he looked unconcerned, sitting quietly with his hands on the table, a small twitch at the corner of his jaw betrayed his anxiety. I allowed my eyes to travel up to his face. His mouth was unusually full for a man yet somehow managed to avoid making him seem feminine. His lips were dark and slightly parted, revealing even white teeth. His nose had a little bend on the bridge, as if it had once been broken and, somehow, this flaw made him seem vulnerable and boyish. His eyes were a deep chocolate brown and were fringed by thick dark lashes most women would envy.

I surveyed his face openly not bothering to conceal my curiosity. It was a technique I often used to disconcert and discomfort but this time I found I was enjoying it more than usual. I couldn't help wondering what his lips would feel like on mine and if I'd be able to feel his beard stubble when we kissed.

Though I often found interrogating a suspect something of a turn-on this was the first time I'd ever found one attractive. If I'm honest, I found the experience exciting and unsettling in equal measure. Somehow it made me feel a little less in control than usual. Something about him was compelling and disturbing, but I had no intention of letting it affect my objectivity.

I was far too professional to allow myself to be influenced by a handsome face but that didn't mean I couldn't enjoy looking at it. I allowed my eyes to wander over his forehead, his cheekbones, his jaw. I let them roam down his throat as far as the opening at the top of his shirt and wondered if those dark hairs went all the way down to his belly. I could see his chest rising and falling as he breathed. I could even hear the soft hiss of his exhalation in the quiet room.

My gaze travelled back to his face and I looked at his dark enigmatic eyes. He met my gaze, staring back at me with a challenge and confidence that seemed genuine and fearless. I was used to the counterfeit confidence of the thief who pretends he's not afraid of arrest and prison but this was the first time a suspect had ever looked back at me with such cool self-assurance. I was intrigued. Under my blouse, my nipples peaked.

He continued to meet my gaze. His eyes seemed bottomless and inviting. I couldn't have looked away even if I had wanted to. Occasionally he would blink languidly and I couldn't help noticing that his eyelids gleamed softly in the harsh overhead light. After several minutes his eyes began to crinkle in amusement and he smiled. Looking back, the smile was what did it. The moment I saw that lopsided grin that quickly turned to laughter, I knew I was lost.

'How long are you going to keep up this staring contest? You won't win, I assure you; I can stare for England. And the silent treatment won't work on me either.' He turned over his hands, showing me his palms, and executed a little shrug with his shoulders that seemed self-deprecating and apologetic but also managed to convey his willingness to engage in the challenge. 'I'm Matthew Molloy, Matt to my friends.' He held out his hand for me to shake and, without even thinking about it, I did so. He gripped my hand for a moment, gently rubbing his thumb against its back. Instantly, I grew goosepimply and tingly. He looked straight at me, a smile on his lips as if he could see the effect his touch was having on me.

'I'm Tess Tyler,' I said eventually, conscious that if I kept silent any longer I risked looking like an idiot. 'I'm the security manager here.'

'Yes, I know that.' He released my hand and I felt instantly bereft. 'You've got a business degree from London University. You started on the shop floor and worked your way up the hard way. You're the first female regional security manager the David Peplow chain has ever employed.' He smiled as he spoke, conscious, I'm sure, of the impact of his words. Somehow, his intimate knowledge of my life seemed both an affront and a thrill. I felt my control unravelling, my self-confidence wavering. But, no matter what, I mustn't show it. If I let him see my confusion I was lost and, even though I felt as though my feet had been swept out from under me, I would not lose control.

'You've obviously done your research. I'm impressed, but so what? You're still a thief.'

He winced visibly. 'That's such a nasty little word, don't you think? And, didn't Marx say property is theft anyway? I'm just doing a bit of freelance redistribution.'

'Robin Hood in a hand-made suit?' I shook my head. 'I'm afraid the police will still class that as shoplifting.'

'Then perhaps you should call them and set the wheels of justice in motion.' He sat back in his chair and crossed his legs, resting one ankle on the other knee. I couldn't help noticing the bulge at his crotch and I quickly looked away. My armpits had begun to prickle with sweat and my hair was growing damp at the nape.

'You think you're clever, don't you? And maybe you are, but I still managed to catch you shoplifting. Perhaps you should think about which of us is cleverer and fortunately you're going to have plenty of time for reflection while you're languishing in prison.'

He laughed out loud and I felt a little shiver of excitement slither up and down my spine.

'You wouldn't have caught me if I hadn't been deliberately careless. In fact, I was beginning to despair of you ever catching me.'

'What do you mean?' The tingly feeling had spread through my body, making my nipples erect and sensitive. 'Are you saying you wanted me to catch you? I don't understand...'

He nodded slowly. 'I've been trying to get you to notice me for months, but you barely even looked at me. I joined your gym and exercised beside you for weeks but you never even saw me. I followed you to the supermarket and deliberately bumped into your trolley but you looked straight through me. Eventually I realised that if I wanted you to notice me I'd have to take matters into my own hands. You seemed so wrapped up in your work that I hit on the idea of getting apprehended for shoplifting. At least that way I'd get to be alone with you for a while. Only, I must be a much better shoplifter than I thought because I've been at it for weeks and nothing's happened. I expected to feel a hand on my shoulder every time I left the store but it never happened. Today I was so desperate and ... well ... horny, if I'm perfectly honest, that I decided drastic measures were required. I stood right in the line of sight of a security camera and made sure they could see me stealing the cardigan. And it worked, because here I am.' He smiled at me, evidently pleased with his story.

I looked at him for a long moment. I didn't know what to think. He seemed to be saying that we'd met socially but how could I have failed to notice him? I had no recollection of ever having seen him before he came into the store. He wasn't the kind of man you could easily forget and yet he'd clearly been following me around – stalking me almost – and I'd never even noticed.

I had to admit that I was rather flattered that he'd been prepared to go that far. I mean, risking arrest and prison just to get a girl to notice you beat a bunch of flowers any day. Realising that he fancied me that much was an enormous turn-on. My skin felt goosepimply and sensitive. My blouse was clinging to my back and, inside my knickers, things had grown distinctly moist.

'If all this is true – and, you must admit, it sounds rather far-fetched – where did we meet in the first place? As far as I remember I never saw you before today.'

'I can't tell you how wounding it is to my ego that I'm so forgettable. Do you remember attending a course at the Midlothian Hotel earlier in the year? Well, I was on the course too. I did my very best to charm you and I'm usually pretty persuasive, but you barely seemed to notice I was there.'

'Yes, I remember the course . . .'

'But not me?'

'No, I don't think so. Though, I can hardly imagine how that happened. You seem extremely . . . memorable.'

'I'm relieved to hear it. I was beginning to think I was losing my touch.'

'Far from it.' I looked straight at him.

He was smiling, his dark eyes sparkled. 'Then, all that remains is to decide what we're going to do about it.' He spread his hands and shrugged again as if issuing a challenge.

I got up and walked over to him. I stood looking down on him. He tilted his head back to meet my gaze, looking at me through thick lashes. I was conscious of my chest heaving as I breathed. I realised that I liked being in a position to look down on him. It felt powerful and authoritative and, for the first time since he'd made his revelation, I felt the balance of power shift back in my direction.

'There's still the small matter of the shoplifting. Can you give me one good reason why I shouldn't call the police and have you arrested?'

He nodded. 'I can do better than that, I can give you two. This one.' He grasped his crotch and jiggled it obscenely. The crudity and directness of this gesture was unspeakably arousing. 'And this one.' He released his crotch and moved his hand up my short skirt and pressed it against the front of my panties, covering my mound. His palm was warm, his middle finger found the groove between my lips. Instantly, my legs felt shaky and I held onto the table for support. He looked up at me, his eyes full of hunger and excitement. I could see he was waiting for permission; he'd gone as far as he dared and needed to feel certain of my consent. I laid my hand over his and pressed it hard against my crotch.

'You think I'd jeopardise everything I've worked for – my job, my future – for a quick orgasm?' I tried to sound outraged and authoritative but my voice was full of breathless excitement and my words might have carried more weight if I wasn't frantically rubbing his trapped hand against my pussy.

Matt kept on looking up at me, his eyes narrow with arousal. He shook his head slowly, never taking his eyes off my face. 'Not at all. But you might swap it for a long, slow, deep one.' He located my clit with his middle finger and stroked it, making me gasp. 'Or even several. Whatever you want. I'm an old-fashioned guy.' His finger moved gently against my hard little bud and my thigh muscles began to twitch. 'I believe it's the gentleman's job to make sure the lady has the best possible time.' His fingers found the edge of my panties and pushed them aside. I exhaled loudly as they made contact with exposed flesh.

'A gentleman thief? How novel. Perhaps I should call you Raffles.'

'I explained all that, I'm not a thief.' His fingertips worked magic on my clit.

'No? It seems to me you can't keep your hands off things that don't belong to you.' I rocked my hips, rubbing my crotch against his expert fingers.

'It doesn't count if you've been invited.' He pressed a fingertip hard against my clit.

'I don't remember issuing an invitation.' My nipples were hard, rubbing painfully against my clothes. A bead of cold sweat trickled the length of my spine.

'Does that mean you want me to stop?' He began to move his hand away and I reached down and grabbed his wrist, holding it in place. 'I'll take that as no, shall I?'

'I don't want you to stop.' My voice was a husky whisper. 'In fact, I'll tell you exactly what I want.'

Matt's cheeks had flushed dark red. His eyes glistened. 'Yes, tell me.'

I don't know what came over me. All I know is that the weirdness of the situation and Matt's expert fingering had brought me to a pitch of arousal. Interrogating a suspect always gave me a thrill of power and control and Matt was obviously eager to please. Suddenly I knew what I wanted with a conviction and certainty that was unshakeable and irresistible.

'I want you to stand up and take off your clothes – all of them – while I watch. And nice and slowly, please, because I don't want to miss anything.'

Matt's face broke into a smile as he realised what I had in mind. His fingers slipped away from my wet slit and the sense of loss was terrible.

He stood up and took off his jacket, hanging it over the back of his chair. He began unbuttoning his shirt, taking his time though the slight tremor in his fingers told me he was using all his self-control not to rip his clothes off and then do the same to mine. As he peeled off his shirt he revealed a sculpted chest covered in dark hair. At his belly there was another patch of hair and a dark trail leading down to paradise.

I assumed he'd remove his trousers next, but he sat down and began to unlace his shoes. Every so often he'd glance up at me and smile. He was teasing me and we both knew it but then I had asked him to take his time; I could hardly blame him for being obedient. He took off his shoes and socks, then carefully placed them under a spare chair. Matt stood up and looked me straight in the eye. He thrust his hands in his trouser pockets and began to lay the contents on the table: a handful of change, a small penknife, an Underground ticket. Somehow, the removal of these mundane objects seemed imbued with the utmost lasciviousness, as if it were a prelude to something dark, forbidden and utterly abandoned.

I was on heat. My pussy ached. My breathing had grown rapid and shallow. I watched as Matt slid down his zip, then bent to step out of his trousers. He folded them neatly, careful to maintain the creases, and laid them on top of his jacket on the back of his chair.

Now he was standing before me dressed only in a pair of grey jersey boxer shorts. The logo on the waistband advertised them as Calvin Klein's and they were the type that are designed to cling. And cling they did. Matt's arousal was obvious. His erection tented the front and there was a small dark stain where he had begun to leak pre-come.

My legs felt weak and wobbly. My damp knickers were clinging to me and my nipples ached for release. Unhurriedly, Matt lowered his shorts, pausing to extricate his manhood, then pushed them down. His cock was thick, standing up proudly almost flat against his muscular belly.

I wanted to fall on my knees and suck it, I wanted to throw him to the floor and sit on it, I wanted to rip of my knickers and press his face against my crotch and hold his head in place until he'd licked me to half-a-dozen orgasms. I wanted to try every sexual act our combined imaginations could think of and I wanted it now.

My hunger and indecision rooted me to the spot. Matt stood in front of me, completely naked, his erection proudly announcing his excitement. The red flush on his cheeks had spread over his neck and chest. The rise and fall of his ribcage as he breathed and the throaty little gasp he made as he exhaled underlined his arousal. As I watched him I realised that, more than anything, I had to come. That was what I wanted; how could there ever have been any doubt?

'I want you to get on your knees in front of me.' My voice was thick with lust. Matt instantly got to his knees and looked up at me, his eyes shining with arousal. 'I want you to take my knickers off and lick my pussy. And make sure you do a good job of it, because I still haven't decided whether or not I'm calling the police.'

Matt reached up under my skirt and slid my knickers down slowly over my hips, pausing to extricate the damp crotch. The expression on his face was pure bliss. He slid my underwear down and I leant against the table and stepped out of them. Matt pushed at my skirt, bunching it up above my hips, exposing my naked pussy to his hungry gaze. As it came into view, he smiled and moaned softly.

'You're beautiful.' His voice was a strangled whisper.

I sat on the edge of the Formica table and lay back. I kicked off my shoes and spread my legs, putting my feet up on the table. Matt sat down in the chair and positioned himself between my thighs. He spread my swollen lips, exposing my excited clit to the cold air. He pressed his face against my moist slit and began to lick. His mouth was unbelievably hot and somehow his body heat seemed to represent the fire of his arousal and mine.

Beneath me, the Formica table was cold and slippery. I could hear the industrial hum of the air-conditioning system. I gazed up at the ceiling, noticing that the tiles were water stained and curling.

Matt circled his firm tongue against my hole, pushing it inside. I could feel his warm breath on my crotch. His strong fingers stretched me wide, allowing him access. He explored me with his eager mouth. He covered every wet millimetre with the tip of his tongue. He nibbled gently on the lips and sucked on my sensitive clit, making me gasp.

A hard little knot of tension settled at the base of my belly. My nipples were fully erect and hypersensitive. They rubbed uncomfortably against my clothes so I unbuttoned my blouse and pulled up my bra, freeing my breasts. The cold air made them tingle. My entire body felt alive with pleasure. Every nerve ending, every follicle seemed sensitised and responsive. Goose pimples covered my arms and exposed breasts.

I was moaning constantly now, emitting excited little gasps of pleasure each time Matt's tongue made contact with my sweet spot. The rickety table had begun to rock. I laid myself flat, distributing my weight more evenly and spread my arms, gripping the edge of the table on either side.

My hips rocked with a rhythm of their own. Every so often Matt would emit a satisfied grunt of pleasure. I had grown so wet that his fingers stretching me apart had begun to slip. He reached up and wiped the slippery digits on my skirt, drying them so that he could get a better grip. Under normal circumstances, soiling my expensive, recently dry-cleaned skirt with his pussy-wet fingers would have outraged me but, in the moment, it seemed erotic and filthy in equal measure and cranked my arousal up a notch.

Blood pumped in my ears. My chest was heaving. I was gasping for breath. My hips thrust, rubbing my excited crotch against Matt's talented mouth. The knot in my belly had spread and tightened. My nipples were on fire. I was sobbing and gasping now, the urgent human sound played counterpoint to the insistent robotic drone of the air conditioning.

My thigh muscles were quivering; my whole body was racked with spasms I couldn't control. The exquisite sensations Matt was creating had brought me to a pitch of arousal. I rubbed myself against his face, utterly wanton.

Matt wrapped his hands around my thighs, pulling me closer. He sucked on my clit, drawing it right into his mouth. My orgasm burst inside me like a bomb, taking me by surprise. Spirals of delicious pleasure shot around my body like fireworks, each small explosion more spectacular than the last.

My nipples tingled with excitement. Waves of ecstasy possessed my body. I gripped the edge of the table, my knuckles white. I was moaning uncontrollably now, abandoned, animal howls I could hear but had no awareness of making. My legs were trembling uncontrollably, shaking the table. Matt held onto me, his mouth pressed against my twitching clit, sucking the orgasm out of me.

He held onto me long after it was over, his face pressed between my legs, his tongue soothing tenderly the places he had so recently excited but were now too sensitive for touch. When I got my breath back I heaved myself up on my elbows and looked down at him. He sat back in the chair and wiped his shiny face with his hand. His cock was magnificent. Even bigger now if that was possible, standing up in front of him like an obscene flagpole, advertising his arousal.

'What do you want me to do now?' He reached down and slid his foreskin backwards and forward, over the engorged helmet, never once taking his eyes off me.

To tell you the truth, I'd been asking myself the same question. Not normally indecisive, I was torn between two irresistible desires: did I get on my knees and suck on it or did I spread my legs and order him to put it where it so obviously belonged? Under usual circumstances I'd have done both but these circumstances were anything but normal. This was my place of work and the door wasn't even locked. What's more, there were two security guards standing sentinel in the corridor outside. While the risk of discovery and being overheard had undoubtedly contributed to the excitement of the situation, I couldn't afford to take unnecessary risks.

But what to choose? Either option would be fantastic and yet choosing one meant I would have to go without the other. I looked down at Matt's hard cock. He was still holding its base in his hand, leaning back in his chair with his legs spread wide. A thin sheen of sweat filmed his upper lip and his chest rose and fell visibly. As I looked down at his crotch he slowly pushed down his foreskin, exposing his shiny dark helmet and I knew I had never really had a choice.

'I want to suck you, Matt. I want to kiss every part of you and explore your body millimetre by millimetre until there's no part of you I haven't touched or tasted. But there's two hairy thugs outside and they're probably already getting suspicious about why I haven't asked them to call the police yet so I think I'm just going to have to get you to fuck me and leave all that delicious exploration for later. How does that sound to you?'

'It sounds like heaven.' He reached forwards and grabbed my hips, pulling my bottom roughly to the edge of the table. He got to his feet and positioned himself between my legs. His fingers were on my pussy, spreading it, and I felt the tip of his cock pressing against me. He thrust his hips forwards and he slid inside in a single fluid movement. 'And that feels like heaven.'

I had to agree with him, but I was too breathless to say it out loud. There's nothing like the first moment of penetration when my body surrenders to the delicious invasion. He was thick and hard. He held onto me and allowed his weight to push his cock home. I gasped as his hot rigid meat claimed me.

He circled his hips, rubbing his crotch against mine. His cock moved inside me and his scratchy pubes rubbed my sensitive clit. I wrapped my legs around his buttocks and squeezed, pulling him into me.

'I don't think I'm going to last very long, I'm afraid. All this has got me rather excited.' Matt began to move inside me, sliding in and out with the inexorable perfection of a piston.

'That's no problem. I'm pretty aroused myself as it happens. In fact, I'm pretty close to coming again.' I tilted my hips up to meet his thrusting cock, causing delicious friction for my clit. 'That feels so good.'

'Oh no, it's much better than that. I told you – it's

heavenly.' He gave a long deep thrust and I felt his balls banging against my buttocks. 'It's ecstasy...' He thrust again, making the table rock. 'It's pure bliss ... rapture ... perfection.' With each word he pressed his cock home hard and deep. I gripped him with my legs, meeting his thrusts. 'In fact I think it's paradise.' He elongated the word, turning it into a sibilant hiss that gradually became an incomprehensible gasp of pleasure.

He fucked me with his eyes closed. His face was filmed with sweat. His lips were berry dark and plump. I could see the tendons in his forearms standing out like rope as he held onto me. His hips moved like pistons, driving his cock home.

I arched my back on each thrust, rubbing my clit against his rough pubes. My nipples were on fire. My hair was damp, clinging to my nape. My bra dug in under the arms where I had pushed it up, but I didn't care. I watched Matt's face as he fucked me. He was beautiful, totally lost in the moment and his sensations, lost in me.

I gasped as the first tremors of orgasm began to build. Matt plunged into me; his strong hands gripped my hips. Our sweat-slicked bodies moved as one. My thighs were trembling again and the table began to wobble. I gripped the edges for support. I ground my crotch against his, relishing the sensation. He filled me, stretched me, moving inside me with a rhythm dictated by his arousal. I was tingling all over again. My nipples were so sensitive they were almost painful.

Matt was groaning and grunting, thrusting into me with short deep strokes. He tilted back his head and howled at the ceiling and I felt his body quiver as he began to come inside me. I'd been riding the edge of my own orgasm and feeling Matt come tipped me over the edge. I held onto the table and allowed it to wash over me. Matt's penknife clattered to the floor, as the table wobbled.

I was panting and gasping, coils of delicious pleasure

spreading through my body like a blood transfusion. Matt held onto me, his fingers digging into my flesh. Little waves of contractions, like aftershocks, kept taking my breath away. The table creaked beneath me; coins tinkled onto the tiled floor as it rocked. Sweat dripped off Matt's face and landed on my belly. He gave one final thrust, pressing deep into me, his head bent and his eyes still closed. I thought it would never end.

Finally he opened his eyes and used both hands to wipe the sweat off his face. He pulled me upright and wrapped his arms round me and kissed me – a long, deep, melting kiss that I felt all the way to my toes.

'Do you think we should put our clothes back on before you call the police, Tess?'

Needless to say, I never did get round to calling them. It turned out Matt had been at the training course because he was head of security for the Godfrey chain of department stores. I told my employers that his shoplifting spree was the result of a co-operative scheme the two of us had secretly organised to test the stores' security arrangements and they were so impressed with my initiative they even gave me a pay rise.

Every couple of months after that Matt and I took turns shoplifting in each other's stores. Sometimes he'd play the criminal and sometimes I would. As it turned out, I discovered that being caught in the act and hauled off to the interview room by two burly men in uniform was a far more powerful aphrodisiac than I could possibly have imagined. I'd always thought there was no greater buzz than the sense of power and control that apprehending an offender had always given me. But that was before I experienced the sheer shame, seediness and illicit thrill as they manhandled me along the corridor never knowing that Matt and I would get down and dirty the minute they'd left the room.

In between, we practised at his house or mine a couple

of times a week and, even though it was never less than fantastic, there was always an extra little frisson of excitement when we did it an interview room with two uniformed guards on the other side of the door. In fact, I grew so addicted to the feel of cold Formica under my bottom and the harsh fluorescent lighting hurting my eyes that we usually ended up doing it on the kitchen table before we even got to the bedroom.

Not that I'm complaining. Before I met Matt my idea of an exciting night in was a prawn biryani and a Brad Pitt DVD. Matt might not be as prettily perfect as Brad but he was far more exciting than an Indian takeaway and he was all mine and, when you think about it, you can't buy that, though – if you're very lucky – maybe you can steal it.

Mae Nixon's first Black Lace novel, *Wing of Madness*, is published in April 2007. Her short stories have appeared in several Wicked Words collections.

Getting Good Designer Outlet
Saskia Walker

We shop for clothes on Saturdays, but we rarely buy anything on these trips. Not any more. That isn't what it's about. It's about the total turn-on that we share while we're there. Will calls it his public, private show: me, trying it on, while he watches. We discovered this new pastime quite by chance and, since then, we go shopping every week, because we can barely get home fast enough to climb all over each other, afterwards.

The first time it happened was in the biggest department store in town. I'd been looking for something to wear to a business function that I didn't really want to attend. Will was waiting outside the changing rooms. As I stepped inside the cubicle, jerking the curtain across behind me, I realised that the dress I'd chosen was almost identical to one I had at home.

I kicked my shoes off, reaching for the hem of my top, to pull it over my head. That was when I became aware of being watched, the skin on the back of my neck prickling with awareness. Turning slightly, I realised that I hadn't closed the curtain properly and it was open enough for Will to see me from where he was standing. And he *was* watching; he was riveted. I met his gaze and something passed between us. Something sexual; the hint of a private, intimate secret. I knew that look, and my body responded instantly, my sex clenching, heat welling between my thighs.

People passed by in the background, moving amongst the rails and displays, but only he was looking my way, down the short corridor and into the cubicle. I felt a rush of deviancy in my blood, and it empowered me. I turned fully towards him as I pulled off my top and I smiled, dangling it over my shoulder, nonchalantly. The other hand rested over the belt of my low-slung jeans. I swivelled my hips in a slow lap-dance style.

He nodded at me, smiling.

I dropped my top, and ran my hands over my lace-covered breasts before reaching around to undo my bra. Turning on my heel so that I had my back to him, I took it off, and dropped it to the floor. Bending slowly over to pick it up, I wriggled my arse at him. It had been a spur of the moment thing; a naughty devil had prodded me into it when I saw the way he was looking.

Chuckling to myself, I stood up and my hand went for the curtain. That's when my mobile phone bleeped. I glanced over my shoulder. Will had his phone against his ear. Mine was in my bag, on the stool in the cubicle. Bleeping insistently.

I stepped behind the curtain and pulled the phone out of my bag, my arms across my bare boobs.

'Don't stop. Give me the whole show.'

'But, Will –'

'Keep going. I'll be enjoying the show.'

That's all he said. I peeped out from behind the curtain and saw him flip his phone shut and shove it back into his pocket. He folded his arms over his chest, leant back against the pillar and stroked his chin as he watched.

Slowly, I closed my phone, dropped it back in the bag. *The whole show?* I had to get down to my G-string for this dress. And he wanted me to leave the curtain open as it was? Between my thighs I was hot, my pussy was tingling with arousal. Someone walked past my cubicle to the next one along the corridor. They barely glanced at me. Let's face it, I never blinked when I saw someone's arse poking out of the changing room. It would never occur to me that their husband was watching, getting a stiffy from the show. I looked out again. A blur of figures moved across the ladieswear department in the background, and my man was standing there egging me on to give him a show, regardless.

And if someone else did see? I smiled at my reflection in the mirror, registering the mischief twinkling in my own eyes. *Let 'em look.*

I ran my hand down the edge of the curtain, edging it back a bit more. Stepping forwards, I pushed my hair up in my hands, watching as my breasts rolled with the movement. When I glanced to the side, I could make out the distant outline of Will's body. I could feel the tension across the atmosphere between us. Lowering my hands, I ran them over my bare breasts, thrilling at my own display. When my nipples were fully peaked, painfully so, I went for the zipper on my jeans. I dropped them to the floor, turning this way and that, giving him an eyeful. Somehow putting the dress on seemed unnecessary, I wasn't going to buy it anyway. I did it all the same, and then did the whole strip thing again as I got out of it, laughing to myself as I realised how good it made me feel, how sexy. Knowing that Will was looking at me, wanting me, made me hungry for sex.

When I came out of the cubicle he was smiling. 'I think the dress is perfect, lover. But why don't you try something else on, while we're here?'

I hung the dress on the reject rail. 'Don't push your luck,' I replied, slapping him on the behind. 'Besides, I want to get home as fast as possible.' I flashed my eyes at him, made sure he knew what I was getting at.

He grinned, a possessive hand against my back as he steered me out of the department store. 'I may have to break the speed limit,' he replied.

He drove us home holding my hand on his erect cock through his jeans, while I wriggled and shimmied on the passenger seat, desperate to be had. As soon as we got home, he pushed me in the direction of the sofa. I could barely get my clothes off fast enough, and he had me bent over the back of the sofa with my jeans hanging around my ankles, fucking me from behind, while I clutched at the cushions. Liquid heat dribbled down the inside my thighs as I squeezed his cock tight inside me. He urged me on, and we worked each other fast and hard for relief of the tension that had built while I was trying on the dress.

Since then, we went shopping most Saturdays. We would go from place to place, with me trying on exotic outfits of all types, while he watched – either surreptitiously, or if the set-up didn't allow it I would come out and parade the outfit in front of him. While he preferred to see the strip, he said it made him feel rich and powerful having me parade up and down in front of him in these outfits. He played his part well, appearing to give serious consideration to each outfit, shaking his head and suggesting I try on another, or go back to a different shop.

All I need is the suggestion, and I run with it. Will was good at being suggestive. I couldn't decide if we were eminently good for each other, or bad to the bone. We were working the system for our own sexual titillation, not entirely a respectable pastime, but somewhat addictive, as it turned out. Whatever it was, the sex that happened afterwards was fucking hot. Sometimes we couldn't even wait to get home, we did it in the car, right there in the multi-storey car park, wanking each other off across the seats, too horny to hang on any longer. Our routine remained, until one unsuspecting day, when events spiralled out of control, upping the ante, changing us forever.

'So, do you want to go shopping?' As he asked me the almost inevitable Saturday morning question, Will had that look in his eyes. He stepped closer, and rested one finger on my collarbone. Smiling, he raised one eyebrow, and ran his fingertip down into my cleavage.

I looked down at his finger and gave a breathless laugh. My temperature had begun to rise, my breasts aching for more than one finger, aching for his whole hands to touch my breasts, to mould them and massage them deeply through my top. 'Whatever did you have in mind?'

He stroked the length of my throat, making me purr and shiver, then pushed my chin up, so that I had to meet his gaze. I didn't really need to ask. I always knew what he was thinking, especially when I saw him with that look in his eyes. Will and I had been together for five years, married for four, and that dark twinkle was very familiar.

'Where do you want to go? The big department store?' My heartbeat paced up a notch.

'No, not the department store.' He raised his eyebrows slightly. 'I was thinking maybe we could go to another one of those exclusive shops down in The Lanes, a proper designer outlet.'

The Lanes is the old fishermen's area of town. Quaint, higgledy-piggledy streets now populated with exclusive boutiques and hand-made gift shops. The clothing shops are characterised by ridiculously expensive outfits in the window, and stuck-up, austere-looking assistants behind the counter. We'd tried one a couple of weeks back. The assistant had looked at Will as if a male shouldn't even be in her shop, let alone be allowed to eyeball her products. He'd faced up to her, but her attitude to him had made me laugh more than anything.

'Oh, Will, you are incorrigible.' I couldn't keep my smile off my face. 'Do you think we dare, after the last time?'

'You dare, lover. You dare.'

He was right. As long as we were both happy with it, I was willing to explore just about everything.

The shop we chose was a corner unit, all glass. Glancing in, I could see a blonde assistant sitting on a stool behind the counter, a bored expression on her face as she filed her nails. There only seemed to be two rails of clothing in there. Four mannequins were paired like twins either side of a pillar in the window. They wore skimpy garments with exorbitant price tags.

Will bowed, his arm sweeping out towards the door. 'Shall we?'

I couldn't help chuckling. It felt so naughty. And yet I suspected a lot of people went into these places and didn't actually intend to buy anything, just window-shopped. We were simply doing window-shopping of a slightly more deviant kind.

The assistant perked up considerably when we came in, smiling and standing up. She was a sophisticated punkette with short bleached hair, gelled upright. Her mouth was wide, and painted vivid red, her smile suggestive. I realised then how very small it was in there, and she dominated the space, attractive and watchful. Had we chosen the wrong venue for our game, yet again, I wondered? But then I noticed there was music playing through speakers mounted on the walls, ambient but sexy.

Perfect for a striptease?

I bit my lip to stop from grinning.

'Welcome,' the assistant said, in a slightly accented voice. Her posture was immaculate, her body swaying with fluid grace as she stepped out from behind the counter.

I couldn't place her accent. Belgian, maybe. She was probably a student, I decided. Maybe this was a Saturday job; she certainly didn't have a possessive, snooty air about her, like the other shopkeeper we had encountered down here.

'Hi,' I replied. 'I'm looking for something for a business function.'

She nodded, slowly, her smile never wavering. She glanced at Will. 'Please, take a seat.'

She gestured to a low leather armchair that I hadn't seen from the window, because it was behind the pillar. I scanned the set-up: the chair had a view into the area of the changing room, where mirrors abounded.

Perfect.

By the time I met Will's gaze, he'd noted that too and was smiling. He strolled over to the chair, sat down, languidly stretching out his legs and folding them at the ankle. With one elbow on the arm of the chair, he rested his chin on his hand. He looked sexy as hell, our little secret echoed in his subtle smile and the twinkle in his dark eyes. His very glance teased me, the entire surface of my body tingling. Then he looked at the assistant. She was drawing my attention to one of the rails, and I moved in her direction.

I made a show of looking at the items on the rail, but my attention kept being drawn back to her instead. She wore a black sleeveless top and a miniskirt, with knee-length boots. Her figure was slim and lean, and suited her style well. She was hot, sexy in an androgynous, upfront way. She was still smiling, her eyes knowing. It was almost like she knew what we got up to. I shook the feeling off, telling myself it was only because of what happened the other time we were down here.

'Why don't you try this one?' She lifted a hanger from the rail and gave it to me.

I took it automatically, glancing down at the twist of red fabric hanging from it. It looked like a scarf, but on closer examination I saw it was some sort of stretchy dress, off one shoulder and pointed at one side of the hem. Presumably you wriggled into it, like a body stocking. It was no more suitable for a business function than going naked, but the fact that she'd put it into my hand affected me like one of Will's suggestions.

I broke into a smile. 'What good judgement you have. It's perfect.'

She pointed to the changing room, standing by with one hand on her hip. Her expression was filled with humour. I could swear she knew. I didn't even dare to look at Will.

There was only one changing room, with a sort of stagey area outside filled with mirrors, presumably for checking the outfit. The changing area itself was a lot more spacious than the one in the department store or any of the other places we'd been. There was a fancy dining chair with a stuffed velvet seat, and more mirrors. I pulled the curtain across to about three-quarters, and noticed that Will was reflected in the angled mirrors outside. Smiling and humming along with the music, I hung the hanger bearing the scarf-dress from the hook on the wall, and relaxed into my surroundings, more at ease now I was alone.

I could feel the heat of Will's stare and ran my hands over my body, revelling in the way it made me feel – powerfully feminine and deviant, all at once. I'd worn stockings, suspenders and high heels, and I shimmied my skirt down, kicking it aside, moving my hips to the music. Swaying in front of the mirror, I glanced out and saw Will's smile. He would be getting hard now; he told me he did, when I moved that way, doing my secret performance for him.

I stuck my tits out and ran my hands over them, before moving down to peel off the skimpy top I was wearing. I looked at myself in the mirror. The heels, stockings and suspenders, skimpy knickers and bra – all black – made a powerful image. I took a moment to enjoy it, before checking on Will. He was watching closely. I turned away to drop my top next to my skirt.

'Please, let me help.'

I nearly jumped out of my skin. It was the blonde assistant. *Had we been caught?*

'It's OK, I can manage.' I reached for the coat hanger,

made a show of fiddling with the dress. She pushed the curtain open and stepped into the cubicle behind me, leaving the curtain wide open. I glanced at Will. He was leaning forwards, his elbows pressing on his knees. The smile was gone; his expression was guarded.

'Don't worry, just go with the flow.' Her voice was close against me as she stepped behind me, her breath warm on the back of my neck. I was about to question what she meant, when it struck me. *She knew.* She knew what we were up to, but she was playing into it. *Oh fuck.* Heat raced over me.

Her hands on my bra strap left me in no doubt as to what was coming next. She was going to undress me; the curtain was open. She was only getting involved. I swallowed – could I deal with this? Then I felt her shift against me; she shimmied up and down against my back in time with the music, and then snapped the hook on my bra. My core melted in response to her sure touch on me, my knees going weak. Glancing at the mirror, I saw her naughty eyes peeping over my shoulder.

'You don't mind me helping you undress, for him, do you?'

For him. My eyes flashed shut for moment. I couldn't have been more self-aware, more on the spot. And yet I didn't want her to stop, because I was on fire for more of it. I shook my head. 'How did you know?' I breathed.

'I saw you last week, when you were over the way, with the stuck-up hag in the shop opposite. I pretty much guessed then, but when you came in and I saw the way you responded to each other, I knew it for sure. You're very sexy together.'

'I see,' I said. *But what was she up to?* 'And you're not going to chuck us out?'

'Are you kidding? I get paid really well to work Saturdays here, but I'm bored out of my mind. This is just the sort of distraction I need.' She chuckled softly. 'Tell me, does he ever put on a show for you?'

I could barely answer because she'd slipped her hands round to the front of my loose bra and eased them under it, cupping my breasts inside the bra as it fell away down my arms. She moved her hands on me, massaging my breasts. Darts of pleasures shot through me. I stared at the mirror. The image of her hands cupping my bare breasts from behind mesmerised me. 'I don't understand what you mean.'

Her fingers moved to my nipples. My heart was thudding, my sex clenching and unclenching with needy arousal. She rubbed my nipples roughly and then pulled on them, making them long and hard. I swayed, rammed my hands up against the wall either side of the mirror to keep myself standing up. Glancing sideways I caught sight of the expression on Will's face. His mouth was open as he watched, his eyes positively glazed. I bit my lip, arousal soaring through me. *Oh yes, this was the hottest it had ever been.*

'He's still watching,' she said softly. 'He likes it this way just as much, I think.'

'Oh yes, he does.' I gave a breathless laugh. 'What if someone comes in to the shop?'

She shrugged, her hands stroking the outline of my hips, as she leant against my back. 'I go to them.'

I found myself praying no one would come in.

'Why don't you ask him to give us a show, in return?' she suggested.

'A show?'

'Yes, ask him to come in here, with us.'

How would he react? Knowing this man that I loved on an everyday basis was thrilling, and yet ... *not* knowing how he would react to this held its own dark seductive charm. I wanted to see what would happen, I wanted to know.

'Will,' I called, my voice shaky. 'Come here.' My throat constricted with arousal. I watched him, while she moved her hands over my breasts. He seemed frozen to the spot.

Then he ran his hand across the back of his neck, before standing up. He glanced around him, presumably looking to see if anyone was approaching the shop. A moment later, he was beside us.

'We thought you might want a closer look,' the shop assistant said, gesturing at the seat.

He was amazed. I could see it on his face, and I also saw the interest that was registered there. He stepped in front of us and moved to the chair, sitting down. The assistant closed the curtain behind us, the three of us now ensconced in the cubicle.

'Are you OK?' he asked me.

She kept stroking me, from beneath my breasts down to my hip bones. I nodded, my pulse racing. Will's gaze dropped from mine, and he watched her hands moving around my hip bones, her fingers following the line of my knickers until they met over my mons. She kissed the back of my shoulder and my head dropped back, my eyes closing. I was aching for her to touch my pussy. I rocked against her and she chuckled softly.

'I'll do you a deal,' she said.

I opened my eyes, rolling my head to look at her over my shoulder.

She was still looking at Will. 'I bet you'd like me to make your wife come, while you watch, wouldn't you?'

Will nodded. She stepped out from behind me and turned me easily in her arms. I was like a mannequin from her window display, pliable under her touch, willing. We were face to face now, and she stood up against me, close, with her body brushing mine. Her face was turned towards Will, so was mine.

'Fair's fair,' she whispered, and her fingers dived inside my knickers. 'We'll give you a show if you give us one.'

'Oh my God,' I blurted out loud, when I realised what she was suggesting. But my clit was throbbing with the need to be touched and her finger was only millimetres away.

One corner of Will's mouth had lifted, and as I glanced down I could see that he was hard, his cock large and defined through his jeans. He rested back in the chair, his hips jutting forwards on the edge. One hand rested over his zipper. 'Sounds fair to me.'

The assistant turned to look at me, her wide mouth smiling. She reached out and kissed me tentatively, her tongue tasting my lower lip. My mouth opened automatically, a whimper escaping me. Desire rolled over me, forcing me to act. I had my hands on her hips, moving my lower body against hers, my mouth open to take her tongue. Once I responded, she kissed me deep, both soft and yet fierce all at once. Then she drew back and dropped down, pulling my knickers down the length of my legs as she did so.

'Let me touch you, open your legs,' she said.

I did so, leaning my back against the wall to hold me up.

Will had his cock out and was stroking it, slow and deliberate, one hand cupping his balls. His cock was standing up from his zipper like a totem pole. I loved to watch him wank at the best of times, and now this woman was touching my bare pussy while I watched. A fever ran over me as she pushed one finger into my slit. She rose against me, straddling one of my thighs, her miniskirt riding up. Her finger stretched over my clit, making me shiver. Then I felt her grinding her pussy against my thigh, and I clutched at her hip, encouraging her. She gave a husky laugh and snatched at my hand, pushing it down between her thighs and over her mons.

'Fuck, that looks so hot,' Will said, shaking his head, his hand moving faster on his cock. I could see the end of it was oozing.

My fingers were inside her underwear, soft cotton, stretchy. When I touched her labia, it was warm and melted against my fingers. She nodded, urging me on as I sought out and stroked her clit, then she pushed her hand deeper against me, resting her palm over my clit to maintain the pressure, and shoving one finger inside me, looping it inside. That sent me into the wild zone. Suddenly we were thrusting and grinding against each other like frenzied creatures, pivoting and sliding against the wall, the pair of us watching Will as he watched us.

'Oh, oh, oh.' I couldn't help myself, I was moaning like a banshee. The pad of her finger had stroked the front wall of my sex. Pleasure, heady blissful pleasure, reverberated through my groin, my sex in spasm as I came. She shoved her pussy against my hand and shuddered, her thighs clenching and unclenching on mine. We held onto each other, swaying.

She looked into my eyes, her expression delighted and filled with laughter, and I thought she was about to say something about Will – who was going at his cock like a madman seeking relief – and then her expression changed. In the distance I registered the sound of the door. She reached to give me a quick regretful kiss, and then reached to pull her underwear into place, shoving her skirt down. She waved her fingers at Will, and then shot out of the cubicle, dropping the curtain into place behind her.

I wavered, watching Will as he shot his load into his hand, his eyes closing, his head sinking back in relief. I made it over to him, and kissed his mouth to bring him back, chuckling softly.

'You are bad to the bone,' he whispered.

'Yes, and you love it.'

I dressed and we emerged from the changing room, with me carrying the hanger bearing the untried dress. In the shop, the assistant was walking along the rail, pointing out particular designer items to the female customer who had arrived. When she saw us, she paused, breaking into a big smile.

'That dress just wasn't quite right for the occasion, was it?' She stepped over and relieved me of the hanger.

'It was a memorable sight,' Will said, giving a dark laugh.

'Why don't you come back next Saturday?' she suggested, breezily, her glance going from one to the other of us. 'We'll have new stock in and I'll remember your size.' She winked and her eyes scanned my body with a familiarity that made me burn up all over again. 'I can pick you out something special to try on, if you'd like me to?'

I looked from her to Will and back, tangible electricity crashing between the three of us. I noticed the customer in the background had paused to observe the exchange, a small frown on her face. Will nodded slowly, his eyebrows rising as he looked at me.

'It sounds perfect,' I said. 'We'll see you then.'

'I look forward to it,' she replied.

Outside the shop, we walked away in the sunshine. Will had his arm around my waist, possessively. After a moment he stopped dead in his tracks and kissed me long and deep, right there in the middle of the street.

'I can't wait to get you home,' he said, as he drew back. 'I want to give you a nice long fuck, while you tell me exactly what she did and said to you.'

I could feel his erection through his clothes. The Saturday shoppers moved around us in an unseen blur.

'And there was me thinking you'd want to go back to the department store, next time around,' I mocked.

'No way. Quality shopping for you from now on, my love.'

What could I say? He was happy, I was happy.

It pays to get good designer outlet.

Saskia Walker's short stories have appeared in several Wicked Words collections.

This Very Boutique
Portia Da Costa

'Good afternoon, sir, and welcome to The Boutique. How may we help you this afternoon?'

Sir strolls into the showroom, then halts right in the centre and slowly looks around. His sharp gaze flits hither and thither, alighting on the various samples set out for display in a studiedly casual arrangement across the sideboard, the occasional tables and elsewhere. We offer a very personal hands-on service here in this bijou little establishment and we like our shoppers to feel as comfortable and relaxed as they would do in their own homes. So they'll buy more . . .

It's hard to tell what Sir really thinks about the risqué items we have on show. His expression is inscrutable, mutable, and hard to fathom. The only indication of any kind of emotion is the faintest hint of super-cool amusement. But even that could be a trick of the imagination.

'Please, won't you take a seat?' I encourage, gesturing to the most comfy armchair.

His hooded eyes narrow, but he moves towards the seat, and lowers his tall, substantial form into it, setting the pink paper carrier bag he's been holding on a table beside him, and making a big show of fussing with the panels of his voluminous dun-coloured raincoat. It's not a plastic mac, thank God, or even a crumpled Columbo jobbie. But it's not exactly an example of metrosexual man chic either, and disturbing thoughts of flashers spring to mind. Especially given the way he's eyeballing me. His face is still bland enough, but there are lights dancing in his intelligent brown eyes.

'Sir?' I prompt, but all he seems to want to do is just sit there smiling slightly, as if he's guarding a special, wicked secret. I get the feeling that he's enjoying the retail experience immensely.

'Sir?' I enquire again, as he looks me up and down, those intensely gleaming eyes doing the grand tour from my boobs to my legs to my general groinal area to my face and then back around again. Suddenly my crisp white blouse feels tight and restricting across my frontage, and to my dismay my nipples choose this moment to want to pop out like organ stops. I can almost hear them go 'Ping ping! Ping ping!' They're acting as if it's cold here in the showroom, when in reality it's already far hotter than it should be and getting hotter with every minute that passes.

'Ah, yes,' Sir purrs at last, focusing that sultry look of his like a technician tuning a high-powered laser, 'I've got a slight problem, my dear.' He taps the pink carrier bag at his side, the one that's been subconsciously bugging me since his arrival. His long fingertips flick at the paper in a way that's vaguely suggestive. 'I bought this item a couple of days ago, from this very boutique, and I'm afraid it's very far from satisfactory.'

I bite my lip, feeling uncontrollable silliness suddenly bubble up inside me for a split second, and then immediately I make every effort to keep my mind on the job. I'm not behaving very much like a professional vendeuse, am I?

Right, back to business . . . and, oh dear, it's a return.

I hate returns. They can be really tricky when you sell the sort of merchandise we do, and half the time people who bring things back are just in here to try it on. I just hope that Sir doesn't turn nasty. Not that he looks nasty. In fact, he looks about as far from nasty as it's possible to be. To my mind, he looks very nice indeed, with his big burly body, and his face that's so boyishly handsome despite the silver grey in his crisp-cut dark hair. My mind goes cantering away from the job in hand like an out-of-control pony, and I imagine what it might be like to kiss Sir and waylay him for a shag.

'Um ... in what way is the item unsatisfactory, sir?' My voice comes out rather like a cartoon squeak, and I cast around for a look of servile solicitude instead of the rampant lust that I'm sure is written large and obvious on my face. 'We very rarely get complaints about our merchandise here, sir. But if there is a problem, I'll do everything in my power to resolve it.'

There, that sounds suitably crawly, doesn't it?

Unfortunately, Sir clearly thinks it's crawly too, suitable or otherwise, and he gives me a rather stern look that induces my knees to tremble.

'That's as maybe,' he continues, and strangely, he seems to be the one who's biting his lip now, 'but I'm very disappointed. I don't expect to be sold substandard goods at these prices and I'm accustomed to better customer service than this.'

'I'm very sorry about that, sir,' I murmur obsequiously, 'please let me take a look at the goods, and if they're faulty, I assure you we'll replace them for you.'

Sir hands me the bag, and his brown eyes lock on mine as he looks up at me. I can see that he's still trying to appear indignant, but there's a strange tricky gleam about him, a sort of smile that's not a smile, and I get a distinct feeling I'm in for big big trouble with this one.

I open the top of the bag and look inside.

Uh-oh ...

There's a very popular item peeking out of the nest of shredded tissue paper. A very popular item indeed, at least with me. I wonder what on earth Sir can possibly think is wrong with it.

'Ah, the Spinetingler Deluxe, one of our best-selling lines ... We don't usually have any complaints about these. They're usually completely reliable and satisfactory.'

The Spinetingler Deluxe is made of sturdy pink silicone, very thoughtfully shaped and very generously sized. It reminds me of another sturdy, thoughtfully shaped and very generously sized item. One that's always completely reliable and so satisfactory that it has a tendency to make me feel as if it's about to blow the top of my head off ... It's also pinkish, after a fashion, but more of a flesh tone.

'I'd better test it, I suppose.' I glance at Sir, and notice that he looks remarkably keen on this idea. His big brown eyes are as bright as two stars, and his nice, rather reddish mouth has now curved into a smile. It appears that the severe demeanour of a moment ago was just an act, and one he's already as good as forgotten.

'That's an excellent idea,' he concurs roundly. 'It may just be that the young friend I purchased it for isn't using it correctly, so you'd be doing us all a service if you could just show me how it works. Unfortunately it didn't come with a user manual.'

I take out the Spinetingler and set the bag aside, conscious of Sir's eyes following my every move with minute attention. He obviously doesn't want to miss a single detail.

I twist the bezel at the end of the Spinetingler.

It buzzes like a box of angry wasps.

I give Sir an encouraging look.

'Well, it seems to work perfectly ... Did your friend try twisting the knob?'

I give said knob another twist, and the wasps get angrier.

'Of course,' he replies, a frown pleating his fine broad brow. 'Are you implying that my friend and I are stupid?'

'No! Of course not! But this Spinetingler seems to be in perfect working order, Sir.'

'Ah yes, but is that all it's supposed to do?' His glittering eyes narrow all of a sudden. 'As I pointed out, there weren't any instructions in the bag with it, and it's not immediately obvious how one is supposed to use it.'

That's true. Items like the Spinetingler aren't generally supplied with an operating manual. But then again, any red-blooded woman – or man – should know almost by instinct what to do with it. I get the feeling that Sir is just being deliberately obtuse. You get characters like this in the retail trade all the time, and it's usually best for business to try and play along with them.

The customer is always right and all that stuff, don't you know?

'Perhaps a brief demonstration would help?' he suggests, in anticipation. For a moment he purses his lips, and seems to find it difficult to meet my eyes. But then his broad face straightens again, and he gives me a long, almost imperious look.

'Of course, if you think so ...'

'Oh, I know so,' he confirms with great authority, settling his large form more comfortably in the chair and tweaking at his long unglamorous raincoat again. He seems to be making certain that it fully covers his lap.

'Well, usually a young lady would tend to use this sort of item at night, in the privacy of her bed, or perhaps in her bath in the case of the waterproof version.' I twist the bezel again, for effect. 'But sometimes, of course, an armchair will do just as well.'

'Do you often use it in an armchair?' Sir enquires.

'Um ... yes. Sometimes.'

'And what about bed? Do you sometimes use it there too?'

'Er ... yes, that too.'

'Which is best?'

'I don't have a preference.'

'Well then ...' He gives me an encouraging nod, then snags his full red lower lip with his snowy white teeth again. He's sitting very still, but somehow he seems as full of dynamic energy as a tensioned spring at the same time.

Setting the Spinetingler down on the chair arm, I take a seat. This is very embarrassing, but – showing immense presence of mind for me – I manage to get a grip on myself. Reaching beneath my neat grey shop-girl's skirt, I fish around and find the elastic of my panties.

Sir's dark eyebrows lift.

I tug at my pants and slide them down my thighs, over my knees and off.

Sir blinks, his rather beautiful eyes widening

I wriggle in my chair to get comfy, just as Sir has, and he nods pointedly at my skirt, which is still covering the aforementioned groinal area.

'Of course, I'm sorry,' I apologise, then hitch up my skirt so he can see my demonstration.

'No problem,' he murmurs, sitting up in his chair all of a sudden, and leaning forwards.

I pick up the Spinetingler from the chair arm. 'Well, some young ladies rather like to … er … insert the Spinetingler, but others prefer to use it externally.'

I suppose I'm stalling for time here, but this *is* rather a personal matter, and it's the first time I've ever had to demonstrate an item for a customer in this way. Furthermore, it doesn't help that I keep getting the distinct feeling that Sir actually *does* know everything there is to know about the use of Spinetinglers and other similar devices, and is actually just sitting there, large as life, and silently laughing his head off as he dares me to make an exhibition of myself.

'Which would you recommend?' he asks, grinning.

'I … I usually start off using it externally.'

'Perhaps you could you show me that then?' he suggests.

I twist the bezel and the Spinetingler buzzes loudly. Too loudly, in fact, so I back it down a notch.

'Sometimes it's best to start off gently and build up.'

'That seems sensible enough. Please continue.'

I close my eyes, and guide the pink silicon tip of the device to the target zone.

When it touches me I can't help but let out a gasp.

The Spinetingler really is an excellent product, and its vibrations are right on my frequency. The buzzing and thrumming makes me pant for breath and compels me to wriggle, but I try to stay as still as I can so that Sir can see exactly where the stimulation should be applied.

'And how does that feel?' he asks, his voice suddenly low and silky.

'Um ... v-very nice,' I stammer, aware that I'm not really going to be much good as a demonstrator. I tend to get pretty inarticulate pretty soon in situations like these.

'You know, I can't really see all that well,' he complains suddenly, although it's not so much a complaint as an observation that comes out in the form of a stifled laugh. 'Perhaps you could open your legs a bit wider? Put your thighs over the arms of the chair, maybe? I'm sure that will provide a much better view.'

I'm sure it will, you wicked old pervert, I want to say to him, but he is the customer, after all, and I'm here to serve. So, trying not to lose my place, I hitch and hutch my bottom around in the chair, and tilt my pelvis so I can drape my thighs across the arms.

The resulting position is not unlike being on a gynae-cologist's couch with all my bits on display for Sir's perusal.

'That's so much better. Please proceed,' he remarks cheerfully.

I apply the Spinetingler to my sex again, keeping my eyes closed so I can't see Sir's avid face. With the vibra-tions on low I play the naughty silicone widget up and down, to and fro, and side to side, expertly goosing my sticky, swollen folds and all my sexy little hot zones.

All except one, that is ... Because if I go there too soon

this entire demo is over and done with before we've barely even started, and I don't want any more complaints from Sir that I'm not doing my job right.

'Is that usually how you use it?' he asks, his voice sounding rather closer than before. My eyes fly open and I find that somehow, moving lightly and silently for such a sizeable man, he's sneaked out of his chair and he's sitting on the carpet right in front of the one I'm in. He's no further than a yard away from the Spinetingler and my cunt, and when I almost fly up out of the chair, he places a large warm hand on the inside of my knee, as if to calm me.

'I do hope you don't mind,' he says blithely, a look of feigned innocence on his stocky face, 'but I really couldn't see all that well from over there.'

'N-no, it's all right. No problem,' I burble, not sure what to do next. The Spinetingler has slipped out of place and is noisily buzzing to itself.

'Do go on,' Sir encourages. 'This is all extremely instructive.'

As I prepare to comply, I notice that his hand stays where it is.

I circle the buzzing tip again, around and around my entrance, up and down the length of my sex, carefully skirting my swollen clit. My eyelids flutter down again because I can't cope with the intensity of his gaze.

'Ah, I see what you're doing now,' says Sir, his voice not quite steady. 'I get it. You don't go for the obvious place straight away in order to prolong the experience . . . That's very clever, my dear. You're clearly a virtuoso with this particular item.'

I nod my head, because I'm not sure I can actually answer lucidly.

His fingertips curve against the inside of my knee, then slide sneakily upwards. His touch is light and almost diffident, but it encourages me. I reach for the bevel, but even before I can make an adjustment, he murmurs, 'Ah yes ... that's good. Now show me how you execute the coup de grâce.'

Coup de grâce? What is he on about?

I need to come now, whatever the hell he chooses to call it.

The Spinetingler seems to howl now, at least inside my head, and as I slide its slick reverberating tip towards the knot of nerves that craves it, my thighs flex and my bottom rises from the chair.

'Good girl,' croons Sir, his hand curling around mine to render guidance.

I hit the red zone and I shout and jerk and come.

The next few moments are a blur of moaning and thrashing and pure dumb pleasure. I forget all about The Boutique, and my sales pitch, and my product. I'm just a bundle of feelings and a throbbing, pulsing clit.

Eventually though, I come crashing down from whatever 'up' place I've been to, and rediscover the fact I've been giving a demonstration. With reluctance, I open my eyes, and meet Sir's ...

They're dark, so dark, and full of wicked mirth and what looks like a genuine sense of wonder.

'That was excellent, my dear.' His voice is arch and full of delight and slightly shaken by that revealing unsteadiness. 'A very clear demonstration.' He takes the extremely fragrant Spinetingler from my trembling, nerveless grasp, and runs his own fingertips slowly up and down it. 'There's obviously nothing whatsoever wrong with this.'

'Um ... no ... It seems to be in perfect working order,' I observe gustily, clutching at the scraps of my composure despite the fact that I'm draped across an armchair with my thighs splayed wide open and Sir's face is barely a couple of feet from my sex.

'Here, let me help you,' he offers as I wriggle and struggle and try to sit up. He offers his free hand to assist me with my efforts, while he springs to his feet with an effortless elegance so surprising in a big man. An instant later I'm back on my pins again too, albeit somewhat shakily, and tweaking my skirt back down to cover my naked thighs. A look of disappointment momentarily clouds Sir's wide handsome face as he looms over me, but then it's gone again, and he's clearly thinking, thinking, thinking ...

'Yes, the Spinetingler is obviously an excellent product for a young lady like you,' he observes, still fondling the stupid thing, 'but what about a gentleman? Could he use it?'

Oh, I can think of a million ways to use it on you, you disgraceful reprobate, I tell him silently, almost hypnotised by the way he continues to examine and as good as caress the silicone cylinder. Beneath my skirt, I get a naughty little renewed tingle in my sex at the thought of some of the things I'd like to do to Sir, and that reminds me that I'm no longer wearing any knickers.

Where the devil are they?

I glance quickly around, and notice a scrap of white lace peeking out of the pocket of Sir's disreputable brown raincoat. I fleetingly consider accusing him of shoplifting, but it's not really stealing, is it, because my panties weren't on sale anyway?

'So?' he prompts, giving the bezel of the Spinetingler a little tweak, then as it buzzes, he casts an almost coy little glance downwards at his crotch.

I glance too. Then feel *really* coy.

There's a prodigious bulge behind the fly of his charcoal-grey trousers.

'Yes, of course, a gentleman could certainly use the Spinetingler,' I say, trying to retrieve my efficient, helpful salesperson mode. Which isn't easy, when I can't stop snatching quick glances at that whopper down below, and speculating what it would look like outside those elegant grey trousers.

Sir fiddles with the bezel a bit more, and the pitch of

the buzz oscillates up and down. 'Perhaps another demonstration would be in order?' he suggests. He doesn't seem to be making any attempt to play the serious shopper any more because he has a wide white grin plastered across his big handsome face.

'Of course, sir.' I'm sure my own grin is just as expansive too, and why wouldn't it be? Any girl would smile at the prospect of getting to grips with a sex toy that promises to be far more impressive than the silicone Spinetingler. 'Take a seat, and make yourself comfortable, and I'll see what I can do.'

He sinks back into the chair that he occupied before and sets the Spinetingler down on the arm, but this time there's no hiding of his light behind the bushel of his drab brown raincoat. This time, he carefully folds it back out of the way, and then, with no further ado, he unfastens his fine leather belt.

When his long deft fingers go to the fastenings of his trousers, I forestall him.

'Allow me, sir,' I say politely, trying to mask the fact that my mouth is watering almost as much as my nether regions are, and that I'm dying to get to grips with his monster.

'Why, that's very kind of you, miss,' he murmurs, then snags his lip again. His wickedly long lashes flutter as I dive for his trouser button, and then tease down his smooth-running zip.

Naughty Sir! He's not wearing any underwear!

And boy does what lives in his trousers live up to my expectations!

The flesh and blood spinetingler easily matches its silicone cousin, and is just as stiff and a good deal rosier and more appetising.

'I'm sorry about that,' remarks Sir, obviously not sorry at all, but proud as any typical male exhibiting his pride and joy, 'I'm afraid your demonstrating had a very stimulating effect on me.'

'No need to apologise, sir. It's perfectly natural. I have to deal with this sort of thing all the time.'

'Really?'

Oops! Does he think I'm a slut?

'Given the sort of merchandise we sell here, these sorts of situations tend to arise.'

Sir licks his lips, and even though I wouldn't have thought it possible, the 'situation' seems to arise even further than it has already arisen.

I reach for the Spinetingler, even though I'm almost certain Sir has forgotten all about it.

'Shall we give it a try then, sir?'

For a moment, the hint of what just might be nervousness flits across those gorgeous features of his, but he nods.

I switch on the mechanism, but keep it at the lowest level. Best not to give the poor man a heart attack, eh?

Very lightly, I allow the buzzing toy to drift up the length of the underside of his shaft. I barely touch his flesh, but still those big, graceful, long-fingered hands gouge deeply at the chair arms and he cries out an impassioned, 'Oh dear God!'

'Are you all right, sir?' I enquire, glad that his long, long lashes have fluttered down and he can't see that I'm grinning like the proverbial Cheshire cat.

'Fine,' he gasps as I delicately circle the Spinetingler's buzzing silicone tip around *his* tip. Which is much bigger and dark as wine with tumescent blood. 'Please continue.'

'But you're not looking, sir,' I point out, withdrawing the toy for a moment.

'I don't need to look, you silly girl,' he growls, his hips lifting as if his marvellous dick is blindly seeking its new playmate. 'Now just get on with it.'

Ooh, getting testy are we?

But then again, who can blame him? He's seconds from detonation and I'm messing about and being very unprofessional. I decide to apply myself – and the Spinetingler – to his predicament. The silicone simulacrum, I slide carefully into his trousers, and apply lightly and delicately to his tender perineum.

And myself?

Well, I apply myself to the real thing. The delicious, gleaming, silky, rampant appendage that's rearing up magnificently in my face.

Sir's eyes fly open as I take him between my lips. I can't speak, because my mouth's full – very full – but I silently challenge him to find better customer service anywhere.

And as I work wickedly and tirelessly with tongue and Spinetingler, he utters a stream of the wildest and most midnight-blue profanity.

But I know he only means it in a nice way...

A long, shagged-out while later, I stir sleepily amongst the fallout of my sales pitch. The Spinetingler, the Naughty Nipple Clamps, the Pink Furry Love Cuffs, the Magic Vibrating Egg and a colourful selection of even ruder 'samples' lie scattered around us on the sitting-room rug, and Sir's capacious brown raincoat is draped haphazardly across our sticky naked bodies. Over on the telly screen, an adult DVD is playing silently, on repeat.

Sir groans and his large warm hand curves drowsily around my breast. His wine-scented breath plays like a zephyr against the back of my neck.

'What would I do without you, my love,' he mutters, levering himself up and kissing the side of my throat and my jaw. 'What other woman would indulge a disgraceful old perv like me and play his daft games with him?'

'You're not old,' I observe, snuggling back against him and pushing my bottom against a rising erection that attests to a sexual stamina that would put a man half his age to shame.

He laughs, and nudges me rudely with the thing. Neither he nor I deny that he's a perv. Because he *is* one.

And with every day that we're together, I'm rapidly catching him up.

'I'm glad you think so,' he says as he suddenly leans right over me and starts to fish about under the adjacent coffee table, 'because I've *really* been shopping.'

Despite the fact that I find his penis poking against my backside very distracting indeed, I feel a tingle of purely retail-related excitement.

Sir does very, very good shopping, especially online, and parcels tend to arrive with a delightful frequency.

Agent Provocateur. The Erotic Print Society. Hotel Chocolat. All my favourites.

But the carrier bag he pulls out from under is unfamiliar. It's made from shiny blue and gold paper, and it's little and dainty. After a moment's hesitation, he puts it gently into my hands.

The retail excitement turns to a different kind of thrill. Even the unflagging erection nudging my bottom becomes temporarily ever so slightly less of a priority.

I lift out a small blue velvet jewellery box with the kind of dimensions that are coded into the genes of almost every heterosexual woman in the western, capitalist world.

'Just a small item for madam's consideration.' His voice is soft and arch, much as it was during our silly sex shop game, but I also detect a hint of genuine nervousness.

I flip up the lid, and breath, 'Oh Bobby,' loving him more than ever when I see the box's dazzling contents.

'I'll take it,' I declare, then roll to face him and seal the transaction with a kiss.

Portia Da Costa is the author of the Black Lace novels, *Gemini Heat*, *The Tutor*, *The Devil Inside*, *Gothic Blue*, *Continuum*, *The Stranger*, *Hotbed*, *Shadowplay* and *Entertaining Mr Stone*. Her short stories have also appeared in numerous Wicked Words collections.

Rummage Elizabeth Coldwell

When Sarah volunteered the two of us to work at St Barnaby's harvest festival rummage sale, I should have known she had an ulterior motive. She may be one of my oldest and very best friends, but that means I know her inside and out and, to be frank, altruism isn't high on her list of positive qualities. She'll buy the odd packet of charity Christmas cards, or drop her loose change into a collecting tin if someone rattles it under her nose at the bus station, but anything that involves giving up a substantial amount of time or seriously putting herself out to help someone else – forget it. So I should have been suspicious.

But I was too busy being annoyed. The rummage sale was being held the following Saturday morning, and I'd already made plans for that day. I'd been working all hours on a vital proposal document, making sure all the numbers added up. A large engineering contract was being put out for tender by the local council, and my boss was absolutely determined that our company should win the bid. For weeks I'd barely seen the outside of my office, and even when I went home, I still had columns of figures dancing in front of my eyes. And in all that time I'd gone without indulging in those two pastimes which are vital to every girl's health and wellbeing – sex and shopping. But now the hard work was out of the way, my pay cheque – including a nice bonus for all the overtime I'd put in – was sitting safely in my bank account and I had been all ready to hit the high street for a much-needed dose of retail therapy. Until Sarah had stepped in.

'We have to do it, Roxy,' she wheedled down the phone line. 'I promised Neil.'

'And who might Neil be exactly?' I asked as casually as I could.

'He comes into the coffee shop every morning, and we've got chatting,' she replied, trying to make it sound as though he was just another customer, though I suspected in her eyes he was anything but. 'He's a really interesting guy, Roxy, you'll really like him. He's a local conservation worker, and he's been involved in this amazing project where they're dredging the canal down by the old biscuit factory to encourage wild birds to breed there again. But he does a lot of good work in the community, too. He's going to be running one of the stalls at the rummage sale, and when he told me they were short of volunteers, I said you and I would be happy to help out. I hope you don't mind.'

So that was it. Sarah hadn't developed a conscience but a crush. I ought to have known. After all, it was hardly the first time she had changed her behaviour because she was trying to impress a guy she fancied. There was the three months we'd spent standing in a muddy playing field every Sunday morning because she was after the guy who played prop forward for the police rugby team. Not to mention the excruciating spinning class she enrolled us both for simply because she thought the instructor had a cute arse. Mind you, that one only lasted a couple of weeks, after she managed to wangle a lift home from the class with him in the hope of seducing him on the sofa, only for him to play thrash metal at top volume all the way back in the car. So, on reflection, losing a morning to a rummage sale wasn't too bad in the scheme of things. If only it hadn't meant me having to give up my longed-for shopping trip.

I could have told her I didn't want to do it, of course, but then I would have just sounded mean and whiny. And there was always the following Saturday, assuming the saintly Neil wasn't going to need a hand organising a cub scouts' jamboree or something.

St Barnaby's church was in one of the more affluent parts of town, an imposing building made of red brick rather than stone, with a Gothic metal spire that dominated the surrounding skyline. Posters on the notice board at the end of the gravel path advertised both the rummage sale and a forthcoming performance by the local choral society of Handel's *Messiah*. When I arrived, Sarah was standing waiting for me in the church doorway, looking thoroughly miserable.

'I've just had a text from Neil,' she told me. 'He's come down with the flu and he's not going to be able to make it. You know, helping out here wasn't the greatest idea I've ever had. Maybe we could just sneak away and take a look round the shops or something. I'm sure we won't be missed.'

Thank you, thank you, I silently mouthed to the god of shopping, who I was suddenly, overwhelmingly convinced was looking out for me. But just as we were about to make a hasty exit, a plump motherly-looking lady with grey hair came up to us. 'Ah, good! There you are. I'm Mrs Whittaker, but you can call me Doreen. Neil told me to expect the two of you. Come round to the side entrance and we'll start setting up the stalls.'

I smiled to myself as Sarah and I trudged after her. At least now I wasn't the only one who was giving up my Saturday for no good reason. I was being deprived of my shopping; Sarah was being deprived of lusting after Neil. We were even, and now I could just get on with enduring the next couple of hours.

And then something happened to make me think the rummage sale might not be a complete waste of my time after all. Doreen took us into the church hall and assigned each of us to a stall. Sarah was on the tombola, presiding over the chance to win an array of prizes from a large tin of biscuits to a kid-leather-backed vanity set, both of which appeared to date from some time in the late 1950s. I was on ladieswear, which consisted mostly of hand-knitted cardigans, from what I could see. Doreen was on the stall next to mine, in charge of jams, preserves and some rather tasty-looking home-made cakes.

'Everything's priced as marked,' she told me. 'You may get people coming in with donations, though, and if that happens, you can take them into the back room and sort them out. You'll soon get the hang of it, dear. And, of course, the best part is at the end when we've cleared everything away, and we all sit and have a nice cup of tea and any of the cakes that are left over. Which we pay for, of course. After all, it's important to raise as much money as we can to restore the church organ. It's such a good cause.'

'Yes,' I murmured politely, wishing I was at least on the same side of the hall as Sarah so we could have a giggle about the sort of organ we'd like to restore. Somehow, I didn't think it was the kind of comment that would go down well with a pillar of the community like Doreen. I turned to sort out the float in the cash box I'd been handed and thought about how long to give it before I faked a strategic migraine.

And then I heard Doreen say, 'Ah, Reverend Delamere. Yes, we're very pleased with the amount of contributions, and with the number of people who've so generously given. You might have seen we've got a couple of new volunteers today. They're friends of Neil Merryweather. This is – er – Roxy Watson.'

I was expecting the vicar to be in his sixties and as fossilised as his parishioners. I was wrong. He couldn't even have been thirty, and I couldn't quite believe how cute he was. He was close to six foot tall, with broad shoulders, sandy hair that flopped into his eyes and a muscular-looking build that wasn't really disguised by his uniform of black V-neck tank top, white shirt with the sleeves rolled up halfway to the elbow and plain black trousers. He smiled, and I felt something inside me go hot and gooey. I felt like I was in one of those cartoons where a character has a little angel sitting on one shoulder and a little devil on the other and, in my case, they stood for the respectful side of my personality and the lustful side. At that precise moment, Lust had got her tiny pointy pitchfork out and was trying to knock Respect's halo off.

'Reverend Delamere,' I said, extending a hand.

'Call me Jon,' he said, and not in that 'I'm down with the kids, hand me a guitar and we'll all sing "Kumbaya"' way some clergymen adopt to try to prove what they do is relevant. No, he was genuinely being friendly, and his firm handshake only served to stoke up the thoroughly inappropriate thoughts I was having about him.

'So you're a friend of Neil's?' he said, finally relinquishing his grasp on my fingers.

'Well, not as such. To be honest, I've never even met him. My friend Sarah, over there on the tombola, she's the one who knows him. She asked me to come along and help.' And now I'm incredibly glad she did, I thought, before sternly reminding myself that you shouldn't lust after a vicar – or if you did, it was best to avoid doing it in his place of work if you possibly could.

'Do you have any questions?' he asked.

Yes, I wanted to say. What time do you knock off for the day and have you taken a vow of celibacy I should know about? Instead, I just shook my head. 'No, I think Doreen's pretty much explained everything.'

'Good, good. Well, I'll be wandering around if you should need me. If not, I hope you'll be joining me in the vestry for a cup of tea later.' And with that, he went to check on another of the stalls, leaving me to think about joining him in his vest for something much more interesting than a cup of tea.

Five minutes later, the doors of the church hall were

opened to the paying public. What followed reminded me nothing more than that scene in *Beau Geste* where wave upon wave of ferocious warriors come marauding down the hill to attack the tiny and frankly petrified ranks of the Foreign Legion as they huddle in their desert fortress. Only these weren't bloodthirsty Arabs brandishing scimitars and shotguns, these were blue-rinsed grannies with umbrellas and walking frames. And they were a hundred times more frightening.

As I've said, I love my shopping, but for me, it's a leisure pursuit. I like to stroll down the high street at my own pace, stopping halfway through the morning for a cappuccino and a *pain au chocolat* at Luigi's in the town hall square. This, on the other hand, was more like all-out warfare. Items on the stall were snatched at, money was flung into my cash box and carefully arranged piles of clothing were sent tumbling to the floor as people fought for the best bargains. If you've never seen one old-age pensioner take out another with a carefully aimed elbow to the solar plexus or squash their toes under the wheel of a tartan-patterned shopping trolley, you've never manned a stall at a rummage sale.

I tried to distract myself from the mayhem of it all by fantasising about the luscious Reverend Delamere wearing nothing but his dog collar as I lay back on the trestle table among the piles of knitwear and he buried his head between my legs. The feel of his breath against my skin would be exquisite as he searched among the juicy folds of my pussy for my clit, and when he found it he would suck on it reverently with his soft full lips, driving me to a peak of pleasure that would have me shouting, 'Hallelujah!'

'Excuse me. Should I leave these with you?'

I turned at the sound of the voice, my erotic daydream brutally interrupted, and saw an elegantly dressed woman of around forty holding three or four dry-cleaning bags. A lace hem peeped out of one, something which looked like a silk nightdress spilled from another.

'Er, yes, sure,' I said, reaching out to take them from her. For a moment, she seemed to hesitate, as though she was about to change her mind and leave, then she shook her head.

She sighed. 'I'm sorry, I shouldn't be so sentimental, but I've had some good times in these outfits. Make sure they go to a good home, won't you?'

I looked around the hall. Two old ladies were arguing over a Fair Isle cardigan one of them had plucked from my stall, stretching it between them as they each fought to take it off the other. I glanced back at the woman clutching her treasured bags and wanted to put my hand over her eyes and steer her carefully away from the carnage around her. Seeing someone grabbing at her much-loved old clothes, more than likely tearing them to shreds in the process, would probably break her heart.

'Thanks very much for these,' I told her. 'They're really appreciated.'

Asking Doreen to keep an eye on things for a couple of minutes, I took the donated clothes into the little back room she had pointed out to me, intending to price everything up as she'd advised me. The room seemed to be the last resting place of dozens of old hymn books, some broken music stands and a couple of painted backdrops left over from the Christmas production of *Jack and the Beanstalk*. I draped the dry-cleaning bags over the upright piano that stood against one wall, and began to open them up. My mouth gaped as I realised what I was looking at. This wasn't ordinary jumble; this was a clothes junkie's dream. Every piece was by a hot young English designer; whoever the donor was, she not only had plenty of money but superb taste to boot. Even in my wildest shopping dreams, I would never be able to afford anything like this, and now I was being asked to put a price on them for buyers who wouldn't know Stella McCartney if she painted her bottom blue and danced up and down the church aisle singing, 'I'm Stella McCartney,' while accompanying herself on the ukulele.

I had already spread all but one of the items out on display, but when I pulled the last dress from the bag I knew there was no way I could sell it to anyone else. It was a gorgeous bias-cut satin evening dress in midnight blue, sleeveless and with a plunging halter neck. I stroked the fabric tenderly, wondering how I would look in this beautiful dress. I knew I should be back at my stall, but I just couldn't resist trying it on. Sarah had deprived me of my shopping trip, but she couldn't deprive me of this. If it fitted, I was buying it.

Quickly, before I could think about the risk I was taking and change my mind, I pulled off my boots and socks, then stripped out of my jeans, T-shirt and zip-up cardigan. The dress would look wrong with the bra I was wearing, so that had to go, too. For a moment, I stood topless in front of the piano, wondering if I should check whether the door was locked, but then decided I'd wasted too much time as it was. I unzipped the dress and stepped into it. There was no mirror in the room, but as I fiddled with the halter fastening at my neck, I just knew it looked good on me. It clung almost indecently to my breasts and hips, emphasising my curves. I caught hold of my hair and twisted it in a knot, holding it at the nape of my neck. I felt like some 1940s femme fatale, about to seduce a world-weary private eye with a clever quip. All I needed was a cigarette in a long-stemmed holder to complete the impression. When the doorknob rattled, I half-turned, ready to ask Humphrey Bogart whether he knew how to whistle.

Except it wasn't Bogie who walked into the room, but Reverend Delamere. He took in the sight of me in the tight-fitting dress, and I wondered if it was only my imagination that made his eyes linger for slightly longer than a man of the cloth's ought to on my so obviously braless breasts. When he looked back up to my face, there was a slight flush in his cheeks.

'Roxy – there you are. Mrs Whittaker was just – er – wondering where you'd got to and was going to come looking for you. I thought it was best if two stalls weren't left unattended –' he emphasised the word 'two', making me feel like a naughty choirboy who had been caught blowing his peashooter at the organist during morning service '– so I told her I'd find you. I suppose I should ask you exactly what you think you're doing?'

'I'm sorry,' I replied. 'I came in here to put price labels on all these clothes, and then when I saw this dress, I – well, I wanted it so much, I just had to try it on. I was going to put a decent contribution into the church funds for it, honestly, but you're right, I should be out there keeping an eye on the stall. Let me just take it off.'

If I'd been a good girl, I should have asked him to leave the room – but then he was supposed to be a good man, and he made no effort to go. Brazenly, I undid the neck fastening of the dress and let the two strips of material simply fall to my waist. This time, he didn't even pretend his gaze wasn't drawn to my chest. There was a hungry, immoral expression on his face as he stared at my full breasts.

'Why, reverend, don't you have a rummage sale to supervise?' I asked, unable to keep the smile out of my voice.

'Yes, but –' His voice seemed to catch in his throat. 'We really shouldn't be doing this.'

'You're right,' I said, walking towards him. The front of his dark sensible trousers seemed to contain a very promising bulge, and this time it was my eyes which strayed downwards and lingered. 'We shouldn't. But you see, I've been working so hard these past few weeks, I've had no time for shopping, which I love, and definitely no time for sex, which I also love, and today – well, it looks like I might be able to put both those things right.'

He stepped back, and I began to think I'd gone too far and that I should just get dressed and forget I'd tried to seduce him. However, all he did was turn the key in the lock, and then he took me in his arms and kissed me with a ferocity that had me panting. His teeth nipped at my lower lip, teasing me, and I found myself wondering where a vicar had learnt how to kiss like this.

When his mouth let go of mine, I thought about framing the question, then almost forgot about everything as his tongue began to snake a wet single-minded trail down my neck and collarbone, towards my exposed breasts. When he caught one of my nipples between his lips and sucked just hard enough to send a bolt of sensation shooting down to my crotch, I had to bite my fingers to stop myself crying out. The fantasies I'd been having about him using his mouth on me didn't even begin to compare to the reality. I wanted to urge him on, wanted to beg for his hand between my legs, touching me where I was starting to feel wet and desperately needy, but I also wanted to use my mouth to return some of the pleasure he was giving me.

I reached for his zip, pulling it down. I saw a quick flash of the sensible cotton of a pair of white boxer shorts. I wouldn't be at all surprised if they were Church of England standard issue, I thought as I reached into the fly hole and grabbed his cock. Hot and hardening under my touch, it reminded me of how long it had been since I'd last done this. Well, not that I'd ever done anything quite like this, as my fingers worked up and down his meaty shaft. Nothing so unexpected, so urgent – so forbidden.

I was barely aware that the evening dress had slithered down to my ankles until Jon urged me to step out of it. Wearing only my decidedly damp pink panties, I got down on my knees on scuffed wooden floorboards that smelled of dust and industrial polish and took him between my lips. I teased his tight balls with my fingers as my tongue flicked over the head of his cock. Every time I glanced up, I caught a glimpse of the blissful expression on his face and the white ring of the dog collar around his throat. Who cared that the rummage sale was still in full swing on the other side of the door, or that people – and more specifically Sarah, bored out of her mind on the tombola stall – might be wondering where I and the Reverend Delamere had disappeared to, and what we could possibly be doing that was taking us so long? All that mattered was the musky tang of his flesh in my mouth, and the small agonised gasps he was giving as I continued to suck him.

'Roxy, I have to fuck you,' he murmured, pulling away.

Lifting me to my feet again, he turned me round so I was resting against the piano, my palms flat on its closed lid. He tugged at my panties, pulling them down until I could step out of them. I was naked. He, on the other hand, was still respectably clothed – only his cock sticking hard and proud out of his flies gave any clue as to what was really going on here – and that contrast made things seem even naughtier.

I heard him moving into place behind me, and looked back provocatively over my shoulder at him. He was holding his cock, stroking it almost absent-mindedly as he guided it towards my soaking hole. Nothing, not the joy of grabbing that last pair of must-have jeans in my size off the rack, not even the thrill of slapping down my gold credit card on a shop counter as the assistant totalled up my purchases, could compare to the feeling of Jon's thick length sliding up inside me. His big hands closed round my breasts, cupping and squeezing them. My nipples were hard as rosary beads between his fingers; my juices were flowing so freely I was sure he could smell me as keenly as I could smell myself. I moaned as his cloth-covered pelvis banged against my bare bum. Time after time he thrust into me, powerful thrusts that shook my whole body, and I wondered how long it had been since he last enjoyed the pleasures of the flesh. And he was enjoying them, there was no doubt about it.

I let go of my fairly precarious grasp on the piano lid and stuck my own hand down between my legs, needing to bring myself to the brink. It only took a few swipes of my fingertip over my swollen clit before I was gasping and my pussy muscles were spasming around Jon's cock. Colours danced in front of my eyes, vivid as light through a stained-glass window. He gave one last convulsive thrust, and I knew he, too, had come.

We held on to each other for a moment, still almost unable to believe what we had done, and then he pulled out of me.

'Well, that was different,' he said. 'Normally at one of our rummage sales all I get is a cup of tea and a piece of Battenburg cake.'

'Don't worry, I'm sure Doreen's saved you a slice,' I told him. 'Let me get dressed, and then I can sort out what I owe you for this dress.'

'Don't worry about it.' He picked up a couple of the other dresses, a little crumpled now after our exertions against the piano. 'I'm sure we'll make enough from these other contributions.'

I shook my head. 'I wanted to shop today, and buying that dress counts as shopping. Plus you need the money more than the people on the high street – unless they're thinking of offering incredible sex as part of the experience, too.'

He laughed and left me to put my clothes back on. Before I left the room, I hugged the blue satin dress to my body, smiling blissfully. This charity lark wasn't the chore I had thought it would be. It really did give you a satisfying glow to do a little good for someone else. And if my cute vicar had some free time, perhaps I could persuade him to come shopping with me, and tempt him into one of the private cubicles in a department-store changing room. After all, he'd fucked me in his place of worship; next time, I could fuck him in mine.

Elizabeth Coldwell's short stories have appeared in numerous Wicked Words anthologies.

WICKED WORDS ANTHOLOGIES –

THE BEST IN WOMEN'S EROTIC WRITING FROM THE UK AND USA

Really do live up to their title of 'wicked' – Forum

Deliciously sexy and explicitly erotic, *Wicked Words* collections are guaranteed to excite. This immensely popular series is perfect for those who enjoy lust-filled, wildly indulgent sexy stories. The series is a showcase of writing by women at the cutting edge of the genre, pushing the boundaries of unashamed, explicit writing.

The first ten *Wicked Words* collections are now available in eye-catching illustrative covers and, since 2005, we have been publishing themed collections beginning with *Sex in the Office*. If you never got the chance to buy all the books when they were first published, you can now complete your collection and be the envy of your friends! Look out for the colourful covers – guaranteed to stand out from everything else on the erotica shelves – or alternatively order from us direct on our website at www.blacklace-books.co.uk

Full of action and attitude, humour and hedonism, they are a wonderful contribution to any erotic book collection. Each book contains 15–20 stories. Here's a sampler of what's on offer:

Wicked Words

ISBN 0 352 33363 4
£6.99

- In an elegant, exclusive ladies' club, *fin de siècle* fantasies come to life.
- In a dark, primeval forest, a mysterious young woman shapeshifts into a creature of the night.
- In a sleazy midwest motel room, a fetishistic female patrol cop gets dressed for work.

More Wicked Words

ISBN O 352 33487 8
£6.99

- Tasha's in lust with a celebrity chef – it's his temper that drives her wild.
- Reverend Billy Washburn needs salvation from Sister Julie – a teenage temptress who's set him on fire.
- Pearl doesn't want to get married; she just wants sex and blueberry smoothies on her LA poolside patio.

Wicked Words 3

ISBN O 352 33522 X
£6.99

- The seductive dentist – Nick's encounter with sexy Dr May turns into a pretty unorthodox check-up.
- The gender-playing journalist – Kat lusts after male strangers whilst cruising as a gay man.
- The submissive PA – Mandy's new job fulfils her fantasies and reveals her boss's fetish for all things leather.

Wicked Words 4

ISBN O 352 33603 X
£6.99

- Alexia has always fantasised about being Marilyn Monroe. One day a surprise package arrives with a sexy courier.
- Bridget is tired of being a chef. Maybe a little experimentation with a colleague is all she needs to get back her love of food.
- A mysterious woman prowls the back streets of New York, seeking pleasure from the sleaziest corners of the city.

Wicked Words 5

ISBN 0 352 33642 0
£6.99

- Connor the tax auditor gets a shocking surprise when he investigates a client's expenses claim for strap-on sex toys.
- Kate the sexy museum curator allows a buff young graduate to make a thorough excavation of her hidden treasures.
- Melanie the interior designer and porn fan swaps blokes with her best mate and gets up to nasty fun with the builders.

Wicked Words 6

ISBN 0 352 33690 0
£6.99

- Maxine gets turned on selling exquisite lingerie to gentlemen customers.
- Jules is stripped naked and covered in cream when she becomes the birthday cake for her brother's best mate's thirtieth.
- Elle wears handcuffs for an indecent liaison with a stranger in a motel room.

Wicked Words 7

ISBN 0 352 33743 5
£6.99

- An artist's model wants to be more than just painted, and things get pretty steamy in the studio.
- A bride-to-be pays a clandestine visit to the bathroom with her future father-in-law, and gets much more than she bargained for.
- An uptight MP has his mind (and something else!) blown by a charming young woman of devious intentions.

Wicked Words 8

ISBN 0 352 33787 7
£6.99

- Adam the young supermarket assistant cannot believe his luck when a saucy female customer needs his help.
- Lauren's first night at a fetish club brings out the sexy show-off in her when she is required to wear an outrageously daring rubber outfit.
- Cat's fantasies about hunky construction workers come true when they start work opposite her Santa Monica beach house.

Wicked Words 9

ISBN 0 352 33860 1

- Sarah gets a surprise when she and her husband go dogging in the local car park.
- The Wytchfinder interrogates a pagan wild woman and finds himself aroused to bursting point.
- Miss Charmond's charm school relies on old-fashioned discipline to keep wayward girls in line.

Wicked Words 10 – The Best of Wicked Words

- An editor's choice of the best, most original stories of the past five years.

Sex in the Office

ISBN 0 352 33944 6

- A lady boss with a foot fetish
- A security guard who's a CCTV voyeur
- An office cleaner with a crush on the MD

Explores the forbidden – and sometimes blatant – lusts that abound in the workplace where characters get up to something they shouldn't, with someone they shouldn't – someone who works in the office.

Sex on Holiday

ISBN 0 352 33961 6

- Spanking in Prague
- Domination in Switzerland
- Sexy salsa in Cuba

Holidays always bring a certain frisson. There's a naughty holiday fling to suit every taste in this X-rated collection. With a rich sensuality and an eye on the exotic, this makes the perfect beach read!

Sex at the Sports Club

ISBN 0 352 33991 8

- A young cricketer is seduced by his mate's mum
- A couple swap partners on the golf course
- An athletic female polo player sorts out the opposition

Everyone loves a good sport – especially if he has fantastic thighs and a great bod! Whether in the showers after a rugby match, or proving his all at the tennis court, there's something about a man working his body to the limit that really gets a girl going. In this latest themed collection we explore the sexual tensions that go on at various sports clubs.

Sex in Uniform

ISBN 0 352 34002 9

- A tourist meets a mysterious usherette in a Parisian cinema
- A nun seduces an unusual confirmation from a priest
- A chauffeur sees it all via the rear view mirror

Once again, our writers new and old have risen to the challenge and produced so many steamy and memorable stories for fans of men and women in uniform. Polished buttons and peaked caps will never look the same again.

Sex in the Kitchen

ISBN 0 352 34018 5

- Dusty's got a sweet tooth and the pastry chef is making her mouth water
- Honey's crazy enough about Jamie to be prepared and served as his main course
- Milly is a wine buyer who gets a big surprise in a French cellar

Whether it's a fiery chef cooking up a storm in a Michelin-starred restaurant or the minimal calm of sushi for two, there's nothing like the promise of fine feasting to get in the mood for love. From lavish banquets to a packed lunch at a motorway service station, this Wicked Words collection guarantees to serve up a good portion!

Sex on the Move

ISBN O 352 34034 7

- Nadia Kasparova sees the earth move from a space station while investigating sex at zero gravity . . .
- Candy likes leather pants, big powerful bikes, miles of open road and the men who ride them . . .
- Penny and Clair run a limousine business guaranteed to STRETCH the expectations of anyone lucky enough to sit in the back. . . .

Being on the move can be an escape from convention, the eyes of those we know, and from ourselves. There are few experiences as liberating as travelling. So whether it's planes, trains and automobiles, ships or even a space station, you can count on the Wicked Words authors to capture the exhilaration, freedom and passion of modern women on the move. Original tales of lust and abandon guaranteed to surprise and thrill!